THE LADIES AUXILIARY

THE LADIES AUXILIARY

Tova Mirvis

W. W. NORTON & COMPANY
NEW YORK · LONDON

Printed in the United States of America
First Edition

The text of this book is composed in Electra
with the display set in Copperplate Gothic and Stuyvesant
Desktop composition by Gina Webster
Manufacturing by Maple-Vail Book Manufacturing Group
Book design by JAM Design

Library of Congress Cataloging-in-Publication Data

Mirvis, Tova.
The ladies auxiliary / Tova Mirvis.
p. cm.
ISBN 0-393-04814-4
I. Title.
PS3563.I7217L33 1999
813'.54—dc21 99-30720
CIP

W. W. Norton & Company, Inc., 500 Fifth Avenue, New York, N.Y. 10110
www.wwnorton.com

W. W. Norton & Company Ltd., 10 Coptic Street, London WC1A 1PU

1 2 3 4 5 6 7 8 9 0

To my parents
and to Allan,
with love

THE LADIES AUXILIARY

BEFORE BATSHEVA MOVED TO Memphis, our community was the safest place on earth, close, small, held together like a carefully crocheted sweater. Little changed in this city where we had always lived, and like our parents and grandparents before us, we couldn't imagine living anywhere else.

We knew the city as well as we knew our own faces, could map each turn and bump in the roads the way we followed the curves of our chins. Memphis is built on a bluff, a high-rising strip of land that overlooks the Mississippi River, shielding us from the tornadoes that sweep across Arkansas every year just as spring is around the corner. When the warning sirens ring, winds hurl and rain pounds against our thick roofs, we breathe easier up here on this God-given piece of land. When it is done with, when the skies lighten again to their usual peaceful blue and the trees stop their frantic swaying, we open our doors to see that once again, we have been passed over.

Memphis folds slowly off the Mississippi, whose murky waters flow on to larger, faster places. Along the riverbanks, tall office buildings, luxury hotels, and parking garages have sprung up only recently, changing the sleepy streets once filled with general stores, rundown music clubs, and pawnshops into a city that could have been anywhere. With this, the city was transformed; cars sped up, people walked faster, too hurried to stop by or wave hello anymore. But Memphis doesn't seem ready for the glass and steel buildings, the eight-lane highway and the new sports stadium. It is like a child dressed in adult clothing, too big and too old, too soon.

From the river, the city spreads out, east, north and south. We aren't the only ones who live in East Memphis—we are the few among the many non-Jews—but still we exist as a city within a city, with fortress walls surrounding us on all sides, drawing divisions in our minds if not in our yards. The only thing that has seeped in is a southern flavor, creating a strange new combination. And after living here for so long, who can remember what originally was ours and what was theirs?

Because no one knows why Orthodox Jews settled in Memphis while everyone else headed to New York or Chicago, the community seems dropped like manna from heaven. It is said that the early Jews came because someone had a cousin here (maybe a dry goods peddler, maybe a textile merchant), but though many have tried, no family has laid definitive claim to this cousin. Once our families came, they stayed, spreading out and multiplying, sinking new roots into this soil and making it their own. After a few generations, the lines between families blurred, melting us into one; in Memphis, Levys become Friedmans become Sheinbergs become Levys again.

The thought of anyone leaving was impossible. We hadn't built this city for nothing, all our history and tradition to end with us. Moving away a few years, we understood. But the children always came back, carrying our community and our history forward. We saw ourselves as the Jerusalem of the South, our families part of a chain of Jewish Memphians that would extend into the future forever, as long and as far away as God in Heaven.

When it didn't happen that way, it was the last thing we had expected. Maybe we heard the warning signs, maybe we saw the darkening skies and felt the pattering of rain. But even so, it was as if we were watching from beneath the green-gray waters of the Mississippi. Later, it was all we could think about. Was it something we had done? Or something we hadn't done? Was it because of us all along? These things we think about now. But at the time, all we could see was that we were losing our children. And so what else was there to do?

1

BATSHEVA APPEARED IN OUR lives on a Friday afternoon as we were getting ready for Shabbos. It was inappropriate that she moved in when she did. Not that there was any religious prohibition against it, but it wasn't something we would have done. Fridays were set aside to prepare for Shabbos, and on the day Batsheva arrived, we were picking up our children from day camp, frying up chickens and doing laundry, the list of last-minute tasks growing as sundown approached. Even in the summer, when Shabbos started close to eight o'clock, there was never enough time to get ready. Each week, when the last glimpses of sun were fading behind the trees, we looked around our spotless houses, smelled the freshly cooked food, and felt a sense of wonder that once again we had finished in time.

We had heard that someone new was moving in, that the Liebmans had finally rented their house to a nice Jewish family as they had hoped to. This is who we were expecting any day now, a husband, a wife, a few children. We had begun speculating: Would the wife want to join the Sisterhood, the Ladies Auxiliary, the Donor Luncheon Committee? And whose carpool would they be in? It was the end of June and car pools for the upcoming school year were already being finalized.

When Batsheva drove down the street in a dusty white car piled high with luggage, her windows rolled down and loud music from a radio station we never listened to pouring out, it didn't occur to us that she might be the new neighbor we had been waiting for. We assumed that this woman had taken a wrong turn, that she was cruising through our neighborhood in search of some other one. On our streets we were used to seeing station wagons or minivans able to transport our many children, our bags of groceries, our mounds of dry cleaning.

But she slowed as she approached the Liebmans' house and leaned her head out the window to check the address. She pulled into the driveway, her brakes squealing as she stopped. She honked several times, as if expecting someone to run out and welcome her. But no one came out, and instead, veiled behind our curtains, we watched her get out of the car, raise her hands over her head and stretch out her thin body. She turned to stare at the street, her eyes moving from house to house, drinking us in slowly like hot tea.

Who knows what she saw when she first looked around. We had lived here so long that it's difficult to imagine seeing it fresh. The shul and school stand in the middle of our neighborhood, and our houses circle around them in homage to what is most important. Our winding streets are quiet, peaceful. The branches of dogwoods, white-budded magnolias and thick oaks curve over the roads in a green canopy, painting a leaf-patterned shield in the sky. The houses, mostly ranch style, large and sprawling, are situated at comfortable distances from each other. The lawns are well kept, the bushes are trimmed, and bright-colored flowers line the brick pathways that lead to our front doors.

Right away we knew Batsheva wasn't one of us. What stood out most was her white-blond hair. She left it loose and it was long, all the way down her back. Her green eyes leapt out at us and her face glistened with sweat. Her features were small and even, her cheeks were carefully sculpted, pale skin stretched tightly across bone. But her lips were full, curving upward like an archer's bow. It was also her clothes that caught our attention. She didn't dress the way we did, in loose skirts and modest necklines that hid our curved female bodies, shaping them into soft masses. Her white, short-sleeved shirt clung too tightly to her chest. The gauzy fabric of her purple skirt, the hem of it trimmed with fringes, swished when she walked, and we could almost see the trace of her legs beneath. And she wore a silver anklet with shiny blue beads and brown leather sandals with thin straps that crisscrossed in tight angles across her skin.

She went around to the other side of the car, opened the door, and out came a barefoot little girl in a yellow sundress. Ayala's face was smudged with chocolate and her hands looked sticky. Something about this little girl's face made us need to look again: on first glance we had seen the face of an adult even though our eyes were telling us it was a child no more than five years old. Her hair was a few shades lighter than Batsheva's and hung in wisps across her forehead and reached her chin. Her eyes had a ghostly quality, giving the impression that no one was behind them. And her skin was so pale we could almost see past it to the blue veins below.

Ayala went to sit on the lawn, which had turned brown and stiff that summer from the lack of rain. She picked the dandelions that had been growing wildly for months and pulled up pieces of grass, splitting the blades with her fingernails, waiting for her mother in a way our children never did; if we kept them waiting for five minutes, they were sure to pull at our skirts and whine. But Ayala was in no hurry. She was perfectly content to just sit there.

Batsheva turned her attention to unpacking. The top of her car was covered by a green tarp, protecting a collection of items tied so precariously to her luggage rack it was a wonder the whole thing hadn't toppled off miles back. She tried to undo the tarp, a job we would have left to our husbands. Every few seconds, she shook her head and let out a choice word. Finally she loosened it and unloaded milk crates, shopping bags and suitcases onto the driveway. Sticking out from the top of a bag we caught a glimpse of paintbrushes tied together with a red ribbon. In the bottom of a milk crate, we detected tubes of paint in all different colors and sizes. And we made note of a shopping bag overflowing with books, a partially opened box of colored candles.

Batsheva took a single key from her purse and unlocked the front door. The house had been cleared out months before when Joseph Liebman was transferred to his computer company's headquarters in Atlanta. The day they moved, the whole neighborhood had come out to tell Joseph and Estie and their two children good-bye. We had hated to see them go—Joseph was born here, at the same Baptist Hospital as many of us, and he had never lived anywhere else. Estie had been a member of the Ladies Auxiliary Executive Board, vice president of decorations, and it was a shame to lose such a hard worker.

Once inside, Batsheva poked her head around the corner for a quick look at the living room. It was empty, but when it was filled with the Liebmans' furniture, it had been one of the prettiest rooms in town: brocade couches with matching chairs, an oak breakfront, and two Persian rugs. The rest of the house was the same, lavishly decorated, not a thing out of place; how Estie managed that, with two kids, none of us knew. Without taking a closer look, Batsheva left the house and carried their things up the driveway, creating a pile in the entrance hall that threatened to topple with each addition.

When she finished, she went over to her daughter and hugged her. Then she took her hand and they walked up the driveway. Ayala turned back to look longingly at Rena Reinhard's three children playing under a sprinkler on the far corner lawn and at the Zuckerman's puppy making its way up the street. When they reached the door, Batsheva lifted Ayala to kiss the wooden mezuzah on the doorpost that the Liebmans had left behind. Perhaps the Liebmans had forgotten about it or maybe they assumed the next occupants would be Jewish as well. Batsheva and Ayala turned around for one last look at the street. Then they went inside and closed the door behind them.

IN the hours between Batsheva's arrival and the beginning of Shabbos, there was a flurry of phone calls. Arlene Salzman thought this woman looked familiar: where had she seen her before? Bracha Reinhard, Rena Reinhard's youngest daughter, claimed (falsely, it turned out—a week later she admitted to making up the story) that she was passing by on her bike when Batsheva called out to her by name; only when Bracha turned around she had disappeared. And Mrs. Irving Levy, her body swelling with curiosity, said she had half a mind to walk across the street, knock on Batsheva's door and ask who exactly she was.

"And that's just what I'll do," Mrs. Levy decided, when her curiosity had reached the point where she could no longer stand it. She fluffed her auburn hair (dyed, but who would dare say anything publicly about that?), straightened her already crisp clothing and filled a basket with food for Shabbos—challahs, a fried chicken, two kugels, and a dish of her famous hush puppies.

Mrs. Levy made it her business to be our eyes and ears, the supplier of all information and news. Her job would be easy this time—she had the good fortune to live directly across the street from Batsheva. She walked over and knocked on the front door, but there was no answer. Mrs. Levy couldn't begin to guess where Batsheva had gone, and she certainly couldn't imagine how she could have left the house without being noticed. Perhaps Batsheva was hiding inside; perhaps she had something to be afraid of. Determined to discover what exactly was going on, Mrs. Levy knocked again, louder this time.

When there was still no answer, Mrs. Levy sighed. "It just goes to show you, doesn't it? You try to do something nice for someone and this is what happens," she said to herself. Filled with the frustration of those who go out of their way to be generous, Mrs. Levy set the basket by the door and was about to start down the driveway when she heard something.

"Wait a minute," Batsheva was calling from inside. "I'm coming."

Batsheva opened the door wearing a white silk bathrobe. When she saw Mrs. Levy standing there with her most welcoming smile, she looked nervous, not sure what to make of this visit.

"Well hello there," Mrs. Levy said. "I thought for sure y'all had already run off somewhere. But you just moved in here, so I couldn't imagine where you'd go. Anyhow, I was watching you move in, and I thought to myself that there's no way this woman is going to have time to cook, seeing as you barely made it here before Shabbos. So I thought I'd bring by some food."

Batsheva stepped out onto the front porch, not caring that she was in her bathrobe and that anyone passing by could see her. She smiled at Mrs. Levy, and when she introduced herself, she shook Mrs. Levy's hand, like two men at a business meeting; this was something certainly not done here.

"That's so nice of you. You didn't even know my name and you brought all this food over," Batsheva exclaimed.

Mrs. Levy smiled modestly as she acknowledged the compliment. It *was* nice of her, she admitted, but then, she did consider herself something of a one-person welcome wagon. And as long as she was here, she decided to ask a few questions; no sense letting this good deed of hers go unrewarded.

"Tell me, Batsheva—is that what you said your name was?—what brings you down to Memphis? It's not every day that new people come along."

"I've always wanted to be part of a small, close-knit community," Batsheva said. "I had always heard what a nice place this was and thought that it would be good for us. And now I see I was right."

"Yes, you were," Mrs. Levy said. "In fact, we pride ourselves on our good ol' fashioned southern hospitality. But you didn't pick Memphis out of a hat, did you? You must have known someone from here."

"I did know someone who used to live here," Batsheva said but didn't elaborate, leaving Mrs. Levy to figure out whom she had meant. She began running through her mental list of everyone who had lived in Memphis at one time or another. Her concentration was interrupted though when Batsheva stuck her head inside the house and called to her daughter.

"Ayala, come see what we have for Shabbos," she said.

Ayala ran to the door in nothing but her underwear, and Batsheva laughed.

"I was about to give her a bath when I heard you knocking," she explained.

Mrs. Levy didn't see what there was to laugh about. Nakedness, even in children, was nothing to take lightly. Ayala shyly stole glances at Mrs. Levy but didn't say a word, and Mrs. Levy swelled with feeling for this little girl. Her own children and grandchildren were, inexplicably, living out of town and it was nice to see a child who needed a little love and care.

"This nice woman brought us over a basket of food. See all the good things we're going to eat for Shabbos?" Batsheva said.

Ayala poked through the basket. She didn't say anything, but she looked so excited to see the food that Mrs. Levy began to wonder if she was getting the homemade nourishment all children need. But there would be time to deal with that. For now, her mission was to find out all she could about Batsheva.

"Anyhow, as you were saying," Mrs. Levy prompted, hoping to subtly return Batsheva to her point about whom she had known from Memphis.

"Was I saying something? I don't remember." Batsheva laughed. "Maybe the heat is affecting me. It's hot as hell out here."

This Batsheva was certainly mysterious, Mrs. Levy decided, not to mention indiscreet with her language, especially in front of a child. God only knew what kinds of things she said when no one was around. But best to let the conversation flow and sooner or later she would find out the other pieces of this puzzle.

"It's always like this in the summer, hot as blazes. Each day I think it's the hottest day we've had and then I wake up the next day and it's even hotter," Mrs. Levy said.

"I can't believe I've let you stand out here sweating and haven't invited you in. Come, let me get you something to drink," Batsheva said.

"No, that's okay. You look like you have your hands full already and I'm sure the house is plenty messy." As much as Mrs. Levy would have welcomed the opportunity to find out more about this woman, it was getting close to Shabbos. "The last thing you need right now is visitors."

"Are you sure? It's so nice of you to come over. It's the least I can do."

"Another time. I have cooking to finish up and I'm sure you have some getting ready to do yourself."

They said good-bye and Mrs. Levy hurried home. There was just enough time to make a phone call or two before sundown.

"I only talked to her for a few minutes so it's hard to say anything for sure," Mrs. Levy reported to her best friend and closest confidante, Helen Shayowitz. "But something about her didn't seem right. I can't put my finger on what it was, but I'm telling you, there was something not right about her."

"Really," Helen said. Being the first to hear the news was one advantage of her friendship with Mrs. Levy. She was constantly amazed by Mrs. Levy's ability to find out about anything going on in Memphis. After years of experience, Helen had learned to trust her opinion without question.

"First of all, she came to the door in a bathrobe. And she practically ran down the driveway in it. You would think she didn't care who saw her. I tried to find out who she was but she was evasive—very, very evasive. I honestly wouldn't be surprised if she's running from something messy." Off the top of her head, Mrs. Levy could think of several scandals that had begun this way. "Then there's the question of why Ayala looked like she hadn't seen homemade food in ages. And the poor child was running around half-naked, like she was living in the wild."

"None of this is surprising," Helen agreed; she always made a point of backing up what Mrs. Levy said, even if she didn't one hundred percent agree. Here though, she had to admit, Mrs. Levy's assessment was right on target. "She doesn't look like your average good mother."

"No, she certainly doesn't. Women like that don't have the time to put into their children." Mrs. Levy was about to expound on all the ways these modern mothers hurt their children when her chicken noodle soup began boiling over. She had to run; there was only time for one final comment.

"Mark my words, Helen. This is going to be a situation to watch out for."

The news of Mrs. Levy's visit spread through the neighborhood. Helen Shayowitz called Tziporah Newburger who called Becky Feldman who conference-called Arlene Salzman and Rena Reinhard, who each called Leanna Zuckerman and Naomi Eisenberg and Jocelyn Shanzer. Even though we were rushing around doing last-minute vacuuming and dish-washing, we knew, in no time, what Mrs. Levy had learned about Batsheva. Our houses were connected by a telephone wire that stretched through our yards, a switchboard underground and all its lights ablaze.

AT sundown, we lit Shabbos candles in our silver candelabras—one candle for each member of our families—and a calm settled over the neighborhood. Cars were parked, televisions were shut off, phones stopped ringing. Children came indoors, men dressed and went to synagogue. We put on flowing skirts, silk blouses and fresh makeup. Our weeks waited for Fridays. We were commanded to set the Sabbath apart and make it holy. We have clothing we wear only on Shabbos, china dishes, sterling silverware, and crystal goblets that are only for Shabbos. We don't turn lights on or off, don't listen to music, go to work, use our ovens, our telephones, our cars. We reserve the day for God and for family, spending those twenty-five hours between Friday's sundown and

Saturday's dusk in a peaceful pattern of prayers, meals, and relaxation. The outside world vanishes, even if only for that one day.

Alone in our houses, we waited for our husbands and children to come home from shul. We could have gone to shul if we wanted; there were always a few wives dotting the women's section. But three hours of shul on Shabbos morning was plenty. And we weren't obligated to go. That was only required of men; we could fulfill our religious obligations at home. We preferred the quiet of our houses. It was the only time that nothing pulled at us, no meetings to attend, no phone calls to make. After the frenzy that filled each Friday afternoon, we loved to sit back, put our feet up and relax.

We took out our siddurs to say the prayers welcoming Shabbos. During the week, it was difficult to make time for the morning prayers, let alone the afternoon and evening ones. We would intend to daven, we would open our siddurs, but one chore or another always pulled us away. The phone would ring, a child would cry, our thoughts would drift to the dry-cleaning we had to pick up, the toothpaste we needed to buy. Even when we managed to say the prayers, we rushed through them, attributing no more meaning to these words than if we were reciting the Memphis phone book.

But on Shabbos it was easier. We felt as if we were standing before God. We thanked Him for giving us this day of rest and praised Him for the beauty of creation. Most of all, we prayed for our families. Springing from the square black letters, we saw the faces of the children, husbands and parents we loved. We closed our eyes, the well-being of the world in our hands.

Even though we davened alone, we always sang the lecha dodi out loud: *Come my beloved to greet the bride, let us welcome the Sabbath spirit.* We invited the Shabbos bride into our houses and imagined her flying in through our windows, sheathed in a white organza dress, the light from our Shabbos candles dancing across it. Her hair, crowned with a wreath of freshly cut roses, sparkled in the light. The words flew from our mouths and escaped out of our houses, forming a chorus of prayer rising to heaven.

When our husbands and children returned from shul, we moved to our dining rooms to begin our Shabbos meals. Gathered around our tables, we sang the shalom aleichem welcoming God and his angels into our homes. This song reminded us of the story we had been told when we were children. Every Friday night, two angels, one good and one bad, follow the men home from shul. As each man enters his house, the angels peer inside. If the table is set for Shabbos, the white tablecloth spread in front of a smiling family, the good angel will be happy and bless them by saying, "May your house have a Shabbos like this every week." And the bad angel will have no choice but to say Amen. But if there are no Shabbos candles burning, if like every other night, the television blares and the phone rings, the bad angel will smile and say that the house should have a Shabbos like this every week. And the good angel will have to hang his head, hold back his tears and say Amen. If we closed our eyes, we could see those two angels looking in our windows, the good one bestowing his blessing upon us.

Next we sang the aishet chayil: A *woman of valor who can find? Her value is higher than pearls. Her husband's heart depends on her and he shall lack no fortune.* As we took in our husbands' thankful faces, we felt appreciated like no other time. We didn't mind doing the housework, but still, a little gratitude was nice. Then our husbands placed their hands on our children's heads and blessed them: *May God make you like Ephraim and Menasheh, like Sarah, Rivka, Rochel and Leah, may He bless you and keep you.* They recited the kiddush over the full cups of red wine, blessing God who created the world in six days and rested on the seventh. Then we went into our kitchens and washed our hands with two cupfuls of water on each loosely clenched fist and didn't speak until our husbands recited the hamotzi and we bit into pieces of the braided challahs.

During the first courses we had prepared, we tried our best not to talk about Batsheva. We didn't want to engage in needless gossip, at least not at the Shabbos table. Instead, we talked about Shira Feldman, Becky Feldman's seventeen-year-old daughter, who had once again been spotted wearing a scandalously short skirt. We mentioned the fact that Yocheved Abraham, already twenty-nine, had returned home from New York without finding a husband. She was so picky, no one was ever good enough for her, and she was no beauty either. And, God help us, the news that Rachel Ann Berkowitz's little boy had come down with chicken pox. Surely that meant an epidemic was imminent. Any day now our children might be covered with the telltale red spots.

But by the time we brought out the chickens, salads, and kugels we had spent all day making, we couldn't stop ourselves from mentioning Batsheva. We had held our mouths for long enough and our curiosity bubbled over like boiling pots of water.

Over fried chicken, green bean almondine, and black-eyed peas, Helen Shayowitz leaned forward to share her news with her two sons, their wives and her grandchildren. After first hearing about Batsheva from Mrs. Levy, Helen had made a few phone calls of her own and had found out something that Mrs. Levy hadn't been able to uncover. She was proud of this coup. It proved that she was not simply Mrs. Levy's right-hand woman; she could be an eyes and ears all on her own.

How she found out her information was a little roundabout, but that didn't matter; news was news. Helen's brother David lives in West Memphis, Arkansas, and is no longer religious, but no one (at Helen's request) speaks about that anymore. It's a long story, but suffice it to say that he went to a secular college and that was the end of that. Anyway, he works for the same computer company as Joseph Liebman and they had happened to speak a few days earlier. The conversation came round to Memphis, and Joseph mentioned that they had finally rented the house.

"I suppose Joseph thought to tell David about the house because he knows I live here," Helen explained. "But you know David. He couldn't remember anything about this woman, only that she's from up north somewhere."

Helen shook her head. What was the point of finding out that the house was rented but not getting information about this newcomer? It was like driving all the way to the grocery and forgetting to buy milk. But Helen did get the one other piece of information David was able to recall. The woman who was renting the Liebmans' house had a connection here. She had been married to someone from Memphis.

UP the street, Edith Shapiro was eating at the Newburgers' house, which she often did since her husband died. Tziporah Newburger had given her a standing invitation. When other people extended invitations, Edith never knew if they were being sincere; she assumed they didn't really want a sad old lady around. Only Tziporah seemed to really mean it. She had invited her not once, not twice but three times until finally Edith had accepted. Tziporah's mother was Edith's husband's third cousin, and that made it easier; being related was, after all, the most important thing there was, and Edith was determined to cling to any branch of her dwindling family tree. And now, after a few months, the Newburgers' living room was her second home. Edith had even grown used to Tziporah's nervous demeanor, to the plastic tablecloths Tziporah spread over her good linen ones, the paper plates she relied on, and the chaos of so many children screaming, running around, knocking things over.

After the youngest kids had been put to bed, tucked in once and then twice, it was finally possible for Edith to reveal what she knew. She felt it was her obligation as a guest to always come equipped with some interesting topic of conversation and a nice bottle of grape juice; that way, the Newburgers wouldn't grow tired of her company.

"This afternoon," Edith said and paused dramatically, "I spoke to my cousin Jeanette who lives in New Jersey, and I happened to mention that a woman with a little girl had moved in."

Wasn't this a coincidence, but a few weeks before, Jeanette had run into Barbara Jacobs, who used to live in Memphis. They were in line at a kosher bakery in New Jersey, and at the time Barbara was looking after her only granddaughter. Her son, Benjamin, had died in a terrible car accident two years before and this little girl was all she had left of him. Jeanette overheard the child—a sweet, blond-haired little girl—talking about the new place she and her mother were moving, somewhere far away. When Jeanette leaned closer, trying to pick out a fresh chocolate babka, she swore she heard the word Memphis. Jeanette's ears perked up and though she didn't ask—she didn't want to appear nosy—she was quite certain the word was Memphis.

According to what Edith and Tziporah pieced together, the girl in the bakery must have been Ayala—how many blond-haired little girls could be moving to Memphis in such a short period of time? And if this was true, then Barbara Jacobs must have been Batsheva's mother-in-law, Batsheva having been married to her son, Benjamin. Edith and Tziporah nodded in satisfaction. Everything was starting to make sense.

AT the Levy household, Mrs. Levy had information which would confirm Edith and Tziporah's hypothesis. As usual, Mrs. Levy had a crowd for dinner; she preferred cooking for big groups and that night, the Berners and the Reinhards had been invited. Mrs. Levy always served buffet style. She enjoyed spreading out a meal on her best serving pieces, the pickles and olives arranged just so, the brisket carved and decorated with sprigs of parsley, the cherry noodle kugel set out on a bed of lettuce so that the colors contrasted with the right amount of drama. And then the excitement of the guests seeing the food all at once. It was more creative; it turned cooking and serving into an art.

Once everyone had piled food on their plates and returned to their seats, Mrs. Levy cleared her throat, making sure she had everyone's undivided attention. At the other end of the table, her husband, Irving, smiled. He was used to her taking control, and he loved seeing her shine like this, all eyes on her as if she were a movie star.

"Something strange happened last week at the Ladies' Night Out Supperette," she began. "The Supperette itself was lovely—the food was delicious and the decorations were perfect. But . . ."

At the time, Mrs. Levy hadn't known what to make of it, but after her visit to Batsheva that afternoon, it snapped into place. At the Supperette—right after the smoked salmon quiches—the Rabbi's wife, Mimi Rubin, started asking how the Jacobs were doing, wondering if anyone had spoken to them since Benjamin died, if anyone remembered where Benjamin's wife was from.

"It's not like Mimi to go around gossiping. But then I realized that she must know something the rest of us didn't," Mrs. Levy explained.

Not one to hold her tongue, she had come right out and asked Mimi why she was so curious. But Mimi said she had been thinking about them, that was all.

"I didn't buy that. Not for a minute. I didn't know why she was asking, I just knew there had to be a reason. And now I know what that is," Mrs. Levy said. According to her now well-documented theory, Batsheva was the Jacobs' former daughter-in-law and she had no doubt called the Rabbi and inquired about the community before moving in. Mimi must have known Batsheva was coming, even if the rest of us didn't. It was common, Mrs. Levy knew, to do this, but obviously there were special circumstances at play here. Batsheva was hardly the usual newcomer, hardly someone who had selected this community because she was a good match for it. Mimi must have been doing a little background work, trying to get the whole story, so she could keep an eye out for this woman.

Mrs. Levy was filled with the satisfaction of once again being able to detect any piece of news, as if she were a seismograph sensitive to every shift in the community. She rose to serve dessert. This week she had gone all out: individual lemon mousse freezes with a pareve whipped-cream topping, in addition to her famous peach pie and her mother's apple spice upside-down cake.

THESE pieces of information about Batsheva and her daughter stirred our memories and at each of our tables we began putting them in order. Jocelyn Shanzer remembered that many years after the Jacobs moved away from Memphis, Benjamin had become engaged to a non-Jewish girl that he met in New York. His family had tried to hush up the news. There were no announcements or photographs of the happy couple in the Jewish newspapers, no engagement parties or phone calls to old friends. Of course we heard about it anyway and knew that even though she was converting, the Jacobs were heartbroken. We too hadn't been sure what to make of the wedding, whether we should be happy for Benjamin or if this was a sign that he was no longer religious, her conversion only an appeasement for his parents.

Doreen Sheinberg recalled that we hadn't called or sent mazel tov cards with glass bowls or crock pots as engagement gifts. It was a small wedding, only their immediate families and a few friends. We weren't offended that we hadn't been invited, even though we had invited them to all our weddings and bar mitzvahs. After that, it was harder to keep in touch. We heard little about the Jacobs until Mrs. Levy got a phone call one morning with the bad news: Benjamin and his wife and small daughter (whose birth we hadn't heard about) were driving in the Catskill Mountains, a weekend vacation. It was raining, and up there the roads are dark, the turns sharp and the edges steep. Benjamin was killed instantly, but his wife and daughter escaped unharmed.

Since then, we hadn't heard much about Benjamin's wife and daughter. We had eventually stopped wondering about them and assumed that they had stopped being religious. Now that her connection to Judaism was gone, she would have returned to her family and her people. Eating our desserts, we shook our heads and drew the only possible conclusion: the woman who had moved into our neighborhood was Benjamin Jacobs's wife, scooped up by some cyclone and deposited here for God knows what reason. This feeling of wonder added a new spice to our Shabbos meals, an extra pinch of excitement.

That night no one saw Batsheva. The crickets chirped in muffled tones, the only sounds on our streets. It hadn't cooled off and the air was full from the relentless heat and humidity. Every once in a while, a shadow passed behind Batsheva's windows, then vanished from sight. A few times, we saw a hand move aside the curtain, revealing the hazy outline of a face. As the night wore on, our houses went dark, our automatic timers switching off our lights one by one. But Batsheva's house was still and her lights burned the whole night like a lonely beacon calling out from the middle of our neighborhood.

2

THE NEXT MORNING, WE walked to shul with thoughts of Batsheva still on our minds. The shul stands proudly at the center of our world like a beloved oldest son. It was built by the first Jews who came to Memphis more than a hundred years before. But this is no ordinary shul. Instead of the simple buildings that exist in Jewish communities twice our size, we have the equivalent of a cathedral that rivals the magnificent steepled structures decorating every corner of this Bible Belt city.

The sanctuary is shaped like an amphitheater, with a mechitza dividing the shul into two, a men's section and a women's. The chairs are purple and the walls are finished with panels of silver. The color scheme is no accident, no passing fad; it was modeled after the mishkan, the tabernacle the Jews built in the desert, made of rich tapestries of red, blue, and purple. Because we had grown up here, we were always surprised when visitors commented that they felt like they were in a disco, that they expected a strobe light to descend and no one other than Elvis Presley to rise from underneath the bima. When we visited other shuls, we took in their dark walls, black chairs and subdued carpeting and felt a swelling of pride, a bite of nostalgia for home.

We arrived at our leisure, sending our husbands and children ahead, not considering ourselves late unless we showed up after Rabbi Rubin's speech; no women were there at eight-thirty when davening officially began. We settled in, flipping through our siddurs to the right page, and took a look around. The men's section looked empty. They were sitting farther apart from each other than we did, wrapped in their black-and-white tallises. Some of them sang along with the cantor, swaying back and forth. Others wandered around or talked to each other or dozed in the back row, letting out a snore every now and then. The women's section was livelier. Brightly colored hats rose around us like a city skyline. We wore straw dyed in every shade, tall like skyscrapers, rounded like sports stadiums, trimmed with pink satin bows, silk flowers, peacock feathers, netted black veils, and cornucopias of fruit.

From her spot in the middle of the women's section, Helen Shayowitz noticed that Mimi Rubin, the Rabbi's wife, wasn't in shul. "Poor Mimi," she said. "She must still be getting over that terrible cold." Mimi was always coming down with one thing or another—she was delicate, more susceptible to whatever germ was passing through town.

"With it so hot out, it's a wonder we aren't all sick," Tziporah Newburger said nervously, having read that week about the dangers of being overheated.

"I'm going to run over a pot of chicken matzo ball soup to Mimi the minute Shabbos is over," Helen decided. Even though Mrs. Levy openly questioned whether Mimi wasn't sick a little too often to warrant soup brought over every time, Helen loved Mimi. She was the one person (besides Mrs. Levy of course) that she aspired to be like.

"How do you make your matzo balls?" Edith Shapiro asked. "I refrigerate the mixture. That way they're so soft you can cut them with a spoon. That was how my husband, bless his memory, liked them."

"What I do," Helen leaned forward to reveal, "is add a pinch of cinnamon and then take a piece of chopped meat and wrap the matzo ball around it so there's a nice surprise inside." Helen believed in being forthcoming with her recipes—asking for a recipe was the most sincere form of flattery—but still, she always left out one ingredient (in this case, the dash of vanilla) so she could keep her chef's edge.

Mrs. Levy couldn't believe they were discussing matzo balls at a time like this. Apparently, if the conversation was going to be focused in the right direction, it would be up to her.

"Speaking of people who aren't in shul today, notice who else isn't here," Mrs. Levy said.

Helen, Tziporah, and Edith stopped talking, all thoughts of matzo balls dissipating. Mrs. Levy was right, Helen realized; she hadn't thought to notice if Batsheva had come. That was the difference between her and Mrs. Levy. While she was often distracted from the things that went on, Mrs. Levy was singularly focused on the day-to-day issues that affected the community. Tziporah looked around, to see if they had missed Batsheva walking in, and Edith viewed Mrs. Levy with renewed respect for being able to command their attention so swiftly; she could only dream of someday occupying such a position in the community.

"You didn't think Batsheva would come to shul on her second day here, did you? I'm sure she needs time to settle in," Helen said, though she, like all of us, was disappointed. Batsheva had been in the backs of our minds all night. Even as we slept, something had nagged at us, the same itching feeling of being away on vacation and worrying that we had forgotten to turn off the oven or lock the back door.

"I'm not saying we should necessarily make anything of this, but I did dream about Batsheva last night. She was like a ghost, wearing this long white dress, and she was floating in and out of our house," Mrs. Levy said. She shook her head. She had woken up in a cold sweat from this dream and had only been able to fall back to sleep after nudging Irving awake and having him put his arms around her.

"It's still early, so we don't know for sure that she's not coming," Edith said. "In the meantime, we'd best take our minds off her."

We tried to forget about Batsheva. There were other things we were supposed to be thinking about. We still hadn't found the right page in our siddurs, we needed to quickly recite the morning service that we had missed, and it was already time for the Torah reading. The Rabbi was standing in front of the ark facing east, our eyes and hearts toward Jerusalem. Originally, the ark was covered with a tapestry depicting the splitting of the Red Sea. But it had become worn and faded, so last year, the Zuckerman family donated new sliding doors shaped like the Ten Commandments—two big tablets made of genuine Jerusalem stone. At the dedication ceremony, Naomi Eisenberg had commented that when the ark was opened, it looked as if the Ten

Commandments were being dropped all over again. We didn't find that funny; on the contrary, those looming tablets reminded us of Whom we stood before.

We followed along as the Torah portion of the week was read. It was one of our favorite sections, a relief after weeks of reading about the boring temple sacrifices. We listened to the story of Korach who rebelled against Moshe's authority in the desert, and we tried to envision the scene, the people assembled, those with Moshe on one side, and those against him on the other. In a show of thunder, lightning and fire that outdid any Fourth of July fireworks we had ever seen, the ground became a monster, its jaws opening and swallowing Korach and his followers alive. As we were getting into this scene, imagining ourselves there, the doors of the sanctuary opened. Our picture of Korach disappeared and we turned to see Batsheva and Ayala in the doorway.

Batsheva didn't flinch as we looked her over. She straightened her shoulders, held her head high and flipped her hair back. She was wearing a dress that was loose and flowy, made of a thin beige fabric. Somehow, even with all that material, it wasn't modest enough. It lacked the propriety of the tailored dresses and summer suits we wore, and it made us all too conscious of her body underneath, her long legs and thin torso. Ayala stood behind her, biting her bottom lip, ready to burst into tears. While Batsheva didn't seem fazed by all the new faces, Ayala looked timid and vulnerable.

When Batsheva saw Mrs. Levy, she waved. This, Mrs. Levy knew, was to be expected; she was the only person Batsheva knew in the entire city. She gave her a nod and waved back. But there were no available seats near Mrs. Levy; she always sat one row behind Helen Shayowitz with Bessie Kimmel, her first cousin, on one side and Edith Shapiro on the other, and some traditions were not meant to be broken. Batsheva saw this and kept going, scanning the rows for two empty seats. They weren't hard to find. The shul only filled up on Rosh Hashanah and Yom Kippur, and on an ordinary Shabbos like this, the room looked like a movie theater showing an unpopular film. Batsheva reached the front of the women's section, and they sat down in the first row where none of us ever sat.

We tried once again to follow the Torah reading. We were in shul, we should be paying attention, we chided ourselves and each other. But we couldn't help it. We kept looking up to steal glimpses of Batsheva.

Helen Shayowitz leaned over toward Becky Feldman, her chumash open to the wrong page. "I heard that she is definitely a convert."

"I don't know about the rest of y'all, but I knew she wasn't Jewish the minute I laid eyes on her," Becky said. She considered herself something of an expert in these matters. Her daughter Shira had been hanging out with some girl she met at the mall and she only had to take one look to know that she wasn't Jewish.

"It's the saddest story I ever heard," Rena Reinhard said. "Benjamin Jacobs dying like that and now she's like a lost soul showing up here."

"I knew it. I'm telling y'all, I knew it. As soon as I saw her, that's who I guessed it had to be," Mrs. Levy said.

The Torah reading ended and we stopped whispering. One of the men lifted the Torah, the parchment open wide, and together we proclaimed in Hebrew: *This is the Torah that Moshe put before the children of Israel, through the word of God and the hand of Moshe.* Then the cantor took the Torah and carried it around the room while he and the men sang: *The voice of God is in the waters, the glory of God thunders aloud. The voice of God is in the deepest waters, the voice of God is majesty.* We didn't sing along. Even though we knew the words, we hummed quietly. That was just the way we did things.

But Batsheva sang, loud enough for everyone to hear. She knew the words, and to our surprise, her Hebrew sounded natural, even better than some of ours. But the fact that she was singing so loudly was evidence enough that she wasn't one of us. Maybe if she had stood in the back and sang that would have been one thing. But she was in the front row and her body swayed to the words, her eyes were closed, and her fists were tightly clenched. She was beseeching God, right at this very minute, right in front of everyone.

"Someone certainly likes to sing," Bessie Kimmel commented.

"I think she's showing off," Edith Shapiro said. In her day, she had been known for having a very nice voice. In fact, years and years ago, she had had a solo in her public school's Christmas pageant, but that was something she didn't go around telling people.

"Maybe that's how they do it in church. Not that I've ever been inside one, but I would guess that they do a lot of singing," Bessie said.

"But why does she have to sing so loud?" Helen Shayowitz asked. "I'm no rabbi, but I don't think that's how things are supposed to be done."

"It sounds to me like she's trying to audition for the cantor's job," Mrs. Levy chuckled.

All this time Leanna Zuckerman had been sitting quietly, not joining in any of these conversations. Leanna was originally from Chicago but had lived in Memphis for eleven years, ever since she married Bruce Zuckerman, a born and bred Memphian. Usually she liked living here, but today, she was tired of hearing what people had to say about Batsheva; she wished they would give the poor woman a break. Leanna didn't dare say this out loud though. The price she'd have to pay for such a comment was too great. News of her rudeness would, in minutes, get back to her mother-in-law, who was either a close friend or a relative of everyone in town. But Leanna enjoyed Batsheva's singing. Her voice was beautiful and it was nice to see someone who had her heart in her davening, someone who wasn't just reciting empty words. It made Leanna want to sing a little herself.

The cantor carried the Torah around the room, the procession of Rabbi, shul president, and four vice-presidents behind him. We reached across the railing and touched the Torah's velvet covering with our siddurs, then brought them to our lips. When he neared the bottom of the stairs, Batsheva picked Ayala up and raised her over the railing, so she could kiss the Torah with her bare lips. Then Batsheva leaned over and did the same.

"How do you like that?" Mrs. Levy said. "Bare lips and all. I'm sure that's not allowed."

"Don't ask me," Doreen Sheinberg said. "I don't know things like that."

"I don't either," Helen Shayowitz said. She hadn't studied in a yeshiva as many girls did these days; she simply did what her mother had done and her mother had certainly never kissed the Torah like that.

We turned to Tziporah Newburger. She was officially the most religious of any of us. If anyone would know, she would.

"Of course it's not allowed," Tziporah pronounced. "It's immodest, calling so much attention to herself."

We nodded in agreement. Modesty, that was a good one. When in doubt, we could always assume there was an issue of modesty. We'd have to remember that for next time.

With the Torah put away, it was time for the Rabbi's speech. We checked our watches and tried to calculate if shul was running faster or slower than usual. But the speech could always throw that off; there was no way to tell how long it would last. Once, the Rabbi had spoken for a full forty-five minutes. Helen Shayowitz remembered it especially well because it was the Shabbos of her son's bar mitzvah and all the out-of-town guests had grumbled.

The Rabbi stood up and took his place at the pulpit. "What did Korach do wrong?" he began. "What is his sin that warranted such a horrific punishment?"

He paused to see if any of us would volunteer an answer as we sometimes did. But not this week. With Batsheva here, we had too much on our minds.

"Let's open our chumashim and see what the real issue is," the Rabbi said.

We followed, shuffling through to the right pages, again trying to keep our minds on shul.

"You don't think," Edith Shapiro said, "that she's planning on staying here permanently, do you?"

"Well my God, Edith, of course she is," Arlene Salzman whispered, hiding her mouth behind her chumash so the Rabbi wouldn't think she was talking during his speech. "She wouldn't have moved all her stuff down if she wasn't planning on being here at least a few months."

"But she doesn't know anyone. She has no family here," Edith said.

The Rabbi began to read. "*They assembled themselves against Moshe and Aaron and said: You take too much authority upon yourselves. Isn't the entire congregation holy and isn't God among everyone? So why do you raise yourselves above the people?*"

"Single women with little girls don't pick themselves up and move clear across the country for no reason. Maybe she moved here because of someone specific," Becky Feldman said. "If you know what I mean."

Could it be true, we wondered. Was there a secret relationship being carried on behind our backs? We glanced at the men's section, at Irving Levy and Alvin Shayowitz and Bruce Zuckerman and Daniel Feldman. As hard as it was to imagine, perhaps one of them knew a great deal more about Batsheva than they were admitting.

"How can you say such a thing?" Tziporah asked. "We're religious. No one we know would do anything like that."

"Stranger things have happened, dear," Mrs. Levy said. "Not in Memphis, of course, but certainly in other places. All I can say is that I don't have a good feeling about this woman."

"And because of that we're supposed to ostracize her? I suppose you have ESP now," Leanna Zuckerman said from her seat behind Mrs. Levy. She hadn't meant to say this out loud, but now that she had, she felt a strange relief; it was almost worth the piercing look she received from her mother-in-law.

Mrs. Levy spun around. "If you must know, I have a knack for getting these things right. Call it what you like, but when you've lived here as long as I have, you know when something isn't going to turn out well." She readjusted her hat, making sure it still sat on her head at the most attractive angle, and turned back around.

It was best not to respond, Leanna decided; one assertive comment was enough for today.

In the silence that followed, our attention returned to the Rabbi. We had missed some crucial element of the speech, and he had moved to a different, presumably unrelated topic. "Which is why we need to support our school and our institutions and our leaders. A community that doesn't has lost the fear of heaven," the Rabbi said.

"What I'm wondering," Rena Reinhard said, "is how the Jacobs feel about her moving so far away. That little girl is their only granddaughter."

"I wonder if she still speaks to them. The way I heard it, they weren't big fans of her when she and Benjamin got married," Naomi Eisenberg said.

"I feel like calling the Jacobs after Shabbos to see how they're doing. I haven't spoken to them in ages," Jocelyn Shanzer said.

"I couldn't do that. I'd feel too uncomfortable," Rena said. "You'd have to mention that Batsheva was here. If you didn't, it would be obvious you're avoiding the topic. But if you did bring it up, they would think that was the only reason you were calling."

The Rabbi closed his chumash, the sign that he was done. "May it be God's will and together we say Amen," he said.

Even though we weren't one hundred percent sure what he was talking about, we were sure it was a good cause. We joined in, our voices merging into a single Amen.

Shul was almost over and, restlessly, we checked our watches: already 11:45. We were in the home stretch. All we had to do was make it through mussaf, which, thankfully, was short. Twenty minutes later, Jeremy Shanzer, the shul president, made the announcements. The Ladies Home Study Circle was meeting the first Wednesday of the month at Doreen Sheinberg's house. This month's topic was Prayer: The Proven Potent Path. Dessert would be served following the class. The clothing drive was still under way. And tickets were on sale for the youth group raffle—buy them and support our children.

When shul ended, we filed out of the sanctuary, wishing each other Good Shabbos, complimenting each other on a lovely hat, a new piece of jewelry. We moved into the social hall, which was also used for bar mitzvahs, weddings, and sisterhood events. Whenever there is a function, the room looks as lovely as the Peabody Hotel. In fact, when Bessie Kimmel's daughter got married, a local florist had transformed the room into a blossoming garden, with bunches of pink roses and sprigs of baby's breath cascading down the walls.

Batsheva had been one of the first to leave, and by the time we got into the social hall, she was standing with Ayala. Other people, if they had no one to talk to, might have left, embarrassed to be seen alone at the edge of a crowd. But not Batsheva. She smiled at each person who passed and said Good Shabbos. We smiled and returned the greeting, meaning to properly introduce ourselves. But each time we were about to, we got caught up in another conversation. Anxious to make peace after her outburst at Mrs. Levy, Leanna Zuckerman let everyone know that the baby had finally slept through the night. Helen Shayowitz had spoken to her daughter, Tamara, up in New York City. Things were getting serious with the young man she was dating; we should keep our fingers crossed and pray for an engagement.

We filled our plates, spooning out pickled herring, gefilte fish balls, crackers and chocolate cake. With plates full of food, we listened to the Rabbi make kiddush: *Remember the Sabbath Day and keep it holy. For six days you may work, but the seventh day is the Sabbath, for Hashem your God.* Standing by the Rabbi's side was Yosef, his only child. The week before, Yosef had come home for the summer, on break from yeshiva in New York City, where he was studying to be a rabbi. No one talked about it anymore, but for years Mimi and the Rabbi had been unable to have children, one miscarriage after another until they had almost given up. We had grown accustomed to watching Mimi daven, holding her siddur in front of her face to cover the tears that streamed down her cheeks. But now Yosef was twenty-two years old and so special that he almost made up for the rest of the children they couldn't have.

The Rabbi smiled at Yosef with the wonder we had seen in our husbands after the births of our children, the look that asked if the existence of this other being was possible. But on the Rabbi, that look was there all these years later. When we looked at Yosef, we understood why. Not only was he exceptionally smart, but he was handsome as well. He was close to six feet tall, and he had filled out recently; his shoulders were broader than we remembered them being. He had the same dark hair that, on the Rabbi, was beginning to thin and gray. His chin, nose and jaw had a regal sharpness, but his smile had the same softness as Mimi's.

We were thrilled to have Yosef home. We remembered the day he was born, when he started first grade, when he fell off a swing and broke his wrist, when he had the chicken pox. We remembered every birthday party of his, as if we were surrogate parents peering in over his shoulder. His bar mitzvah was a day we would never forget. Yosef led the services, read from the Torah and spoke from the pulpit. He had an ease and confidence unusual for a thirteen-year-old, as if he had been standing in front of the shul his whole life. Afterward, the kiddush was the biggest we had ever seen. Mimi had baked for weeks, creating a mountain of cakes and pastries to celebrate Yosef's passage into manhood.

In the midst of eating, we went over to wish the Rabbi a Good Shabbos and compliment him on the insightful speech he had given.

But more than talking to the Rabbi, we relished the opportunity to speak to Yosef. We gathered around him, jostling to get closer. He told us how much he was enjoying yeshiva, that he was getting along nicely with his roommates, that it was wonderful to be home. He looked each of us in the eye and his voice was filled with warmth. He remembered to ask how Tziporah Newburger's allergies were, he was sensitive enough to remember that Rachel Ann Berkowitz's mother had been unwell. He carried around these pieces of our lives, and that made us feel like he was always with us and we were always with him.

Of all of us, Edith Shapiro had the strongest connection with Yosef. It began years ago, when her husband, Kieve, was alive. He and Yosef sat near each other in shul, and with his own sons grown and moved away, Kieve watched him with pride.

"This boy," he used to say, putting his arm around Yosef, "this boy is going to be something special."

Kieve died the year before Yosef graduated from high school—liver cancer, there was nothing the doctors could do—and Yosef started visiting Edith on Shabbos afternoons. His visits were all she had to look forward to, the only break from the monotony of so many days alone. Even after he went away to yeshiva, he continued these visits whenever he was home. Yosef would arrive after lunch and Edith would have a plate of cookies waiting. They would talk, mostly about Kieve, and before he left, Yosef would say a few words of Torah in Kieve's memory.

"It's good to have you home," Edith said to Yosef that morning, full of these memories. "We miss you when you're not here." She took a good look at him. For a second, Edith thought he looked tired. But it was probably a result of traveling, she decided. There was no cause for worry.

"I've missed you too," Yosef said.

"Are you happy in New York? It's not like Memphis. It gets very cold up there."

"I am happy, but it's great to be home. There's nowhere like Memphis."

"You're a very smart boy. Kieve and I always knew that about you," Edith said, relieved that even after all the time he had spent away, Yosef still realized that Memphis was a special place. He hadn't been lured away by the glamorous hustle and bustle of life in the big city. In his heart, he was and always would be a Memphis boy.

The Rabbi tapped Yosef on the shoulder, bringing him into his conversation with Mayer Green. "Listen to this, Yosef. Mayer has a question for you," the Rabbi said, eager to show off his son.

Every time he saw Yosef, Mayer came up with a question to try to stump Yosef. He would spend hours preparing it, and each time Yosef answered without a problem. Mayer described the situation: a piece of meat falls into a pot of milk, breaking the laws of kosher. Could the milk still be drunk?

It was an easy question for Yosef, but even so, he nodded his head with great seriousness, making the old man feel good about himself and the question. Not only was Yosef smart, but he was kind and modest as well. Even if Mayer had been able to come up with harder questions, there was no doubt Yosef would be able to answer those. The Rabbi's eyes sparkled with pride as he watched his son say that it depended on the ratio of milk to meat. This was what he had been raising his son for, and it was only a hint of the greatness that lay ahead. We also saw this as a glimpse of what was to come. Ever since Yosef was a little boy, we had harbored the hope that one day he would succeed his father here, the rabbinate passed down like the kingship from David to Solomon.

In the middle of this conversation, Mrs. Levy went over to Yosef and the Rabbi. "Shabbat Shalom, y'all," she greeted them. "I'm sorry to interrupt, but I haven't had the chance to welcome Yosef home. It's not everyday that we have him here so y'all are going to have to share him with the rest of us."

Mrs. Levy had a way of saying things that made it difficult to argue, so the Rabbi did what the rest of us did: he moved aside and let her continue.

"What are your plans for the summer?" she inquired.

"I'll be learning with my father," he said and glanced in his father's direction. The Rabbi met Yosef's eyes and smiled. The Rabbi had been looking forward to this for months. Every time we had asked how Yosef was doing, he would tell us that Yosef would be home for the entire summer and they would be learning together.

"And then you'll be going back to yeshiva?" she asked.

"After the holidays, in October."

His visits home were longer than most children's. The obligation of being the only child made a big impression on him, and he enjoyed fulfilling the commandment of honoring his mother and father.

"Oh good, a nice long visit. And I'll bet it won't be long before we're calling you 'Rabbi.'"

Yosef looked down, uncomfortable at all the attention she was heaping on him. "Another year," he said.

"I can hardly wait. Our own Rabbi Yosef. And then one day, our own Rabbi Yosef right here in Memphis."

Before Yosef could respond, Mrs. Levy wished them a Good Shabbos and went off to fetch Irving, who was, no doubt, eating too many sweets when he was supposed to be watching his weight.

Batsheva was still at the kiddush, standing next to Ayala. The little girl's plate was overflowing with cake, crackers and gefilte fish, and she was dropping crumbs everywhere. Batsheva talked to her daughter as if she were an adult, pointing out the memorial plaques hanging on the walls, the photographs of recent shul functions tacked to a bulletin board. Even though there were plenty of other kids, running around the social hall, Ayala made no move to join them. She just nodded and listened to what her mother was saying.

Naomi Eisenberg was also standing by herself, a few feet from Batsheva. Her husband hadn't come to shul that morning—he found it hard to sit through so many hours—and she had already chatted with the few people she was in the mood to speak to. Even though Naomi had gone to the Hebrew Academy with us, attended Stern College in New York, and after getting married, moved back home, she had, somewhere along the way, breathed in another world. She worked part-time as a social worker and left her children with a babysitter. And she was always disagreeing with the rest of us, about the school, the role of the Ladies Auxiliary: every year or so there was some incident.

Naomi couldn't stand seeing Batsheva alone. She was sure everyone was planning on introducing herself, but everyone probably thought that someone else would make the first move. Determined to make Batsheva feel welcome, she put down her plate and walked over to her.

"I was standing there watching you and even though I'm sure everyone is planning on coming over, it takes a while. That's how this community is. Of course Mimi, the Rabbi's wife, isn't here this Shabbos. She would be the first one over, I can promise you that."

Batsheva smiled at Naomi and in that space, a hundred more thoughts came rushing into Naomi's mind. It had been ages since she talked to someone new and she felt invigorated.

"I heard you're living in the Liebmans' house. A very nice family, if a little uptight. Once I happened to spill a little soda on the carpet and it looked like Estie was going to cry. Anyway, they moved because he got a big promotion, a lot of money I was told. I'm sure you've heard about them. News travels fast here. Trust me, I'll bet everyone in this room knows your life story and you haven't been here twenty-four hours."

"Actually," Batsheva said, "it's nice to be in a place where people know each other. It's one of the reasons I came here. You've heard what they say about New York: you could die and your neighbors wouldn't notice until they smelled you decomposing." She laughed at her own joke and Naomi joined her, already knowing that she was going to like this woman.

"That wouldn't happen here, that's one thing you can be sure of. Everyone would know about it at least an hour beforehand," Naomi said.

Naomi noticed that people were looking her way, taking note of the fact that she was talking to Batsheva. She could almost hear what they must be saying: how nice, the two outsiders becoming friends. She hated to give everyone the satisfaction of being correct, but Naomi sensed that she and Batsheva had many things in common. She was only a few years older than Batsheva and it would be nice to have a new friend.

"Did you move here because of Benjamin? Like maybe if you lived here you could get over him?" Naomi asked.

Batsheva looked surprised that her connection to Benjamin had already been established. "It was just this feeling that I had to go somewhere. Losing Benjamin made me feel like I had nothing to hold onto, and I needed to be rooted inside something."

"I know what you mean. Sometimes I wonder if I would feel tied to anything if I didn't live in Memphis," Naomi said.

Naomi had been thinking about moving her whole life. She yearned for new faces and new scenery. Her life seemed to be in reruns, except that she was now the parent instead of the child. She lived five blocks from the house she had grown up in, she was friends with the same people she had gone to elementary school with, her children went to the same Torah Academy with the same teachers and the same problems. But even so, she didn't know if she could ever leave. She had been here too long and had set down too many roots.

As Naomi took in Batsheva's eagerness to make a place for herself here, she had the urge to give her a warning that things might not be as ideal as she thought. Memphis was great only if you were like everyone else. If not, it could be tough. But she hated being the one to ruin Batsheva's enthusiasm; that would come soon enough. And she wondered if maybe she had grown so cynical from feeling like an outsider that she was unable to appreciate what was special about the community.

"You let me know if I can help out," Naomi said. She wished Batsheva a Good Shabbos and went home to her husband.

Bessie Kimmel and Estelle Marks, her sister, saw Naomi walk away and because not being the first one to approach a newcomer made it easier, they went over to Batsheva.

"You look like you're new," Bessie announced, and her sister nodded in agreement. "I always go over to anyone I don't recognize. In fact, that's how I met my husband, fifty-six years ago. We were at kiddush and I looked up and saw this nice-looking young man. I went over to him and said, 'I thought I knew everyone in Memphis.' It turned out that he had just moved here. A year later, we were married," she said, smiling at how nicely things had turned out. "So tell me, are you from up north?"

"I was living in New York for a few years before I came here, but I'm not from anywhere in particular. I'm a mix of a lot of different places," Batsheva said.

What kind of answer was this? You were either from somewhere or you weren't. Well, she must be from up north, Bessie decided. Even if she wasn't going to admit it. She could hear it in the way Batsheva spoke. She had only needed to hear a few words.

"We, of course, are from Memphis," Bessie said. "Fourth generation. Our family came down right after the civil war. They were among the first Jews here, maybe even the very first, and we've been here ever since."

"I haven't lived in one place for more than a few years," Batsheva said.

"But Memphis isn't any place. This is a wonderful community. Everyone knows each other. We have for years. It's the only home we've ever known," Bessie said.

"That's what we're hoping it will be for us too," Batsheva said.

Bessie looked down at Ayala, who had taken a stack of Styrofoam cups from one of the tables and was using them to build a pyramid. Batsheva hadn't done anything to address the situation except to smile encouragingly. Such lackadaisical attitudes, Bessie knew, could only lead to trouble. But perhaps with a little guidance, Ayala might blossom into a proper young lady. It wasn't that Batsheva seemed like a bad mother, at least not as far as Bessie could tell. But she did seem a little careless: one of Ayala's small white socks had a rip, her Shabbos dress had a stain, and her hair wasn't pulled back neatly with a ribbon or a barrette. The community could give them some much-needed structure and provide them with a good example of how one ought to be.

"It's been a pleasure meeting you but we need to be going," Bessie said and with that, the two sisters moved off toward the schnapps table.

When the crowd thinned out and most of the food and conversation were finished, Yosef walked in Batsheva's direction. We had seen him take note of her presence earlier, but he hadn't made any move to talk to her. This was exactly as it should be. It would hardly be appropriate for him to be the one welcoming her to Memphis. He scanned the tables for a piece of herring or cake. He had been so busy saying hello to everyone that he hadn't had a chance to eat. With a red toothpick, he speared a remaining piece of gefilte fish. As he was popping it into his mouth, he stepped back and bumped into Batsheva, who had appeared right in his path.

"Hello," Batsheva said to Yosef.

Yosef looked down and shifted his weight from one foot to the other. He wasn't accustomed to talking to girls. Batsheva was more than ten years older than him, but she wasn't a lady of the community and those were the only females he was comfortable with. With girls his own age, any socializing was supposed to wait until he was ready to get married. Not that we weren't thinking about who we might fix Yosef up with; the sooner he got married, the sooner he could move back to Memphis. We already had a few ideas, a cousin's cousin in St. Louis, a very pretty girl from a nice (not to mention wealthy) family who might be right for Yosef. And because St. Louis was so close to Memphis, we couldn't imagine that she would object to living here. And Becky Feldman thought that her seventeen-year-old daughter, Shira, might get along nicely with Yosef. True, Shira was a little young, but everyone was always commenting how sophisticated she was for her age.

"You must be the Rabbi's son. You're attracting as much attention as I am," Batsheva said. "I'm not sure if it's you or me everyone's looking at."

"Don't worry, it's probably me. It's my first weekend home," Yosef explained. "Did you just move in?"

"Yes, and I live right down the street," Batsheva said. "From what I've been told, I'm sure you'll hear sooner or later that I was married to Benjamin Jacobs."

"I did hear that," he said.

"Did you know Benjamin? He must have been a few years ahead of you."

"He was a lot older than me. He was actually my camp counselor one summer."

"That's funny, I remember him talking about being at camp." Batsheva laughed. "God, that was a long time ago. What was it, twelve or thirteen years ago?"

"I think so. I was ten years old," Yosef said. "And I was also at the funeral. I was in school in New York, so when I heard what had happened, I wanted to go," Yosef said.

"That's so nice," Batsheva exclaimed. "Maybe that's why I feel like I know you."

We expected Yosef to be thrown off, to blush and stammer and not know how to respond. We still thought of him as being a little shy, comfortable with us only because he had known us his whole life. But watching him talk to Batsheva, we saw a glimpse of another side of him. He had become confident and poised. He knew exactly what to say.

"Even though I hadn't seen Benjamin in a while, I felt a connection to him," Yosef said. "When I was growing up, he was always so nice to me. He used to come up to me every Shabbos in shul and shake my hand as if I were an adult. And in school, whenever he passed by my classroom, he would wave to me and make a funny face. I always felt like he was looking out for me."

Batsheva smiled wistfully. "I love hearing about his life before I knew him. We were only together for five years, so there's so much that I never knew."

"That must be hard," Yosef said.

"It is. But I thought that if I came here I could be more connected to him and that I could raise Ayala the same way he was raised."

Batsheva was about to say more when she looked over at the Rabbi. Even though Alvin Shayowitz was telling him about the board's plans to fix the shul's roof—he was chairman of the building committee and the roof was their top priority—the Rabbi was looking at his son.

"I think your father is looking for you," she said.

Yosef caught his father's eye and a guilty look passed across his face. We remembered this look from his childhood; whenever the Rabbi had seen Yosef misbehaving, he would seem surprised that his child would do anything wrong. He would narrow his eyes and shake his head slightly and Yosef would snap to attention.

"I'd better be going," Yosef said. "It was nice to meet you."

"Bye," she said. "I'm sure I'll see you around."

He walked away, not turning around to look back at Batsheva. She took Ayala's hand and watched him as he walked up to his father and touched the back of his arm. The Rabbi smiled and put his arm around Yosef's shoulder. They walked home, their arms swaying in sync, their legs perfectly in step.

3

WE SPENT THE NEXT FEW weeks watching Batsheva. It was easy to do so—every morning, she stepped out her front door, headed down the driveway and went for a walk. Even though she walked for over an hour in humid, near hundred-degree weather, she never looked tired. She moved as if there were light music playing in the background, lightening each step. Batsheva's arms swung freely by her sides and her hair flew behind her, until she disappeared inside a hill or around a corner.

At first, Ayala went with Batsheva, her small legs struggling to keep up with her mother's long ones. She went because there was nowhere else for her to go. School didn't start for another few weeks, the Jewish Community Center day camp was halfway through its second session, and Batsheva wouldn't have been able to find a babysitter for that one hour. But we marveled that she was able to get Ayala to go. Long walks in this heat were the last thing we could have convinced our children to do. Maybe because it was just the two of them, but they seemed to spend every second together. Ayala clung to Batsheva, afraid to be without her. And as far as we knew, she had barely spoken to anyone besides her mother. We didn't have a hard time imagining why. Losing a father and moving to a new city were enough to upset any child. And to top it off, she had such an unconventional mother: that couldn't be easy.

Batsheva's walks weren't for entertainment or exercise. No, she was a woman on a mission. She ignored the passing cars, instead scanning the rows of houses, their triangular roofs rising into sharp peaks. She turned right, cutting through the empty field, down a small dead end street. From there she either walked toward Shelby Farms, the park near the city outskirts, or in the other direction toward the main shopping area. For us, Memphis was little more than our own streets and the stores and offices lining Poplar Avenue, the main street that bisects Memphis. But right from the start, Batsheva walked past the parts of the city we frequented. She didn't hold back, didn't wait to see how things were done. It was as if she had lived in Memphis her whole life.

No matter which direction Batsheva turned, she always ended up in front of the house where her husband, Benjamin, had lived. It was farther out than most of us lived and there was no shul nearby, not even ten men for a minyan. Before the Jacobs moved away, we had grown accustomed to seeing them trudge the two and a quarter miles to shul, no matter how hot and humid it was, no matter how hard the rain was falling.

At first, Batsheva paused in front of the house and looked longingly at it. A few times, we saw her wipe away tears and give Ayala a hug. We wondered if Batsheva felt closer to Benjamin by being there, if she wished she could will herself back in time to see a school-aged Benjamin emerge from the red brick house and run around the yard. Since Batsheva had been here, we too had been thinking about Benjamin, remembering the last time each of us had seen him. When he was a little boy, he had none of the rambunctiousness that ran through our boys. He was quiet and gentle, he always said "please" and "thank you, ma'am" when he spoke to us. And he would cry easily, he took everything to heart. Ayala reminded us of him; they had the same innocent faces and gentle manner.

On the last day of July, Batsheva went inside. When the Jacobs moved, they sold their house to the Ackermans, who were not technically part of the Orthodox community. They didn't keep kosher, they hadn't sent their children to the Torah Academy, and when they did attend shul (on special occasions like Rosh Hashanah or for a bar mitzvah) they drove. But Marilynne Ackerman still had a connection to us. She was Jocelyn Shanzer's third cousin and she had gone to Central

High School with Mrs. Levy and Helen Shayowitz, and they still played mah-jongg on Monday nights.

When Batsheva knocked on the door and introduced herself, Marilynne realized who she was; even though mah-jongg was taken very seriously, there was usually enough time for gossip breaks and, on the previous Monday, Mrs. Levy had filled her in. Batsheva explained that her husband had grown up in this house and had died two years before, would it be okay if she and Ayala came inside.

"I want Ayala to see the house so Benjamin can seem real to her," Batsheva said. "Ayala was only three when he died. I hate the idea that she's going to grow up remembering nothing of him."

Marilynne was, of course, surprised. Such requests didn't happen every day. But she didn't mind having Batsheva come in and look around. They walked into the living room and Batsheva stood in the doorway and took in the room.

"See, Ayala, this is the house Daddy lived in when he was your age. Can you imagine him that small? And see the backyard? That was where he played," Batsheva said and Ayala looked around carefully.

Batsheva held Ayala's hand as she walked down the hallway, peeking into each bedroom.

"Do you know which room was Benjamin's?" Batsheva asked.

"It's hard to say," Marilynne said. "It was so many years ago."

"It's okay," Batsheva said. She leaned her head against the doorpost of one of the rooms. "Something tells me it has to be this one."

Batsheva sat at the edge of the bed facing the window, lost in her own world. She stared as if Benjamin were on the other side of the pane of glass, his body floating in the sky, his limbs shaped by the clouds. She explained to Ayala how Benjamin was now part of nature, in the flowers and trees around them. Ayala nodded and patted Batsheva's arm, as if she were the mother giving comfort, and it broke Marilynne's heart.

Batsheva turned away from the window, the vision outside vanishing. "Can I trouble you for a glass of water?" she asked.

"Of course. Come sit down." Marilynne motioned to the living room couch. Batsheva and Ayala sat down and Marilynne brought a glass of water for Batsheva and a cup of juice for Ayala.

Marilynne sat next to Batsheva. Neither of them spoke and

Marilynne noticed a tiny spot on the armrest of the sofa and rubbed it clean with her finger.

"It feels good to be here," Batsheva said at last. "I almost feel like I've been here before."

"I'm happy to have the company," Marilynne said. Her husband was a lawyer at one of the most pish-posh firms in Memphis, and this meant that she never saw him; it wasn't unusual for him to work until ten o'clock at night. She had taken up hobbies to pass the time—needlepoint and gardening had become her specialties—but still, she often went stir-crazy from so many hours alone.

"I've thought about this house so many times," Batsheva said. "We never visited when he was alive but I always wanted to. I thought we could take a road trip through the South and end up in Memphis."

Marilynne touched Batsheva's hand sympathetically. "But Benjamin didn't want to?"

"He used to talk about how everyone knows everyone and is related three different ways. 'I could sneeze and everyone would know about it,' he would say. For him, it was too much. He grew up feeling suffocated. He loved living in New York, where he could do his own thing. But hearing him talk about Memphis made me want to be part of it."

Marilynne vaguely remembered Benjamin, his sandy brown hair and thin body. When he died, two years back, the news had spread rapidly, and she had felt a special connection to it, living in a house now tinged with tragedy.

"I remember when he died," Marilynne said. "Such a terrible thing. None of us could believe it."

Batsheva shook her head. "All of a sudden, I was without him, and I looked for any way to keep a connection. I called his old friends and talked to them about Benjamin. I looked at his baby pictures. I kept all his things in the apartment. I wasn't ready to accept the fact that he was gone. It was hard to keep doing the things we had always done together. We loved preparing for Shabbos together, and we would invite lots of people over, hoping we could have the kind of home where people always felt welcome. But when he died, I couldn't imagine doing that anymore. Ayala and I would be alone and when I lit Shabbos candles, I always lit an extra one for him to remember how special our Shabboses used to be."

"Like a yahrzeit candle," Marilynne said, proud of herself for knowing a Jewish term to throw in.

"Yes, except that instead of lighting it only on the anniversary of his death, I did it every week. I was looking for a way to create my own rituals to remember him and this was the most meaningful way."

All this time Ayala hadn't made a sound. She was sipping her juice, listening to the conversation. But as Batsheva continued talking about Benjamin, Ayala climbed off Batsheva's lap and went to look out Marilynne's bay windows. She stared at the backyard, at the brand-new barbecue pit and the wood deck with matching porch furniture. She took hold of Marilynne's creme damask curtains and wrapped herself in them. Batsheva smiled, not worrying that Ayala might ruin the curtains or that Marilynne might not want anyone pulling on the heavy fabric.

Many things went through Marilynne's head, but the idea that kept coming back was how did Batsheva still believe in God after what had happened. She remembered something from Hebrew school so many years ago: the story of God testing Abraham, heaping problem after problem upon him to see how righteous he really was. That was one of the justifications Marilynne gave for not being observant: she couldn't believe in a God that would allow so much suffering. Then there were the other reasons she had for not being Orthodox, the difficulty of such a strict lifestyle, the over-attention to details, the outdated nature of so many of the laws.

"Can I ask you something?" Marilynne asked. She didn't want to upset Batsheva, just as she was afraid of offending her religious friends, never sure what would be seen as disrespectful. "I don't mean to go and be personal, but when your husband died, I would think that you'd be angry at God and it would be hard to stay religious."

"I *was* angry," Batsheva said. "With Benjamin, I had this beautiful relationship and I couldn't believe he was gone. But Ayala and I walked away from the accident completely unharmed. For whatever reason, we were being watched over. That has to mean something, doesn't it? I felt like I had a purpose that I hadn't yet fulfilled and I tried to use that to ease my grief."

"That makes sense," Marilynne said. "But it still seems so hard to understand."

"I know. But I had to find ways to draw closer to God so I wouldn't feel like He abandoned me. When I pray or when I eat kosher food, I try to remember that the purpose of my actions is to seek this closeness with God and spirituality. Otherwise, I'd be completely lost."

This wasn't what Marilynne usually heard when people described being Orthodox. Helen Shayowitz and Mrs. Levy spoke about the importance of obedience and discipline, of following all parts of a rigorous system, of being connected to the past. What Batsheva was describing sounded a lot more appealing, almost something she could be part of.

Batsheva stood up to leave, and to Marilynne's surprise, she gave her a hug. "It was nice talking to you. I feel like a piece of Benjamin is still here," she said.

"Then you come back and visit whenever you want, you hear?" Marilynne said.

As Marilynne watched Batsheva and Ayala walk down the front walk hand in hand, she struggled to put her finger on what made Batsheva different from the other Orthodox women here. Batsheva had none of the reserved mannerisms that she saw in many of the other women, as if a strong barrier was always being preserved between her and them. Batsheva's demeanor was easygoing and relaxed. She smiled easily and seemed comfortable with herself and those around her. Marilynne hadn't felt the need to hide the fact that she wasn't observant, as she did when Mrs. Levy and Helen Shayowitz were visiting; worried they were looking down on her. And just in case they were, she would make a point of mentioning something Jewish, even if it was just an apple strudel she had baked.

WHEN Batsheva and Ayala were a few blocks from home, Ayala stopped walking and began to cry.

"Come on, Ayala. We're almost home," Batsheva said.

Ayala sat down on the sidewalk and refused to budge. If it had been us, we would have called her name until she understood that we meant business. If need be, we would have resorted to threats, no dessert tonight or an earlier bedtime. But Batsheva had her own way of dealing with it. She went over to Ayala and crouched down.

"Talk to me, Ayala. Tell me what's the matter," she said.

Ayala shrugged her shoulders and looked at the ground. Batsheva wrapped her arms around her, like she had known all along that this was exactly what the poor child needed.

Leanna Zuckerman was walking by just then. She was having Bruce's family for dinner, and she needed a break from cooking. Her baby boy, only four months old, was tucked into the carriage she was pushing. Even though Leanna had three children, and one of them so recently, her body had the slimness of a teenager. (How did she do it? we asked her. Did she eat enough? we wondered privately.) She was immaculately dressed, in a crisp white T-shirt tucked smoothly into knee-length navy culottes.

Leanna's culottes were something we often commented on. Pants were considered immodest and wearing culottes walked a dangerous line. It was one thing to dress this way when no one would see. Becky Feldman and Rachel Ann Berkowitz (and possibly Tziporah Newburger, although no one had ever been able to prove this) even went mixed swimming, but only when they were away on vacation, where the chance of anyone they knew seeing them was lessened. But to publicly appear in culottes showed a certain disregard for the way things were done. Which was, truth be told, exactly what Leanna intended. She didn't think there was anything wrong with culottes, or even pants for that matter—they were certainly more modest than some of the skirts people wore. Wearing the culottes was her way of saying that though she seemed like everyone else, she really wasn't. And they were the easiest way to do this. They weren't as obvious as pants, not as radical as shorts. They sent a quieter message. They still allowed her to belong.

When Leanna saw Batsheva, she smiled. Even though she hadn't reached out to Batsheva as much as she should have, she had been wondering how she was doing. Leanna knew what it was like to be new to Memphis. She had married in, and Bruce's family had lived here forever. She would never forget the first time she came to Memphis, right after she and Bruce got engaged. There had been so many different names to remember, so many relatives and friends to keep straight. She had tried to come up with ways to remember them: Mrs. Levy was wearing the giant strand of pearls, Cousin Renelle had on the flowered silk dress. But the next day when they had changed their clothes, she confused everyone and found it hard to think of a single thing to say.

"Are you enjoying your walk?" Leanna asked.

"No," Ayala said before Batsheva could say anything.

"You don't sound like a happy little girl," Leanna said.

"She's a little sad today," Batsheva explained.

Leanna wished she could come up with a way to cheer her up. She could only imagine how hard it must be for Ayala, with so many changes one after another.

"Do you like to swim?" Leanna asked Ayala. "Last week," she turned back to Batsheva, "my husband set up our pool, one of those above-ground types, and I was thinking, maybe Ayala could come over sometime. All the kids from the neighborhood come."

"Ayala, how does that sound? Would you like to go swimming?" Batsheva said.

Ayala didn't say anything, but she did eye Leanna with interest, and Leanna knew enough about kids to take this as a good sign.

"Great, then," Leanna said. "Is tomorrow good?"

In the eager way that Batsheva said yes, tomorrow was perfect, Leanna saw a flicker of loneliness. She hadn't thought of it before, but this was a perfect opportunity to get to know Batsheva better, to test the waters, so to speak, before jumping head-first into a friendship with her.

The next morning, the children who usually gathered in the Zuckermans' backyard were there—the Newburgers' two girls, Chani and Basya; Rena Reinhard's daughter, Bracha; and of course, Deena, Rivkie, and Jonathan Zuckerman. Leanna was outside watching the kids; she spent most of her day out there. Sometimes she toyed with the idea of getting a job. At night when the kids were sleeping, she and Bruce made lists of things she might like to do. She would think back to college, how she had enjoyed math and really was very good at it. But she hadn't finished her accounting degree because Bruce came from such a wealthy family and she had been excited about not having to work.

Leanna looked up to see Batsheva and Ayala standing on the other side of the fence that surrounded the yard. She hadn't known if they would really come, but now that they had, she found that she was pleased. She walked over to the fence and let them in.

"I'm so glad you came," Leanna said.

"We've been excited about it all morning," Batsheva said and smoothed Ayala's hair. "I'm hoping that being in such a nice environment will reassure Ayala. She's been this quiet since the accident. She wasn't hurt but she was shaken up and then she had to adjust to not having her father."

"How do you manage alone?" she asked Batsheva. Leanna couldn't believe she and Batsheva were the same age—both thirty-four—but Leanna's whole life was already set. She owned a house and two cars, she had three children. Batsheva still seemed to have everything ahead of her, no paths ruled out.

"It's tough with all there is to do, and being in the Orthodox world, where most people are married, it's even harder being on my own. But I can't imagine my life without Ayala. She grounds me and gives me purpose," Batsheva said.

Before Batsheva left, she hugged Ayala good-bye. "I'll be back for you soon," she said.

Ayala stood there, not sure what to do with herself now that her mother was gone. Deena, Leanna's nine-year-old, went over to her.

"Do you have a bathing suit on?" Deena asked.

Ayala bit at her lip and looked like she was about to cry.

"Don't worry. It's okay," Deena said and put her arm around Ayala. Ayala smiled shyly at her and peeled off her yellow shorts and faded blue T-shirt, revealing a red-and-white polka-dot bathing suit. She lowered herself into the small pool, landing without a splash. The other children gathered around her, and Ayala looked like any of them. Her eyes shone a little brighter and her face was newly alert. Only her hair—so light in the sunshine that it appeared translucent—singled her out.

AYALA had grown so accustomed to swimming at the Zuckermans that she was surprised one overcast day to look into the yard and find it empty. Leanna had taken her kids to the library, forgetting about Ayala. At first Ayala stood patiently outside the fence, but after a few minutes of waiting, she walked across the grass to the Levys' house and knocked on the door. Mrs. Levy, still dressed in her red-and-yellow-flowered housecoat, answered.

"Is there swimming today?" Ayala asked.

Mrs. Levy couldn't believe her ears. Swimming, in weather like this! Of course there wasn't. Why just yesterday she had read an article in *Reader's Digest* about the terrible likelihood of being struck by lightning while in a swimming pool.

"It looks to me like it's about to pour. And I saw Leanna's station wagon pull out of the driveway half an hour ago," Mrs. Levy said. The poor child's face was so crestfallen that she couldn't stand it. "There's no point in having you stand outside. Come on in."

Ayala peered inside the house and looked up at Mrs. Levy.

"Don't be shy. No one's going to bite," she said.

Ayala walked into the kitchen. Thursday morning was Mrs. Levy's time to bake, and the smell of fresh bread, cookies and summer fruit pies filled the house.

The first thing Mrs. Levy wondered was who was taking care of this poor girl. Even in a place as safe as Memphis, it wasn't good for a child to wander the streets alone.

"Ayala dear, where is your mother?" she asked. "Don't tell me she's letting you run around alone like this!"

Ayala shrugged, which made Mrs. Levy's heart break even more. She didn't understand why people brought children into this world if they weren't prepared to care for them. This certainly wasn't how Mrs. Levy had raised her children. They never once came home to an empty house, never had a non-family member for a babysitter, never missed out on a home-cooked dinner. For Irving too, she had made sure that he had everything he needed, every button carefully sewn on, every shirt meticulously ironed, every brown-bag lunch hand-packed.

"Sit here," Mrs. Levy instructed. She cleared off the table, moving aside oil and brown sugar, cracked eggshells and peach pits. With a blue-and-white-checkered dishtowel, she wiped the table clean. Then she took a small white china plate and placed on it two strawberry tart cookies and a challah roll fresh from the oven.

"Let me know how they are," she said. "My children are grown and gone, so it's nice to have a little girl tasting my food again."

Ayala tasted a cookie. After licking her fingers, she bit into the challah roll. "It's the best challah I ever had," she said.

"Aren't you just the most precious thing!" Mrs. Levy ruffled Ayala's hair. Today was the first time that she had heard Ayala speak and she took it as no small victory that it happened at her own house. No matter what she thought of Batsheva, Mrs. Levy decided that, with a little help, Ayala could turn out just fine. Maybe one day it would be almost impossible to tell that she hadn't grown up with a conventional mother. And luckily, Mrs. Levy had enough time left after all her other projects to work with her; as she liked to say, you could never have your fingers in too many pies.

"Tell me, Ayala, what does your mommy do all day?" she inquired.

"I don't know." Ayala shrugged.

"You must have some idea. Does she clean up the house and make nice food for you? What did she fix y'all for dinner last night?

"Pancakes."

"Pancakes?" Mrs. Levy repeated; last time she checked, they were breakfast food.

"They were very good," Ayala said.

"I'm sure they were, sweetheart. I'm sure they were," Mrs. Levy said and sighed; without the proper nutrition, it would be an uphill battle. "Why don't you tell me what else she does?"

"She paints pictures."

"Oh, really. What kinds of things does she paint?"

"Colors."

"Of course she uses colors but what are her pictures of? Does she make pictures of people or scenery?"

"Just colors."

As far as Mrs. Levy knew, colors alone did not count as art. But she was getting nowhere with this line of questioning, and she decided to pursue a different subject. "Your mommy must be lonely. Does she ever have company?" she asked. She could just envision the various men who might pay visits to Batsheva in the dark of night.

"No, not anymore," Ayala said.

"Well, I'll be," Mrs. Levy said. Even though she had suspected that something like this was true, she hadn't thought it would be so easy to get confirmation. It would certainly be something to look into.

Ayala took another bite of her cookie. "My daddy is dead," she announced.

"Poor thing," Mrs. Levy murmured as she bent down to hug her.

"You must miss him so much. I remember when he was a little boy. In fact I think he looked a lot like you. He had the same sweet eyes and soft voice." Mrs. Levy busied herself with putting away the vanilla and baking powder. "Is that why you moved here?" she asked.

"Yes. So we can be close to him," Ayala said, parroting back what Batsheva must have told her.

"And how did your grandparents feel about this?"

"They said we didn't know anyone here."

"Yes, I can see that," Mrs. Levy said. This was exactly as she had suspected. It wasn't unlike her own situation, Mrs. Levy realized. She had three grown children, and not one of them lived in Memphis. She had never imagined it would end up like this, and it was her private shame that she couldn't convince them to move here. Every time she spoke to her children—Raphael in Baltimore, Rebecca in Houston, and Anna Beth (who now went by her Hebrew name, Chana Bayla) in Monsey—she held out the hope that they would announce their plans to return home. They had presumably valid excuses for living away—Raphael was the principal of a day school in Baltimore, Rebecca's husband was doing his medical residency in Houston, and Anna Beth/Chana Bayla felt that Memphis did not offer the proper right-wing schools for her children. These were the reasons Mrs. Levy was always quoting to her friends; no, it had nothing to do with Memphis, it was just one of those practical necessities. But still, Mrs. Levy sometimes felt a fleeting fear that at the heart of these reasons lay a dissatisfaction with Memphis, that her own children found something missing in this community she had worked her whole life to build. She pushed the thought away. Dissatisfied with Memphis? It was impossible.

Still thinking of her children and grandchildren, Mrs. Levy felt a rush of sympathy for Ayala. "I made too many challahs for Shabbos and they'll get stale if I save them for next week. Let me pack up two of them for you to take home."

It was the least she could do. Mrs. Levy wasn't going to stand by and let the poor child go hungry. She recalled a sermon the Rabbi had given a few weeks before: In a place where there is no man, you should try to be a man. There was no reason why that couldn't apply to women as well. (Or was there? Should she check with the Rabbi before assuming this applied to her? She didn't want to be presumptuous or, God forbid, feminist. She would add it to her list of Questions for the Rabbi.) In the meantime, she wrapped each challah in aluminum foil, careful not to shake off the sesame seeds that dotted their tops. She put them into a plastic shopping bag and gave them to Ayala, hoping this would give her a taste of what it had been like to grow up in her house.

A week or so later, Helen Shayowitz saw Batsheva in the dressing room at Loehmann's. She had spent the morning running a few errands that Mrs. Levy had asked her to do, but now it was Helen's time for herself. Helen loved to shop, even though she pretended to her husband and friends that it was a burden she bore bravely. Losing herself in the colors and textures of all these clothes was the best way to block out the things that weighed on her mind. She considered whether Mrs. Levy was once again taking advantage of their friendship by having her pick up the centerpieces for the upcoming donor luncheon instead of doing it herself. And she thought about her daughter in New York. Would she ever get engaged to the nice young man she had been dating for three months already? And she worried about the occasional pain in her shoulder. Who knows what sort of disease might be lurking there?

Only shopping could alleviate these concerns. Helen made sure she had nowhere to be for hours; she couldn't shop under pressure. She dressed up, feeling more comfortable in her nicest clothes. And she didn't ask for assistance from the salesgirls. It was too hard to explain why her skirts needed to cover her knees, why she didn't wear dresses that dipped low in the front or that revealed her back and shoulders. It was better to be on her own. That way, no one would know that she was different from any other Memphis lady. Orthodox women could pass easily. Which was why she often encouraged her husband, Alvin, to wear a cap over his yarmulke when they were in public.

"All I'm saying," she would argue, "is that it's easier this way. You don't have to worry what people are thinking. It's not like we live in New York."

In New York, there were men in yarmulkes everywhere. But not in Memphis, where most people had never seen a yarmulke. It was easier to blend in. But Alvin wouldn't listen to her. "I've lived here my whole life and I'm not going to start being ashamed of who I am now," he would say. In fact, Alvin was one of the few who had always worn his yarmulke in public, even in the forties and fifties when people just didn't do that.

With a pile of dresses over her arm, Helen walked into the Back Room, which doubled as both the place where the fanciest clothes were kept and a communal dressing room, no curtains sectioning off private changing areas. All around the room, in between the fancy evening dresses, women were taking off their clothes and trying things on. And in the far corner, next to a rack of the prettiest red satin gowns Helen had ever seen, was Batsheva. She was standing in front of a three-way mirror, a collection of small blouses and tight velvet skirts hanging on the rack by her side. Batsheva didn't look up, her attention focused on the black dress (no sleeves and no back!) she was trying on. Like a fashion model being photographed for *Vogue*, she put her hands behind her neck and pulled her hair to the top of her head. Who she thought she was, Helen wasn't sure.

A glimpse of Helen's face passed across Batsheva's reflection and she turned around while unzipping herself.

"This one doesn't fit, but I was just trying it on for fun. I had a little time to myself, and I was driving around and decided to stop in," she said.

"Oh, where's Ayala?" Helen inquired.

"Mrs. Levy offered to look after her. I was going to say that she didn't have to do that, but Ayala was so excited, I couldn't bear to disappoint her."

"How nice." Helen remembered that Mrs. Levy had been carrying on about what a precious child Ayala was and that she was determined to do whatever she could for her. At the time, Helen hadn't realized how seriously Mrs. Levy intended to take this, but if Mrs. Levy was going to go all out, then she should as well. Helen didn't know any other single mothers, but part of being a community, she reminded herself, was pitching in, even in situations you wouldn't expect to have to deal with.

"I'll be happy to help out too. You give me a call if you need anything."

"Thank you," Batsheva said. "It makes such a difference, having people around who are willing to help."

Batsheva unzipped the dress she was wearing and this jolted Helen back to reality. There was shopping to be done and it was time to get started. Helen hung her pile of clothing on the rack in front of her, the items she had selected suddenly seeming frumpy.

"That looks like you," Batsheva said, pointing to a red-and-navy plaid dress, its hem falling below the knee, its neckline high above the collarbone.

Helen bristled: just what she wanted, to be thought of as old, stodgy. She longed to wear the kind of clothing Batsheva was trying on: tight little outfits that would show off the figure she still prided herself on. But the laws of modesty prevented Helen from doing so. She had to do the best she could. She had been known to show up at shul wearing a knee-length black leather suit or a leopard print hat instead of an ordinary wool one. She had more freedom when it came to shoes; there were no laws of modesty (at least that she knew about) governing footwear. She wore stiletto heels, gold open-toe sandals, and orange suede loafers. Her closet was a testament to all the ways shoes could spice up an otherwise modest outfit. But it wasn't enough. Helen still dreamed of walking into shul in a tight, sequined dress or wearing a strapless gown to the school's Annual Scholarship Banquet. Everyone would marvel at how young Helen looked. They would exclaim that at the age of sixty-one, she looked as beautiful as she had as a teenager.

Batsheva stepped out of the dress and left it in a pile at her feet. In the middle of buttoning, unzipping, fastening and snapping, Helen stole a few glances of her. Helen is not one to be indiscreet, but she did, to the best of her ability, describe to the rest of us what Batsheva looked like. Batsheva did not wear ordinary underwear, none of the full, plain white cotton that we preferred. Her underwear was the sort meant for spectators. All it was, really, was a few straps and a patch or two of black lace. Her bra matched exactly: it was the same lace and barely covered her.

But that was the least of it. When Batsheva pulled a short-sleeved maroon sweater over her head, Helen caught sight of something peeking out from the left side of her bra: a tattoo in the shape of a rose. No one we knew had a tattoo, no one at all; it was forbidden to desecrate our bodies in such a way. Helen turned away, worried she had been caught staring. She tried to focus on the clothes in front of her. But while Batsheva was deciding what to try on next, Helen seized the opportunity to get another look, to convince herself that her eyes weren't playing tricks on her, that it wasn't a fluke of the lighting reflecting the pink wallpaper. This time the tattoo was more pronounced, a darker red than she had first suspected. Trying to be subtle, Helen studied the details, how big it was, how many petals, what the green leaves were shaped like.

"I see you've noticed my tattoo," Batsheva announced, sending Helen into a flurry of denials as she busied herself with a wayward zipper, a stubborn button.

"No, no, I barely noticed it until you said something," Helen protested. But free to take a closer look, she walked over to Batsheva. As she looked it over, her mind was filled with the things she believed to accompany tattoos—big-muscled men on motorcycles, seedy dance clubs, and leather, lots of leather. So that was the world Batsheva was from.

"How unusual," Helen finally said, realizing it was rude not to make some sort of comment. Her heart began racing. She hoped that Batsheva wouldn't hear the discomfort in her voice and peg her as hopelessly old-fashioned.

Batsheva laughed. "No, I guess it's not the usual thing here."

Just then, Jocelyn Shanzer walked into the dressing room. Helen rushed over and gave her a peck on the cheek. Jocelyn and Helen had never been the best of friends. Years back, they had run against each other for Ladies Auxiliary president, and when Jocelyn won, Helen's hurt feelings had taken a while to heal. Helen really had had no chance of winning—Jocelyn had more relatives here than Helen did, and all those cousins assured her a voting bloc. To make it worse, Jocelyn was one of those people who were popular from the day she was born. Helen had taken her loss as an indication that her position in the community was precarious, in need of Mrs. Levy's constant patronage and support. And though she usually went out of her way to avoid Jocelyn, in a situation like this, Helen believed in working with what she had.

"What a coincidence bumping into you. And look, here's Batsheva," Helen said.

"Helen was just admiring my tattoo," Batsheva said and winked at

Helen, who blushed a deep pink, almost the exact shade as the wallpaper. Now Jocelyn would tell everyone that Helen had approved, or at least pretended to approve, of such a thing.

Jocelyn put down the dresses she was carrying and went to get a good look. "At least it's a rose. That's pretty. When did you get it?"

Helen nudged Jocelyn in the side. It wasn't nice to ask directly. Better to hint at it and let Batsheva tell them on her own. Jocelyn shot her a look that said don't worry, I know what I'm doing. When there was information to be had, it was necessary to throw politeness to the wind.

"I got it when I was in high school," Batsheva said. "A friend of mine had one, and I thought it was beautiful. I liked the idea of using my body as a space for art."

"What about your parents?" Jocelyn asked. "What did they say?" Even if the Torah didn't forbid it, Jocelyn would never let a daughter of hers get a tattoo.

"They let me do whatever I wanted. They assumed I would eventually figure things out for myself."

That didn't sound like a very good idea, Helen thought, but she decided at the last second not to say it out loud.

"How do they feel about the fact that you decided to convert?" Jocelyn asked.

"They thought I'd gone off the deep end. But when I converted, I had to cut those ties in some way. I guess that's what the Torah means when it says that a convert is like a new baby. You have to make these connections again."

"But you still speak to them, don't you?" Helen asked. The idea of a child cut off from her parents made her nervous.

"Every once in a while, I call my mother and let her know I'm alive. She met Ayala once, right after she was born. I felt like I was visiting someone I used to know. Being an Orthodox Jew was the last thing in the world my mother could imagine. But for me, it never seemed that far away."

In more ways than Jocelyn liked to admit, this reminded her of her own background. She had grown up with nothing Jewish. Her parents were immigrants anxious to become Americans. When Jocelyn was a teenager, she had come to it on her own. With all the teasing she had endured in public school about her parents' accents and old-fashioned clothing, she thought she should at least know what Judaism was about. She had walked one Saturday morning to shul and felt at home.

Once she made this change, she had never looked back. Being observant came naturally to her. She liked feeling that her life wasn't so different than her ancestors' lives had been. But there was one small thing that she couldn't bring herself to give up: shrimp salad. She ate it in secret, whenever she had the urge. She had a separate treif pot and knife she used, and she kept the finished product in a special container in the freezer, behind the frozen veal chops and broccoli florets. No one, not even her husband, knew. Her husband had always been religious and she worried he would think she was slipping back into the lifestyle of her childhood. But she had an arrangement with God: He would overlook her one transgression and she would take care of the rest.

Instead of trying to make conversation with Jocelyn and Batsheva, Helen wandered over to the red satin gowns and checked to see if they had her size—a six, if she held her stomach in the tiniest bit. She fingered the material. Maybe after Jocelyn left, she would try it on. She had been known to bring home something that she could never wear and let it hang in her closet for a few days until she returned it. As she was imagining what she would look like in the dress, she realized that if she had a tattoo (for whatever inconceivable reason) it would be fully visible with this low-cut neckline. She looked at Batsheva; did she have to think about this with everything she wore?

"There's no way to get the tattoo off?" Helen asked. "I hear there's some new surgery they can do."

"I don't mind it. It reminds me of where I come from. It's not like I can erase who I used to be," Batsheva said.

To Helen, it seemed that such an attitude would only make life harder. Everyone had to make compromises in order to fit in. Helen certainly had—she was always swallowing what she really thought in order to keep the peace. Letting go of her past didn't seem like too much to ask of Batsheva. With constant reminders that Batsheva had grown up in a different world, it would be hard to act like she was part of this community.

After that, there wasn't much to say. Jocelyn and Helen tried on their suits and skirts and waved a polite good-bye to Batsheva when she finished dressing and left the room.

ANOTHER time, when most of us were ready to turn in for the night, shutting off lights, locking doors and closing curtains, Batsheva left her house and walked down the street to the small, windowless building behind the shul. Except for a bare bulb above the doorway, no sign indicates its presence. This is the community mikvah, and each night, a few of us descend upon it in strict privacy to use the ritual bath. We are commanded to immerse, seven days after the completion of our periods, and only then can we be intimate with our husbands again.

That night, Tziporah Newburger was sitting in the mikvah's waiting area on one of the pink plastic chairs donated by the Levy family in honor of Mrs. Levy's sixtieth birthday. Without the long brown sheitel she usually wore (so natural-looking, from the back you could hardly tell it was a wig; but then, she had paid three thousand dollars for genuine human hair and she should at least get her money's worth), Tziporah looked like a different person. Even though no one else was there, she had her hair pinned up under a scarf. She was one of the few women in the community who covered her hair—for most of us, this was a mitzvah that had fallen by the wayside—and she was determined to prevent even a single strand of hair from creeping out uncovered.

Although she didn't discuss this with anyone—the mikvah was supposed to be done in private—Tziporah hated going to the mikvah. She had read stories of women who loved it, how refreshed they felt, spiritually and physically reinvigorated. Certainly Tziporah wanted to feel this way. She was ashamed of herself for having negative thoughts about one of God's commandments. And she would do it no matter what; the whole point of being Orthodox was to obey God's word even if she didn't want to. If He was omniscient and omnipotent, certainly He knew better than she did. But the mikvah was such a hassle: the careful cleaning of her body beforehand, having to tuck the kids into bed before she went, and then the fear of running into someone she knew on the way. If one of the men from the community saw her and guessed where she was going, he might imagine what happened afterward between Tziporah and her husband.

What happened afterward though was the part Tziporah looked forward to; it almost made the hassle of the mikvah worth it. If the kids were asleep and her husband was home from teaching his adult education classes, if the phone wasn't ringing and there were no dirty dishes in the sink, and no papers and clothing scattered on the bed, Tziporah and her husband could finally be alone. For twelve long days and nights, they hadn't touched, hadn't slept in the same bed, hadn't undressed in front of each other, hadn't even passed each other a dish or a book for fear of arousing any sexual feeling. This separation was a throwback to the days before they were married, when they hadn't touched, not once, not ever; it had even been forbidden for them to be alone in a closed room together. On mikvah night, Tziporah felt that same tingle of a first touch all over again. Her body still quivered when her husband's hands moved across her skin. It was hard to believe that such a pleasure was allowed, that, in fact, it was considered a mitzvah, it was something God wanted them to do.

Trying to focus on the intimate moments that lay ahead, Tziporah came up with ways to enjoy the mikvah more. She took a bubble bath before getting ready. She promised herself manicures the day after. She hired a baby-sitter to look after the kids even though she was home. But it didn't work. No matter how scrupulously she cleaned her body, she knew that she wasn't fulfilling the spirit of the law. It was a physical cleansing, not a spiritual one. The anxiety she carried into the mikvah tainted those pure waters.

Tziporah leafed through the stray copies of *Southern Living* and *Ladies Home Journal*, skimming articles about how to look younger, how to care for problem skin, how to prepare Sunday brunch on fifteen minutes notice. She had been waiting for almost half an hour for her turn in the mikvah when she heard a knock at the door. She had no idea who it could be; she knew who was on the same cycle as she was and could figure out who would be there. For years Leanna Zuckerman and Tziporah had identical schedules, and when Leanna wasn't there one month, Tziporah had known she was pregnant.

Tziporah opened the door. Batsheva was standing there, her face scrubbed clean, her cheeks shining red. Her hair was wet, and instead of covering it with a scarf as we usually did so no one seeing us would know where we were going, she wore it loose.

"I hope I'm not too late. It was impossible to get away earlier," Batsheva said.

She sat down, acting as if her being at the mikvah were the most normal thing in the world. But only married women were supposed to use the mikvah, and Tziporah could think of no possible explanation for Batsheva to be there. She didn't say anything, hoping her startled glance would convey the inappropriateness of what Batsheva was doing. She waited for the explanation. Surely Batsheva would realize that her presence required some kind of justification. But none was offered, and the silence began to weigh on Tziporah.

"Has it started raining?" Tziporah asked.

"Not yet. It's quiet but about to let loose," Batsheva said.

"Well, I hope it waits until I get home."

Batsheva kicked off her sandals and took out a pumice stone from her crocheted purse. "I forgot the bottom of my feet," she said. She crossed one leg over the other and scraped the stone along her heels, the loose skin falling away. "I love walking barefoot, but it kills my feet." She slipped the stone back into her bag. "Do you think I got the nails short enough? The laws are so precise and I always feel nervous about doing them right."

Even though she didn't want to, Tziporah leaned over to look at Batsheva's toes. "They look good enough to me," she said.

In fact, Batsheva's nails could have been a lot shorter; most of the white of the nail was supposed to be cut. But Tziporah would not be sidetracked from the issue of what Batsheva was doing here. The mikvah was one of the pillars of Judaism, as important as observing Shabbos and keeping kosher. Once you started bending laws, shaping them according to whatever fad arose, they lost their legitimacy. Instead of being the word of God, the laws became the word of man. Tziporah thought of the sons of Aaron, the High Priest. They had been so excited to serve God, they hadn't followed the detailed laws of the temple service. Angry at their overeagerness, God had consumed them in His fire. The situation with Batsheva was at least as bad. As the minutes ticked by, Tziporah grew angrier. What was next, she wondered, religious anarchy?

Finally it was Tziporah's turn. She had bathed at home and all she had left to do was shower. She did this quickly, letting the hot water work its way down her tired back and legs. She wrapped a terrycloth bathrobe around herself and ran through a checklist in her mind to make sure she had done everything: cut her cuticles, flossed her teeth, scrubbed her elbows, cleaned her belly button, her ears, between her toes. Satisfied that she had thoroughly prepared her body, she said the prayer that hung on a laminated card next to the shower: *May these purifying waters wash away all my sins and transgressions, all my sorrow and sadness.*

When Tziporah entered the room with the mikvah, she removed her robe. She looked down self-consciously, still not used to standing naked in someone else's presence. She waited nervously while the mikvah lady, Bessie Kimmel, checked her fingernails for any remaining speck of dirt, her toes for any loose piece of skin.

"What's new, dear?" Bessie asked while picking off a few stray hairs that had fallen onto Tziporah's back.

"Oh, nothing," Tziporah sighed.

Being the mikvah lady was not a job Bessie took lightly. "The job is not as simple as you think," she would explain. "You think all I have to do is make sure there are clean robes and fresh towels? That's the easy part. What's hard is the responsibility, making sure you go under the water all the way, that your arms and legs don't touch the wall. And you can't imagine the secrets I have to keep: if you're pregnant, if you gain some weight, if you have a scar from a C-section. Anything that happens here passes before my eyes."

We remembered the first time we had been to the mikvah, a night or two before our weddings. We had been nervous, all too aware that we were passing into the grown-up world of our mothers. As we surveyed the small room, feeling too young to be there, Bessie had squeezed each of our shoulders and said that we were going to make a beautiful kallah; she had seen many brides pass before her and she knew when she saw a beautiful one.

Tziporah walked down the steps into the water. She dunked once and said the blessing: *Blessed are you God, King of the universe who sanctifies us with His commandments and commands us to ritually immerse.* She went under twice more as Bessie stood above her, like a lighthouse guiding the ships that passed through her waters. When Tziporah finished, she stepped out of the water and breathed in, hoping to feel a sense of renewal, some glimmer of rejuvenation. But she felt nothing. She was the same Tziporah as before.

While Tziporah dried off, Batsheva went into the bathroom and started the shower. Bessie saw Batsheva and raised her eyebrows. "What's going on?" she asked Tziporah.

Tziporah shook her head. "I have no idea. If it were up to me, I'd send her home."

"So she'll dunk a few times," Bessie decided. "A little swim." She didn't think there would be any harm in letting Batsheva use the mikvah even though she didn't need to. Now if she wasn't using it when she was supposed to, that would be another story.

Batsheva entered the room with the mikvah and removed her robe, not self-conscious to stand there naked. There was no need for Bessie to do such a careful inspection for stray hairs or hangnails. Batsheva wasn't fulfilling any religious obligation, so it would make no difference to God if every part of Batsheva's body was not completely immersed. Bessie's eyes did of course rest longer on the tattoo, which was exactly as Helen Shayowitz had described it; this was certainly a first for the mikvah.

Batsheva walked down the three steps into the water and floated on her back. "I like to spend time in the water so I can take in the whole experience," she said.

Bessie decided to tolerate this. Everyone had a different way of using the mikvah, and she had found that it was best to allow the women to dunk however they chose. Some women liked to get used to the water for a minute or two before going under. Others went under right away, so fast she barely had time to watch. Some spread their limbs out from their bodies so that they accidentally touched the walls of the mikvah. When Bessie still needed to use the mikvah, before she had reached menopause, she had loved to curl into a fetal position as she went under the water. She felt at peace with herself for those few seconds, believing that anything that was wrong would eventually work itself out. Night after night of watching other women use the mikvah made her miss the experience, and sometimes, when no one was looking, she would take off her shoes and stockings and dip her legs into the warm water to remember what it felt like.

Immersed in the water, Batsheva looked like she had fallen asleep. Her hair spread out behind her, and her arms fell loose in the water. It was one thing to get used to the water, but this looked like a full-fledged swim. Bessie cleared her throat to get Batsheva's attention. Batsheva made no response, and in all fairness, with her ears underwater, maybe she hadn't heard her.

"Nu." Bessie snapped her fingers. "We don't have all night."

Batsheva got the message, and she stood in the center of the mikvah. She went under for longer than anyone else did and when she came up, she said the blessing carefully, emphasizing each word.

Tziporah was still in the waiting area, blow-drying her hair so no one who saw her would know where she had been. When it was one hundred percent dry, she brushed it out. She felt pretty, almost glamorous. She was so used to seeing her face surrounded by a wig that sometimes she forgot she had hair of her own. After taking one more look, she twisted her hair into a bun and pinned it up under her scarf. She imagined how when she got home, her husband would unfasten it. He would wrap a few strands of her hair around his fingers and goose bumps would rise all over her body. He loved seeing her hair uncovered, and he loved that he was the only one who saw her this way. It made him feel special; it was one more way in which he alone knew her.

When Batsheva left the mikvah, Tziporah was just getting into her car. From her car window, she watched Batsheva walk down the street. Tziporah wasn't sure whether she should offer her a ride. Some people preferred to walk; they enjoyed the quiet of nighttime. And it was perfectly safe—this was Memphis after all. But what if Batsheva did want a ride and she thought Tziporah was being rude? Tziporah would have to pass right by Batsheva's house on the way home. She couldn't drive by without offering.

"Can I give you a lift?" Tziporah called.

Batsheva walked closer to the car to see who was there.

"Hi Batsheva, it's Tziporah. I was wondering if you wanted a ride."

"I couldn't tell who was there—I thought some stranger was trying to pick me up," Batsheva said.

Tziporah laughed; it was the first time she had been mistaken for that. "No, it's just me."

"That's nice of you, but I'm okay," Batsheva said.

"It's no problem. It might start raining any minute now. And I'll feel bad if you walk when I have all this room," she said, motioning to the empty seats in her minivan.

"Okay," Batsheva said and got in the car. "Don't you love going to the mikvah? I feel so refreshed," she said. "Anything that's bothering me is washed away and I can start over. After Benjamin died, I couldn't give it up. It had become such a part of me."

Tziporah's chest tightened. It wasn't right, an unmarried woman using the mikvah. The Torah made it perfectly clear that it was only for married women, for the purpose of making sex permissible. Perhaps Batsheva didn't realize the impropriety of it. Maybe no one had ever told her. Tziporah remembered that the Torah commands us to offer rebuke when we see someone committing a sin, if we believe our words will be well received. And how do you know, she decided, unless you try? They were almost at Batsheva's house and Tziporah knew that if she didn't say something, her chance would be lost, and she would have to live with herself for not seizing the opportunity to fulfill a mitzvah.

"You know, Batsheva," she began nervously, "I don't want to embarrass you, but I don't think it's appropriate for you to use the mikvah. It doesn't look right."

"I realize that it's not what's usually done, but I don't think there's a problem with it. How can it be bad if it makes me feel more religious?"

"The whole point of the mikvah is so you can have . . . relations with your husband. So I don't see why you need to go," Tziporah said.

"But I want to even though I don't have to. When the water closes over me, I feel like any impurity is being carried out of my body. Doing it only because it's commanded would take the joy out of the mitzvah. Anyway, I think that we need to emphasize the spiritual aspects of Judaism more. Sometimes they get left behind, and when that happens so much of what it's about gets lost."

Batsheva spoke with confidence; she acted like there was no problem with what she was saying. And she didn't seem to care that Tziporah was explicitly disapproving of her behavior. Maybe it was fine to have these kind of discussions where she was from, but to Tziporah it sounded close to heresy. Judaism wasn't about self-interpretation; it wasn't a new age religion where you were supposed to create your own meaning. It was a very old tradition with very old laws. Batsheva had been Jewish for what, five years? Who was she to say what it was and wasn't about?

Tziporah tightened her grip on the steering wheel; maybe giving Batsheva a ride wasn't such a good idea after all. But she held her tongue. No point getting into a fight with Batsheva. Better to remain on good terms so she would have an opportunity at a later date to broach the topic again. They reached Batsheva's house and Tziporah waited until she got inside, then hurried home to her husband.

The next morning, Tziporah awoke with an unsettled feeling in her stomach. Her encounter with Batsheva weighed on her all morning and when she spoke to Mrs. Levy, she mentioned that Batsheva was still using the mikvah.

"That's interesting," Mrs. Levy exclaimed. "Hardly the ordinary thing. It's certainly going to make a splash."

"Please don't say anything," Tziporah begged. "Or everyone will know that I was also at the mikvah last night. And that wouldn't be modest."

"Certainly, dear," Mrs. Levy said. There was no reason Tziporah's name had to be attached to the news. The source could simply be anonymous.

The news of Batsheva using the mikvah traveled the neighborhood. We all had something to say. How unusual, how surprising that she would want to go to the mikvah even though she didn't have to. Becky Feldman wondered if Bessie Kimmel could forbid Batsheva from using the mikvah. Arlene Salzman thought that it was best to pretend that we knew nothing about it; if we ignored it, maybe it would go away. And of course we all marveled at the lack of concern for what people would think, the inappropriateness of it, the potential for lewdness.

HEARING the talk about Batsheva and the mikvah, Naomi Eisenberg decided to find out for herself what it was about. She lived several blocks away from Batsheva, on a street with no other Orthodox families, and she wondered if this was why she hadn't bumped into

Batsheva, as everyone else was apparently doing on a regular basis. These constant references to seeing Batsheva made her feel left out and she decided to give her a call.

"I wanted to see how y'all were holding up," Naomi said to Batsheva. "I know it can be hard to move into a place where everyone knows each other, and I was wondering if maybe you wanted to go for a quick yogurt."

The Yogurt Shoppe was around the corner and when it first opened, it wasn't kosher. We would drive by and steal glances inside, wishing we could eat there. It's hard to keep a kosher restaurant in a community as small as ours. Every few years, the only one closes down, and a few months later, another opens in its place, the new owner wide-eyed with optimism that he'll be the one to succeed. These days, the restaurant was The Posh Nosh. There were no waiters and no menus. But there was no need; we all knew what they had. The fried chicken, collard greens, hash browns and salami salad were the closest thing we had to nonkosher southern cooking. As good as it was, we did sometimes tire of the same food and same decor and we longed to visit New York or Chicago or Los Angeles, where keeping kosher was hardly a sacrifice—so many restaurants to choose from, Chinese, Mexican, French, even kosher sushi.

A little over a year ago, the Rabbi announced that he had important news and we had snapped to attention: Was he leaving the shul? Had there been some scandal in the school, maybe one of the teachers fired? But instead, the Rabbi revealed that he had closed a deal with The Yogurt Shoppe and beginning next week, all frozen yogurt flavors would be kosher. What good news it was. There was, finally, some other place we could eat. The first few weeks, frozen yogurt was the only thing we consumed. Whenever we were in the vicinity, we swung by, enjoying the opportunity to be like everyone else.

Naomi offered to have Ayala stay at her house with her kids while they went out, but when she came to pick them up, Batsheva got into the car alone and said that Ayala had been invited over to Mrs. Levy's for the afternoon—they were planning to bake apricot rugelach.

"Ayala loves Memphis," Batsheva said to Naomi. "She feels so at home."

Naomi smiled as she remembered when she too used to feel this way. As a child, she had always felt safe, part of a large extended family. Even with the restlessness she now felt, it had been a wonderful way to grow up.

Naomi and Batsheva found a table in the corner and set down their yogurts. There were so many things she wanted to ask Batsheva. With most people here, she felt like she knew their entire life stories.

"Why did you leave New York?" Naomi asked. "Don't worry, you can tell me what happened. I know how it is. Sometimes things get out of hand and the best thing to do is start fresh."

"No, it wasn't like that," Batsheva said and looked a little embarrassed. "I wanted to leave New York. I was so lonely there. Before I decided to move to Memphis, I had a dream that I was standing in front of a map of the United States, closing my eyes, and placing my finger wherever it fell. No matter how many times I did it, it always landed on Memphis."

"So you just picked up and left?" Naomi asked.

"It took two weeks from the time I decided to move to the day I left. When you want something badly enough, things fall into place. I found out about the house for rent and I packed whatever we had, loaded up my car, and that was it," Batsheva said. "When we got to this neighborhood, it looked perfect. It was exactly as I had imagined."

"Does it still seem that way?" Naomi asked.

"No, not exactly. When I first got here, I was so excited by how close-knit the community seemed that I didn't care about anything else. I just wanted to be taken in. I still want that, but I realize it's going to take time to adjust."

"It must be a big change from New York," Naomi said.

"In New York, it was easier to do your own thing, which was good in a lot of ways, but bad also. I never felt like I was part of a community, and it's harder to be religious without the support of people around you."

Naomi remembered all the times she had decided to daven because she saw someone else with an open siddur, when she had made a bracha before eating because someone else did. Naomi had cousins who lived in a small town in Mississippi, and they were the only Jews there. She couldn't imagine how hard it was to do these things on your own. But at the same time, there must be a certain freedom that came with it. You would know that you were doing the mitzvot because you wanted to. And if you decided not to do them, that was your own business too. But it seemed like Batsheva was looking for a place where it wasn't only her business, where the presence of a community would help her be religious.

"I don't want to disappoint you, but it isn't always so easy in a small community," Naomi said. "Maybe I shouldn't be telling you this, but I've had my share of problems here."

As Naomi began to tell Batsheva about how often she felt on the outs here, how it was possible to feel alone even though she knew everyone, she realized that she was doing the same thing that had once gotten her into trouble. A family (the Shinebergs? the Reinbergs? who remembered their names anymore?) had visited Memphis, thinking about moving here from Philadelphia. They had seemed lovely and everyone made a point of telling them what a wonderful community this was: the people were friendly, the housing inexpensive, the Jewish day school top-notch.

Everyone except for Naomi. She had taken the wife to lunch and answered her questions without holding back. The truth was, the school wasn't academic enough; standardized test scores for the high school kids were frightfully low. And there was no culture in Memphis, nothing to do but go to the movies. And if you weren't related to anyone, you might have a tough time fitting in. After all Naomi told her, it was no wonder that this family had decided instead to move to Boston. It hadn't taken long to chase down the source of this information and we had been furious. How dare Naomi speak badly about our school and our city. Even if the things she said were true, there was no need for her to air our dirty laundry in public.

Batsheva didn't respond and Naomi wondered whether once again she had gone too far. "Of course that's not the way it is for everyone. Some people love Memphis and can't imagine living anywhere else," Naomi said.

"I hope so." Batsheva laughed nervously. She knew what it was like to stand out and also what it was like to need roots. But for Naomi, talking about other places reminded her that she could leave Memphis. It reawakened her desire to be somewhere where there would be no past tying her to something she didn't choose on her own. When they finished their yogurt and stood up to leave, Naomi was still thinking about the possibility of a new city waiting for her.

A week later, Rena Reinhard was cleaning out her family's closets as she did every August. She prided herself on her organization and neatness. She liked everything to be just so. That way she knew where everything and everyone was. In the pile of clothing that Bracha, her youngest, had outgrown was a blue velvet Shabbos dress with a white lace collar, a dark green princess-style dress, a pink turtleneck with a matching skirt. The clothing was in mint condition; the Reinhard girls were, like their mother, extremely neat. Rena hated the idea that these clothes would go to waste. She usually gave them to her nieces, but they didn't really need them; they had closets full of their own expensive clothing. If she could find someone who would really benefit from them, she wouldn't feel as guilty.

Then she thought of Ayala. Rena was always noticing when Ayala's dress had a stain or when she wore the same outfit two days in a row. She couldn't imagine that Batsheva had much money, and this made her feel even worse, ashamed of her husband's large salary, her spacious house, her children's brand-name clothing. Determined to help out, Rena folded the clothes into a shopping bag and stopped by Batsheva's house.

"I'm glad I caught you. I have these clothes that Bracha outgrew, and I was wondering if they might fit Ayala," Rena said when Batsheva answered the door. As Rena spoke, she blushed, worrying that Batsheva would be embarrassed or offended by the offer.

"That's nice of you to think of us," Batsheva said.

Rena followed Batsheva inside. "Come here, sweetie," Rena called to Ayala. "Let's see if this fits." She took the blue velvet dress from the bag and held it against Ayala. "Perfect. I'm so glad Ayala will get some wear out of these. Bracha is growing so fast, I can hardly keep up with her."

Ayala fingered the velvet and rubbed it against her cheek. Even after Rena held the rest of the clothes up to her and folded them back into the bag, Ayala didn't let go of the dress.

"Would you like some tea?" Batsheva asked Rena. "And I have some cake leftover from Shabbos. It might be a little stale, but I think it's still good."

"Just tea is fine," Rena said.

While Batsheva was in the kitchen putting water on, Ayala took the bag of clothes and sat on the floor. She unpacked the pieces of clothing and spread them out on her lap, touching the different fabrics. With Batsheva and Ayala both busy, Rena made use of the opportunity to look around. "A person's house is like a photograph of themselves," Rena was known to say. She had read it in one of those home magazines, but as far as she was concerned, it was one hundred percent true. By spending five minutes in someone's living room, she could learn so much. For example, in Helen Shayowitz's house, the furniture was covered with slipcovers, the wood tables with thick plastic mats; this showed Rena how nervous Helen was. And Bessie Kimmel's living room was filled with tiny glass miniatures of every place she had visited. According to Rena's theory, Bessie was afraid of forgetting any place she had ever been. She bought these souvenirs so that the past could not escape from underneath her.

Rena began her tour in Batsheva's entrance hall. It was lined with bookshelves, cluttered with books that Rena had never heard of. She scanned the titles. There were books on Jewish spirituality, Judaism for beginners, comparative religion, books on finding yourself, on meditation, on using art to heal the soul. These weren't the kinds of books Rena was used to and, convinced that she wouldn't understand them, she left them alone.

The living room was Rena's next stop. The room was sparsely furnished, with just an old red couch, its velvety fabric shiny with age, and a coffee table made of a piece of glass balanced on a white milk crate. Even though Batsheva had been here for almost a month, she hadn't finished unpacking. Open boxes sat in each corner, spilling over with shoes and afghans and small framed paintings. The room looked like it could use a good cleaning; not only were the boxes everywhere, but a pair of Batsheva's sandals sat in the middle of the floor, a few of Ayala's toys were scattered about, and the tabletop and wooden floor were dusty.

The walls of the room, on the other hand, looked like something out of a museum. All available space was covered with oversized paintings. They were abstract, no people in them, no landscapes. Instead, bold streaks of color zigzagged across the canvases. Rena stood in front of a painting and squinted her eyes. Maybe if she stood a little farther back she would get it. She backed up and was still staring at it when Batsheva came into the room, holding two chipped mugs filled with tea.

"What do you think?" Batsheva asked.

"I don't know," Rena confessed. "I'm not good at understanding art. It all looks the same to me."

"Of course you can understand it. Think about how it makes you feel," Batsheva said. She put down the tea and stood right behind her, so close that Rena could feel the warmth of her breath against the back of her neck.

"It makes me feel confused," Rena decided. "There's so much color and disorder."

"That's what I hoped people would feel. It's from what I would call my disorientation period," Batsheva said and laughed.

Rena's hand flew to her mouth. "Oh my God, I didn't realize you made this. I knew you were some kind of artist, because we saw those tubes of paint and the canvases when you moved in but I had no idea that . . ." Rena let her sentence dangle, not sure what she might say to smooth things over.

"I'm glad that you felt something. Sometimes I paint things to get a reaction out of people. I hate seeing them move through life as if they've left their emotions behind." Batsheva gently touched the back of Rena's arm. "Come, sit down before the tea gets cold."

"So you're an artist. Wow," Rena said. When she was a child, her teachers had commented that she was artistic, and she had used those skills for decorating her home, baking fancy birthday cakes for her children and designing flyers for the Ladies Auxiliary. But she had never met a real artist before. Most women here didn't have careers and those who did certainly didn't do anything that exciting. Rachel Ann Berkowitz was a kindergarten teacher, Doreen Sheinberg was the secretary at the school, Jocelyn Shanzer ran an invitation business from her home, and Norelle Becker sold hats in her living room. Rena did volunteer work, devoting her time to the shul sisterhood and the Ladies Auxiliary. Last month, in fact, she had been elected president of the Auxiliary for the upcoming school year.

"I don't know anything about being an artist. How did you become one?" she asked.

"I always loved to draw. When I was little, I spent a lot of time alone drawing imaginary houses and cities. When I got older, I still loved to create on paper all the things I saw in my head. I took a bunch of art classes in college and then took a few years off and worked in a gallery in California, and then I went back to school to get a master's degree in art."

Rena was starting to feel out of her league, and she decided to look for some common ground that they could discuss.

"What are your plans for the house?" Rena asked, assuming that Batsheva wasn't planning on leaving it this way. "You know, to decorate or fix it up a little."

"Oh, I don't know. I like it this way. The mess makes me feel more comfortable. I'd hate to have a house that I was afraid to live in," Batsheva said and leaned back into the couch. "Before we moved, Ayala and I were taking a walk and we found this couch out by the curb. I couldn't believe that someone had thrown it away. I called a friend of mine and he came and we brought it back to my apartment. It was so funny—he sang the whole time so we wouldn't think about how heavy it was and everyone on the street was watching us and laughing."

Rena nodded and shifted in her seat, moving to the edge of the cushion so as not to dirty her skirt. She was trying to act as if finding a sofa on the street was something any of us would do.

"Was this friend someone special?" she asked.

"No, not really," Batsheva said and looked away. "He was just a good friend, someone who had been close with Benjamin."

"I'm sorry, I hope I haven't upset you," Rena said, taking in the faraway look on Batsheva's face.

"No, it's okay. I miss Benjamin, but it makes me feel less lonely to talk about him. At night, Ayala and I go out in the backyard, and look up at the stars and talk to him. I get Ayala to tell him about what she did that day and then I talk about how we're building a new life for ourselves here," Batsheva said and drew her knees into her chest, her bare feet on the couch.

Rena's eyes filled with tears. Hearing Batsheva talk about Benjamin made her think about the situation with her own husband. She pressed her fingers against her eyelids and tried to think happy thoughts, but in the end, she couldn't help it. She burst into tears.

"I shouldn't burden you with this, but I can't stand it anymore," Rena said, her words nearly lost in her sobs.

"You can tell me," Batsheva said. "It's okay."

"Marty and I are talking about getting a divorce," she said and began to cry harder.

Rena wasn't sure why she had chosen to confide in Batsheva. She had friends she had known much longer. But the fact that Batsheva was separate made her feel safer. Whatever she confided would have a greater chance of staying a secret.

"I have this feeling that he's, you know, doing things he shouldn't be. Not that he would ever tell me," Rena said bitterly, "because we hardly talk anymore."

Batsheva listened as Rena told her that she and Marty went for weeks at a time without speaking. The only break from these periods of silence was when they would scream at each other, throwing out their anger all at once. But none of this was the worst part. It was also suspected that Marty had a *friend.* No one wanted to say anything because Marty was respected, on the board of the school and the shul, even a former vice president, and it was impossible to believe that one of our own would do such a thing. But on more than one occasion, he had been spotted at the Peabody Hotel having a drink with an unidentified red-haired woman.

Rena thought back to her wedding. She wasn't the same person as the innocent bride she saw on the video, beaming with the happiness and fulfillment marriage was guaranteed to bring. She had met Marty when she was nineteen. He was handsome and sophisticated and charming. He knew what he wanted out of life; he had been working in banking for two years. Exactly one year from the day they met, they had gotten married.

"If we get divorced, everyone will be talking about us. I can't stand the thought of being the topic of conversation around everyone's Shabbos table," Rena said.

Batsheva hugged her. "I know how hard it is to feel like people are talking about you, but if there's one thing I've learned, it's that sometimes you have to let things happen as they will. There's no point trying to please everyone around you."

Rena sniffled. She wished that she could shake off the worry of what people would say about her. But she had an image to uphold: the perfect daughter and now the perfect wife. She was supposed to be pretty, put together, a smile always on her face.

Batsheva put down her mug and stood up. "I want to show you something I painted after Benjamin died. I hung it next to my bed so I can wake up and remember that no matter how sad I might be, things will always be good again."

She took Rena by the hand and led her to the bedroom. Batsheva's bed filled the room and the sheets and bedspread were disheveled. Tiny glass bottles, dried flowers and gauzy scarves covered the dresser. But Batsheva wasn't embarrassed by the mess. She didn't make excuses, that she had been about to clean when Rena stopped in, that Ayala had torn apart the room that morning looking for a toy. She didn't try to quickly straighten up, to shove stray pairs of pantyhose under the bed, to bury her other unmentionables under her pillow.

"This is it," Batsheva said. "This is my favorite painting."

To Rena, the painting looked like the others. It was a huge unframed canvas and running across it were wavy lines in blue and greens, the colors of the sea. The brush strokes were angry, thick paint swirled together. In the center, a blurred figure painted in white was rising from between these lines.

"After Benjamin died, Ayala and I would drive to the ocean. My favorite time was during the winter when we were the only ones there. I would wade into the water, even though it was freezing and somehow, feeling the waves crash against me made me feel better, like there was still a force so much bigger than me in the world. That was the feeling I wanted to evoke here," Batsheva explained.

Rena stared into those colors, trying to find what Batsheva was describing. But all she saw was a swirl of blue and green. Not wanting to hurt Batsheva's feelings, she forced a smile onto her face.

"Thank you for sharing it with me. I feel better, I really do."

As she was about to stand up and thank Batsheva for her hospitality, the thing that had been nagging at her came into focus. There was not a single photograph displayed in the house: no family portraits by her bedside, none of Ayala, or even of Benjamin. She thought she had seen a few photo albums at the bottom of a bookshelf, but they seemed hidden away, not something Batsheva would flip through everyday. It was so different from her own house, where every surface was crowded with pictures of smiling family members, as if she could preserve only the happy moments and block out the rest. Batsheva had come here without a past, no witness to whatever had come before. Maybe pictures only reminded Batsheva of things she wanted to leave behind; any remnants from the past might taint the future.

Rena looked out the window opposite Batsheva's bed and through the almost-sheer white curtains, she saw the familiar maze of streets spreading out on either side. More than being a real place where real people went about their complicated lives, it looked to Rena like a city of dollhouses, where everything was bright and cheerful and carefully arranged. The houses and yards were in order, the families inside appeared safe and peaceful. She imagined Batsheva lying alone in her bed looking out this window, and for the first time, she understood why Batsheva had come to Memphis.

4

THE FOLLOWING THURSDAY, many of us were at Kahn's Kosher-Mart moving through the aisles, noting the new items Mr. Kahn had recently ordered. The store was small, the shelves piled so high with kosher products that it seemed as if they might overflow onto the street in a flood of Streit's matza, Manischewitz gefilte fish, Miller's cheese, Kedem wine, and Empire chicken. The regular grocery stores carried some kosher food, anything marked with the kosher symbols—the O/U, the O/K, the Star-K—like secret codes only we understood. But there were other kosher products the grocery stores didn't carry, so we were always stopping by for fresh chickens and cornmeal for frying them up, low-fat salad dressing, matzo meal, beef fry, and pickled tomatoes.

"I've never seen this before," Rena Reinhard exclaimed. "Preprepared mock chopped liver." She put two containers into her basket. Her husband loved homemade chopped liver, and in the past she had slaved away making it, but with the way they were fighting these days, she wasn't going to do it anymore. He could make it himself if he wanted it that badly.

Tziporah Newburger looked over her grocery list, pulled a pencil from her purse and began checking off what she already had in her basket. "Only three more things." She shook her head. "But they're out of scouring pads again."

"Doesn't Piggly Wiggly have scouring pads?" Rena asked. "I think I saw them there yesterday."

Tziporah shuddered. She never shopped at Piggly Wiggly. Even if the store carried products that were certified kosher, she was sure that the very name rendered the entire operation treif. She had been there once, and it was as bad as she had feared: there were giant pictures of smiling red pigs on the walls, on the shopping carts, even on the milk containers. She had felt as if they were trying to tempt her into tasting just a little of bit of bacon, a single slice of ham. Her heart had raced uncontrollably and she had had to flee the building.

As Tziporah was asking Mr. Kahn when he expected the shipment of kosher scouring pads to arrive from Brooklyn, Batsheva breezed into the store. She grabbed a cart and lifted Ayala into it. She made her rounds quickly, not stopping to compare Shabbos menus, to ask for a recipe for a new appetizer, a special dessert. Her basket was filling up with the things someone who didn't cook would need: frozen fish sticks, a can of bean and barley soup, a package of crackers, grape jelly, and two challahs.

"Someone is certainly in a hurry," Bessie Kimmel said.

"She's from New York. What do you expect?" Helen Shayowitz shook her head.

"I didn't know she had anywhere that exciting to run off to," Bessie said.

"I certainly wish I did," Helen said. Even though she had been racing around all day—from the dentist to the dry cleaners to the low-impact aerobics class she had recently enrolled in—none of it seemed likc anything to look forward to.

Bessie patted Helen on the shoulder. "Is something bothering you?"

"I'm tired, that's all. Tired of cooking for Shabbos." She rubbed her fingers against her forehead, trying to fight off a headache.

It was a feeling the rest of us knew well. Week in, week out, we spent half of Thursday and all of Friday cooking and cleaning and just once, we wanted a break. The minute one Shabbos was over, it was time to think about the next: a new menu to come up with, more guests to invite, more silver to polish and tablecloths to press.

"Buy takeout," Bessie advised. "I do it all the time. I buy food from the Posh Nosh, doctor it up with salt and pepper, and then put it in my own baking dishes."

"But what if someone asks for a recipe?" Helen asked.

"Make it up. A few eggs, a cup of oil, a scoop of flour here or there, what's the difference?" she said. To reassure Helen, Bessie decided to tell her the one story she had never told anyone. "Once, I was having the Levys over for dinner and I hadn't had time to make the potato kugel. I had a very complicated recipe, with egg whites and all kinds of spices. I was fixing to make it, but I looked at the clock: Shabbos was starting in an hour. I grabbed a mix and whipped up one of those instead. I served it without saying anything. Well, wouldn't you know it, Mrs. Levy started carrying on how good the kugel was, the best she'd had in her life—and you know she's comparing it to a lot of kugels. She asked for the recipe and what could I do, I gave her the complicated one. The next week, she called me. She couldn't get hers to taste like mine, what was she doing wrong? I said to follow the recipe exactly and it should come out the same. To this day, she thinks she's doing something wrong."

Helen and Bessie laughed, and Helen imagined the thrill of putting one over on Mrs. Levy. Even though they were best friends, she wouldn't mind bringing her down a notch or two. But she would have been unable to go through with it as Bessie had. Deliberately withholding one ingredient from every recipe she gave out was one thing, but she would never tell an outright lie. Such treason could destabilize the entire system of trading recipes.

In the meantime, Batsheva finished her shopping and went over to the checkout counter. She was lining her food up on the counter when Mimi Rubin, the Rabbi's wife, walked in. Mimi was wearing a pale pink blouse with tiny pearl buttons, a long flowered skirt and a matching scarf tied over her hair; this was the way she usually dressed and her soft pastels were soothing, exactly what we wanted our rebbetzin to look like. The fact that all her hair was covered didn't make her look severe, as other women who covered their hair often did. On the contrary, it allowed her brown eyes to stand out even more and her kind, welcoming smile to leap off her face.

Bessie and Helen waved excitedly; it was always a treat to see Mimi. No matter how often we bumped into her, we always felt as if we hadn't seen her in ages. Mimi returned the wave, but instead of coming over, she saw Batsheva and ran over to her.

"I'm Mimi Rubin," she said. "We spoke on the phone before you came."

"Of course. It's so nice to meet you in person," Batsheva said.

"And this must be Ayala," Mimi said. Ayala was sucking a lollipop she'd swiped off the shelf (whether Batsheva was planning to pay for it, who knew).

"Say hi to Mimi," Batsheva said, ignoring the fact that all the children, even the teenagers, called her Mrs. Rubin.

"I feel terrible I haven't welcomed you yet to our community," Mimi said. "I've had cookies sitting on my kitchen table that I've been meaning to bring by, but I've been so busy. Still there's no excuse. I hope I can make it up to you."

It was the truth. Mimi had been busier than usual. She had been under the weather for the past two weeks, and before that, she had been in Birmingham, taking care of her sick father. Not to mention the extra cooking she was doing now that Yosef was home.

"It's fine," Batsheva said. "What you told me has been so helpful. It's exactly like you said—I can definitely see making a home for ourselves here."

"I'm glad. Before long, I hope you'll feel like you've lived here forever."

"I hope so. But ever since Benjamin died, I've realized there's no point in planning so far ahead," Batsheva said.

"One day at a time," Mimi agreed.

"Exactly," Batsheva said.

They smiled at each other, and Tziporah, Rena, Helen and Bessie felt abandoned. So Batsheva had called Mimi and asked about the community before she moved here, exactly as Mrs. Levy had deduced. And now the two of them seemed to have a bond. Caught up in her conversation with Batsheva, Mimi didn't notice how Helen and Bessie peered out from behind the carefully stacked cans of soup, how Tziporah and Rena listened closely from the freezer section, trying to fight the jealousy they were feeling. The Rabbi might have been our soul, but Mimi was our heart. We loved her as if she were our sister, mother or daughter. In her shining face, we saw goodness, reminding us of who we wished we were.

"Why don't you and Ayala come for Friday night dinner? That way we can get to know each other," Mimi said.

"We'd love to," Batsheva said.

"I also invited the Feldmans. Have you met Becky yet? Her husband is out of town, but she and her daughter Shira are coming," Mimi said.

Batsheva paid for her groceries in cash—she didn't have a charge account yet—and as she was walking out, Mimi called to her, "See you tomorrow. I don't go to shul on Friday night, so come by after candle lighting."

ON Friday afternoon, we called Mimi to wish her a Good Shabbos. We tried to bring the conversation around to Batsheva. To inquire directly was out of the question; that wasn't how we did things. It was better to drop hints and ask the right questions so the subject of Batsheva would be raised naturally.

"I'm sure you're running around getting ready, but I wanted to wish you a Good Shabbos. Are you having company this week? Oh, really? How nice," Rachel Ann Berkowitz said an hour before candle lighting. "How did that come about? I've been meaning to have her myself, you know."

"I saw you at Kahn's yesterday. I was running in for some ground beef for the kids' supper, but you seemed so deep in conversation, I didn't want to bother you," Rena Reinhard said, a dangerously close twenty minutes before Shabbos.

But Mimi offered no news and though her voice was kind and patient, we detected a hint of reproach; she was warning us in her soft way to give Batsheva a chance. On many occasions, Mimi had spoken about our power to change the world, first by fixing our small corner of it. You never knew, she would remind us, when a smile or a kind word could change someone forever. Mimi would never say anything harsh to us outright, but she would quietly urge us to be more than we were.

After the men went off to shul, Mrs. Levy decided to visit Mimi. It would be a good opportunity to further question Batsheva, and she looked forward to spending more time with Ayala. But just so she wouldn't be accused of being excessively nosy, she made an effort to conceal her intentions.

"Of course I'm not going over there to spy on Batsheva," she said. "I haven't visited Mimi in ages, that's all. And if Batsheva happens to be there, what can I do?"

She walked down the street and around the corner in the green velvet housecoat with gold trim that she wore on Friday nights, even when she had company. "It's like a dress," she would say when one of us commented on her practice of wearing it outdoors, even for a quick trip to the grocery. When her daughters criticized her for this practice, her husband assured her that she looked beautiful no matter what she wore. In fact, Irving loved the way she looked in these robes so much that he bought her a new one every year for Chanukah.

Mrs. Levy arrived at the front door as the Rabbi and Yosef stepped out on their way to shul. "Hello there, Rabbi. Hello, Yosef. I'm paying a surprise visit to your lovely wife," she said.

"Go right in," the Rabbi said as he and Yosef hurried down the driveway.

"Yoo hoo," Mrs. Levy called through the screen door. "Anyone home?"

Mimi came to the door and when she saw who was there, she smiled. This in itself was a good thing, because not so many years back, there had been some hurt feelings. It was a long story but it had come down to the fact that Mrs. Levy had decided that it was she, and not Mimi, who was really the heart of this community. Mrs. Levy didn't think that just because Mimi was the Rabbi's wife she should have an automatic claim on this position; to her, that smacked of favoritism. It was unusual for anyone to be angry at Mimi, and we hadn't known how to handle it. In the end, we had decided not to dwell on the unpleasantness, so much better to let it fade away.

"What a nice surprise," Mimi said.

"I was out enjoying this beautiful evening and I wanted to say hello," Mrs. Levy said.

"Come sit down. I'm expecting the Feldmans and Batsheva any minute now."

Mrs. Levy followed Mimi into the living room. "How nice. I didn't know you had invited Batsheva. What an interesting woman she is. Seems like she has quite a story behind her, don't you think?"

"I suppose we all do," Mimi said. Mimi certainly did. She was the daughter of a rabbi in Birmingham and the youngest after five brothers. Her father had taught her as he had his sons—this was at a time when no one did that—and we were always surprised at how much she knew. She had gone to public high school because there was no day school in Birmingham and then she went to Barnard College in New York. All the while, she had stayed religious; she was never susceptible to outside forces.

What would her own story be, Mrs. Levy wondered. She was born in Memphis, raised in Memphis, married in Memphis, gave birth to three children in Memphis, raised them in Memphis, and as far as she knew, she would die in Memphis. There didn't seem to be much drama to that.

"But none of us has a story as unusual as Batsheva's, I'm sure," Mrs. Levy said. "Just the other day I was wondering how someone like that would do here. She's used to a different kind of life, I would presume."

Mrs. Levy settled into the sofa and looked at Mimi, hoping she would supply her with some much-needed information. She had, after all, gone to the trouble of walking over here when she still had a salad to make and a table to set. But Mimi wouldn't budge. She gave a mysterious smile which made Mrs. Levy more certain that there was some terrific secret being hidden from her. As she was deciding upon a strategy for uncovering it, Becky Feldman and her seventeen-year-old daughter, Shira, arrived. They were clearly in the middle of a fight. Shira's cheeks were flushed in anger, and she was standing as far from her mother as possible. But Becky, concerned about putting up a proper appearance, smiled and acted like nothing was wrong.

"Good Shabbos," she said brightly.

The conversation began again, but the issue of Batsheva had receded, too far off the topic for Mrs. Levy to return to it. Instead, the usual subjects were touched on. About the results of the youth group raffle and the clothes at Goldsmith's: so few long skirts, what would we do? And of course about the heat wave. It had never been this hot as far as anyone could remember and everyone was languid, barely able to leave the air conditioning of houses and cars.

Shira wasn't interested in the conversation. She leaned back against the couch and stared at the ceiling. With her skirt so short, her shoes clunky, her short sleeve sweater tight as can be, she looked as if she had stepped off the page of a fashion magazine. This past year, some tough exterior had grown over Shira's sweet face. She was still making straight A's, everyone still talked about how smart she was, but she had a new way of speaking, with her jaw locked and her eyes averted.

"How has your summer been?" Mimi asked Shira. "It's probably hard to see it end."

"Yeah," Shira said and gave a sour look.

"Shira, every time I see you, you look prettier and prettier," Mrs. Levy said, hoping to soften her up a bit.

Batsheva and Ayala arrived at Mimi's house in the middle of this. Instead of knocking with great hesitancy and respect, as we would have had we been new to a community, they walked right in. We kept our doors unlocked, but even so, there were certain unsaid rules about when it was okay to walk in: at family's and friends' homes, it was fine, but at the Rabbi's house, never.

"Anyone home?" Batsheva called from the entrance hall.

Mimi rushed to greet her. "I'm so glad y'all could come," she said.

Batsheva walked into the living room and squeezed herself onto the couch between Mrs. Levy and Becky. She was about to lift Ayala onto her lap when Mrs. Levy waved hello to her. Ayala pulled away from Batsheva and went over to her for a hug.

"Hi, dear. How would you like to sit on my lap? I have all this extra room and it's going to waste with no little girl on it," she said in her sweetest voice, which she saved for children.

Ayala nodded and smiled at Mrs. Levy, who picked her up and placed her on her lap.

"Don't you just look darling!" Mrs. Levy exclaimed. She straightened out Ayala's pink shirt, which was a little creased around the collar. It was one of the hand-me-downs that Rena Reinhard had given her and it fit perfectly.

"I think Ayala has a new friend," Mimi said. She turned back to Batsheva. "Do you know everyone?" she asked, and without waiting for an answer, she made introductions. "This is Batsheva and Ayala. And this is Becky Feldman and her daughter, Shira, and you must have already met Mrs. Levy."

"How do you do," Mrs. Levy said and nodded at her.

Mrs. Levy cleared her throat while Becky busied herself with a piece of Shira's hair that wouldn't stay out of her face. The previous conversation could not be resumed—about the redecoration of the Torah Academy, whether it would be finished in time for the first day of school, two weeks away. It didn't seem like the kind of thing to talk about with Batsheva—perhaps it was too provincial for someone like her. But what kind of thing she would be interested in, no one knew.

"Tell me again where you're from, Batsheva," Mimi said.

"We were living in New York. I had just moved there when I met Benjamin," Batsheva said. She looked around the room at everyone sitting there. "You must have all known Benjamin."

"Of course we knew him. I went to high school with his mother and his grandparents lived on the same street as my parents. And his uncle was married to my third cousin for a short while. But that's another story," Mrs. Levy said and bounced Ayala up and down to keep her happy. "So tell me, Batsheva, where are you from originally?"

This was always asked of newcomers; there was so much to be learned from it. When anyone asked Mrs. Levy, she replied with pride: her family was *from* Memphis. Not just living here for a generation or two, but deeply and certainly from the innermost core of this city.

"I've only been to New York once but I can't understand how anyone lives there," Becky interjected. "Everyone is always rushing around, and it's so crowded and dirty." She was about to launch into the story of how she had nearly been mugged in New York when Mrs. Levy shot her a look.

"Hush, Becky. Now Batsheva, where did you say you were from?" Mrs. Levy asked.

"A lot of different places, but I was born in Virginia," Batsheva said.

"Where in Virginia?" Becky inquired. "My cousin is from Newport News. His father was the rabbi of the shul there. Maybe you know him."

"I grew up in Hampton. It's right near Newport News, but I probably didn't know the rabbi," Batsheva said.

Even though the fact that Batsheva had converted was in the forefront of our minds, there was considerable effort being made to pretend that she had always been Jewish. And here the uncomfortable topic had been raised anyway. Of course Batsheva wouldn't know the rabbi of the Newport News shul. We, of course, could play Jewish Geography with the best of them, comparing whom we knew from where, from which youth group convention, summer camp or college.

Becky was so embarrassed at her mistake that she wished she would fall through the floor. And she could have sworn she heard Shira mutter something, probably "smooth move, Mom," or "way to go," one of those sarcastic remarks she was always making. The normally spacious room seemed to close in on her, the soft couch cushions became her prison, the silence around her a reminder of her faux pas. But for Mrs. Levy, Becky's indiscretion provided a much-needed opportunity to unearth some information. Now that the subject had been touched upon, it was possible to broach the question. We had been tiptoeing around it for weeks, and if Batsheva wasn't going to be forthcoming with the information, Mrs. Levy would have to uncover it herself.

"If you don't mind my asking," Mrs. Levy began, "what made you decide to convert?"

There, the question was out and asking it had been easier than she anticipated. No lightning bolts had descended from heaven, no astonished gasps had filled the room. Even Batsheva didn't act like the question was that surprising. In fact, she smiled at Mrs. Levy, happy to have a chance to talk about it.

"I was always pulled toward Judaism, like God was calling to me," Batsheva said.

"Really," Mrs. Levy commented. She had never felt God calling out to her, and in fact, she distinctly remembered learning that He no longer called out to people so directly in this day and age.

"I was walking in the city on a Friday afternoon and I passed by a shul, although at the time I didn't know what it was. The doors were open and I walked in. I had never seen anything like it. The room was alive. The people were singing and clapping and swaying back and forth. I also started swaying to the singing. I didn't know the words. I couldn't even understand them because they were in Hebrew. But I didn't care. Maybe they had been buried in me all along, maybe they were a part of my experience from some other time or place."

"That doesn't sound like any shul I've ever been in. Are you sure it was Orthodox?" Becky asked. "From what I hear, in New York those shuls all look the same from the outside." Becky had never been in a non-Orthodox shul, but she did have a third cousin who was Conservative and this, she believed, gave her a certain authority on the subject.

Mrs. Levy cut her off. "Go on, Batsheva. What happened next?"

"A woman came over to me and reached for my arm. We swayed back and forth together. The words had ended and the tune was sung over and over. It no longer sounded like individuals singing. All the voices had melted into one. When the next prayer began, the woman took my hand and led me to a seat at the front of the women's section next to her. She handed me a siddur and I followed along in English. Soon everyone started dancing and I was swept into a circle of women. I felt like I had been doing this my whole life. Right then, I knew that I had found what I was always missing."

"You were always missing something?" Mrs. Levy inquired, to clarify.

"Before I converted, I felt this giant hole in my life, like hunger, only deeper in my body."

"But how could you be sure you wanted to be Jewish?" Mrs. Levy said. She couldn't understand why anyone would voluntarily take on so many commandments. She had enough trouble remembering all of them and she had been born into it.

"It just felt right. I knew a Jewish family when I was young. The mother would light candles on Friday night and I started going over to watch. She lit one for each of her children and she asked if I wanted her to light one for me too. I loved seeing my candle burn next to theirs. Years later, when I ended up at this shul, everything fell into place. I have to believe that there was always a hand guiding me toward Judaism."

Hearing this, Mrs. Levy felt a renewed sense that Orthodoxy was indeed correct. If someone like Batsheva wanted to be Orthodox, there was surely something to it. Not that she doubted it (or at least she didn't ever really and truly doubt it), but it was nice to have outside validation. Whenever Mrs. Levy heard about people who left Orthodoxy, she felt a pang of insecurity. Did they know something she didn't? Were they smarter than she was? Did they now look at Orthodox Jews as silly, backward, superstitious? But with Batsheva choosing it on her own, she could breathe a little easier. She gave Batsheva a genuine smile. Maybe this newcomer would fit in better than she had anticipated.

"But let's get back to your story," Mrs. Levy said, not wanting to leave any thread hanging. "What happened next?"

"When davening ended, the woman kissed me on the cheek and invited me to join them for Shabbat dinner. There were so many things I wanted to ask, but I decided to feel it and worry about all the questions later. Her living room was filled with a huge table. No places had yet been set because she never knew how many people were coming. The guests were from all over. Some were like me who had never celebrated Shabbat before and others did every week. It didn't occur to me to mention that I wasn't Jewish. No one was worried about where I was from. All that mattered was that I was there and was happy to be.

"The meal lasted for hours, and finally, after midnight, there were only five of us left. The conversation was growing more intense and I was ready for it. How does one ever feel God, one of the men was asking. How can we reach something so far from us? I caught this man's eye. That was the first time I saw Benjamin. When I left that night, he walked me home. I went back to shul the next week and introduced myself to the rabbi. We began learning together, and I converted a year later. Benjamin and I got married right afterward. By then, it felt like we had spent several lifetimes together. Even though he had grown up Orthodox, we had the same attitude toward being religious. He agreed that it was important to explore what he really felt and to always be growing in his spirituality. I had never met anyone before that I could share this with and for the first time, I was with someone who really understood me."

Hearing about Batsheva and Benjamin's relationship, a sense of sadness descended over the room. Batsheva seemed smaller than she had before; her excitement as she described coming across the shul on Friday night disappeared. Mrs. Levy considered how devastated she would be if she lost Irving. He was her soulmate; she was sure of that. And Batsheva had to deal with this loss on her own. She didn't have a family she could fall back on.

Becky looked for a way to change the subject, to at least move on to a different aspect of Batsheva that wasn't as tragic. "I assume the name Batsheva is new?" she inquired; no sense letting Mrs. Levy do all the asking.

"I picked it when I converted," Batsheva said. "Once I was becoming Jewish, I wanted to take a Hebrew name. It was my way of sealing this new identity inside me."

"But why Batsheva?" Becky asked. Once you were choosing your own name, there were so many possibilities. If she had been given the choice, she certainly wouldn't have selected Becky; she would have gone for something more dramatic, maybe Shoshana or Ariella.

"I loved the way it sounded and also, it has a special meaning for me. Batsheva means 'the daughter of seven' and I decided to convert because of Shabbos, the seventh day."

For the first time, Shira joined in. "That's cool. I'd like to change my name too."

"What are you talking about? Shira is a beautiful name," Becky said and turned to the other women. "She's named after my grandmother. She's just saying that to upset me." Becky sighed. She was tired of dealing with Shira alone. Her husband always managed to be out of town whenever things flared up.

Becky looked to Mrs. Levy and Mimi for sympathy and Mrs. Levy offered her most encouraging smile. She had raised two daughters, and she knew how hard it could be. She thought back to the terrible fights she had had with them when they told her they had no plans to move back to Memphis. She looked at Shira, who was pouting; in fact, she could have sworn she rolled her eyes at her mother. What a contrast it was to Ayala, who was happily playing with the gold bracelet Mrs. Levy was wearing, leaning back against her for some much-needed cuddling.

"I'm sorry if we're asking too many questions. It must be hard to talk about such personal things to people you barely know," Mimi said to Batsheva, certainly thinking that the Torah says once someone converts, you aren't allowed to single her out and make her feel like a stranger, because we too were once strangers in the land of Egypt. And living here in Memphis, we could certainly relate to that.

"I don't mind," Batsheva said. "It's nice to have people to talk to. Sometimes when I'm home alone and Ayala is asleep, I look out my window at all the houses, and I feel so lonely."

Mrs. Levy tried to imagine what she would do if she had no one in the world except for one quiet little girl. She couldn't picture it. Even though her children didn't live here, in Memphis alone—in a one-mile radius actually—she had a husband, a sister, two brothers and two sisters-in-law, five nieces and seven nephews and countless first, second and third cousins, even more if she included fourth and fifth cousins, but that far out, she had stopped keeping track.

"Do you know what you're going to do here?" Mimi asked Batsheva. "It's easier if you keep busy."

"I was so excited about coming that I didn't have a chance to make plans," Batsheva said. "But I'm going to look for a job in art—maybe teaching in a school or working in a gallery."

"Oh, that's right," Becky said. "Rena Reinhard was telling me about your paintings. She said they're very interesting." Rena had told Becky the part about Batsheva wanting to get a reaction from what she painted, how she wanted to move people to feel and Becky was wondering if that was true of more than just her artwork.

"Lena Hurwitz is also an artist. She does the most beautiful calligraphy I've ever seen and she also embroiders throw pillows. I have two of them in my living room," Mrs. Levy said. "Maybe you could go into business with her."

"I don't do that kind of artwork. I'm a painter," Batsheva answered, in the sort of voice that didn't want to insult anyone but still made it clear that she was above calligraphy and embroidery.

"Well," Mrs. Levy said. She cleared her throat. "Well, that is very nice."

Becky laughed nervously and again turned to fussing with Shira's hair. Shira swatted her mother's hand away.

"Leave me alone," Shira said and Becky looked down; she could never do or say the right thing.

Averting the awkwardness, Mimi looked at her watch. "The Rabbi and Yosef should be home any minute."

Shul was running later than usual that night; the cantor's parents were visiting and he was probably showing off in their honor. By the time the Rabbi and Yosef walked in, everyone was more than ready for their arrival. Mimi introduced the Rabbi to Batsheva and he nodded without really looking at her. He wasn't being unfriendly; that was the way he was, especially with women—a little uncomfortable, a little abrupt. Yosef was a few steps behind his father, and Mimi went over and kissed him on the cheek.

"Good Shabbos," she said. She took in his dark hair and crisp white shirt and glowed with pride. "Have you met Batsheva and Ayala?"

Before he could say anything, Batsheva interrupted. "It's nice to see you again, Yosef." She turned to Mimi. "Yosef was so friendly to me my first week here."

Yosef looked so uncomfortable that Mrs. Levy could barely stand it. "That's our Yosef," she said, hoping to deflate some of the tension.

"It certainly is." Mimi put her hand on Yosef's shoulder. "We're very proud of him."

Mrs. Levy looked around: everyone who was coming to dinner had arrived, and there was no way she could stay without being rude.

"The time has come," Mrs. Levy announced, "for me to be on my way. Irving is probably home from shul and wondering where I've run off to."

As Mimi walked her to the door, Mrs. Levy called out how nice it had been to see Batsheva and get a chance to really talk to her, more than the casual hellos they exchanged when she dropped Ayala off. She thanked Mimi for her hospitality, lovely, as always, and the front door closed, leaving her outside and Batsheva inside.

MIMI invited everyone into the dining room to begin dinner. With the arrival of Shabbos, the room was transformed. The table was set with a perfect white cloth, the all-white china gleaming against it. Mimi's silver candlesticks, passed down from her grandmother, stood on the buffet, three candles lit, one for each member of their small family. The silver kiddush cup was filled with wine, the challahs were covered and the bread knife was ready and waiting. We all loved being invited here for a Shabbos meal; this was how Shabbos was supposed to be celebrated. Even though we too lit the candles and carefully laid our tables, at Mimi's house everything felt holier, as if they lived a little closer to heaven.

On this night though, Becky couldn't get into the right mood; she couldn't let the spirit of Shabbos wash over her and erase all the tensions of the week. They had followed her right into Shabbos. Shira was as difficult as ever. No matter what Becky said or did, it was always the wrong thing. Here, for example, she had tried to nudge Shira to stand near Yosef, to position herself so that she would end up sitting near him; this was the sort of thing Becky had known to do as a teenager. But Shira rolled her eyes and laughed.

Everyone took their places, and as luck would have it, Batsheva happened to sit directly across from Yosef and next to Mimi, the seat Shira should have had. As they began the shalom aleichem, Becky watched Batsheva close her eyes in concentration and sway back and forth. Ayala stood by her mother's side, not swaying or singing but carefully watching everyone. As far as Becky could tell, the little girl was embarrassed by her mother's overenthusiasm. Becky made a face and looked around, wondering if anyone else was bothered by Batsheva. But everyone was involved in singing aishet chayil and listening to the Rabbi make kiddush.

When Mimi rose to serve the meal, Batsheva started to stand as well. Mimi motioned for her to sit back down: she liked to serve by herself, she could work faster that way.

"I guess I'll have to help with the clearing off," Batsheva said.

Though she hated letting Batsheva take the lead, Becky sat back down as well. No point leaving Batsheva alone with the Rabbi and Yosef. Not that anything unusual would necessarily happen, but why take chances?

Yosef looked down shyly at his plate. He had been so comfortable talking to Batsheva in shul, but it was another thing in front of his father. Shira was staring off into nowhere; Becky had no idea what she was thinking about. Batsheva wasn't saying anything either, and after a few more seconds of this silence, the Rabbi realized the task of making conversation had fallen to him.

"How do you like Memphis?" he asked Batsheva.

"We love it here, don't we, Ayala?" Batsheva said. "Everyone has been so friendly, especially to Ayala."

"I'll never forget the day we moved in, almost thirty years go," the Rabbi said. "We pulled up to our house and there were ten women waiting out front with enough food to last a month. And the same thing happened when Yosef was born. People here pride themselves on their hospitality."

"They don't call us the Jerusalem of the South for nothing," Becky said. Her mother had been one of those women standing out front of the Rabbi's house and she was proud of it.

"That's great," Batsheva said and laughed. "The Jerusalem of the South."

On the off chance that Batsheva was being sarcastic, Becky launched into a defense. "Maybe you don't realize this, but we're not like any community. We have an elementary school, a high school, a shul"—she counted these out on her fingers—"a restaurant, a kosher grocery, even a bakery. How many communities our size can say that?"

"I agree. When I told a few people in New York where I was moving, they had a lot to say," Batsheva said.

"Oh really? Like what?" Becky asked. She rarely heard about Memphis from an outsider's point of view and her curiosity was piqued.

"Some people are surprised there are Jews here. They think this is the middle of nowhere and couldn't believe I would leave New York for such a small place," Batsheva said.

"I hope you let them know that we are a very old and distinguished community," Becky said.

"That was what my rabbi told me. He had heard very good things about the Memphis Jewish community," Batsheva said.

The Rabbi leaned forward. This was a perfect opportunity for him to find out more about her. "Who was your rabbi?" he asked.

"Rabbi Abrams, at the Carlebach Shul," she said. "Have you heard of him?"

"Of course," he said, relieved that he could place her inside some definite background.

Hmm, Becky thought, the Carlebach Shul. It had a reputation for being a little outside the mainstream, for attracting an eclectic crowd, for singing and dancing. And as luck would have it, Becky had an old friend from college who lived close to the shul and sometimes went there. Perhaps she knew Batsheva. If it became necessary, Becky wouldn't hesitate to use the connection.

"The hardest part about being down here is that I don't get to learn with my rabbi anymore. I still call him once a week though," Batsheva said.

That didn't sound like any relationship Becky had ever had with a rabbi. When she had a question, she had her husband ask it for her. She was about to ask Batsheva for more details when Mimi began serving dinner. She had outdone herself, as usual. There was honey mustard chicken and barbecue beef ribs, broccoli pie in a homemade crust, noodle kugel with fresh peaches, and baby carrots and sliced kishka sprinkled with dots of brown sugar. For many of us, this kind of cooking was part of a competition over who could make more, who could be fancier, more like a gourmet restaurant. But Mimi never looked like she was doing it for those reasons; she seemed to be doing it out of a love for Shabbos.

Becky watched as Batsheva helped herself to everything but the chicken and beef ribs. That figures, she thought. She must be a vegetarian. People like her always turned out to be. She tried to envision what Batsheva made for Shabbos—tofu? tuna fish? Everyone knew you were supposed to have chicken or roast. It was like a religious law by this point. As Becky cut into her piece of chicken, she grew more annoyed with Batsheva. It was as if she had decided to be vegetarian just to irk everyone. But Becky was not going to let it bother her. She ate her chicken with as much fervor as possible.

"Everything is wonderful, Mimi. Especially the chicken. I'll have to get your recipe for it," Becky said. "How in the world did you have time to do all this?"

"It's nothing," Mimi said. She did this with everything—she was the driving force behind so many projects (the clothing drive, the food pantry, the list was endless), but whenever anyone tried to give her credit, she sweetly brushed it off.

"Don't be silly. Isn't this unbelievable?" Batsheva said. "You must have cooked all day. Benjamin used to do all the cooking and now Ayala and I wing it, don't we?" She looked down at Ayala and the two of them laughed, no doubt thinking of the pancakes and other breakfast foods she tried to pass off as dinner. "Before I was Jewish, I used to eat out all the time. But when I started keeping kosher, it was hard to remember. Once, I walked into a nonkosher restaurant before I remembered."

Becky couldn't imagine that. Keeping kosher was so ingrained in her that it wasn't something she thought about anymore.

"I can imagine," Mimi said. "It's such a big change. Being raised orthodox, I think we don't always realize how hard it is."

"Shira loves to cook," Becky said and nudged Shira in the side. "Don't you?" She waited for Shira to say something, hoping she would tell everyone about the delicious lasagna she had made last summer.

"Not really," Shira said and looked down at her fingernails, polished a bright shade of pink.

"What about you, Yosef? Do you cook?" Batsheva asked.

"Not very much, do you, Yosef?" Mimi said and laughed.

"I know how to," he said. "At yeshiva, I used to make breakfast with some of the other guys if we slept late." He looked shyly at Batsheva. He wanted to talk to her but wasn't sure what to say.

"I'll bet the rabbis loved that—sleeping late and then hanging out in the kitchen." Batsheva laughed.

Yosef smiled at Batsheva, and Becky nearly choked. She put down her knife and fork and folded her hands primly in her lap. Just when the meal was starting to go more smoothly, Batsheva had to say something inappropriate.

"Let's sing something," the Rabbi suggested and Becky, for one, was glad.

The Rabbi began a song and everyone joined in. *God nourishes His world, our shepherd our father. We have eaten His bread and drunk His wine. Therefore we thank His name, His praise is in our mouths.* Batsheva sang loudly, and she put her arm around Ayala, getting her to join in even as she was struggling to stay awake. By the time the song was over, Ayala had fallen asleep, her head leaning against Batsheva's shoulder.

"Look at that," Mimi said. "She must be exhausted."

Batsheva picked Ayala up and carried her to the living room couch. She laid her down and stood over her for a few seconds, watching her sleep. Then Batsheva came back to the table. Not waiting to take her cues from the hostess (as was proper, according to both Mrs. Levy and Miss Manners), she offered to clear the table.

"Good idea," Mimi said and stood up.

"No, sit down. You've done enough work already," Batsheva said.

"Of course not," Mimi said.

"I insist." Batsheva took the plates from Mimi. "Don't worry, Yosef will show me where everything goes."

She stood up and began clearing off the table. "Take these," she said, handing the dishes to Yosef, "and I'll bring in the rest."

The two of them carried the dishes into the kitchen, stacking them on the countertops and the kitchen table, which was covered with cooking pans and aluminum foil. Through the clanking of silverware and glasses, their laughter could be heard in the dining room.

"I'll bet you've never helped clear off," Batsheva teased.

"I have too," he insisted.

"Why don't I believe you?" she said and they laughed.

When they returned to the table, Becky gave them a pointed look, hoping they would realize how inappropriate their behavior was. It would be one thing if Batsheva was flirting with Yosef in private, but quite another for her to be flaunting it in front of everyone.

"Yosef, will you honor us with a d'var Torah?" the Rabbi asked.

The Rabbi asked him to do this every week. It was expected that a yeshiva boy would always carry some words of Torah on the tip of his tongue.

"My father and I have been learning about the parah adumah, the red heifer," Yosef began. He looked around, making sure everyone was familiar with the topic. Looks of recognition appeared on everyone's faces but Batsheva's. It was something we had learned about at some point in school, but who could remember anymore when or where.

He turned to Batsheva. "God commands the high priest to take a cow that is entirely red and without any blemish, slaughter it, and burn it to use the ashes to purify the people so they can enter the bet hamikdash, the holy temple." Yosef was so patient and clear; he was going to be a wonderful rabbi someday. "But there's a paradox. People become impure from touching dead bodies, yet ashes from a dead animal make them tahor, pure, again. This mitzvah is the archetypal law for which we have no reason. We're supposed to obey God's command without asking why. At the same time, this is a powerful message that nothing is absolutely good or bad—anything can be changed depending on its context. From bad, good can come, just as bad can sometimes emerge from good."

When Yosef finished, he looked to his father for approval. The Rabbi gave the slightest nod, one that Becky would have missed had she blinked. But even in that quick look, she saw how his eyes glowed with pride. Yosef too saw this and his lips turned into a relieved smile.

"I have a question," Batsheva said. "I don't understand what the Torah means by 'tahor.'"

"It doesn't necessarily mean pure in the way we think of. It has nothing to do with physical cleanliness. It refers to ritual purity, what would qualify someone to serve in the bet hamikdash," Yosef said.

"I thought it was a perfectly nice d'var Torah," Becky said, under her breath. Why couldn't Batsheva leave good enough alone? That was the kind of d'var Torah Becky liked: everything crystal-clear and easily digestible, no need for follow-up discussion or questions.

"But even ritual purity has to have some symbolic meaning. It seems like purity has to do with life. The more we cling to life the more pure we become," Batsheva said. She looked around the table and Mimi smiled encouragingly.

"That's a nice way to put it, Batsheva," Mimi said.

"Benjamin and I used to learn together and we would discuss the symbolism behind the rituals we did. Since he died, I've tried to keep up with my learning. But I'm always realizing how much I don't know."

"It takes a while," Mimi said. "I've been doing this my whole life and there are still so many things I need to learn more about."

"I wish there was some way I could keep learning. In New York, I belonged to a group that met twice a week in people's apartments and in the summer, in Central Park. Each of us would bring a question and our rabbi would teach us," Batsheva said.

"We have a class that meets once a month," Becky said. "The Ladies Home Study Circle. We're learning about prayer." Now *that* was a class: It was only forty minutes and she could sit back, relax, and listen.

"I have so much catching up to do. I need to find someone who has time to learn with me more frequently." Batsheva looked around the table. When her eyes landed on Yosef, she stopped.

No one said anything and Becky couldn't believe that Batsheva would dare suggest a private tutorial with Yosef; surely not even she would be so nervy. Yosef gave a class every once in a while, on a holiday or when he was here on vacation, and we all made sure to attend. But Yosef's time was something to be guarded. He was so beyond our level that we would never imagine learning with him one-on-one.

"I'm learning with my father in the afternoons, but maybe I can learn with you in the morning," Yosef offered.

He glanced at his father, making sure the idea was acceptable to him. Becky was shocked that he hadn't asked first. She was certain that the Rabbi would never approve. As far as she knew, one-on-one coed learning was not allowed. In fact, years back there had been some discussion about making the high school coed, but in the end, it was agreed that such a move would be inappropriate. And the Rabbi had, on many occasions, tried to protect Yosef from bad influences. She distinctly remembered that when Yosef was in high school, he had discouraged him from attending R-rated movies with the other boys. And Yosef never had anything to do with the girls in his class; he wasn't involved in the Saturday night coed outings that went on in semisecret.

As Becky had expected, the Rabbi was surprised by the idea. Mimi noticed this as quickly as Becky had, and she smiled reassuringly at her husband, to let him know that it was fine. This was how it often was between the Rabbi and Mimi: as much as he was officially in charge of the community, she was always behind the scenes, tempering his decisions with her kindness and wisdom.

"What a great idea," Mimi said to Batsheva. "You can learn in the shul and I'll look after Ayala. It will be fun for me to have a little girl here."

Seeing Mimi's excitement, the Rabbi smiled as well. But Becky couldn't understand what Mimi was thinking. The only possibility she could come up with was that maybe Mimi was so eager to help Batsheva that she was willing to overlook the problem of coed learning. Or maybe she trusted Yosef so implicitly that she knew nothing bad would come of it.

"You wouldn't mind?" Batsheva asked him.

"No, I'm home anyway," Yosef said.

"Then that would be great."

Batsheva smiled at Yosef, as if this were the most ordinary thing in the world, as if Yosef was always volunteering to be a private tutor for women who had just moved in and whom we really knew nothing about.

"Now that that's settled," Mimi said, "it's time for dessert."

She disappeared into the kitchen and returned with a marble cake. It was the same kind of cake that she made and donated each year to the Ladies Auxiliary Midsummer Night's Bake Sale. It was always purchased right away and had once even caused a quarrel between Helen Shayowitz and Mrs. Levy over who had gotten to it first. (In the end, Mimi had settled the issue by cutting the cake in half and promising that next year, she would make two cakes, one for each of them.)

As Mimi dished out pieces of cake, the Rabbi tried to make conversation with Shira. She had been sitting without a word, bored and anxious for the meal to be over.

"Are you looking forward to starting school?" the Rabbi asked her.

"Not really," she answered.

It was public knowledge that Shira was unhappy at school. Last year, she had gotten it into her head that she wanted to go to public school. The fighting between her and her parents continued all summer, and it wasn't unusual to find her sitting on the front curb, Becky's angry voice streaming out of the house. Her parents eventually won: they told Shira that she was going to the yeshiva and that was that. But her attitude was as bad as ever, and some of us suspected that Shira had a part in making the other girls unhappy. The school had grown smaller in recent years: there were only three girls in the ninth grade and five in the tenth. There were a few other problems as well. Some of the students weren't getting along with the principal, and the science teacher had quit the year before and a new one hadn't been found. But whenever people complained, we reminded them and ourselves that with a community as small as ours, we were lucky to have a school at all.

The teachers had tried all sorts of things to get the girls excited: Spirit Week, where the girls took class time to go roller skating, bowling, and on a Mississippi Queen Boat ride. They arranged a mother-daughter luncheon, a fashion show, an after-school aerobics class. They even created a musical extravaganza entitled "Destiny: An

Inspirational Evening of Song and Dance for the Women of Memphis," with a live piano and dance routines. Helen Shayowitz had sewn costumes for the girls—long sarong skirts and matching blouses—and they had looked darling.

"You know how it is. The girls are having a hard time," Becky said. "Sometimes it seems like nothing will make a difference."

"Destiny" had been a failure; the singing and dancing hadn't gone as well as planned—there had been a few missed notes and off-key tunes, several forgotten dance steps, and an unfortunate mishap when one of the dancing girls had fallen off the stage and crashed into the piano. After that, the girls had been unhappier than ever, and Becky had lost hope.

Batsheva was listening to Becky describe the problem and watching Shira roll her eyes at what her mother said.

"Maybe the girls need to do something different," Batsheva suggested. "Mother-daughter luncheons and fashion shows are fine if that's what you like, but when I was a teenager I wouldn't have been into those things either."

Becky stared at her: how could Batsheva know what nice yeshiva girls would like?

"When I was in high school, I needed some kind of creative outlet where I could let loose and get out everything I was feeling," Batsheva said. "That was when I started to take drawing more seriously. I felt like it was the one thing that kept me sane."

Becky started to laugh—obviously letting loose wasn't what the girls needed—and she turned to Mimi, expecting her to be amused as well. But Mimi was giving Batsheva a smile.

"You're right, Batsheva. That is what the girls need," Mimi said. "Why not solve two problems tonight? Yosef will learn with you and you can teach the girls art."

Mimi and Batsheva began discussing the logistics of her teaching, if she could do it in the morning when Ayala would be in school, how the principal would react to such an idea. Any chance Becky had to raise the question of whether Batsheva was the right person to help the girls had passed her by.

When dinner ended, Batsheva picked Ayala up and carried her against her shoulder. Mimi said that it had been so nice to get to know each other, they would have to do it again soon, and before Batsheva stepped out of the doorway, she leaned over and placed a kiss on Mimi's cheek.

"I'm going to speak to the principal right after Shabbos," Mimi said and squeezed Batsheva's shoulder. "I know it's going to work out. You'll see."

After that visit, there were still those of us who whispered about Batsheva's clothes, sent suspicious glances her way at shul, and pretended not to see her when she passed by. But for most of us, Mimi's friendship was a kosher seal newly printed on Batsheva's forehead and it changed everything. We nodded warmly and said Good Shabbos to her, we smiled when we saw her in the grocery store, we even began inviting her to our houses for Shabbos meals.

5

IT WASN'T SO SURPRISING, WE decided, that Batsheva wasn't like us. After all, she had grown up in a different world. We remembered what the Rabbi said about those who came to Judaism on their own: life is like a ladder and each day you climb up one rung at a time. If you climb too fast, you might fall off altogether. The important thing though was to always be moving up. And who better to help Batsheva up this ladder than Yosef?

Batsheva and Yosef met for the first time in the shul. It was only proper that they learn in public. Not that we would have suspected Yosef of anything then, but it was forbidden for them to be alone. When a man and woman were together behind closed doors, there was only one conclusion to draw. And even if nothing was going on, it was still improper. That was another law the Rabbi spoke about when some of us had started buying coffee from the McDonald's nearby: you shouldn't do something people might misinterpret and assume to be allowed. If someone saw you buying coffee from McDonald's, maybe he would think that everything in McDonald's was kosher and, because of you, eat a cheeseburger.

Yosef arrived at the shul earlier than the time they had arranged. Unsure of what Batsheva wanted to learn, he brought with him a stack of books: commentaries on the Bible, a translation of the prayers, guides to keeping Shabbos and kosher. He went into the bet midrash, the small room that was supposed to be a place of communal learning. But whenever we wandered past, it was empty except for the two or three elderly men who studied Talmud there for a few hours in the afternoon.

Yosef sat at one of the tables and waited for Batsheva. Batsheva had been so excited about learning with him that we couldn't imagine she would forget. But even so, she was late—fifteen minutes and counting. It was quickly becoming apparent that Batsheva had no sense of time, no inner urgency moving her along. Yosef drummed his fingers against the table, he flipped through a book, he glanced at his watch for the third time. When he stood up to check the hallway, to see if she was waiting out there, he looked relieved not to see her. We could hardly blame him for being nervous. He barely knew Batsheva and he was going to have to spend all this time alone with her.

After another five minutes or so—who was keeping track anymore?—Batsheva rushed into the room, out of breath.

"Oh my God, I'm so sorry I'm late," she said.

"Don't worry, I just got here myself," Yosef said.

She sat down across from him. She was wearing one of the outfits we had come to expect—a flowy, gauzy skirt covered with small, colored flowers, a shirt that had one too many buttons left undone, a filmy scarf hanging around her neck, beaded jewelry that tinkled when she walked. Not that we really expected her to dress differently for learning with Yosef, to maybe wear a nice denim skirt and a tailored blouse, but it certainly would have been nice.

"I was caught up in my painting and I had no idea what time it was. When I saw the clock, I couldn't believe it. You're sweet not to be angry," she said. "I owe you one already."

She looked eagerly at him, excited to begin learning. But Yosef looked so uncomfortable you would think he had never learned in his life.

"So what do you think we should learn?" he asked.

"Everything," she said with a smile.

"That sounds like quite a task," he said tentatively.

"I'm kidding, don't worry. I don't expect to learn everything at once. But there's so much to choose from. In New York, my rabbi and I learned Jewish philosophy. We went through Maimonides' Thirteen Principles of Faith and tried to understand each one of them."

He showed her the books he had brought with him, and she picked each one up and looked it over.

"I don't know," she said. "I've learned a lot about the details of the laws but they don't have as much meaning to me on their own."

"Those laws are what Orthodoxy is about. It's the details that make up the system."

"I know. It's just hard to always find the meaning behind them."

"I think everyone feels that way sometimes," Yosef said. "Maybe it would be helpful if we studied the larger issues behind why we do these things."

"That would be great," Batsheva said. "There are so many things I wonder about. Once I went camping in the Sierra Nevada mountains and I woke up early and took a walk. I sat at the edge of one of the trails overlooking a waterfall. All around me it was quiet. I felt like I was the only one awake in the whole world. I was amazed by the beauty around me and I felt this incredible urge to understand God and the world He created."

She stopped and looked at him. "You're not saying anything. Is this making sense? Some people stare at me when I tell them about this. They think I can't be serious. But I am. I wouldn't have converted if I didn't feel it."

"No, it makes a lot of sense," Yosef said. "It's good to think about the bigger issues. The details of the laws are important, but you need some context for them."

"I'm so glad you understand. Maybe we could explore a different topic each time. I'll think of issues that I don't understand and we can go through them," Batsheva said and smiled at him. "Okay?"

Instead of answering, he looked down and blushed. The more comfortable she was, the shyer he became.

"I have to tell you," Yosef said, looking down, "this is a little strange for me. I'm used to learning with my father or with the guys from yeshiva. Most guys I know would laugh at me if they saw me here. Even my father would have a hard time learning with a woman." He paused and looked sheepish. "I'm not exactly used to being around girls."

"Do you think there's a problem with men and women learning together?" Batsheva asked.

"I don't know. It's just not part of a certain lifestyle." Yosef looked confused, not sure if he was doing the right thing by learning with her and not sure if he should be telling her this. "I'm not saying there's anything wrong with it, I'm just not used to being in a coed environment."

"Would you raise your children in such a strict way?" Batsheva asked.

"I guess so," Yosef said. "It creates a certain seriousness and intensity."

"It must be so hard though. Especially as a teenager, I would think you must have been going crazy. It seems unnatural, like it would force you to separate yourself from part of who you are," she said.

Yosef shook his head. "The whole point is that learning should be your main priority and that you should separate from anything that will make it harder to learn. It doesn't always work, but I've never been as focused as I was in yeshiva. Everything else falls away and there's just you and a text. You're part of this continuum that goes back thousands of years."

Batsheva looked at him. "Are you sure you're okay learning with me?" she asked. "I don't want you to feel like you were forced into it."

"I wasn't telling you this to back out. I was just struck by how strange it was. But anyway, why don't you take these books with you. They might be a good place to get some questions."

"Thank you. I really appreciate it." She gathered up the books. "Are you walking out?"

"I think I'm going to stay here for a while," Yosef said.

As she left the room, Yosef opened his Talmud. Instead of concentrating on the words, he stared off, as if he were still thinking about his conversation with Batsheva.

As Batsheva was cutting across the parking lot on her way to pick Ayala up from Mimi's house, Helen Shayowitz was driving up to make arrangements for the kiddush she was sponsoring in honor of her fortieth wedding anniversary. Alvin had given her permission to go all out and she was determined to do so. Her mind was filled with plans: she would serve individual portions of noodle kugel, marinated vegetable salad, and bite-sized pieces of fried chicken. She still had to see to centerpieces and tablecloths, and the issue of colors had yet to be decided. Mrs. Levy had used gold last year for the kiddush in honor of her daughter's engagement, and blue was so obvious; perhaps fuchsia would lend a glamorous touch. Helen was momentarily distracted from these plans by the sight of Batsheva. She remembered that this was the day Batsheva was supposed to start learning with Yosef. Mrs. Levy had reminded everyone of this on the phone the night before, wondering how it would work out, trying to decide if there was technically anything wrong with Yosef being Batsheva's private tutor. Helen honked her horn, and Batsheva looked up and waved.

"Hi there, Batsheva. Let me guess. You're coming from learning with Yosef," Helen said as she got out of her car.

"Yes and it was wonderful. I always worried that I would never be able to catch up and that I was always going to be missing a chunk of knowledge. But now I feel like I'll have a chance."

All that day, as Helen sorted through color swatches for tablecloths and napkins, Batsheva's excitement weighed on her. Helen, like most Jewish children of her generation, had attended public school. Her brother had studied in the afternoon with Jacob Levy, Irving Levy's grandfather, but she had learned to run a Jewish home from her mother. Until recently, Helen had thought this sufficient. But these days, learning had come into fashion for women. She was always hearing from her daughter in New York about women studying Talmud and Chumash and philosophy. At the seder last year, her daughter had launched into a lengthy analysis of the seder plate and though Helen had listened, she hadn't understood everything. When she was done, Helen had mumbled how nice and how very learned, but in case she was expected to say more, she excused herself and went to the kitchen to prepare the bitter herbs and saltwater.

But now, Helen wondered if it was too late for her, or if like Batsheva, she also might have the chance to catch up. She could see herself learning, maybe even spending a few weeks in New York studying with her daughter. Her Hebrew would improve, she would learn to read through the various commentaries, maybe she would even take a crack at Talmud. She tried to imagine it: Helen Shayowitz, Torah Scholar. But then she laughed. She was sixty-one years old. Who knew if it was still possible?

THE next day, Batsheva arrived early to learn with Yosef. We had seen her rushing to Leanna Zuckerman's, where Ayala was going to play for a few hours, and then hurrying the rest of the way to the shul. When Yosef got there, she was ready to begin.

"See, I told you I'd be on time," she said.

"Now I have to make sure I'm on time," Yosef said, for her sake; he was always on time.

"I even came prepared," Batsheva said. "I was reading one of the books you gave me . . ."

"That was fast," Yosef said.

"I couldn't fall asleep and instead of lying in bed letting my mind wander, I decided to get up and read. It's amazing how quiet it is here at night. It was never like this in New York. There's something nice about reading when it's pitch-dark outside and completely silent."

"I know. Sometimes I'll be reading and I'll lose track of time and before I know it, it's the middle of the night."

They smiled at each other and for the first time, Yosef seemed comfortable.

"Anyway, I was reading the book you gave me about repentance. I figured it made sense to start with that since the holidays are next month, and I was so struck by the idea that it's always possible to repent and start over."

"I know. That's the point of the high holidays. They remind us of the opportunity God is giving us to change," Yosef said.

"What I was wondering, though, was even if God forgives you for your sin, can you really change who you are? Does the process of teshuvah have the power to do that?"

"There are two kinds of teshuvah—one is repenting for acts that affect just you and God and the other is for actions that affect you and other people. For those, you have to ask forgiveness from the person you wronged before God can forgive you. But if you do, then it's like starting with a clean slate. There's even an analogy made to a vase that breaks. In life, you can glue it back together, but if you look carefully, you can always see the line where it was once broken. But teshuvah isn't like that. It's possible to fix something so that the break isn't there at all."

"Do you really believe that?" she asked.

"I do. It would be pretty sad if there was no way to make up for things in the past. That would mean that we're stuck with who we used to be and nothing we can do can ever change that."

Batsheva smiled. "I like that idea. It makes me feel like Judaism really understands that people can change. It means there's always hope that things can be better in the future."

They continued talking, and after an hour, the Rabbi poked his head into the bet midrash; it was time for him to learn with Yosef. "Lost track of time?" he asked. "I suppose that's a sign that you're learning well."

"We're learning very well," Batsheva said. "Yosef is the best teacher I've ever had."

The Rabbi smiled at his son, and Yosef blushed.

She gathered her things to leave. "I don't want to keep you from your learning," she said as she slipped out the door. "See you next time, Yosef. Bye, Rabbi."

During another session, Batsheva and Yosef discussed the laws of Shabbos. She was familiar with the basic concept—that we refrained from work, but it was a technical definition of work that the rabbis were using: the thirty-nine categories of activity used to build the mishkan, the tabernacle used to serve God in the desert. But Batsheva wanted to know the meaning behind these different categories. Yosef explained that we didn't necessarily know the reasons for the mitzvot. We obeyed the Torah because it was the word of God. If we started ascribing specific reasons for the laws, then it was possible to come up with reasons not to follow them.

"People used to think that keeping kosher was for health reasons, because there was a disease spread by pig meat. But if that was the only reason to keep kosher, we could argue that there was no reason to do it anymore," Yosef said.

"To me, Judaism is meaningful because I think about the reasons. When I light Shabbos candles, I think about how we need to bring more light into the world and Shabbos is the time to do this," Batsheva said. "What about you? Do you ever think about why you do all these things or do you just do them?"

"Sometimes I think about that," he said. "But I believe God gave us the Torah and that we're supposed to serve Him and follow His will, no matter what the specific reason is for the command."

"I don't know if that's enough for me. I need to really feel it. I don't want to just go through the motions. Don't you ever worry about that?"

Yosef checked his watch, and seeing what time it was, he closed the book in front of him. Then he looked up at Batsheva, who was still waiting for an answer.

"I don't know," he said and she looked carefully at him.

THEY continued like this until the sight of Yosef and Batsheva engaged in conversation was common. Yosef no longer looked down and blushed; he didn't hesitate before he spoke or shift nervously when she looked him straight in the eye and asked him a probing question. Even after their sessions ended for the day, Batsheva couldn't stop talking about how much she was learning. When we saw her at the grocery store, at shul, even at the mikvah, she was always telling us what Yosef had said about the weekly Torah portion, or how he had finally given her a good reason for why it was important to daven even if she wasn't in the mood. At first, we attributed her excitement to her personality: she was naturally enthusiastic about things, she was searching for something, and it made sense that she would respond eagerly to whatever filled that need. It wasn't that we didn't like to learn—we recognized its importance, in the proper place and time—but we had never thought about it as something to get worked up over.

But Batsheva said that her learning filled in those moments when she wondered why she had adopted this lifestyle. She said that she never wanted to feel like she was blindly following a certain set of rules, but that every day she was actively involved in choosing it again for herself. We realized that we too wanted to answer the questions that lingered in the backs of our minds. Why, for example, were we not obligated in all the commandments men were? And did God really see every tiny action that we did? Wasn't He too busy with more important matters?

Anxious to know more, we asked questions during the Ladies Home Study Circle, and we pressed the Rabbi to better explain the concepts that he glossed over. We asked our daughters if we could help them with their Hebrew homework, and we told them how important it was that they take their classes seriously. We looked at our husbands' Jewish books to see if there was anything that might interest us, and we even considered attending the Rabbi's Shabbos afternoon class. Leanna Zuckerman asked her husband to set aside an hour a week to learn with her, and Helen Shayowitz wrote away for a catalog for a women's learning program in New York City. As much as we wanted Yosef to help Batsheva be more like us, we also found that we wanted to become a little more like her.

6

ON THE FIRST DAY OF SCHOOL, Batsheva, like all of us, woke up early, packed a lunch for Ayala, and headed to the school. Those of us who lived a block or two away walked with our children, while those who lived a little farther out drove, our carpools lining the streets, mixing in with the streams of children all heading for the same place. From the back, in their school uniforms, the children looked almost identical. The boys' navy pants and white button-down shirts and the girls' black-and-red plaid jumpers were crisp and newly washed. The school uniforms had been in place since the 1970s, when the Ladies Auxiliary president (Bella Shayowitz, our very own Helen's mother-in-law) thought it made the children look so neat and well-groomed, like little angels. St. Catherine Academy, down the street, had the same plaid jumpers, and although ours were a good few inches longer, people were always confusing our girls with theirs.

The Torah Academy was founded in the 1950s, and many of us had gone there ourselves. When it was first built, it had been gorgeous, with polished linoleum floors and freshly painted cinder-block walls. Over the years though, the building had become dingy, and the low ceilings and hanging fluorescent lighting that used to be in fashion had taken on an oppressive look. Every summer, the Ladies Auxiliary embarked on a project to liven it up. We hung posters, added green plants to every classroom, painted the walls a different color. In the far corners of the walls, where it was hard for the painters to reach, there were streaks from past years, and we imagined if we sliced through them, extracting a cross section of color, we could see our history.

As far as schools go, this one was tiny. There were 150 students from nursery school through twelfth grade. That was to be expected—most communities our size were lucky to have a good Sunday School, let alone an elementary and high school. But the generation before us had been determined to create a Jewish oasis in the desert of Tennessee. Our parents and grandparents started the school in the Reeses' house with twenty kids. They watched it grow like one of their own children, until finally, after two years, the school outgrew its space. They raised money for a building, bought the empty lot behind the shul, and began building on an unusually sunny day in October.

The groundbreaking had been a day to remember. The whole community turned out to witness history in the making. Even the local media was there. The *Memphis Commercial Appeal* sent a reporter, and the next day, a small article appeared on the last page of the metro section. And though the story hadn't made the TV news, Edith Shapiro (then a young woman) spotted a Channel Five news truck parked across the street. There had been a few speeches, by the principal and by the president of the school board, but no one is sure anymore what they said. Probably something about how we were erecting our own miniature bet hamikdash, a place where God might dwell if only we let Him; that kind of thing was always said at these events. But here, it was true. The future of the community was in our hands as we stood on the ground where our children, grandchildren, and great-grandchildren would go to school. If they were to stay religious, it would be because of this building.

When it was time to break ground, Sue Ellen Goldberg, the first-ever Ladies Auxiliary president, took hold of the shovel, its rusty metal handle decorated with blue and white ribbons. Pressing her black patent-leather high-heeled shoe against the shovel, she stuck it into the ground and came up with a scoop of dirt. The applause spread through the crowd, and Sue Ellen lifted her hands over her head and blew a kiss to those around her. The building took nine months to complete, and before school started the next year, the students, sixty in all, moved in.

This year, on the first day of school, we too felt a turn of excitement in our stomachs. When we closed our eyes, we could smell the lingering mustiness in a classroom recently aired out after a long summer. We could hear the tight crackle of brand-new textbooks opening, imagine the freshness of unused notebooks and newly sharpened pencils, feel the flutter of nervousness as the teacher pronounced our names for the first time. Many of the teachers were the same as when some of us were students. Mrs. Kaplan still taught kindergarten, Rabbi Bloomfield still taught second grade. The same wooden desks and chairs stood in those rooms, the initials of our own classmates carved into their surfaces. Seeing our children enter these classrooms made us feel young and old all at once.

We got to the school in time to see Batsheva walk through the doors of the building. She took Ayala to the door of the kindergarten classroom and kissed her on the cheek. Ayala wasn't nearly as shy as she had been a few months before, and she went into the classroom with no clinging or crying. Batsheva watched her go; then she walked down the hallway to her own classroom. The room had previously been used as a teachers' lounge, audiovisual room, storage closet, and science lab. In back corners and in cabinets, there was an old coffeemaker, a few stained mugs, a broken slide projector, some cracked test tubes, a pile of spare school uniforms, and extra rolls of toilet paper.

None of this made a difference to Batsheva. She had spent the few days before school began scrubbing the blackboard, cleaning out old cabinets, wiping off tabletops. She and Ayala cut out pictures from magazines, hung art posters across the back wall of the classroom, and covered the tabletops with butcher paper. And when Ayala needed a break from helping, she would run through the empty hallways, exploring this new school of hers.

Batsheva had only found out that she would be teaching art a week before school started. Mimi had called the principal that Saturday night, a few minutes after Shabbos was over, like she said she would. Even with Mimi pushing the idea, it wasn't easy. Rabbi Fishman said he would be in favor of such a thing, but there would have to be money for it: supplies and salary were expensive. Worried that the idea would get buried under all the other things that had to be taken care of before the school year began, Mimi called Rena Reinhard, who had recently been sworn in as the new Ladies Auxiliary president.

"I know the Auxiliary sometimes sponsors school programs," she began, "and I can't think of anything more worthwhile than an art program."

Even though Rena was grateful to Batsheva for listening to her talk about the terrible situation with her husband, she was taken aback. It was the first she had heard of the idea. "I don't know. We've never had an art program before and we seem to be getting along fine."

Mimi wouldn't be put off. She listed her reasons: it was important for the kids to be creative, they could use a break from so many academic classes. The best private schools in the city had art class, and we were losing enough kids to these schools already.

"And it would be a mitzvah to help Batsheva out. She's all alone and could use our support," Mimi said.

Rena remembered how kind Batsheva had been to her when she had broken into tears. This was her chance to return the favor, to offer a helping hand to someone who really needed it. If Rena ended up getting divorced and moving to a new community, she would want someone to do the same for her. Before they hung up, Rena promised to bring up the subject at the Ladies Auxiliary executive board meeting, only two nights away.

With Mimi behind the idea, no one wanted to speak against it. We trusted Mimi's opinion without question; no one knew this community as well as she did, and if she thought it was a wonderful plan, why shouldn't we? And we had started to like Batsheva. We were growing used to the things about her that were different; we had started thinking that she could eventually fit in here. With this good feeling in the air, the plan was approved unanimously, as easily as if we were deciding to have a luncheon or a Tupperware party. In fact, it passed with so much support that the Auxiliary hired Batsheva to teach art to the elementary school as well.

BATSHEVA'S first class of the day was the high school girls. While the boys school and elementary school were more stable, our only hope for the girls' school was that it survive another year. Its size was always fluctuating. Some years it stayed at around twenty girls and some years it grew smaller, dipping to a dangerously low fifteen, but it never grew larger. Every year, before school began, there was always something to throw us into a tizzy. Two years before, the Sheinbergs had considered sending Nechama away to Beis Rivka Academy in Monsey, New York, and if she went away Ariella Sussberg would too, and if we lost both of them, then Leah Weissberg was sure to leave. And that would only leave two girls in the tenth grade. In the end, thank God, it hadn't happened, but it made us realize how precarious the existence of the school was.

Even when we managed to have enough girls for a class (five students was considered respectable, ten a miracle), there were still problems. This year, the twelfth-grade girls were difficult. The trouble had started when they were in eighth grade, at a school shabbaton, of all places. Once each year, the fifth through eighth graders spent the Shabbos at school, sleeping in the classrooms, eating meals, and davening together. Naturally, the boys and girls were kept separate at night; the rabbis had worked out a schedule to patrol the hallway. But the girls had snuck past Rabbi Horowitz, and though he swears he didn't fall asleep at his post, he is known to be a little lax. They went into the elementary school wing, where the boys were sleeping. Who knows what really went on—maybe they were just talking, as a few of the girls later insisted—but there were reports of Truth or Dare, Spin the Bottle, and God knows what else.

This was hardly what we expected and we had talked about it for days. Should the kids be punished? And if so, which ones? In the end, the principal called the ringleaders into his office (not to name names, but everyone knew that Shira Feldman and Ilana Salzman were among them) and lectured them about what it means to be a bas Torah, a good Jewish girl, about obedience and respect and modesty and holiness. We had hoped that this would be the last we'd hear of such behavior.

But it had only been the beginning. Every year there was another scandal: a coed swimming party at the Berners' when Ruth and Yaakov were out of town, only discovered because Tziporah Newburger happened to be passing by. The following year, Ilana Salzman and Nathan Reese were caught kissing behind the shul during Friday night davening. And, of course, there were the cigarette butts and bottles of beer Becky Feldman unearthed in her garbage can one morning.

That morning, the high school girls filed into the art room, followed by Yocheved Abraham, their new Hebrew teacher. It was only the first day and Yocheved already looked exasperated. She had never married—she was already twenty-nine—and she had finally come home, having given up on finding a suitable husband in New York. The girls didn't have to wear uniforms as the elementary school kids did—this was another change made in recent years to please them—but they still had rules: skirts below the knee, necklines above the collarbone, sleeves to the elbows, no writing on shirts, and nothing outrageous. They managed to look stylish anyway. Along with their denim skirts, they wore clunky shoes with thick heels, long earrings, jean jackets, and silver bracelets that clinked as they walked.

Batsheva watched them as they sat down. She tried to make eye contact, to strike up a friendly rapport. She had made no effort to dress like the other teachers; even the non-Jewish teachers wore conservative clothing. Her dress wasn't exactly immodest, but it was certainly different. It hung loosely around her and it had quiltlike squares of stripes and dots and flowers in every color imaginable, her own coat of many colors. The girls gave Batsheva the blank stares they gave all their teachers, and they whispered, cupping their hands over their mouths.

"If they think this is going to make us like this school, they really don't have a clue," Shira Feldman whispered.

"Wasn't this your mother's idea?" Ilana Salzman asked. Her mother had told her that Mimi Rubin and Becky Feldman had come up with the plan to have Batsheva teach the girls.

"So? My mother has less of a clue than anyone," Shira said. This wasn't the first time a new project had been planned to get the girls excited, and Shira had long ago given up the hope that any real improvement would be made.

"That's what I heard too," Ilana agreed. She put her head down on the table. She was exhausted, having stayed up too late on the phone the night before, even though her mother had warned her a thousand times to get to bed early, that she was going to have to start taking school seriously, they didn't want a repeat of last year. Ilana had heard this before. Her mother was referring to the dismal grades she had received in just about every subject. But she found it hard to apply herself. What was the point of studying? It wasn't like she would be going to a good college. She would probably spend a year or two studying in a seminary in Israel and then get married and have babies. She had no idea if this was the kind of life she wanted, but she did know that it was what was expected of her.

Batsheva had her work cut out for her and she wasted no time. She stood in the front of the room and smiled. "Can I have your attention, please?" she asked.

The girls ignored her. But Batsheva didn't seem to notice. She busied herself passing out sheets of white paper and pastels.

"I want you each to draw a self-portrait," Batsheva announced. "I don't want you to look in a mirror, just portray the way you see yourself in your mind. You can draw your whole self or a part of yourself or you can depict some aspect of your personality that is central to who you are."

The girls stared at the blank sheets of paper. They were used to more concrete assignments: writing book reports on an assigned novel, translating a page of chumash, memorizing Hebrew vocabulary words. After much whispering, a few of them began to draw. Nechama Sheinberg made two eyes, so big they took up the entire page, and inside them, she drew pictures of her favorite things: a pair of ice skates, musical notes and a piano. Hadassah Berner drew herself as a flower, growing in a garden of roses and violets. But mostly, the girls sat there and rolled their eyes at each other. Shira Feldman made a few dashes of color and then stared at Batsheva, trying to provoke a confrontation; she had upset more than one teacher this way. She was expecting Batsheva to have the same reaction as teachers had in the past: to send her from the room, to force her to speak to the principal about her bad attitude, or even on one infamous occasion, to burst into tears.

But Batsheva returned Shira's stare with a smile, and she looked at the other girls, who had stopped drawing and were watching to see what would happen. Batsheva planted herself on top of the desk at the front of the room, her legs dangling over the edge. She swung them back and forth, making no effort to create a sense of teacherly authority.

"This isn't working, is it?" Batsheva said. "I don't blame you. I'm the new teacher here, and you don't know why you should listen to me. I'm sure you have a lot of questions about who I am. So why don't I let you ask me whatever you want to know."

The girls said nothing; they weren't buying any of this fake friendliness.

"Don't be shy. It's not everyday you get this chance. I bet Rabbi Fishman doesn't let you walk up to him and ask whatever you've always wondered about him."

The girls laughed nervously but still didn't say anything.

"If you don't ask me anything, I'm going to have to start asking you some questions of my own," Batsheva said, but they still didn't say anything.

"Okay," Batsheva said. "Everyone stand up."

The girls stared at her.

"I mean it," she said. "Everyone get up and come with me."

They reluctantly did what she said. They followed her as she walked out of the classroom, down the hallway, through the back doors of the building and out onto the playground behind the school. She kept going until she was at the far edge of the fields where they would be the least visible from the principal's window.

She sat down on the grass and the girls stood around, staring at her.

"Sit down," she said. "We're going to have class out here today. It's a shame to waste this gorgeous weather."

They spread out around her, some of them lying back, their eyes closed. It was as hot as ever outside. Shira Feldman pulled up her skirt, trying to keep her tan lines even, and Ilana Salzman rolled up her already short sleeves. Batsheva didn't say a word about these infractions, and she stretched out her legs like the girls were doing and she kicked off her sandals and twisted her hair into a bun at the top of her head.

"Are we going to get in trouble for being out here?" Hadassah Berner asked.

Batsheva laughed. "If anyone has a problem with it, they can talk to me. But I figured it was easier to talk openly out here."

The girls looked refreshed from being outside the building. They acted like it was torture to have to sit inside the classrooms, even though the Ladies Auxiliary had taken great pains to redecorate in pink and purple, just for them.

"So, what do you think of school?" Batsheva asked.

The girls looked at each other and began muttering under their breaths.

"I can't stand it," Shira Feldman said, emphasizing each word, expecting Batsheva to draw back in surprise, to be horrified at her bluntness.

Batsheva met her gaze, then looked around at the other girls. "How about the rest of you? Does that pretty much sum it up?"

A few of the girls—the nicest ones—tried to defend the school, saying that if everyone had a better attitude, it would improve, that it was good to have such individual attention. And they couldn't imagine going to public school, where it would be hard, if not impossible, to maintain their Jewish identities. But the complaints rose above these points.

"It's too small. Eighteen people in the whole school is crazy," Ariella Sussberg said, and the other girls chimed in. It was hard to take it seriously with so few students; they felt like it didn't count as a real school; they had been going to school with the same few people since kindergarten.

"I don't blame you for feeling stifled. I know I would have," Batsheva said.

"It's more like day camp than a real school," Aviva Berkowitz said, sullenly picking at the grass. "You could skip school for a month and no one would notice."

"And we aren't allowed to have anything to do with the boys," Ilana Salzman complained. "They act like we're not supposed to be interested in each other."

Batsheva listened carefully, nodding and sympathizing. She ignored the fact that Rabbi Bloomfield was squinting through his open window trying to figure out what was going on, that Yocheved Abraham had strolled by the art room, just checking to see how things were going, and had discovered to her great alarm that the girls were missing.

"How do you deal with it?" Batsheva asked.

"Count the days till we're out of here," Shira said, still lying down.

"That sounds fun," Batsheva answered. "Is that what all of you are going to do? Just bide your time and hope it passes quickly?"

"What are we supposed to do?" Shira asked, sounding irritated.

"I'm sure we can come up with a few ways to make the school a little more exciting," Batsheva said.

"The way I see it, the size of the school is both the best and the worst part about it. And there's no way this is going to be like public school, so you can forget about football games and senior proms."

The girls laughed, trying to envision a yeshiva senior prom, all eighteen girls in their fanciest dresses, dancing alone in an empty gym.

"But that doesn't mean you can't take advantage of the good parts about being in a small school," Batsheva said. "We can go on trips and do projects that would be impossible if we had more people. It's certainly better than sulking, don't you think?"

The girls began talking about what might make the school year better: they had always wanted to put on a real play, not a stupid song-and-dance performance, but a drama with scripts and scenery and costumes. Some of the girls wanted to organize a hiking trip, and a few of them wanted to be allowed to take classes at Memphis State, anything that would offer them a change of venue. Batsheva offered a few ideas of her own: a community service program in which the girls would work one day a week at a homeless shelter, a soup kitchen, or a hospital; independent study on a subject they were interested in; a weekly meeting with the principal so the girls could voice their opinions about what should be done in the school.

When there was twenty minutes left to the class, Batsheva told the girls that she wanted them to come back inside and finish their self-portraits. This time, they listened to her. They went inside, and though they still were unsure of what to draw, they were interested in the project. They asked her for suggestions, they sketched out a few things, they said they wanted to continue working on the drawings during the next art class.

THAT night, Rena Reinhard called Batsheva on official Auxiliary business. "I'm checking to see how things went today," she said in her most presidential voice.

"I think it went well. But the girls seem so restless and unhappy," Batsheva said.

"Really?" Rena asked. She knew there was a problem with morale, but no one thought it was anything to take too seriously.

"Trust me, I know what that kind of unhappiness looks like. I used to see it in the mirror everyday, this feeling that so many things were going on inside me and no one knew about it. But I know I can help them. They need someone they can trust. They're dealing with so many issues, and they probably don't have anyone they can really talk to."

"Do you think art classes will make a difference?" Rena asked.

"I think it will be just the thing," Batsheva said and explained to Rena that the girls needed something to get excited about, something that might make up for the normal teenage lives they couldn't have.

"I want to help them realize how special it is to be in such a small school, where everyone knows them and cares about them. And I want to find a way to make their education more meaningful, so they don't just concentrate on the things they can't do."

Batsheva sounded so certain that she would be able to help the girls that Rena was swept up in her enthusiasm. As Rena prepared a positive report for the first Ladies Auxiliary meeting of the year, she agreed with Batsheva. Maybe it would be just the thing.

BATSHEVA didn't just reach out to our children. She extended an open invitation to us as well. One morning we opened our front doors to find a note rolled into a scroll, our names in calligraphy along the outside of the beige stationery. Careful not to smudge the writing, we unrolled the sheets of paper and discovered that we were invited to a women's only, Rosh Chodesh celebration in honor of the new moon. At the bottom, in small curly writing, Batsheva had signed her name.

We couldn't decide whether or not to attend. On the one hand, it seemed like some feminist innovation that we, thank God, didn't have to think about living down here. We had heard about what was going on in New York, the Ladies' Minyans and all; even in the Orthodox community, women were trying to do more, reading from the Torah and whatnot. These Rosh Chodesh celebrations had also sprung up recently, their organizers calling Rosh Chodesh a special woman's holiday, a time to celebrate the role of women. But as far as we were concerned all the holidays were women's holidays: we certainly worked hard enough for them.

"Do you think it's even permissible to attend?" Tziporah Newburger asked her husband, Shmuel.

"I don't know. It isn't the best idea," he said. "And I certainly wouldn't eat anything at her house if you do go."

Tziporah agreed. She and Shmuel were particular about whose standards of kashrut they trusted, and Batsheva was certainly not on that very short list.

"Batsheva told me that she wants to do this every month," Naomi Eisenberg said to her husband. "She used to go to a group like this in New York, and she's hoping to start one here."

"Good for her. It's nice to see someone doing something a little different," he said. He was originally from Detroit, and he had never adjusted to living in Memphis; it was too small, he complained, suffocating really. He liked it when some little event was blown up to grand proportions and he could sit back and marvel at the fact that he had lasted so long in this place.

Leanna Zuckerman had taken to speaking to Batsheva on the phone, and they were becoming friends. "I think it sounds exciting. At least it's something different." When she was starting to worry if she would be able to find a baby-sitter for the evening, Bruce had offered to cancel his racquetball game so he could take care of the kids, and Leanna swelled with love for him.

"Sounds a little far out for my taste," Mrs. Levy commented. Batsheva would probably try to get them to prance about in the backyard in some ceremony bordering on idolatry; she had heard about such things.

"I don't know," Helen Shayowitz said. "Maybe we need a change of pace. It might be fun."

"Now Helen," Mrs. Levy warned. "I'm no rabbi, but I don't think we're supposed to be messing with tradition just because it might be fun."

But when we spoke to Mimi on the phone, she asked if she would see us at Batsheva's Rosh Chodesh celebration. Hearing our hesitations, she said she was so excited that Batsheva was starting such a nice program. When Tziporah Newburger wondered out loud to Mimi whether Batsheva's kashrut could be trusted, Mimi said that she wouldn't hesitate to eat at Batsheva's house. When Mrs. Levy expressed surprise that something so new-age was allowed, Mimi reassured her that of course it was; in fact, it would be a wonderful opportunity for religious growth. And she agreed with Leanna Zuckerman that Batsheva was a wonderful resource for the community, that it was good to have someone come in and bring new ideas and fresh enthusiasm.

The fact that Mimi was so behind the idea made us feel better about going. We realized that it was sweet of Batsheva to invite us. Surely this was her way of trying to pay us back for having her over for Shabbos meals, for looking after Ayala. As we discussed it back and forth, it became clear that the only proper thing would be to attend.

On the night of the party, we dressed up, hoping our skirts and blouses would be appropriate for whatever she had planned.

"I'm so happy you could come," Batsheva greeted us, squeezing our hands as we walked in. We were struck by how pretty she looked. She was wearing a long white dress, with white ribbons woven into the top, and she had fixed her hair into a long braid and tied it at the end with a shimmery white scarf.

We walked into the living room. The lights were dimmed and the furniture had been pushed aside. Batsheva had set out vases of wildflowers, and at the edge of the room a table was covered with small, water-filled glass canisters with unlit wicks floating inside. Mimi had gotten there early and had helped Batsheva set up. As we walked in, Mimi looked so proud of us for coming, and we basked in knowing that we had lived up to what she expected of us. She made a special point of going over to Mrs. Levy and Tziporah Newburger, who had been the most nervous about the evening, and she squeezed their hands and said how lovely it was to see them.

Once we had removed our jackets and set down our purses, we stood around. If this had been the kind of function we were used to, we would have known what to do. If it were a bridal shower, we would have added our gifts to the pile and made sure to get a front-row seat for the opening of the presents. We would have sought out the bride-to-be, kissed her on the cheek, and said how excited she must be. But here we weren't sure how to behave.

Batsheva sensed our uneasiness and came over to us. "Before you sit down, I'd like each of you to light a candle."

"How do you like that?" Mrs. Levy commented under her breath. "Next thing you know she's going to invite us to howl at the moon."

If Batsheva heard her, she paid her no attention. "Candle lighting is something we do to usher in Shabbos, and I think it's fitting that we do the same ritual to begin the celebration of the new moon," she said.

With a candle, Batsheva lit one of the wicks. She recited a blessing we had never heard before: *Blessed are You, who gives us the new moon and guides us to renew ourselves.* We repeated after her, trying not to catch each other's eyes for fear we would blush with embarrassment at going along with something so unusual.

Watching everyone read this blessing out loud made Jocelyn Shanzer's heart skip a beat. Not having grown up religious, she hated reading Hebrew out loud and still had to sound out words that weren't familiar. But she protected this secret carefully, worried about what everyone would have to say. She wondered whether it was possible to sneak out or would everyone know what had gotten into her? When it was almost her turn and she was closer to the table, she saw that Batsheva had written the blessing out in transliteration as well, as if she had somehow known it could be a problem. Jocelyn sighed with relief. Her secret was safe for the time being.

When we finished, Batsheva invited us to sit on the floor, and seeing as there was no choice, all of us (even Mrs. Levy, who didn't usually do things like that) obliged. While we waited, the conversation naturally turned to our children. It always ended up there, as if in having and raising children, we had traded our lives for theirs.

"It sounds like the girls are much happier," Becky Feldman said. She didn't have any specific evidence of this. Each time she asked Shira how things were going, she would shrug her shoulders and offer a flippant "fine." But still, Becky had a sense, or maybe a wish, that morale at the school was higher.

"We know who we have to thank for that," Mimi said and motioned in Batsheva's direction.

"I never believed any of the rumors about how wild the girls were becoming. These are good religious girls we're talking about," Tziporah Newburger said.

"Sometimes kids need to test the boundaries and get it out of their system," Mrs. Levy explained. "That was always the attitude I adopted with my children."

We looked up from our conversation to see Batsheva surveying the room, excited at how many people had shown up. There were even some women that we didn't recognize, and we realized that she had invited people from outside our community; who knew if they were religious or even Jewish?

When the room could hold no one else, Batsheva stood in the middle of the circle and we quieted, ready to see what this was about.

"Tonight we welcome Rosh Chodesh Elul," she said. "And we, as women, have a special connection to this holiday. This day was given to us to celebrate our faith in the future. After the Jews left Egypt and were standing at the foot of Mount Sinai for forty days waiting for Moshe to return from his encounter with God, the men grew afraid and thought he wasn't coming back. Searching for a substitute God, they built the golden calf. But the women didn't worship the golden calf because they weren't afraid of Moshe's absence. They didn't think the end had come. They still saw possibilities for renewal. And that's the message of the new moon. There is the potential during each cycle of the moon for new life, just as there is potential in our own bodies every month for new life. This month, with the high holidays coming so soon, offers us a special chance to renew ourselves by repenting and bringing ourselves closer to God. So as we celebrate together, let's think about the ways we can renew our lives."

"Very nice, very nice," Bessie Kimmel said, as she did at the end of every d'var Torah.

"Yes," said Helen Shayowitz. "Very interesting."

Batsheva disappeared into the kitchen and returned with bowls of dried figs, sunflower seeds, pieces of pomegranate, and a tray of crescent-shaped cookies. Mimi helped pass them around and Batsheva explained their significance. "The foods we eat on Rosh Chodesh should remind us of the waxing and waning of the moon, and the seeds remind us that there is always the potential for rebirth." Batsheva bit into a fig, holding it up to show the tiny brown seeds inside.

She joined us in the circle, and her dress fanned out over her legs. Without saying a word, she began to sing. *Open the gates of righteousness so that I may enter and thank God.* We were used to hearing her voice in shul as it rose louder and more beautiful than any of ours, but we had never heard her alone. The song seemed to flow out of her, and it was hard to believe she hadn't been singing these words her whole life. When she finished, Batsheva asked us to join her in the next song. *From the straits I called on God, and He answered me. When He is with me, I have nothing to fear.* With all she had been through, it sounded as if this song had been written with her in mind. If we had been in her situation, who's to say if we would have had the strength or desire to stay religious. We saw in her a kind of faith that eluded us, one that would allow us to lose ourselves in it. We followed the mitzvot; we didn't have a problem with the doing aspect. But the believing part—the loving God with all our hearts and souls and mights—was something else.

We looked to Batsheva to start another song. To our surprise, we wanted to continue. We were no longer focusing on the fact that this was not the sort of activity we were accustomed to. But instead of just singing, Batsheva stood up and took the hands of the two of us closest to her and tried to get us to start dancing. She smiled encouragingly and we started to move with her. At first, our steps were measured, slow and precise, doing the circular horah we always did at weddings and bar mitzvahs. After a few times around, we expected to break into the more complicated dances that we had had to take classes in to perfect: the lines that moved to the right and then left, the kicks and spins and one-two-threes. But Batsheva didn't seem interested in these dances; she just kept us going in circles.

We watched Batsheva, her body so fluid, her arms like two birds flying off. We longed to be like that, loose and free inside ourselves, not worried about how we looked or what anyone thought of us. We imagined our worries falling from our shoulders. Some small piece of us that was usually hidden away would escape from the tight casing that held our bodies together and fly away unencumbered. Filled with this longing, we started to move a little more. Helen Shayowitz added a twirl to her footwork, Mrs. Levy shook her hips as she went round, and Jocelyn Shanzer kicked off her high heels so she could shimmy more freely. As we spun round and round, the room grew hotter, the pictures on Batsheva's walls grew larger, the colors brighter. We felt vaguely aware of the noise around us, and only then did we realize it was our own voices we were hearing, singing louder than we ever had before.

The more we danced, the more we started feeling as if we could send time spinning backward. If we danced fast enough, our growing older might be reversed, and we would be young again. We would shed our wrinkles and the heavy makeup we used to cover them, be rid of our coifed hair, unloosen our respectable, ladylike clothing, remove our sturdy bras and sensible underwear. We would wear our hair long and loose again, our dresses would be soft and flowy, our skin smooth and glowing. We would become the young teenagers we had once been, when our husbands were the shy, skinny boys whose eyes we caught across the room, whose looks made us blush, and our bodies were pink and ripe and bursting with excitement at all that lay ahead.

When we reached the end of the song, we stopped and stood around, looking at each other, our faces flushed and hot, our breath still heavy, our hearts racing. In the dim lighting, we could just make out the outlines of each other's faces, all lines and angles softened into each other, and we felt, for that one second, that we had slipped out of who we usually were.

In the middle of this, Tziporah Newburger glanced at her watch. Without our noticing, the clock had struck ten. It had gotten late and it was time to go home. We smoothed ourselves out, flattening hair, uncreasing clothing, and wiping away sweat; we couldn't very well come home looking a mess and have our husbands wonder what we had been up to.

As we were getting ready to leave, doing up the last buttons on our jackets, Batsheva stood in the middle of our circle. "There's another renewal I'm grateful for," she said. "I want to thank you for welcoming Ayala and me into your community and giving us a chance to start over."

She scanned the circle, taking in our faces. We looked up at the wicks we had lit earlier, the tiny flames like so many new moons in a dark sky, and we clapped, for her, for each other, and for ourselves.

7

AFTER A MONTH OF TEACHING, Batsheva had become close with the girls as no other teacher had. During class, they smiled at her, looked for her to praise their paintings, and asked her for suggestions. They complimented her clothing, her shoes, her hair, and told her that she was the funkiest dresser in the whole school. Who knows what else they talked about—our daughters told us only bits and pieces. They said she was *so* cool, we wouldn't understand: she knew about the music they liked, their favorite movies and television shows. Anytime we walked by the art room, a group of girls was gathered around Batsheva. They had even begun dressing like her. Over the past few weeks, they had started wearing long gauzy skirts (usually close to see-through on her, but we made our daughters wear slips under theirs), dangling earrings, strands of colored beads. And a few of them were talking about growing their hair long, when only a month or two before, they had insisted that short hair was in.

One week, Batsheva invited the girls over to her house on a Shabbos afternoon. When other teachers had suggested an out-of-school activity, the girls were hardly receptive. When Yocheved Abraham arranged a Saturday night outing to the bowling alley, they had all claimed to have baby-sitting jobs, and only Hadassah Berner, who was too nice to say no, accompanied her. And when the principal's wife invited the girls over for a barbecue (as well as a little baby-sitting for her five children), they said they had too much homework. But with Batsheva, they were eager to go.

They showed up at Batsheva's house in small groups, knocking shyly at her door. Even though they were so comfortable with her at school, it was strange to see a teacher outside of class. She called out to them that the door was open, and when they went inside, she said how wonderful it was that they had come. Ayala too looked thrilled to have the high school girls in her house. She took their hands and smiled as they fussed over her, saying how sweet and how cute she was.

Taking food from the trays she had set out, they gathered around Batsheva. She didn't try to make them sing as Yocheved Abraham had done the one time she had gotten them to come over on a Shabbos afternoon. How mortifying it had been: Yocheved, with her slightly flat voice, had been the only one singing, and the girls sat there watching her struggle to make it to the end of the song. But Batsheva took her cues from the girls and let them do what they wanted.

They wanted to hear about her life—where she was from and how she had ended up here. They could hardly imagine how anyone outside the Orthodox world grew up. What they knew came from books and television and movies. Sometimes they tried to pretend they were like everyone else. Once, Ilana Salzman and Ariella Sussberg had gone to a department store and tried on prom dresses, telling the salesclerk that they went to Ridgeway High. Looking at themselves in the slinky gowns, they almost believed that they did.

"What was the wildest thing you ever did?" Ilana asked, her eyes wide with excitement as she imagined the raunchy tales Batsheva would tell.

"Oh, I don't know," Batsheva said. "I guess there was the time when I was sixteen, I snuck out in the middle of the night with some guy and we ran off to see how our parents would react. We stayed away for a week, driving around and sleeping in cheap motels."

"Who was he?" Ilana asked.

"Oh God, what was his name?" Batsheva said. "I can't remember. Obviously he wasn't very important."

Shira was leaning back into one of Batsheva's chairs, lost in her own world. She remembered something she had overheard her mother discussing on the phone and decided to ask Batsheva about it.

"Is it true that you have a tattoo?" she asked. The other girls had also heard about it from their mothers (either directly or by eavesdropping), and they were glad Shira had asked about it, though they wouldn't have had the nerve to do so themselves.

Batsheva laughed in surprise. "I'm glad you don't feel like you have to hold back with me."

"What, is it a secret? I heard about it from my mom," Shira said. "I thought everyone knew about it."

"It's fine. I'm just surprised. But I don't mind talking about it. Yes, I do have a tattoo, from a long time ago." No one was saying anything, but Batsheva could see from the looks on their faces that there was something more they wanted to ask. "Let me guess," she said. "You want to see it."

"Our mothers got to," Shira said. "So I don't see why we can't."

"It's not like I've been parading it around," Batsheva said. "A few people happened to see it, that's all."

"But they all know about it," Hadassah said.

"What do they think?" Batsheva asked, looking a little nervous.

"Of course they disapprove. But I think it's cool," Shira said.

Deciding that there was no harm in showing them, Batsheva unbuttoned the top two buttons of her blouse and pulled aside the material to reveal the tattoo. The girls stared: they too had never seen such a thing this close-up, certainly not on someone they knew.

"Ilana, you should get one of those," Shira said.

"Sure," Ilana said. "We can get them together."

The girls began planning how they would all get tattoos, a yeshiva class trip to the tattoo parlor. They laughed as they discussed the designs they would choose—hearts with imaginary boyfriends' names written inside, snakes curling up their ankles, the name of the school printed on their backsides. And as long as they were at it, they decided that they might as well pierce their noses and belly buttons, spike their hair and dye it magenta, anything to shake their good yeshiva girl images. They talked loudly and screamed with laughter. At Batsheva's house they weren't afraid of anyone overhearing them. They felt completely at home.

While the other girls were coming up with wilder and wilder scenarios, Hadassah Berner grew uncomfortable. She had nothing to add—no new piercing to suggest, no outrageous hairstyle she was dying to try out—and she felt self-conscious, worried she might be seen as a goody-goody. She went over to Batsheva's bookshelves and scanned the titles, feigning great interest in them. When she noticed the photo albums Batsheva had lined up on the bottom of her bookshelf, she picked one up.

"Is it okay to look at these?" Hadassah asked Batsheva, and the other girls chimed in, asking to see them.

Batsheva hesitated. "I don't believe in keeping my past a secret. I'm not going to lie to you and pretend like I never did the things I did. But keep in mind that I left that life," she said.

The girls flipped through the pages of photographs of Batsheva at the beach in a bikini, Batsheva as a little girl in Halloween costumes, next to a fully decorated Christmas tree.

"Oh my God, look at this one!" Aviva Berkowitz exclaimed. She pointed to a picture of Batsheva wearing spandex pants and a tiny black shirt that ended a few inches above her stomach.

"Do you still have these clothes?" Hadassah asked.

"No. It's not like I was planning on wearing them," Batsheva said.

"Why not? They're awesome," Shira said.

Instead of the nice Shabbos clothes they were wearing, the dresses and tailored suits and sweater-and-skirt outfits, they imagined themselves in these clothes: Ariella Sussberg in black spandex, Aviva Berkowitz in a halter top, Hadassah Berner in fishnet pantyhose, Nechama Sheinberg in a sheer red blouse, and Shira Feldman in a skin-tight mini-dress.

"Don't you wish we could wear these things?" Ilana said.

"Definitely. I am so sick of wearing skirts," Shira said. She was so sick of skirts, in fact, that she had taken to rolling a pair of jeans (that she had bought secretly) into her backpack and changing into them when she left the house.

"I know you girls think dressing like this is really cool, but you have to remember that I've chosen something else for myself and for Ayala," Batsheva said. "I really believe that there's something to the idea of dressing modestly. I feel more comfortable with my body now, like it's special and belongs only to me."

"Give me a break," Shira said. "The whole dress code is so superficial. It's like if you wear long skirts then you're religious. And if you don't, then you're not."

"I'm not saying that clothes are the most important thing. I'm much more concerned about what's going on inside. But that doesn't mean it's not important. Look, some of you are in this school for just another few months. And after that, you can do whatever you want. That's what you should be thinking about. If you're just reacting to the rules, you're not going to be able to figure out what you want."

"How are we supposed to know what we really think? Everyone is so busy telling us what to do, but they never give us a reason for anything," Ariella Sussberg said.

"I know. It's hard to figure it out. But you still have to try. When I was your age, I was overwhelmed by a sense of meaninglessness. I floated from place to place and person to person looking for something," Batsheva said. "But when I stumbled into Judaism, I felt whole. Have you ever experienced that? When you feel so completely taken in and you can join in with a community for a higher purpose."

"But it seems like you're making everything so much harder than it has to be. Don't you miss your old life?" Ilana asked.

"Sometimes. But my whole life, it never felt like me. I felt like a soul born into the wrong body. By being religious, you're connected to a tradition that goes back thousands of years. You're always part of something larger than yourself. Think about it—if you could decide right now to walk away from everything, are you sure you would? Maybe for a while it would feel exciting, but don't you think you'd eventually feel like you'd lost something special?"

They nodded, as if they knew what she meant, and when they left her house, they were still thinking about what she had said. Sometimes our girls looked so young and vulnerable, and we couldn't imagine them being on their own. Other times, they seemed wise, as if they had already seen and understood more than we had. Since they had become teenagers, there were so many times that we tried to figure out what they were thinking. In their sullen and angry looks, we looked for glimpses of the happy young girls they had once been. We saw their restlessness when they came home from school, when they accepted yet another baby-sitting job for Saturday night. We knew that they longed for something more exciting, something that looked like the R-rated movies they were always renting in secret. We saw how they read *Seventeen Magazine* and answered surveys about what kind of boy (the football player? the student council president? the punk rocker?) was right for them, experimented with makeup guaranteed to make *him* notice you, fantasized about what kind of prom dress they would wear if only the school had a prom.

Even with the other Jewish but non-Orthodox kids in Memphis, they were anomalies, a minority within a minority. In cities with larger Orthodox communities, there was no need to ever go outside this world of like-minded people. The Jewish schools in New York had their own yeshiva high school basketball leagues. There were hundreds of kids in every age group. Memphis was too small for that, and we were involved with the Jewish Community Center, which was a gathering place for all the Jews in the city, the Conservative, the Reform, the barely affiliated. We went to the occasional speaker, our kids played on their sports teams, we sent our younger children to the summer day camp. But as much as our daughters longed for something beyond the twenty or so girls in the school, we were nervous about them being too involved with nonreligious teenagers.

One year, Hadassah Berner had signed up to play basketball at the Jewish Community Center. The other girls, all non-Orthodox, went to school together and she had been shy. To make it worse, her mother had forbade her to wear shorts but did give in and let her wear sweatpants (Hadassah had said she'd rather not play than play in a skirt). But even so, she was constantly answering questions: Aren't you hot? Why don't you put on shorts? At first she had tried to mumble that she was fine, she got cold easily. But the questions had persisted and she was too self-conscious to state the real reason and she eventually quit the team. Maybe an adult would have been able to answer straighforwardly, proud of who she was, but for a teenager, such a difference was excruciating.

It made us remember our own teenage years, when we had felt the awkwardness of standing out, the shame of being unable to be fully part of the crowd. And back then, it had been easier. Many of us had gone to public school, and being Jewish, regardless of how observant, was a lot in common right there. We had been allowed to join the B'nai Brith youth group; our parents were happy that at least our friends would be

Jewish. The Orthodox world wasn't as strict as it was now. Candy bars that we used to think were kosher were no longer considered so, the synagogue dances we used to hold were now considered scandalous. It wasn't only here that we were becoming more stringent. The whole Orthodox world had taken a giant step to the right, and like partners in a dance, we had followed.

But even so, we were constantly having to explain ourselves, having to say that no, we couldn't go to the basketball game on a Friday night, that we wouldn't be at school for the minor holidays that most Jews hadn't even heard of. Rachel Ann Berkowitz remembered the time she had gone to a youth group barbecue when she was sixteen. She had requested a kosher hot dog ahead of time, hoping that she would be able to blend in. While everyone else was getting their nonkosher hot dogs, Rachel Ann had stood around, trying not to draw attention to herself. But as everyone was sitting down with plates of hot dogs, potato salad, and pickles, the organizer of the event had screamed out "who has the kosher hot dog?" and raised the bun and meat over her head. Rachel Ann had wanted to die, right then and there.

When we were teenagers, we would imagine that when we had daughters of our own, we wouldn't be so strict. We would give them room to explore, let them decide for themselves if they wanted to follow this way of life. But once we were in the parental role, it wasn't as simple. We wanted our daughters to grow up and get married, to have Jewish homes and raise Jewish families. We wanted them to pass on this tradition to their children and to their children's children. We didn't want them to be exposed to bad influences, ones that might make them steer from this path that had been set out for them since birth. We wanted them to avoid the confusion of the modern world, where no one seemed to believe in anything anymore. We wanted them to always feel rooted in their tradition, to be close to their families, their community, and God. And we didn't know how to do that if we made no ground rules, set down no boundaries.

WHEN Batsheva was straightening the art room the next week, she looked up to see Shira Feldman standing in the doorway, her cheeks flushed and her mouth curled into a scowl. Batsheva took Shira by the arm and led her into the room.

"What happened?" Batsheva asked.

"I'm not allowed into class until I call my mother and have her bring me a longer skirt." Shira looked down at her knees sticking out from the bottom of her black denim skirt.

Every year, the girls' skirts got shorter. We didn't know what they would try to get away with next. The teachers had come up with a few solutions: make chronic offenders keep extra skirts in their lockers, or have a few long, shapeless skirts in the office for them to put on. Neither of these plans had been put into practice yet, but the way things were going, it was only a matter of time.

"It looks pretty close to your knees," Batsheva said.

"I told Rabbi Fishman that he shouldn't be looking at my knees anyway," Shira said. "But he said that if my knees weren't showing, he wouldn't have to look. And I can't call my mom. I'm already grounded for the rest of my life."

"I think I can help you," Batsheva said.

She rummaged through a cabinet and pulled out a sheet of gold fabric. With scissors and a few safety pins, she shaped a new skirt that tied at the waist and draped around her hips. Shira looked more like a Roman statue spray-painted gold than a nice yeshiva girl, but the skirt was certainly long enough—it reached all the way to her ankles. When Batsheva finished, she sat down and told Shira to do the same.

"I assume this isn't just about skirts," Batsheva said.

"No, it's about everything," Shira said. And she told her: she was sick of being told what to do, she felt like she was being kept in a small box with no air holes and one day she wouldn't be able to breathe anymore. She was craving open spaces, she wanted to go somewhere where she could be herself. When Shira finished speaking, she was almost in tears.

"What do your parents think?" Batsheva asked.

"My mother thinks she can force me into being exactly like her. But I'm just biding my time until I can do whatever I want."

"It gets easier, I promise you. You'll figure out things for yourself and then you won't have to worry about what other people want you to do."

"My older sister goes to Stern College and my mom also went there and now she's trying to force me to go. But the last thing I'm going to do is sign up for four more years of a religious, all-girls school."

"What do you want to do?" Batsheva asked.

"I wrote away for applications to Columbia and Brown, but my mom found them in my room and said that there's no way I'm applying to them. She thinks that if I go anywhere but Stern, I'll end up not being religious. But she doesn't get the fact that I'm not going to be religious no matter where I go to college. It doesn't mean anything to me."

"It's not always easy to feel it. There have been times since I've converted that I've wondered if this is what I really want. And even if I know that it is what I ultimately want, I've found it hard to keep everything. But I think we're always supposed to be grappling with what we believe."

"Can I quote you on that?" Shira asked. Her mom would have a fit if she heard this, and she would do anything to provoke a good fight.

"Sure. It's okay that you're struggling with it. It shows you're thinking."

"What would you say if I struggled with it and decided I don't believe in it? You must have done that with whatever religion you came from."

"I didn't grow up with any religion so it's not really the same." Batsheva met her eyes. "But if you really thought about it and came to that decision, I would say that you have to do what makes you happy. Obviously I think this is a good way of life, but that doesn't mean it's for everyone."

Yocheved Abraham poked her head into the room and gave Shira a pointed look; she was missing class for the third day in a row.

"Don't worry, I'm coming," Shira said to Yocheved, who was unable to take her eyes off Shira's new outfit. "Do you like it?" she asked. "My mother brought it over. It's the longest skirt I had."

Yocheved couldn't imagine that Shira's mother would have brought over such a thing. She glanced at Batsheva who had the faintest hint of a smile on her face. Perhaps she was responsible for this. It looked like the kind of skirt she might own. She checked Batsheva's face again: the smile had disappeared.

Shira waved good-bye to Batsheva and went off to class, leaving Yocheved alone with Batsheva. Yocheved was trying to be nice to Batsheva, but they had so little in common. Even though Batsheva was just a few years older, she seemed to Yocheved to be years away, having experienced so much more. This made her nervous—she was always afraid that Batsheva might laugh at what she said. In addition, she was starting to feel replaced. She was supposed to be the one closest to the girls, she was supposed to be their role model. Yocheved had left New York because she had a place here. She had thought she would be appreciated, unlike in New York, where she was seen as another near-thirty-year-old woman dying to get married. But now all the talk was about how much the girls liked Batsheva; Yocheved was once again being overlooked.

"These girls." Yocheved shook her head. "What are we going to do with them?"

"They're just having a tough time. It's hard to be at such a small school," Batsheva said.

Afraid that her fear of Batsheva laughing at her was about to come true, Yocheved protested that she hadn't meant anything derogatory, and she hurried out of the room, now late to her own class.

THE more time the girls spent with Batsheva, the more we noticed changes in them. Rachel Ann Berkowitz commented that Aviva was more willing to help out in the kitchen; she didn't put up a fuss when asked to dry the dishes. Ruth Berner was struck by the way Hadassah davened on Sunday morning without being nudged. Nechama Sheinberg began talking about going to Israel for a year after high school when a few months before, she wasn't considering the possibility. Shira too had calmed down. She started coming to classes on time, she skipped school less frequently. She even went to shul on Shabbos mornings, when for the past few months, she claimed to have overslept. We were gratified to see these changes and hoped that Batsheva might be the right influence. As much as we adored Yocheved Abraham, the girls didn't click with her. Batsheva wasn't the role model we would have chosen, but God works in strange ways and maybe, just maybe, she had been sent here to save our daughters.

8

ONCE AUTUMN CAME ROUND, our lives were consumed with the upcoming high holidays. It was a whirlwind: Rosh Hashanah arrived first, then ten days later there was Yom Kippur, and a few days after that we were thrown into the holiday of Sukkot.

Usually Rosh Hashanah was only about the cooking and getting ready. But when the holiday arrived this year, it was unlike any other we had experienced. Batsheva was the first woman in shul, and when we got there, she was deep in prayer. Her body swayed and her eyes were closed in concentration. Watching her made us pray harder. Instead of imagining God as far away in some distant part of the sky, we saw Him all around us. As we were getting tired of standing, feeling our feet grow weary, the cantor began the prayer that was the center of the davening. The tune stirred in our stomachs and rose up through our hearts. *On Rosh Hashanah it is written and on Yom Kippur it is sealed, how many will pass away and how many will be born, who will live and who will die, who a timely death and who an untimely one. But repentance, prayer, and charity cancel the stern decree.* If any bad decree had been set forth against us, we prayed for it to be replaced with a good one. When we dipped our apples in honey and tasted the sweetness in our mouths, we prayed for a sweet year for our families and our community.

That afternoon, we gathered for tashlich, the symbolic casting of our sins into a body of water. The Mississippi was too far from our houses to walk to, so instead, we gathered by the shallow stream of water that passed through the Shayowitzes yard on its way to the river. We stood in front of it and recited the prayer: *Who is like you God who pardons iniquity and overlooks our transgressions . . . He will be merciful and cast our sins into the ocean.* We tore off pieces of bread to symbolize these sins and tossed them into the water. Mrs. Levy's gossip mixed in with Helen Shayowitz's lack of concentration during davening and Tziporah Newburger's trouble remembering to give the benefit of the doubt and Becky Feldman's improper thoughts and Jocelyn Shanzer's secret indulgence in shrimp salad. Soon the stream was full with white dots of bread, and we imagined a rush of water passing through and carrying our sins to sea.

On Yom Kippur, we began the fast with our bodies full from the meal we had eaten, the last food we would take in for twenty-five hours. We stood before God, a single congregation. We wore white dresses, covered our heads with white berets and white scarves. Our husbands wore the simple white shrouds they had worn under our wedding chuppahs, the same ones we buried our dead in. We dressed this way to show the purity inside us, the purity we aspired to attain in the coming year. We looked around the shul, its usual color blanched into a sea of white, and it was like catching a glimpse of heaven.

Sukkot, the holiday of the harvest, is the last of this string of holidays and a relief after the solemnity of Rosh Hashanah and Yom Kippur. The Torah commands us to build sukkahs—temporary huts like the ones the Jews built when they traveled in the desert for forty years—and live in them for seven days and seven nights. When the rest of the world moves indoors, picnic season over for the year, we go outside to eat our meals.

We build our sukkahs out of all sorts of things: aluminum walls, canvas tarps, and metal poles, boards of plywood, old vinyl shower curtains. The sukkahs must have at least two and a half walls and the roofs must be made out of material that grows from the ground—small tree branches, clusters of leaves, or bamboo poles—spaced thinly enough that we can see the stars shining through at night but thick enough that there is more shade than sun during the day. We'd been doing this for so many years that we knew exactly how to build our sukkahs, which corner of the roof to attach the supporting beams to, how big they'd have to be to hold the entire extended family, how sturdy to withstand any rain or wind. Fifteen years back, there had been a terrible storm and many of our sukkahs were uprooted, some flying clear across the neighborhood.

When our children were younger, we spent more time decorating our sukkahs, making paper chains from construction paper, threading cranberries, cutting out shapes from felt. Helen Shayowitz had bought a create-your-own stained-glass window kit, Mrs. Levy had taught her Anna Beth how to make a mobile of hand-sewn fruit, and Bessie Kimmel had her daughters draw individualized placemats for each of the guests who would eat in their sukkah. We laminated the drawings—some of us even Scotchgarded—in an attempt to prevent the rain from ruining them, and at the end of the holiday, we carefully stored them away for the next year.

These days we still pulled out the boxes of supplies from our garages, bought sheets of felt, construction paper tablets, and bags of cranberries. But by the time we finished cooking and cleaning, the space set aside for decorating had shrunk, so small that we wondered if one day it might vanish altogether. Instead of making new decorations, we hung only the ones from past years, trying to salvage what we could. But the paper chains had started to wilt, the paintings had become faded, the lamination was coming off at the corners.

This year, two days before the first night of Sukkot, Batsheva knocked on our doors and told us that she was planning to decorate her sukkah the next day, would our children be able to join her? We saw her excitement as she explained that this was the first sukkah she had ever built, because in New York, she hadn't had a space for one. We felt a rush of compassion for her, an aching to be as enthusiastic as she was, and we said we would be sure to tell our children; we might even stop by ourselves.

The next day, we made our way over to Batsheva's backyard. She had built her sukkah of plain white wood. On top, instead of the light brown bamboo poles we used for our roofs (they had been in fashion a few years back and now we couldn't go back to tree branches, the bamboo was so much easier and cleaner), she had covered hers with magnolia leaves, some of them still sprouting white flowers. Batsheva was standing in the middle of a circle of children. It was a sunny day, one of the last of the year, and the Indian summer sun shone a golden orange off her hair.

"So many kids," Tziporah Newburger said. "Doesn't it make her nervous?"

"I feel like a bad mother just watching her," Rena Reinhard said.

"Nonsense," Helen Shayowitz said. "You're a perfectly good mother."

Ayala was holding a coffee tin filled with paint brushes, their black bristles neatly lined up. Batsheva motioned for her to pass them around to the other kids, and Ayala carefully placed one in each of their hands.

"We're going to paint scenes from the Torah onto my sukkah," Batsheva said. "I want you to close your eyes and pretend that God came down to my backyard and asked us to illustrate the Torah."

Our children walked through the narrow entrance of the sukkah, which was covered with strands of white beads. Inside Batsheva had set out cans of paint in different colors. At first, our kids were unsure of what to do. Some dipped their brushes into the paint and made tentative marks on the walls as they glanced around to see what everyone else was doing. Benjy Reinhard painted a small blue Jewish star toward the bottom of one of the walls. His sister Bracha painted a brown Torah scroll.

"Ayala and I are going to make the splitting of the Red Sea," Batsheva called out. "Who wants to do Noah's ark?"

She began drawing a giant sun on one wall, and Ayala filled it in with streaks of yellow, not worrying if paint dripped down the walls onto the grass, if her hands became stained with color. The kids looked at the bold strokes Batsheva and Ayala made. Then Yechiel Newburger got started on Noah's ark. He painted a honey-colored ark looming large over a row of animals—red cows and green horses and yellow birds. His sister Chani stood on a folding chair and painted a rainbow in the blue sky. The Zuckerman girls worked on a picture of the giving of the Torah. Rivkie drew Mount Sinai, a brown triangle with green around the edges while Deena painted Moshe, a bearded man with the ten commandments on his shoulders.

Mimi and Yosef arrived in the middle of all the activity. She had her arm wrapped through his and they stood at the edge of the lawn watching. When Batsheva saw them, she ran over.

"I'm so glad you could come," Batsheva said.

"Batsheva, this is wonderful. Everyone looks like they're having so much fun." Mimi had often talked about the need to re-energize ourselves so that our observances didn't become rote. She told us that it wasn't enough to observe the holidays and keep Shabbos and kosher if our hearts weren't in it; we needed to look for ways to internalize their messages and this, apparently, was what she had in mind. "Isn't this great, Yosef?"

Yosef nodded. "It really is," he said.

"I have a job for you," Batsheva said to Yosef and handed him a bucket filled with gray water. "You can be in charge of getting clean water. Use the hose by the back door and spill the dirty water onto the grass."

He did as she had said, and Mimi came over to join us, still exclaiming how she had never seen the whole community get so into the spirit of Sukkot, that we should be doing things like this before every holiday. We agreed with Mimi: we had never seen anything like it either. Yosef too was getting involved. He rushed from child to child, admiring their work. He didn't paint a scene of his own, but every once in a while he walked over to the Zuckerman sisters, picked up an extra paintbrush and painted the light blue sky around their mountain.

The sound of Batsheva's laughter caught Yosef's attention. We understood why he couldn't take his eyes off her. She was running back and forth, her hair flying behind her as she offered suggestions, opened cans of paint, and laughed with the kids. She was also busy with her own scene, the splitting of the Red Sea. The sea curled in blue and green swirls around men, women, and children filing through on dry, yellow sand. On one side of the sea was a band of Egyptians on black horses chasing after the Jews. Next to Moshe was Miriam, his sister, in a long turquoise gown holding a tambourine and leading a line of women as she danced across the dry land.

But when we took a closer look, we realized that this Miriam looked suspiciously like Batsheva. She had the same long blond hair and peering green eyes. And we could have sworn that one of the men looked like the Rabbi, that a woman in the back had the same face as Helen Shayowitz, that another woman had the exact hairstyle as Bessie Kimmel. We didn't say anything—it wouldn't have been polite, especially when we were guests in Batsheva's backyard—but we wondered among ourselves if the similarities were purely coincidental. Maybe it wasn't a big deal, even if she had intentionally drawn herself into the Torah; there was no explicit law against this, at least none we could think of offhand.

"How do you like that," Helen exclaimed. "Don't you think that woman looks a little like me?" She couldn't decide whether she ought to be flattered or insulted.

"You're much prettier, Helen. I wouldn't worry," Leanna Zuckerman said and snickered, whether at the painting or at Helen we weren't sure.

"Maybe, but I still think that's me up there," Helen said.

Batsheva left the sukkah, taking a break from her painting to get a drink. Instead of going inside, she went over to the garden hose and drank. The water sputtered across her mouth and she rubbed the water into her face and let the hose wet the top of her hair. When she finished, she noticed us watching her. She walked over to us, her lips and face still dotted with water.

"This is quite a party you have here," Mrs. Levy said.

"I was hoping that the kids would be as excited about it as I am," Batsheva said. "And I want Ayala to have the Jewish memories that I didn't have. It's different when you don't grow up in it. All you can do is hope that you're doing it right."

Mrs. Levy smiled knowingly. "That's very nice. But take it from me, dear. I've been doing this for almost fifty years and after a while it stops being exciting. That's the way it is. Everything in life is like that. There's nothing you can do about it."

We agreed with her as we remembered how, when we had first gotten married, we had been so excited to have homes of our own, to prepare fancy Shabbos meals using our shiny new dishes, our sterling silverware and gleaming crystal.

"I don't know about that," Batsheva said. "It's hard for me to imagine that I wouldn't always be excited by this."

Batsheva busied herself with directing a few children to the unopened cans of paint, and she shouted to Yosef that they needed more fresh water. Having let Mrs. Levy's cynicism pass, she turned back to us. "Don't think I'm going to let you get away with just standing here. I have a job for you." She handed us a shopping bag filled with strands of beads. "I didn't have a chance to finish hanging these. I thought they would look good on the outside walls, so there's something to look at when you first come into the yard."

Batsheva passed us a ball of yarn and two pairs of children's scissors with rounded tips and green rubber handles. Then she ran off, leaving us to our task.

Unsure of what we were getting ourselves into, we walked over to the walls of the sukkah.

"Why don't we tape the beads to the wall?" Helen said. "That should be easy."

"No, that won't look right. They need to be tied on," Tziporah Newburger said. With four children, she had done many an art project, and she considered herself something of an expert.

We got to work, untangling the different strands, cutting pieces of yarn to tie them to the wooden beams of the sukkah, using the ladder that Batsheva had left nearby. We weren't dressed for climbing, but holding our skirts down, slipping out of our low-heeled pumps, we climbed up anyway, tying, cutting, untying.

"This isn't half bad. I'd almost say I'm enjoying myself," Mrs. Levy said. It was too bad that Irving was at work; he would have enjoyed seeing this. She remembered the first sukkah of their marriage, how Irving had built it all by himself and she had held the ladder for him as he hammered the walls together. How young and eager they had been. How proud they had been of their makeshift sukkah with its lopsided walls and homemade decorations. These days Irving hired someone to put up their sukkah, which was ordered from a store in Brooklyn that sold easy-to-assemble kits. And she ordered the decorations from a catalog that specialized in out-of-season Christmas decorations; no one would guess that the blue-and-white metallic stars she hung were intended for something else entirely.

"Look at that," Helen Shayowitz exclaimed. She discovered that by intertwining a few strands of beads she could make a rainbow. She hung her creations in between the single strands Mrs. Levy was busy fastening.

"This may be fun, but I still have work to do," Tziporah Newburger said. She had cooking and cleaning to finish, children to bathe and dress, out of town guests to tend to. It was too much, just too much.

"Loosen up, Tziporah," Mrs. Levy said. "You'll have plenty of time to finish when you get home. And even if you don't, I'm sure you've cooked plenty already."

Rena Reinhard wandered away from where the rest of us were working. Batsheva had left an extra white board leaning against one of the back walls of the sukkah. Rena stared at it and her mind began coming up with shapes and colors that she wanted to paint. She thought back to the paintings Batsheva had shown her when she brought clothes over for Ayala, and she wondered if she could paint something like Batsheva had. Hoping no one would see her, she grabbed a spare paintbrush and a red can of paint. She dipped the brush into the paint and began. Her strokes were angry as she poured out the rage that had been building up inside her. These past months, Rena had worked hard to keep up the pretense that everything at home was fine, that her marriage was as good as anyone else's. In these lines of red, she imagined herself announcing to the world that her husband was cold and neglectful, that he hadn't touched her in months, that he was almost certainly having an affair with someone from his office. She would be the one to reject him; she who would go off without once looking back, leaving him a house full of children and laundry and dirty dishes.

With us caught up in our decorating, Yosef walked over to Batsheva and began adding specks of light green in the waves she was painting.

She put her hands on her hips and smiled. "What do you think you're doing?" she asked.

He laughed and added a small blue fish with bulging black eyes to her picture. "It looks better this way."

"Oh, does it?" With no warning, Batsheva reached out her paintbrush and dotted a circle of red paint on his cheek. "Well, I think you look better this way."

In retaliation, he added a dot of blue to her forehead and they laughed. What struck us most was how relaxed they were with each other, as if they had been friends for years.

Ayala walked over to Batsheva and Yosef. "What are you doing?" she asked.

"We're painting funny faces," Batsheva said. "Do you want one?"

Ayala nodded and Yosef painted two small circles of blue, one on each of her cheeks.

"Now you look like your mom," Yosef said.

Batsheva handed Ayala a paintbrush and she added to the swirls of the ocean like Yosef had done. When she finished, Ayala wrapped one arm around her mother's legs and stretched her hand up to Yosef's. If you weren't from here and didn't know better, you could have mistaken the three of them for a family.

WHEN we went home to our own sukkahs, they seemed old, dull, like bread that had gone stale. The laminated posters of Jerusalem tacked up, our children's faded drawings, the plastic oranges hanging from our bamboo, the Jewish New Year's cards strung together and taped to the walls—these were the same decorations we hung every year and they paled in comparison to what Batsheva had created. We tried to explain to our husbands what was so special about her sukkah but they didn't understand. They reassured us that our sukkahs were as pretty as ever; nothing could compare to all the work we had done preparing for Sukkot.

That night, the first of the holiday, we had dinner in our sukkahs. Even though we were in our backyards, we ate off our finest china and used our sterling silver. We had tried to come up with foods that were special for Sukkot, ones that reminded us of the harvest and autumn. We did everything imaginable to squash: we made squash-nut breads and sweet potato–squash pies, stuffed squash and squash scallopini. We sculpted centerpieces from butternut squash and acorn squash. We even used tablecloths and napkins in yellows and oranges and reds.

When we looked around our tables, we swelled with pride at the faces of our children, grandchildren, grandparents and parents shining under the yellow lights we'd hung to keep away the moths. Through the narrow spaces between the bamboo poles, we saw the black sky and the glimmer of so many stars and felt God looking down at us. No longer sheltered inside the brick and concrete of our houses, we rested more tangibly in His hands. When we finished eating, we sang the birkat hamazon out loud, thanking God for the food He had provided. The voices of our neighbors singing the same words to the same tunes rose up around us. As if we had all eaten together, our voices unified into a single prayer, calling out to God almost visible above us.

We heard voices coming from Batsheva's backyard as well. She had invited an odd group of people to her house—a non-Jewish woman who lived a few blocks away and had never seen a sukkah before, two college students from Memphis State whom she had somehow met, and Mrs. Ganz, who lived alone at the end of the block and was, unfortunately, often forgotten on the holidays, with all the out-of-town company we had. We imagined Batsheva in her sukkah, surrounded by the pictures our children had created and wished that we had also been invited. As we were clearing off the tables, about to go inside for the night, their singing floated toward us, filling our air with a sweetness that was fresh, like a new fruit we had never tasted before.

9

YOSEF WAS SCHEDULED TO go back to yeshiva a few days after Sukkot and we were already thinking about how much we would miss him. When he was away, Mimi was a little sadder and the Rabbi looked lonely, out of sorts. We comforted ourselves with the thought that Yosef would be home to visit before we knew it, for Chanukah, two months away.

A few days before he was supposed to leave, Edith Shapiro was in the men's department at Goldsmith's. She was buying a bar mitzvah present for her nephew, and she had no idea what he would like; men's clothes all looked the same to her, so much black and navy and gray. Having to buy this gift on her own reminded her of how much she missed her Kieve, rest his soul. Just as she was about to sink into another bout of depression, she spotted Mimi across the aisle. She waved eagerly; it was nice to see someone she knew when she was feeling down. Mimi was carrying a pile of undershirts, socks, and white dress shirts and was looking at a rack of pants.

"New clothes for someone?" Edith asked.

"Yosef hates shopping so I'm getting him a bunch of things he needs," Mimi said.

"For yeshiva." Edith nodded. "Boys go through clothes so quickly. It was the same with my sons. As soon as they went away, they started getting taller. Each time they came home, I could have sworn they had each grown another foot."

"Actually," Mimi said, choosing her words carefully, "Yosef has decided that he wants to spend the year at home learning with his father."

"Really," Edith exclaimed. Based on the nervous way Mimi was speaking, Edith assumed that it wasn't as easy a decision as Mimi was making it sound.

"We haven't said anything because we wanted to give him a chance to think it through. But he really wants to stay. He says this is what's best for him."

"But you're not so sure," Edith filled in what Mimi left unsaid.

"I was worried at first. But I trust Yosef. If he says this is what he needs, then I support him."

If the Rabbi's relationship with Yosef had a certain intensity to it, Yosef and Mimi were naturally close with each other. We remembered when Yosef was a little boy, how he would come find Mimi in the women's section of shul and sit on her lap, snuggling against her as she explained what the davening meant. When he was older and no longer allowed in the women's section, he would wave to her from his seat up front, and we could see his longing to still be that little boy on her lap.

"Good for you," Edith said. "That's exactly what you should do. With us, we had a different problem. I wanted my boys to go to the high school here but my Kieve wouldn't hear of it. He thought they needed to be in a real yeshiva."

Edith remembered as if it were yesterday how it felt to send her oldest son away. Reuven was just past his bar mitzvah, only thirteen years old and small for his age. He had never been away from home, not even to sleep-away camp, and she didn't know how he would manage. When she hugged him good-bye, she felt as if she wouldn't see him again for years. She often wondered whether it had been worth it. She knew she was supposed to say that of course it was, a sacrifice for the sake of Torah. All her sons had become rabbis; what more could she want? But once they left, it had never been the same. If Reuven had asked to come home even once, she would have insisted to her husband that a thirteen-year-old still needs his mother. But he had easily blended into the yeshiva world. Their second son, Baruch, had followed and then Naftali when his time came and finally Eliezer, her youngest. Each time, it was as difficult as the last. But she steeled herself to the pain and tried to remind herself that her sons were gifts from God, only hers until they were old enough to be dedicated to Him.

"Appreciate him while you have him. Take it from me, it goes so fast," Edith said. She grasped Mimi's hands in her own. She would give anything to bring back the days when she had her husband and sons at the table for dinner every night. If Mimi was being given the chance to have this for one more year, she should seize it.

Before leaving the store, Edith ran into Tziporah Newburger in the shoe department; there was a big sale that week, all fall shoes marked down 20 percent.

"I'm so glad I bumped into you," Edith said. "I have the greatest news." She moved aside several boxes of shoes and sat down next to Tziporah. "I ran into Mimi in the men's department and she told me that Yosef isn't going back to yeshiva this year. He wants to stay home and learn with his father," she said.

"No, that can't be," Tziporah said. "I'm sure it's just a rumor."

"I swear," Edith said. "I heard it straight from Mimi."

Tziporah thought this over. Learning at home wouldn't be the same as yeshiva. She loved to listen to her husband tell stories of his years in yeshiva in Brooklyn, how focused he had been, how the ancient world of the Talmud loomed larger and more real than the rest of the city. She pictured the young men in crisp white shirts and black pants rising with the sun, eager to get back to the pages of Talmud they had reluctantly left the night before. It was the kind of world that, had she been a boy, she might have liked to belong to. The fact that Yosef was choosing not to return to yeshiva made her wonder how serious of a student he really was. But the benefit of the doubt, she reminded herself; she was supposed to be giving the benefit of the doubt. It was the mitzvah she had chosen to work on this year in her unending quest to perfect herself.

The two women said good-bye. Tziporah went back to trying on a pair of blue suede flats and Edith went to get the tie she had bought gift-wrapped.

THE news that Yosef was staying home began to spread. We turned to one another and asked: Who knew? Who suspected? None of us had had any idea, it seemed, until Esther Abramowitz, the Rabbi's secretary, admitted that she had known and had been holding her tongue.

While she may not have been cut out for secretarial work, Esther had developed a close relationship with the Rabbi and his family. Esther had never married, and at sixty-nine years old, she had resigned herself to the fact that she never would. Yosef was the closest thing she would ever have to a grandchild.

A few days before, she'd brought the Rabbi his afternoon coffee. She didn't knock—after working for him for nineteen years, she had learned to slip in and out of his office unseen—and there was Yosef, looking uncomfortable, almost afraid. Esther knew that the Rabbi and Yosef cared deeply for each other, but they had a hard time expressing that love. At first, she attributed the discomfort to that. But as she was leaving the room, Yosef began speaking, his voice cracking with nervousness. Esther couldn't help herself: she didn't close the door all the way and she could hear every word.

"I was thinking that I would stay home this year," Yosef said.

"What!" the Rabbi exclaimed, completely taken by surprise.

"I feel like I need a break from yeshiva. Maybe it would be better if I had some time away."

As far as the Rabbi knew, Yosef loved yeshiva; he was happy there, he was doing what he had always wanted. And he was excelling—he had already taken his first smicha exam and only needed to pass the remaining two before officially being ordained. "What about becoming a rabbi? What about finishing smicha?" the Rabbi asked.

Yosef looked at his father, trying to decide what to say.

"Tell me what's going on. Is something the matter?" the Rabbi asked. All his hopes that his son would follow in his footsteps became uncertain, and for the first time, he worried that his son might not be who he had always thought he was.

Yosef saw the pain on his father's face; he must have, because he stammered and then swallowed whatever it was he had been about to say. Instead, he looked pleadingly at his father and tried to reassure him. "Nothing is the matter. It's just that I've loved being here this summer and I think I'll get more out of learning with you than I will from yeshiva. And I'll go back next year and finish smicha. Lots of guys take time off to learn in Israel for a year. I'll be doing the same thing, only I'll be here."

"What made you decide to do this?" the Rabbi asked.

"I've always wanted to learn together like we used to when I was in high school. And now that I'm on a higher level, I feel like I'll be able to get so much more out of it.

We too remembered how they had learned. Every day, Yosef would leave his regular classes at school and spend two hours learning with his father. He was on a more advanced level than the rest of the boys, and this was the arrangement that the school had worked out. Not wanting to miss out on a minute of their time together, Yosef would rush from the school to the shul. He hung onto every word his father said, and at night, he would review what they had learned so it would stay sharp in his mind.

Yosef's reasons were enough to convince the Rabbi. He stood up and hugged his son. His initial worry had turned to relief, and he felt more certain than ever that his son would follow in his footsteps.

Neither the Rabbi nor Yosef had noticed Esther behind the door. This wasn't the first time she had positioned herself just so in order to overhear a conversation. Having no husband or children of her own, Esther considered it her duty to look after the Rabbi's family, and if this meant a little eavesdropping, so be it. As Esther went back to preparing the weekly announcements, she couldn't bring herself to feel the same excitement as the Rabbi did. There was nothing she wanted more than Yosef's happiness, but she didn't have a good feeling about this latest development. She had learned to read Yosef's face and she had seen the new uncertainty that had shown up there. Though she didn't know what to attribute it to, she assumed that it was connected to his decision.

The rest of us felt the same ambivalence. We didn't doubt that he would return to Memphis to live, but we had assumed that he would spend several years in yeshiva and then, with his rabbinical smicha in one hand and a wife in the other, he would return to Memphis. This was the path we expected from all our children. They could go away to yeshiva or college in New York: Yeshiva University for the boys, Stern College for the girls. Then they would get married and return to

Memphis. Any time they spent away from Memphis was a small detour from our line of continuity. We didn't dream they would settle anywhere else for good, and we had trouble imagining what those who moved away were hoping to find. Memphis was peaceful, it was pretty, the houses were large and inexpensive, there was a school, a bakery, a shul, and a restaurant. What more could they want?

When the children hadn't returned, the parents had been forced to launch full-scale campaigns to convince them of the error of their ways. Mrs. Levy had gone all out to convince her children to move here: she had screamed that they were being ungrateful and disloyal; she had tried scare tactics, pointing out how terrible crime was in the cities where they lived. On one infamous occasion, she had gotten down on her hands and knees and begged. Not as prone to dramatics as Mrs. Levy was, Edith Shapiro sent each of her children a recent article from the Memphis newspaper describing how the city was growing into the financial center of Tennessee. Bessie Kimmel made sure her oldest son (the only one who didn't live here) knew that there was talk of Memphis getting a professional sports team any day now. When Bruce and Leanna Zuckerman considered settling in Chicago, Ethel Zuckerman had even gone so far as to offer to buy them a house two blocks away from her. And that, in the end, had been enough to convince them.

"I went to school in New York but I knew that nowhere but Memphis would be home," Becky Feldman would often explain. "When I dated, I always thought about whether this person would move to Memphis. I asked it on every date I went on. Later when my husband was doing his residency matching program, he was thinking about Denver. But I told him that if he didn't put Memphis as his first choice, I would never forgive him."

"We lived in Brooklyn when we first got married," Tziporah Newburger recounted. "I hated it. Everything is so crowded up there and no one knows you. It's no place to bring up children." The only advantage of Brooklyn were the stores—there were hat stores and wig stores on every corner. But that alone hadn't been enough to make up for the horror of living there, especially since she could make a pilgrimage every year and stock up.

To make it worse, Tziporah had had to endure a lot of teasing. "Are there really Jews in Tennessee?" the New Yorkers would ask her. "Do you live on a farm? Have you seen Elvis recently?" Though she knew they were joking, it made her realize even more that she never wanted to become a New Yorker, never wanted to be a part of this teasing, pushy mass of people. When she and Shmuel moved back to Memphis, their homecoming had been glorious. The house right next door to her parents happened to be for sale and they had snatched it up. Within their first few weeks home, she was elected Decorations Coordinator of the Ladies Auxiliary. It was as if they had never been away. Within two months, Shmuel too had adjusted; he said he could never imagine moving back to Brooklyn.

Years before, everyone simply used to stay put. There was none of this traveling back and forth. Nashville and Birmingham were considered a long way off. And New York and Los Angeles were worlds away, no closer than the Europe our great-grandparents had left behind.

"How can I explain it?" Mrs. Levy would say. "In past generations, we married each other. Cousins paired off with cousins if need be. We made do with what we had." It was so different from kids today, who were always seeking something they would never find.

"There were no fur coats and Mercedes Benzes then, let me tell you," Helen Shayowitz said. "I grew up over my parents' grocery store and I worked from the time I was a little girl." Even though she and Alvin were now well off, Helen couldn't shake the feeling that at any second their money could disappear and she would once again be that poor little girl who had had to wear the same outfit to Fairview Junior High School every day.

"And another thing," Edith Shapiro said. "You think it's hard being Jewish today. Well, it was a different world back then. We didn't go around saying we were Jewish. We were proud of who we were, but we didn't announce it to everyone we met. We tried to fit in as best we could." Edith had experienced her share of anti-Semitism in Memphis. When she was ten, she and her brother were playing in their front yard and two boys from next door rode by on their bicycles and called them kikes. At the time, she hadn't understood what that meant, but since then, she had had plenty of opportunity to learn. This was the South, after all; as at home as she felt down here, it didn't have the reputation for being the most accepting of regions.

While we were thrilled that Yosef saw Memphis as a good enough place to stay, we worried about him. We thought back to the times we had seen him recently. We agreed that he seemed tentative, as if he no longer knew exactly who he was and what he wanted. And there was another change we talked about. Yosef usually invited his friends from yeshiva down for Simchat Torah to liven up the celebration and lead the congregation in the dancing in honor of completing the reading of the Torah. But this year, he hadn't invited them. At the time, we hadn't thought much of it, but now this too seemed important.

"I'm wondering if he's homesick. His whole life Mimi's done everything for him and maybe he's having a hard time with the separation," Edith Shapiro said. She had wished, just once, that her sons had shown such signs. Whenever they went back to school after the holidays, she had packed up chicken and kugel for them. She sent them cookies for Shabbos and offered to do their laundry if they wanted to mail it to her. Now those days were over—they had wives to take care of them—but before they were married, she would have done anything to feel like they still needed her.

"I wish it were that simple. But I think it's something much worse," Mrs. Levy said. "It usually is." She didn't want to be overly negative, but reality was reality; nothing she could do about that.

"What I think," Helen Shayowitz paused for dramatic effect, "is that Yosef has some horrible disease and he's here for treatment." Images of sickness danced through her mind. She saw fevers and rashes, coughing fits and yellowed skin. "God forbid, of course, but maybe."

When Naomi Eisenberg saw Yosef on his way to learn with Batsheva, she fell into step with him. Even though she herself had moved back to the same city she had grown up in, it was a wonder that Yosef didn't want to seek out new places. He was so smart, he could go anywhere he wanted and doors would open for him.

"How's it going?" Naomi asked, trying to sound casual. She didn't want Yosef to think she was trying to interrogate him or catch the latest piece of gossip. She really wanted to know how he was.

"I'm fine," he said in a noncommittal way.

"I'm glad to hear that. Are you looking forward to your time here?" she asked.

"I am. I haven't lived here in a long time, and I like the idea of being at home for a while. I miss Memphis when I'm away."

"I'm sure your parents are thrilled to have you," Naomi said. She didn't know what else to say. Could she ask him if he ever thought of leaving and not coming back? Could she confide that not a day went by without her wondering if she would ever leave Memphis?

"I think so. Of course they were a little surprised, but now they're as excited as I am."

To Naomi, it sounded like Yosef was trying to make everyone, including himself, believe this version of events. He reminded Naomi of an actor reciting his lines. His whole life, he had played the part of the dutiful son and it was hard to know where the role ended and the real Yosef began. But when the rest of us heard what Yosef told Naomi, we were reassured.

"If he's home, we'll get to spend more time with him," Edith Shapiro said. She was already imagining how frequently Yosef would visit her, maybe even for dinner during the week. She would fix him her specialties, steaks with fried onions, turnip greens, home-fried potatoes, and for dessert, her world-famous green grasshopper pie.

"If he wants to stay, so be it," Bessie Kimmel said, feeling that sometimes, it was best to let things happen as they would.

For Jocelyn Shanzer, who still had hopes that Yosef might be interested in her niece Miriam, who lived in Nashville, his presence at home was ideal. This would be the year to make the match happen. "I wonder if Miriam would like to come for Shabbos next week. It's been ages since she was here," she said to her husband, already envisioning the honor that would come her way if she were related to Yosef. She would be like royalty, invited to every single wedding and bar mitzvah in the city, maybe even asked to sit at the head table alongside the Rabbi.

"Yosef can give classes at the shul and lead youth groups like he used to," Tziporah Newburger said. "He can practice being the rabbi." Her children could use a role model like Yosef, especially her two little boys: Moshe and Yechiel were so wild that she didn't know what to do with them. Instead of staying in Junior Congregation, they ran around with no supervision. It was enough to make Tziporah pretend that she didn't know them.

Now that Yosef would be staying in Memphis, we couldn't understand how we could have ever let him leave. Anything he might learn at yeshiva, he could just as easily learn from his father. He could get smicha from him, he could become the assistant rabbi at the shul. And he could go to New York on weekends for shidduch dates. He could find a bride and bring her here. Because this was his home, this was where he belonged.

10

AFTER THESE FEW MONTHS, we could barely remember what our community had been like without Batsheva. She had become so woven in that she seemed inseparable. She had even begun to talk like us, her words elongating into a southern accent. No one could pinpoint an exact moment when this happened; every day her words had changed the smallest bit. But after a few months, there was no mistaking it. She sounded as if she had lived in Memphis all her life.

Ayala too had become part of the community. It was a common sight to see her running down the street with our children. She was always playing over at our houses, she made herself at home in our kitchens and living rooms. We helped Batsheva with Ayala whenever she needed—picking her up from school if Batsheva was going to be late, inviting her to stay for dinner, making sure she had a sweater on when it was chilly. Because of this, we felt more attached to Ayala than we did to any of each other's kids; we felt a motherly sense of pride that we were taking part in raising her.

Of course there were times when we were reminded that Batsheva wasn't one of us. She still dressed more provocatively than we did, sang too loudly in shul, held herself too freely and said things with an openness we never would. But we reminded ourselves that these differences only showed how far she had come. The Rabbi told us that Jews who had been raised Orthodox could never reach the same heights as those who had come to it on their own; they would always see farther, as if they were standing on our shoulders. Even though we had always kept kosher, even though we had observed every Shabbos, we hadn't chosen it on our own.

It was to Batsheva that Rena Reinhard turned when the situation with her husband got worse, no reconciliation in sight and the possibility of divorce looming larger. She went over to Batsheva's house and poured her heart out. She never felt like she was complaining too much, never worried that Batsheva would grow irritated at always hearing about her unhappiness. Batsheva listened, her face sympathetic and unjudging. She reminded Rena that she had choices, she could decide on her own if she wanted to leave this marriage and the community would support her.

When Leanna Zuckerman was having problems with her in-laws, when she felt that she had no identity separate from them, she would call Batsheva for advice. She told Batsheva how she didn't know who she was, and Batsheva talked about the importance of finding a center within yourself, some space where you existed just for yourself. She encouraged Leanna to branch out, to sign up for a class at Memphis State, to maybe finish her degree in accounting and get a job she would find fulfilling—not because anyone else wanted her to, but because she, all on her own, wanted it.

On Shabbos afternoons, we all ended up at Batsheva's house, bored with our usual conversations. We asked her to tell us again how she had come to Judaism; there was no story we would rather listen to than the one of her walking in New York and stumbling across a shul. We asked her if McDonald's really was as good as the commercials made it seem, if our imitation pepperoni pizza tasted anything like the real thing, if Friday night television was the same as television on any night. All our questions about the outside world came pouring out, and Batsheva answered with great honesty: that it was Mexican food she missed the most, that no, our pizza didn't even come close, that giving up Friday night TV was the least of it. Hearing Batsheva speak about the life she had emerged from was like looking out a window at a place we would never go.

When we needed someone to be in charge of decorations for the kindergarten play, the Book Fair, the Tenth Annual Italian-Style Spaghetti Dinner, we turned to Batsheva. She didn't want an official Ladies Auxiliary position—maybe Decorations Coordinator or Design Co-Chair—but she said she was thrilled to help; it made her feel like she belonged. As soon as we described the project, she had so many suggestions, her voice bubbling with excitement as she told us how we could transform the gym into a miniature Venice for the Spaghetti Dinner, how the kids could come dressed as their favorite characters for the Book Fair.

Batsheva was doing so much for us, we wanted to do something for her. We worried about her as if she were our own daughter. What if she never remarried? What if she was alone for the rest of her life? We tried being subtle. We mentioned that there was a Jewish singles weekend in Knoxville later that month, would she be interested? Or that the *Jewish Press* had loads of personal ads in the back. Out of curiosity we had read through them, and wouldn't you know it, some of those men sure sounded interesting. But Batsheva never showed any interest. She laughed at our efforts and said she could manage on her own. Which only made us double our efforts. Clearly the only way Batsheva would remarry was if we found her a husband.

One Shabbos afternoon, a few of us were gathered in Helen Shayowitz's house. Helen's daughter, Tamara, had, thank God, gotten engaged that week, and all the talk was about marriage and weddings.

"His name is Joshua Kalb and he's from a very nice family in Miami and he's in law school and very good looking. We're planning a May wedding at the Peabody Hotel and for colors, we're talking peach and gold," Helen informed us.

Tamara was her only daughter, and Helen had been waiting for this event her whole life. When both of her sons had gotten married, the weddings were out-of-town. She had had no say in anything; she was, according to the rule for mothers-of-the-groom, supposed to wear off-white and keep her mouth shut and her checkbook open. But this time, Helen would be running the show. There was enough planning and organizing to keep her busy for a year, but she only had six months to do it. Luckily, for the past few years she had been clipping articles from *Southern Bride* on flower arrangements, centerpieces, wedding cakes, and mother-of-the-bride dresses. Several years ago, Helen had even considered buying Tamara a wedding dress that was on sale, because even though she wasn't dating anyone just then, she surely would be sooner or later.

With all the talk of marriage, the subject of fixing up Batsheva was raised. We had been setting up people for years. We would come up with a list of the single men and women we knew. Then the complicated work of matching them up began, deciding who would look good together, who came from the same kind of families, who had similar personalities. Coming up with a good pair was no easy task; even God found matchmaking to be difficult business, more complicated than the splitting of the Red Sea.

"What about the Posmans' son?" Jocelyn Shanzer asked.

Mrs. Levy shook her head. "He never married," she sighed. "What a shame."

"I don't know," Leanna Zuckerman said. "He's very straight-laced. I think Batsheva needs someone a little more laid-back."

"You never know," Jocelyn insisted. "They're both perfectly nice, both religious, both unmarried. That's a lot in common right there."

"Let's see if we can think of anyone better, and if not, we'll give him a try," Helen suggested.

"What about Alan Kranzler?" Mrs. Levy asked. "He comes from a good family."

"You can't set him up with Batsheva," Naomi Eisenberg exclaimed. "He's at least fifty."

"Batsheva's no spring chicken," Mrs. Levy said. She had married Irving when she was twenty, and to her, that seemed the perfect age to get married, not too old and not too young. She didn't understand why women these days waited until they were older; weren't they afraid their best years would be gone? She had a granddaughter who had recently turned eighteen and already she was encouraging her to keep her eyes open, while she was still in her bloom.

"Wait a minute," Helen said. "What about Aaron Fox?"

Mrs. Levy clapped her hands together. "Perfect. Perfect. I don't know why I didn't think of it myself."

Aaron Fox was from Blytheville and he had moved to Memphis to work in a computer store run by a cousin of his. In Blytheville, there isn't an Orthodox shul and Aaron had known nothing about being

Jewish. But once he was in Memphis, he had grown curious—he met the Rabbi and they had gotten into an interesting conversation—and he had started coming to shul. After a few months, he had become Orthodox, more religious than many of us.

How nice it would be if it worked out. We could already picture the wedding. It would be in Memphis of course, and since Batsheva had no family that she was close with, we would step in and make it. It would be at the shul, and afterward we could have the dinner in Jocelyn Shanzer's backyard, which was big enough to seat at least a hundred people. Batsheva would look radiant in her white gown, a simple cut in silk (she probably didn't go for too many sequins or beads) with fresh-cut flowers in her hair. Ayala would be darling as a flower girl, in a pink-and-white dress, carrying a basket of rose petals. After Batsheva and Aaron Fox were married, any remaining differences between Batsheva and us would fade; the propriety of marriage would smooth them away. And it would only be a matter of time before they had brothers and sisters for Ayala. With this image fresh and sweet in our minds, we could hardly wait.

Jocelyn was put in charge of calling Aaron Fox. She had the most experience in this area. When she was a teenager, she had enjoyed a string of boyfriends, and she had never passed a Saturday night without a date. And since she had gotten married, she put these skills to use by fixing up other people. Years ago, she had set up the Zuckermans. Bruce, like her, was from Memphis, and Leanna was from Chicago, and Jocelyn had been her advisor at a youth group convention. And she had fixed up the Berkowitzes' niece Tanya with Edith Shapiro's youngest son, Eliezer, even though they were second cousins and had known each other their whole lives; a match was still a match. With two successful marriages under her belt, Jocelyn only needed a third to assure her a spot in The World to Come.

After she had tucked her kids into bed, she called Aaron and after a few minutes of chatting, she came right out and asked him. "I think I have someone for you. Would you be interested? She's very pretty, and she has a good heart, and she's just the tiniest bit unusual."

Aaron agreed right away. He had noticed Batsheva in shul and wondered who she was. There were very few single women in the community, except for the high school girls, and he had figured that they were probably too young for him. He was serious about finding a match—he had already been to New York for several shidduch dates, arranged by a rabbi there who knew our Rabbi. He had met each of these girls in a hotel lobby and the conversation had been very serious, the sole purpose to determine if they would be suitable mates for each other. But none of these girls had worked out and he was willing to give anything a try.

"Just to keep this nice and casual, why don't I have the two of you over for Shabbos dinner, and if you like each other, you can take it from there," Jocelyn said. She hoped that they would feel more comfortable with her and her husband to help things along.

It was settled. All Jocelyn had to do was make sure Batsheva would be there as well. She called to invite her on Monday, very early for issuing Shabbos invitations. Batsheva agreed to come, but before hanging up, Jocelyn realized that she had better tell Batsheva more specifically what she had in mind.

"There is one small thing I should mention," Jocelyn said. "I also invited Aaron Fox for dinner. He's a very nice young man, and I thought that maybe you'd like to get to know him better."

"I don't know," Batsheva said. "I know who he is, and I can't see it working."

"Why not?" Jocelyn demanded. "We all think it's a great idea."

"It's just the feeling I get. We don't seem to have anything in common."

"Listen, Batsheva. You barely know him. He is a fine man, and all I'm asking is that you give him a chance. And I've already invited him and told him you'd be coming."

People often said no when Jocelyn asked to set them up. They had just ended a relationship, they needed a break from the dating scene, they had heard bad things about this particular person, or else they were plain shy. It was her job as matchmaker to convince them, even if it meant stretching the truth. She had, on occasion, been forced to call light brown hair blond, to refer to five foot seven as very close to six feet tall, to claim that someone had plans in the very near future to attend medical school. But Jocelyn didn't know what to make of Batsheva's reluctance. Batsheva wasn't shy, she hadn't recently ended a relationship, she wasn't dating someone else, and those were the only reasons Jocelyn could come up with to explain any hesitance. Filled with this uncertainty, Jocelyn reported to the rest of us that Batsheva had agreed, but barely.

"That's ridiculous," Edith Shapiro scoffed. "Batsheva needs to give Aaron a chance. When Kieve first asked me out, I took one look at him and thought that there was no way it would ever work. But we were happy for fifty-three years."

"Date 'em until you can't stand it anymore," Helen Shayowitz said. "That was what my friends advised me. That way you'd never have to worry that you'd let the right one get away." With Alvin, she had been ambivalent. He had seemed nice enough, but she didn't know how she was supposed to be sure. If marriage was forever, as her friends were always reminding her, that was a very long time. But Alvin had been patient. He said it was worth the wait. And after breaking it off several times, Helen had mustered her courage and said yes.

"Maybe she's already dating someone, if you know what I mean," Becky Feldman said.

"No, I don't think that's it," Naomi Eisenberg said. She hated hearing these reasons for Batsheva's lack of interest in Aaron Fox. From the way everyone was talking, it sounded like Batsheva had been reluctant just to spite their good intentions. Naomi was so determined to set the record straight, that in a moment of weakness, she slipped up and revealed what Batsheva had told her.

Naomi had started joining Batsheva on her walks; she knew she could benefit from the exercise as well as the company. They were walking down Poplar Avenue and Naomi had raised the subject of men.

"Has there been anyone since Benjamin?" Naomi had asked. Batsheva was so pretty, so full of life; surely men must have been interested in her wherever she went.

But Batsheva, who was usually so forthcoming, grew silent and looked away.

"You don't have to talk about it if you don't want to," Naomi reassured her. "I was wondering, that's all."

"No, it's okay. I know you didn't mean anything by it."

In a low voice, Batsheva began to tell Naomi how, a year after Benjamin died, she had become close with a man who had been one of Benjamin's good friends. He was married, and he and his wife went to the same shul as Batsheva. At first, Batsheva and this man had shared their grief. He was kind and sympathetic, she said. They would stay up late talking, sometimes all night, and he would listen as she described her memories of Benjamin. She could tell him how hard it was, how alone she felt in the middle of the night when she would wake up surprised to find Benjamin not there beside her. And Ayala had loved him too. He took her to the park and held her on his lap during shul, just as Benjamin had done.

"At first, I just felt lucky that I had this wonderful friend who understood what I was going through. He also missed Benjamin and he would tell me what Benjamin had been like before I met him, and we would laugh at the good memories we had of him."

As she listened to Batsheva, Naomi had started to feel nervous. Even though there was nothing wrong with what Batsheva had said so far, she was starting to get the feeling that there was going to be more to this story.

Batsheva took a deep breath. "But after a few months, it just sort of happened. I never meant for it to be anything more than a friendship, but we had become so close and had shared so much . . ."

Batsheva's voice trailed off, and she gave Naomi a look begging her to understand. As much as Naomi wanted to believe the best of her, there was no way around it: this was definitely an affair Batsheva was describing.

"I never meant for it to end up like that. But I felt like I couldn't stop it from happening. Everything I had with Benjamin was gone and I was all alone. I kept thinking that if I had someone with me, it would make it easier."

"What happened?" Naomi asked.

"Eventually we decided that we had to stop, that the main thing between us was Benjamin and we both needed to let go."

Batsheva looked so sad and confused; Naomi had never seen her this way before.

"Afterwards, I needed to get away," Batsheva said. "There was too much going on, and I thought that by coming here, I wouldn't feel as lonely and I could make a fresh start."

Pulling herself out of these memories, Batsheva shook her head and tried to force a smile onto her face. "Who knows anymore?" she said.

Upon hearing this from Naomi, we were stunned. We had come to expect more from Batsheva. Maybe before she converted she would have done these things. But afterward, she was supposed to be religious, and having an affair with a married man certainly didn't fit our definition of religious. We tried to come up with reasons to explain her behavior. She was lonely, she had been through a terrible tragedy; who's to say what any of us might do in the same situation? But no matter how understanding we tried to be, there would be no way to look at Batsheva and not see this aspect of her.

"I guess that settles it," Mrs. Levy pronounced. "She's not religious after all." As far as Mrs. Levy knew, there was no way to be religious and have had an affair; the two just didn't go together.

"No, I guess not," Helen Shayowitz was forced to agree.

As this news was being disseminated, Mrs. Levy happened to pay a visit to poor Mrs. Ganz. She was so quiet, so old, that sometimes she was forgotten about. But she had been a close friend of Mrs. Levy's dear mother, rest her soul, and this made Mrs. Levy feel an obligation to look after her. Before going over, she baked one of her special hospitality cakes that she always brought with her on these visits like a calling card.

Mrs. Ganz was pleased to see her—for any of us, a personal visit from Mrs. Levy was a special occasion. After the usual chitchat, Mrs. Levy reported the latest gossip about Batsheva in an attempt to make Mrs. Ganz feel part of the community.

"Oh, I heard about something like that," Mrs. Ganz said, trying to remember where it could have been.

"You don't say." Mrs. Levy decided to humor her. It was impossible that Mrs. Ganz would know more about this than she, Mrs. Levy, would.

"Yes, I think it was the other day at the park. Mimi was talking about it," she said, trying to get her memories to snap into clarity. "Maybe it was a TV show she had seen where someone had had an affair and she was telling Batsheva about it."

Mrs. Levy sat up a little straighter. Was it possible Mrs. Ganz had overheard something important and didn't even realize it? If Batsheva and Mimi were talking about affairs, it must be this same one. After Mrs. Levy plied Mrs. Ganz with more cake and hot tea, the old woman slowly told her everything that had been said.

Mimi and Batsheva were sitting on a picnic blanket in Audobon Park on a Sunday morning, and Ayala was feeding the ducks in the pond leftover bits of challah. Mrs. Ganz fed these same ducks every morning, exactly at ten o'clock; she liked knowing that they were counting on her. She hadn't gone over to say hello because she was busy with the ducks, and Batsheva and Mimi were so involved in their conversation that they didn't notice her on the bench in front of them.

"I knew it was wrong," Batsheva had said. "I even decided to go to the mikvah because at least that way I wouldn't be completely cut off from being religious. But knowing it was wrong didn't make it easier to stop. When we were together, it was the only time I didn't feel lonely. But as soon as he'd leave, I'd feel even worse."

"Batsheva, you can't let it eat away at you," Mimi had said. "Everyone makes mistakes and it's important to learn from the past and move on. You should concentrate on how far you've come and not dwell on what you still have to work on."

"I know. But I feel like I should have been able to hold back. When I converted, one of the ideas that moved me most was that there was beauty in restraint, that you can feel more free by setting limits than when everything in the world is wide open to you."

We understood why Batsheva would tell this to Mimi. Whenever Mimi asked how we were doing, we felt as if she could see beyond any surface answer we might give into the most private chambers of our hearts. When Edith Shapiro spoke to Mimi, she didn't feel the need to say that she was getting over the death of her husband. These pleasantries were what she assumed everyone else wanted to hear—no one was interested to know that the pain hadn't subsided, that four years later, she sometimes woke up in the morning and felt a stab of disappointment that she hadn't died in the night. But Mimi let her know that it was okay to talk about the unpleasant, the sad, the truth. Rena Reinhard felt the same way. Besides Batsheva, Mimi was the only one she could really talk to about her problems with her husband. Mimi called her every few days to see how she was, to let Rena know she wasn't alone.

But still, as much as Mimi took us in with our problems, we were surprised that she was so forgiving towards Batsheva. We had always assumed that committing adultery was a line that once crossed, there was no turning back. But Mrs. Ganz went on about how supportive Mimi had been, so unwilling to judge, and we wondered if there was anything that would shock Mimi, any sin too great for her compassion and understanding.

Despite Mimi's willingness to forgive and forget, Tziporah Newburger felt vindicated: there was something inappropriate about Batsheva using the mikvah after all. She had taken a mitzvah and corrupted it by using it for sin. Tziporah had heard about women who had sex outside of the holiness of marriage and tried to justify that sin by using the mikvah. Perversity, if you asked her. Tziporah also knew enough to read between the lines of what Batsheva had said to Naomi and Mimi. Even though Batsheva tried to pretend that her affair had to do with her grief over Benjamin, Tziporah could tell that Batsheva was the type to go after any man, even a married one. And adultery was as bad as you could get. It was the sort of thing that first-rate scandals were made of.

For Leanna Zuckerman, hearing about Batsheva's affair confirmed what she had always sensed about Batsheva. She could tell how lonely Batsheva was, how she seemed so eager to be close to anyone, even the high school girls. Leanna knew what it was like to feel this way. On the surface, she had everything Batsheva didn't: a husband, a large extended family, a community she was a part of. But it didn't make a difference. If this loneliness was inside you, nothing would appease it.

The news of Batsheva's affair hit closest to home for Rena Reinhard. Here she had turned to Batsheva for advice about her marital problems, and it turned out that Batsheva had caused these same problems in someone else's marriage. She thought of this poor wife. Had she known for sure about the affair? Or had she only suspected it, as Rena did? Did she drive herself crazy every time her husband came home a little late? Did she try to pick apart everything he said looking for clues? As much as Batsheva had made her feel better about her own situation, she wouldn't be able to turn to her in the future. Everything Batsheva said would be tainted by her past.

With this aspect of Batsheva fresh in our minds, it was hard to be excited about our plan to set up Batsheva with Aaron Fox. Apparently,

Batsheva had been withholding what she knew we wouldn't want to hear and it started us wondering: What else was she keeping from us? And who knew if Aaron would be interested in her now? He had become quite religious; we couldn't imagine he would want to marry someone who had done such a thing.

Mrs. Levy turned her interest to setting up the other single people that she knew. Part of her God-given mission in life, she believed, was to find a husband for Yocheved Abraham. She considered whether placing a personal ad in the *Jewish Press* on Yocheved's behalf would be overstepping her role. Helen Shayowitz realized that with all she had to do for her daughter's quickly approaching wedding, she had no business thinking about anyone else. So far it had been one crisis after another: the photographer she had her heart set on had another wedding that same day; it was hard to find a mother-of-the-bride dress to match the exact shade of peach of the wedding hall; and the only way to get the perfect wedding cake would be to have it FedExed in from New York.

Only Jocelyn Shanzer was able to put aside her frustration and distrust and do what she needed to do. The only way to create successful matches, she knew, was to act as if the two of them were destined for the marriage chupah. And, she reminded herself, you never knew. She could think of less likely couples than Batsheva and Aaron Fox. If they did end up together, we would be able to overlook Batsheva's recent past with that man. And as long as Aaron didn't find out about the affair we could hope that the purity of marriage would wash it away. Jocelyn began planning the menu for Friday night dinner: her famous mock crawfish for an appetizer (almost the same recipe as her shrimp salad), followed by barbecue chicken, vegetable fritters, and sweet potato pie with a marshmallow fluff topping. A full, satisfied stomach might be enough to convince someone to go out a second time.

WHEN the big night arrived, Aaron walked home from shul with Jeremy Shanzer. In preparation for the evening, Aaron had shaved, gotten a haircut, and dressed in his best suit. He was wearing the black hat he had recently bought, and he looked as if he had spent his whole life in yeshiva. He shifted his weight back and forth in the entry hall, not wanting to enter the living room for fear that Batsheva might be there and he wouldn't know what to say.

"Is she here?" he whispered to Jocelyn.

"Not yet," she said. "Relax, I'm sure everything will be fine."

Aaron sat in the living room with Jocelyn and Jeremy. Each time Aaron heard a noise, he jumped. For the first time, Jocelyn noticed that he was the slightest bit awkward. Maybe Batsheva wouldn't notice, at least not right away.

Twenty minutes later, Batsheva and Ayala knocked on the door and Jocelyn hurried to open it.

"I'm sorry we're late," Batsheva said, but she didn't seem to be in any rush. She wasn't the slightest bit out of breath.

"It's fine. I was just finishing up some last-minute things in the kitchen," Jocelyn said, trying to hide the irritation she felt.

She checked out what Batsheva was wearing and she was disappointed. When our daughters went on dates, they went all out, a fancy outfit, a fully made up face and not a hair out of place. But Batsheva was wearing something we had seen her in hundreds of times—a black sweater dress, a bit clingy, with small silver buttons down the front, an okay outfit (despite the places where the material was pilling), but nothing special.

"Batsheva, this is Aaron. Aaron, Batsheva," Jocelyn said. "Why don't y'all sit next to each other and we can get started."

They sat down, Batsheva and Aaron next to each other as Jocelyn had instructed. Jocelyn had done everything she could to ensure a successful evening. She had lit her Shabbos candles on the table instead of on the buffet, dimmed the lights and placed a dozen long-stemmed red roses in the center of the table. She glanced at her husband sitting across the table. When he smiled at her, she blushed; she was feeling a little romantic herself.

Jocelyn glanced at Batsheva and Aaron. Not a single word had been exchanged. Batsheva was busy helping Ayala settle in and Aaron was looking down at his plate. A warning bell went off in Jocelyn's head: if Batsheva was going to be preoccupied with Ayala, she wouldn't be able to give Aaron a fair chance. To prevent this from happening, she excused herself and came back with the box of toys she had saved from when her children were young. With the toys to keep Ayala occupied, Batsheva could concentrate on Aaron.

"Look at what I have for you, Ayala," Jocelyn said brightly and she unloaded Barbie dolls and stuffed animals onto the carpet.

Without a word to Aaron, Batsheva walked Ayala over to the toys and started to play with her. Aaron glanced her way a few times, hoping she might come back to the table, but Batsheva paid him no attention. Jocelyn thought about the advice she had given her own daughters when they started dating, the same advice she had followed as a teenager: Always make the man feel important. Always act as if what he has to say is the most fascinating thing you've ever heard. Batsheva, though, was going out of her way to do the exact opposite; she wasn't giving Aaron a chance to say anything.

But there was still time to get the evening started on the right foot. Jocelyn politely but forcefully invited Batsheva back to the table and the meal got under way. When everyone was involved in the mock crayfish, Aaron smiled nervously at Batsheva. He cleared his throat a few times, wrung his hands, and finally mustered up the courage to speak. "I hear you're from New York City," he said. "That must be exciting."

"And you're from Blytheville. That also sounds pretty exciting," Batsheva said with a smile.

"I was born there and lived there my whole life. But now I hope I'll be able to make my home in Memphis," he said and gave Batsheva a meaningful look.

Batsheva didn't respond to his glance. She held up her spoonful of pink mock crayfish. "You know, this tastes exactly like real crayfish," she said.

"Thank you. I'll take your word for it, I suppose," Jocelyn said, trying not to think of the contraband shrimp salad hidden in the freezer just a few feet away.

"Keeping kosher was one of the biggest adjustments when I converted. Shabbos came easily to me, but with kosher I had to remind myself all the time. And I had to work harder to make it meaningful. What about you? Was it hard to start keeping kosher?" Batsheva asked Aaron.

He looked down, mortified. He wanted to block out his past and pretend like it had never happened. All those years of breaking the word of God stuck out as his terrible, private shame.

"Aaron, why don't you tell us about your work at the computer store?" Jocelyn asked.

He described his job: he was in charge of keeping track of the accounts. He spent all day poring over columns of numbers. "I love my work," he said. "It's nice making sure everything lines up perfectly."

Batsheva laughed. "I can't imagine doing something like that. I'd go crazy."

As he continued talking about the beauty of accurate accounts, Batsheva hardly paid attention. The neckline of her dress fell into a sharp V and would have plunged far too low if it weren't for a small pink barrette holding the two sides together. Instead of listening, or even looking at Aaron, she played with the barrette, twisting it between two fingers. It finally came loose and fell onto the table.

"One of Ayala's," she said with a smile, as if that explained everything.

Aaron stopped talking and coughed in embarrassment. Batsheva grasped the two sides of her dress together and reattached the barrette.

"Batsheva, why don't you tell Aaron about your teaching?" Jocelyn asked. This evening was turning out to be harder work than she had anticipated. But she hoped Aaron and Batsheva could find some common ground in this conversation. Aaron had been pleased when Jocelyn told him Batsheva was a teacher; he said it sounded like a job that wouldn't interfere with raising children and making a Jewish home.

Batsheva described the creative projects she was doing with the girls, how she was encouraging them to express their feelings through art. And already she could see the difference in them; they were more sure of themselves, more spirited.

"It's wonderful to see this change in them. It's like seeing them come to life," she said.

Aaron narrowed his eyes, trying to figure out if this was a good thing. "What does the school think?" he finally asked. He didn't know much, but he was pretty sure that Orthodoxy didn't encourage free expression and creative inner spirits.

Batsheva smiled at him. "Why? You don't think you can be religious and still be free and creative?"

"No, it's not that exactly," he said and shifted uncomfortably in his seat.

As Jocelyn listened to the two of them, she realized what a terrible idea this setup had been. Batsheva and Aaron had absolutely nothing in common. The roses and the candles that had burned out seemed comical now, a sharp reminder of how excited she had been. After that, the meal only went further downhill. The few pieces of conversation were punctuated with long pauses. Jocelyn tried to make conversation about the nicest Memphis tourist spots that both Aaron and Batsheva, as newcomers to the city, would have to check out, perhaps together. But nothing caught on. In the end, Jocelyn decided that silence was better than an out-and-out fiasco. She rose to serve the chocolate cream pie, hoping that they might attribute the silence to the richness of the dessert.

Aaron left without so much as an "I'll call you" to Batsheva, and Jocelyn began to work on Batsheva. If Batsheva was interested, maybe she would be able to convince Aaron to give it another try.

"So, what do you think?" Jocelyn asked.

"He's nice, but not for me," Batsheva said.

"Why not?" Jocelyn demanded. She couldn't understand why Batsheva was being stubborn; you would almost think she had no interest in remarrying. "You can't stay single forever. What will you do if you don't remarry?"

"I'm not going to force something that isn't there," Batsheva said.

"But what about Ayala? She needs a father, like you need a husband."

"We're doing just fine on our own," Batsheva said as she helped Ayala into her fuzzy red coat and crouched down to button her. It was cold out and she pulled up Ayala's hood and tied it under her chin. Then she thanked Jocelyn for dinner, wished her a good Shabbos, and was gone.

Batsheva's refusal to give poor Aaron a chance started us thinking. We had been sure that it was only a matter of time, that sooner or later Batsheva would become one of us. We had grown to like her, and many of us even considered her a close friend. We tried to hold on to the image of how nice it would be if she remarried and settled down. But every time we tried to smooth away one of Batsheva's sharp edges, a new one appeared. We started wondering if maybe Batsheva wasn't interested in remarrying because she saw no need for something so traditional. Apparently she had no problem carrying on a sexual relationship outside of marriage. Maybe that was what she was looking for again.

Mrs. Levy took Batsheva's lack of interest in Aaron as a sure sign that she didn't want the same things that we did. It was one thing to be unmarried out of a lack of options, but Batsheva was choosing to remain this way on her own. And that could be a very dangerous influence on the high school girls. They might get the impression that someone could be both happy and single. Yocheved Abraham was a perfect example of the inherent unhappiness in being single. As she thought of poor Yocheved, bells and flashing lights went off in her head. She slapped her hand to her forehead: Yocheved Abraham and Aaron Fox. They were perfect for each other, a match made in heaven. It had been right under her eyes all this time, and she had been too busy trying to help Batsheva to see it.

For Edith Shapiro, the failure of the setup gave her more reason to worry about Yosef. She had noticed how comfortable Batsheva and Yosef were together. Maybe Batsheva had her eye on him and that was why she had shown no interest in Aaron Fox. Edith had been so excited about the setup because with Batsheva safely dating Aaron, everyone would be neatly paired up, leaving Yosef to concentrate on his studies and his future. Batsheva still being available made her feel as if the community was on loose footing, a table with one of its legs too short.

To Tziporah Newburger, this seemed like a good time to once again raise the question of why Batsheva was using the mikvah. Perhaps there was a connection. Maybe Batsheva didn't want to be set up because she was secretly having an affair here. And that was why she was still using the mikvah. If she had done this once (or more than once—who knew anymore?), what would stop her from doing it again?

We tried to busy ourselves with other things. We reminded ourselves that we needed to be patient; Batsheva was still taking her time climbing up the ladder to greater observance. And after what we had heard about her, we knew it was no easy climb. But we couldn't stop thinking about her past. We imagined the way she must have flirted, how she had probably tossed back her hair and smiled, how comfortable she probably was opening up to anyone. With these thoughts filling our heads, we doubted that Batsheva could ever be one of us.

To make it worse, this time of year was a dry spell, no holidays to occupy our time. All we had was the routine of our everyday lives. Each day was the same as the one before, loads of laundry to wash and rewash, children to carpool here and there, and meals to prepare. And it had grown cold. The sun was barely visible for days on end, and we spent our time indoors, hurrying from houses to cars to stores. With the trees bare, the grass stiff and brown, Memphis no longer looked beautiful. It was dismal and gray. It could have been any city in the world.

11

ONCE CHANUKAH WAS ONLY A week away, we were busy again, our minds on presents and decorations and parties. But all around us, the city was consumed with Christmas. It wasn't easy to celebrate Chanukah in a city blanketed in red and green. We tried to block this out by imagining ourselves like the Maccabees, the few pious Jews who resisted Hellenism and defeated the many, mighty Greeks. As a reward from God, their one pure carafe of oil burned in the temple menorah for eight days. But there was still something exciting about the Christmas lights, so many shiny colors and designs zigzagging across lawns and houses. We took our children to different neighborhoods to see them, driving slowly, stopping to admire the houses with the most spectacular displays illuminated Santas pulled by reindeer, Styrofoam snowmen covered with white lights, trees that flashed red and green.

This year, though, something caught our attention in our own neighborhood. One Sunday morning, a few days before Chanukah, Batsheva got into her car, put Ayala in the back, and started down the street. First she stopped at Yosef's house. She honked once, but before she took her hand off the horn, he came running out and jumped into the front seat. Then she drove the few blocks to the Feldmans' house and honked, expecting Shira to come running out as well. But there was no sign of Shira, and Batsheva gave a loud insistent beep that Shira would have heard even if she was asleep. There was still no Shira, but Batsheva would not be deterred. She got out of the car, leaving it running, and she jogged up to the door and knocked.

When Becky answered, she wasn't surprised to find Batsheva there. Batsheva and Shira had been spending lots of time together, both in and out of school. Shira said she could really talk to Batsheva, that she didn't bug her about what she was or wasn't doing, and even though Becky was relieved that Shira seemed happier, she took this comment as a direct swipe at her.

"I'm here to pick Shira up. She's helping me with a project I'm working on," Batsheva said.

Becky was about to press Batsheva for more details, but Shira came out of her room. She was wearing an old baggy sweatshirt and long underwear under her jean skirt; that was how all the girls were dressing these days.

"I'm ready," she said to Batsheva, barely looking at her mother.

Batsheva smiled at Becky and said good-bye, leaving Becky with the sense that she was being left behind. Becky remembered how, as a little girl, Shira had loved to spend time with her. Becky longed for the days when the two of them went shopping and cooked dinner and Shira would turn to her with an adoring look on her face.

With everyone in the car, Batsheva drove off. None of us knew where they went, only that an hour later, they were back. The car was piled high with packages, and sticking out the side window were several long planks of wood. They unloaded their purchases and carried them around to Batsheva's backyard. We heard hammers and saws and laughter that continued all day long, but we didn't know what they were up to; we hadn't been told about this project in advance and we hadn't been asked to join them.

The only other person Batsheva had included was Mimi. She dropped by Batsheva's backyard with a bag of cookies and her voice joined in with all the chattering that was going on back there. Maybe we should have been used to that by now; Mimi and Batsheva were together all the time now. We tried not to feel excluded, we reminded ourselves that we were the ones who had known Mimi longer. But still, their friendship weighed on us and we looked for ways to make sense of it.

"Mimi's there. That means it's probably okay for us to go over too," Helen Shayowitz said.

"I wouldn't count on it. Obviously, Batsheva is willing to make an exception and include Mimi in her little plan," Mrs. Levy said.

"But maybe they need some help. We could go over there and offer," Helen said.

"Helen, if Batsheva wanted our help, she would have asked," Mrs. Levy said. "Obviously we're not wanted."

We hated that there was something going on in the community that we weren't a part of. That wasn't how things usually worked, and filled with the sense that we were being deliberately excluded, we had to know what Batsheva was up to. Living directly across from Batsheva usually afforded Mrs. Levy the most reliable information, but now her strategic position was useless; there was no way she could see past Batsheva's house into the backyard. Doreen Sheinberg's backyard bordered Batsheva's on the far right corner, but years before, the Sheinbergs had installed a high fence and now they could see nothing.

The closest we got to an actual peek was from Helen Shayowitz's yard, three houses away. Hoping to be the one who could provide the rest of us with an answer, Helen stood on her tiptoes during the darkest part of the night and peered over several fences. In the middle of Batsheva's yard, a huge object, maybe seven or eight feet tall, was draped with old flowered bedsheets. It was tall and wide, but beyond that, it was unrecognizable. We racked our brains, but we couldn't figure out what this unlikely trio of Batsheva, Yosef, and Shira could be up to.

The next day, Tziporah Newburger bumped into Batsheva outside the school. As soon as Tziporah saw her, she felt irritated. She still didn't understand why Batsheva had to be so different. She had been here long enough to see how things worked; why couldn't she do a better job of blending in? Since that time at the mikvah, Tziporah had treated Batsheva with restrained politeness. She hadn't had a chance to broach for a second time the inappropriateness of Batsheva's using the mikvah, and she was biding her time until an opportunity came along.

Tziporah forced a smile onto her face and went over to Batsheva. "There was so much noise coming from your backyard yesterday that I was starting to worry if everything was all right."

Batsheva gave her a smile. "Everything is fine."

Not to be put off, Tziporah asked again: what was going on out there?

"Don't worry, Tziporah. What I'm doing is perfectly kosher." Batsheva laughed and gave Tziporah a wink.

Tziporah left, feeling even more justified in her distrust of Batsheva. If she had nothing to hide, why was she being elusive? If Leanna Zuckerman or Naomi Eisenberg had asked, Batsheva would have told them. She was always with them, laughing and talking away. Mimi too had been let into this clique. But apparently Tziporah wasn't part of this inner circle. Batsheva really had a lot of nerve, she decided. She had tried to help Batsheva be more scrupulous in her observance of Judaism, and this was how she was repaid. Tziporah only felt better when she remembered that the prophets in the times of the Bible weren't always well liked by their own communities either.

Ayala too could not be coaxed out of secrecy. After school one day, she was wandering the hallways waiting for Batsheva to finish cleaning up the art room, and Becky Feldman passed by and saw her.

"It sounds like something exciting is going on in your backyard," Becky said.

"Yes," Ayala said excitedly.

"You can tell me what it is, sweetheart. I won't tell anyone. My own daughter is helping you, so I'm sure there's no harm in my knowing."

"No. It's a surprise," Ayala insisted and she ran off to find her mother.

Later that day, Mrs. Levy ran into Yosef at the shul as he was coming from learning with his father. "You seem to be keeping yourself busy," she remarked.

Yosef nodded but didn't say anything.

"It looks to me like you have your hands full with Batsheva and whatever she's been up to in her backyard."

"I'm helping her with something, that's all," he mumbled.

Mrs. Levy noted how uncomfortable Yosef seemed. He had probably been roped into participating. But that was the way he was, always willing to help someone out even if he didn't want to. She remembered how he had led the shul youth groups all through high school because none of the other teenagers would do it.

"But you must know what she's up to," she persisted.

"I promised Batsheva I wouldn't say anything," Yosef said.

If he was going to be that way, there was nothing Mrs. Levy could do. But she would get to the bottom of this mystery. Batsheva suddenly seemed to think that she was the one in charge of planning community activities. But she would have to learn that *nothing* went on in Memphis without Mrs. Levy being included, or at least being consulted for advice.

ON the first night of Chanukah, we were setting up our menorahs in the front windows of our homes when we saw Batsheva, Yosef, and Shira pushing something into the front yard of Batsheva's house. Ayala was trailing behind them, holding onto one of the sheets that covered their project. When they reached the middle of the lawn, they stopped. It was cold out and Batsheva didn't have a coat on. She was wearing a green velvet dress that fit her tightly across her chest and then flared out around her legs, barely reaching her knees. Though her hair was blowing every which way in the wind, she didn't seem bothered by it. She was too focused on this surprise to think about anything else. Shira was standing next to Batsheva, also without a coat on. She and Batsheva were talking and laughing, as if they were the same age and old friends. Yosef kept glancing at our houses, hoping we would be too busy with our own lives to notice. Of course that wasn't the case—how could we miss something right in front of our noses?

We assembled at our windows, blinds pulled up, curtains pushed aside, waiting to see what was going to happen. Not content with the view from inside, our children gathered at the edge of her lawn. We didn't have the heart to stop them, and even if we had, we doubted they would listen. We felt a small itching to let everything be all right again between Batsheva and us. We remembered how nice Sukkot had been when we were all gathered in her yard. But we reminded ourselves that this time we hadn't been invited to join and we stayed in our houses.

"Don't be shy," Batsheva called to the kids, who were confused by our reluctance to join them.

They listened to her, as they always did; once again, she had our children gathered around her. She was enjoying the attention and wouldn't unveil her surprise until she was satisfied that she had all our kids close by. Mimi too had shown up and she was standing behind our children, watching the scene unfold. With our children around her and us watching from our windows, Batsheva pulled the sheets off and there was the biggest menorah we had ever seen. It was made of wood painted silver, and on top of each of the eight branches was a lantern waiting to be lit.

We tried to tell ourselves that this menorah wasn't so special. We came up with all the problems it presented: it was ostentatious, showy. Even though we were commanded to publicize the miracle of Chanukah, we were different enough from our non-Jewish neighbors, and we didn't need to stick this in their faces more than it already was. And maybe it set a bad example for Ayala. She would grow up thinking that this was perfectly normal, that everyone built larger-than-life menorahs. We wondered if it was even in accordance with Jewish law. For all we knew, maybe there was some sort of prohibition against such displays.

But even so, we couldn't stop staring at how tall and proud this menorah stood against the darkening blue-gray sky, how pure and simple it was. It brought this miracle from so long ago into our front yards, and we began to wish that we had thought of doing something like this ourselves. Batsheva's menorah made us feel that we no longer had to stare longingly at the Christmas decorations in the rest of the city. We finally had something of our own to look at.

"It's time to light the candles," Batsheva announced to the children around her, and she handed a book of matches to Yosef.

Yosef used the match to light the shamesh candle while Batsheva lifted Ayala onto his shoulders. Stretching up as high as she could, Ayala took hold of the shamesh and lit the first lantern. The three of them began singing the blessings: *Blessed are you God who commanded us to light the Chanukah candles, for doing miracles for our ancestors and for us, for renewing us and sustaining us and bringing us to this time.* Batsheva put her arm around Shira and tried to get her to sing with her. Shira rolled her eyes, but it was in a good-natured, friendly way. However reluctant she was, she too began to sing, having a good time despite herself.

When Batsheva began singing the maoz tzur, our kids joined in. They had been practicing this song in school and they knew it by heart. They swayed back and forth as they sang, copying Batsheva's movements. She was singing her heart out and didn't care if her voice floated down the street, through the neighborhood, clear across town.

We would be singing these same songs in our homes as soon as our husbands came home from work, and we wondered whether our kids would sing with such gusto, if it would still feel like the first night of Chanukah. As much as we tried to convince ourselves that it would, that our own candle lightings were special no matter what Batsheva was doing, we knew that it wouldn't be the same; the uniqueness of seeing just one of the eight candles burning was over for this year.

When Batsheva finished singing, we went back to our own candles. We set them up in the front windows, peeled the colored wax left from last year, put aluminum foil down to protect the wood buffets and tables we placed our menorahs on. Our children set up the handmade menorahs they had made in art class with Batsheva. Each one was different. There were menorahs made out of clay, old pieces of scrap metal and soda cans, painted in bright colors, with beads and pieces of ceramic tile glued onto them.

Later that evening, when we looked out our windows, these handmade menorahs were the ones we spotted first. They stood out against the other menorahs, as if they had been lit with stronger candles, drawing a brighter light from the menorah in Batsheva's yard. We continued our Chanukah celebrations, we grated potatoes for latkes, fried them until they were golden brown, we distributed gifts to our children. But we couldn't overlook Batsheva's presence, because here she was in every window, mixed in among every one of us.

12

WHO KNOWS THE WAYS OF God, who is to say why things follow one from another? But all we knew was that after Chanukah, things in our community began to go awry.

Every January, the high school girls went on a school trip, an attempt to prevent the winter blues from sinking in. Last year, the girls went to St. Louis, the year before to New Orleans, and the year before that, all the way to Chicago. This year they were going to Gatlinburg, Tennessee, a town in the Smoky Mountains. They spent much of the year raising money for the trip; all those pizza sales and mother-daughter luncheons went to pay for these five days.

In previous years, different teachers had gone with them, but as arrangements were being made, it became clear that no one wanted to go. The principal's wife was pregnant and didn't want to take any chances. Yocheved Abraham decided she wasn't up to it. She made excuses—she hadn't been feeling well, she had developed a tendency to car sickness—but the truth was, she was starting to suspect that the girls were tired of her, and she certainly wasn't going to go where she wasn't wanted. And Rachel Ann Berkowitz, Ruth Berner and Arlene Salzman had ready excuses for not going: they had husbands and children to take care of, carpools to drive, Ladies Auxiliary events to plan.

As we were wondering what we were going to do, Mimi suggested that Batsheva go with the girls. "She would be so much fun and the girls would be thrilled," Mimi said as she began talking up the idea.

Tziporah Newburger couldn't believe that Mimi didn't have reservations about sending a group of impressionable teenagers off with Batsheva. Like Tziporah, Mimi was supposed to be religious, really and truly frum. Surely she would understand the problem of bad influence, of exposing the girls to foreign ideas and inappropriate behavior. Tziporah called Mimi one evening and laid out her concerns: Batsheva didn't seem to be a proper role model, and it was unclear whether her judgment could be trusted.

"I understand what you're saying," Mimi said. "And I realize that Batsheva may not be the kind of person you're used to, but I've seen how much she cares about the girls and I think she's having a wonderful influence on them."

Mimi spoke in such a soothing way. She only saw the best in people—she trusted their intentions even if they weren't always backed up with actions; she recognized the good that could arise from any situation. Everything she said was gentle and sweet, and yet, at the end, it left Tziporah feeling frustrated.

"But what about all the inappropriate things she's done? How can we know that she isn't doing those same things here?" Tziporah protested.

"Tziporah, I know you believe in the power to transform oneself through teshuvah. Think about the message of Rosh Hashanah and Yom Kipper—God gives us a clean slate and we're supposed to do this for one another as well."

"Of course, of course," Tziporah was forced to say. She couldn't very well argue with what Mimi had said, even though it had made her feel no better about Batsheva. As Tziporah hung up, she was left with the same feeling that she had had after she was unable to convince Batsheva that it was inappropriate to use the mikvah: she knew, in no uncertain terms, what was right and what was wrong, but somehow she wasn't able to get her message across.

"I don't know what's gotten into Mimi, but I still wouldn't let my daughter go off with Batsheva," Tziporah Newburger warned later that day and clutched her two-year-old daughter closer to her.

"Maybe you should go with them," Mrs. Levy suggested. "You're a lovely role model for the girls. It would do them a world of good to spend some quality time with you."

Tziporah laughed. "Are you kidding? I have four children. I'm not going anywhere."

All along Leanna Zuckerman had been thinking that Batsheva would be a great chaperone for the trip. Even though she didn't yet have a daughter in the high school, she was sure that Batsheva would provide a much-needed break for the girls. She could see how tired they were of being told what to do. Batsheva would no doubt let them have a good time, certainly a better time than Yocheved Abraham would ever allow. Even if that meant a few rules were broken, it was worth it. But after hearing from everyone about Batsheva's potential to be a bad influence, she felt alone in her opinion. When she remembered, though, that Mimi was the one who suggested that Batsheva go with the girls, she decided to give her a call.

"I wanted to know that I'm not the only one who feels this way," Leanna explained to Mimi. "Sometimes I feel like I must be missing something that everyone else is seeing, and maybe I shouldn't trust my own judgment."

"Of course you should trust yourself," Mimi assured her. "And I agree with you completely. Batsheva is just what the girls need. Sometimes I worry that the girls aren't getting a positive enough sense of what it means to be religious. It's so hard at that age to accept any kind of authority, and I hope Batsheva can help them see the beauty in it."

"I'm so glad to hear that," Leanna said. It was so nice to know that even though she might be in the minority, she was in good company.

Her confidence bolstered by her conversation with Mimi, Leanna began letting the rest of us know what she thought. "I'm sure she'll do a wonderful job," she said. "She's just what the girls need."

Naomi Eisenberg agreed with her. "The girls love her," she said. "I've never seen them this excited about one of their teachers." Every time Naomi looked at her sixteen-year-old daughter, Kayla, she felt more certain that Batsheva was a good influence. Normally, Kayla was painfully shy. Even with the classmates she had known her whole life, she found it hard to speak up. But in the past few months, she had started to emerge from her shell.

Given the support for Batsheva that Mimi had drummed up, we begrudgingly asked Batsheva if she would accompany the girls. Batsheva said yes right away. It would be fun, she said, as if she were in high school all over again. She had no idea about the rumblings of tension we had started to feel toward her these past few weeks, and she took the invitation to accompany the girls as another sign that she was fitting in. She wanted Ayala to come as well; she said it would be nice for Ayala to feel like she had a family of sisters.

Still nervous about sending Batsheva off with our daughters for five days, we made sure to establish some ground rules. The girls were supposed to have a curfew; there was to be no running wild. They had to wear skirts and dress modestly. And Batsheva needed to keep an eye on them at all times. We were trusting her with our daughters and we expected her and them to behave responsibly.

The morning of the trip, we dropped our girls off at the school. There was so much energy in that parking lot, their bright-colored coats and overnight bags bringing to life the overcast skies. To our surprise, Batsheva had arrived on time. The girls were already crowding around her, even though they would be spending the week together. And they were picking up Ayala and fussing over her, saying how cute she was, that she could sit on their laps the whole way there. They loaded their things onto the bus and quickly kissed us good-bye. As the bus pulled away, we stayed behind and waved to our girls until they were out of sight.

All week, we wondered how they were doing. Ariella Sussberg called to say they had arrived safely, and Nechama Sheinberg called in the middle of the week for a few minutes, but that was it. The only thing for us to do was hope the trip was serving its purpose and would return the girls energized and cheerful.

When the girls came home, all they could talk about was how it was the best trip ever, not because of the tobogganing or the Dollywood amusement park, but because of Batsheva. She had them wake up early so they could daven together in her hotel room, instead of flying through the morning prayers alone, or worse, not saying them at all. And she was full of boundless energy. She was the first one awake every morning, the last to go to sleep at night, and during all the hours in between, she was encouraging them to hike up to the next waterfall, to take the ski lift to the top of the mountain. They had become closer with Ayala too, all of them eager to take care of her. And when she went to sleep at night, they had stayed up late talking with Batsheva about religion and marriage and what they wanted to do after high school.

"How did you know he was the one?" Ilana Salzman asked, eager to hear details of her marriage to Benjamin. "Weren't you worried you'd meet someone better?"

Batsheva laughed. "You'll see. You can't imagine being with anyone else. With Benjamin, I had everything I wanted. With all the others, I could always tell right away why it wouldn't work out. Sometimes I would continue the relationship, but it always ended for the reason I had seen in the beginning."

"Why did you keep going out with them?" Hadassah Berner asked. She had grown up with the idea that dating was only for the practical purposes of marriage; there was supposed to be no point in viewing it as a recreational activity.

"I don't know. I suppose I learned something from all my boyfriends. And I learned things about myself that I would never have known otherwise," Batsheva said.

Hearing these details of the trip, we were relieved. Perhaps Batsheva was coming along after all. It was always good for the girls to hear positive things about marriage, especially from someone like Batsheva. And it was nice that they had looked after Ayala; baby-sitting was certainly valuable, and we felt gratified that our daughters were taking part in making Ayala feel at home. All these things seemed to have made a difference, because after the trip, there were fewer complaints about the drudgery of school, less rolling of eyes when we asked how classes were. We had entrusted our girls to Batsheva and she had returned them invigorated.

Or so we thought, until we saw the pictures. We couldn't imagine that we shouldn't look at them; the pictures were from a school trip and we wanted to see what fun our girls had had. It wasn't like reading their mail or their diaries, which none of us (except for Becky Feldman) had ever done. At first, the pictures were as we had expected: the girls in front of the Great Smoky Mountains, hiking the many trails, next to the waterfalls. And pictures of them in town, in front of the candy store, the long strands of saltwater taffy in the front window. And on the ski lift, coasting down the mountainside on yellow toboggans, their skirts tucked underneath them.

But after taking a closer look though, we began to worry. We couldn't pinpoint what exactly was wrong, but we all agreed: the girls just looked like they were having too much fun. They had never enjoyed themselves this much on previous trips, so it was impossible to believe that no rules had been broken. We tried to draw clues from the pictures. But the only evidence we could come up with was that in one picture, the girls' faces were covered in makeup, their hair in shocking arrangements, their skirts rolled up so that they landed somewhere in the middle of their thighs. If they were dressed like that, there must have been a reason.

When we interrogated our daughters, they insisted that the trip had been exactly as they had said. It was the lighting, they claimed, they were barely wearing any makeup. And their skirts only looked short because the wind must have blown them up as the pictures were snapped. Nothing was revealed until one night Hadassah Berner broke down and told her mother the truth about the pictures.

For most of the trip, Hadassah had felt left out. The girls were talking about boys and movies and rock groups, and she didn't know much about these topics. She could never keep straight which singer went with which group, she could never remember the lyrics to songs that all sounded the same to her. Her discomfort reached its height on the last night of the trip. The girls had been experimenting with wild hairstyles and heavy makeup. Hadassah too had tried a little red lipstick and black eyeliner, but had never planned on going out in public like that. But the other girls decided to go out wearing the makeup they had applied and Batsheva hadn't objected. She said that it wasn't up to her to tell them what to wear; they were adult enough to make those decisions for themselves. And that had freed them to put on their tightest blouses and to roll up their skirts so they looked even shorter.

Hadassah didn't want to go along with them, so she had volunteered to stay behind and baby-sit for Ayala. Batsheva had tried to convince her to come; she said she didn't mind bringing Ayala along even though it was late. But Hadassah had insisted and she had watched with resentment as the other girls went out in their wild getups. They came home talking and laughing about how fun it had been, the stares and catcalls they had attracted. And Batsheva had laughed along with them; she had treated the whole thing as a joke.

Once Hadassah was relieving the guilt that had plagued her for the previous few days, she decided to tell her mother everything. Yes, Batsheva had talked to the girls about marriage, but from there the conversation came round to sex. It was late at night and Batsheva had changed into her pajamas, a sleeveless white night shirt, not expecting the girls to come back to her room. The girls had been discussing topics they shouldn't have even been thinking about, comparing their experiences with boys, trying to imagine the things they had not yet done. They decided to see if Batsheva was still awake, and she had gladly welcomed them in; she said she had been lonely since Ayala had fallen asleep. The girls gathered around her on the bed, whispering so they wouldn't wake up Ayala.

"We wanted to ask you something," Shira Feldman had said. She paused and looked at the other girls, hoping she wasn't crossing a line by asking what they had been wondering about.

"You can ask me anything," Batsheva said.

"We were talking about, you know," Ilana Salzman said nervously.

When Batsheva saw how they were blushing, she smiled. "Let me guess. You want to ask me about sex."

The girls looked at each other sheepishly. No one said a word. They weren't used to talking about these things with a teacher, even if that teacher was Batsheva. Such topics were officially discussed once a year. This year, Yocheved Abraham had been the one to give the girls a class on being shomer negiah. She explained the laws forbidding physical contact—no hand-holding, no kissing, no touching at all—until marriage. She would point out how serious these laws were, in her opinion, the most important in the whole Torah. Then she would give them other reasons for the laws: you never knew what those boys were thinking, they were using you to fulfill their bodily urges, and it was best to have nothing to do with that. When she finished, she asked for questions. To her relief, there never were any and she took this as a sign that she had presented the issue perfectly, with no ambiguities.

"It's okay that you're talking about these things. I'd be worried if you weren't at least curious," Batsheva said.

"Some of us are shomer negiah, but not by choice. We're not

around the guys so it's not like we have that much opportunity," Ariella Sussberg said. She was embarrassed that at the age of seventeen, she had never kissed a boy. If someone from public school knew that, she assumed they would think there was something wrong with her.

"That's not true," Ilana said. "If you really want to, you can." Everyone knew what Ilana was talking about. She had been caught, on more than one occasion, with Nathan Reese. "I don't see what the big deal is. It's not like we're having sex."

The girls turned to Shira. She had more experience than any of them. There were always rumors of Shira hanging out with kids from public school, maybe even dating some of them, but Shira had sworn them to secrecy.

"Don't look at me," Shira said. "At least I'm not a hypocrite."

"So what about you?" Ilana said to Batsheva. "Before you were religious." The lights were dim in the room, making them feel as if their curiosity was hidden and it was safe to ask what they wanted to know.

"I know you girls are probably thinking that it's a different world out there. Well, it is." Batsheva paused before she said anything else. "I guess it's okay for me to talk to you about this, right?" she asked hesitantly. "I don't want to upset anyone."

"We're not as sheltered as everyone thinks. You think we don't talk about it or see movies?" Shira said.

"You're right," Batsheva said, "and I want to treat you like adults."

"How old were you when you first did it?" Ilana asked.

"I was fourteen, which was young even in my school. I was wild and willing to try anything."

"Fourteen," Hadassah gasped. "I barely even knew about sex when I was fourteen."

"It was different," Batsheva said. "I didn't grow up in such a strict household, and I didn't feel any sense of expectation about what I should be doing."

"Do you regret it now?" Ilana asked.

"No, not really," Batsheva said. "I try not to think about it like that. At the time, it was what was right for me. I was doing what I felt like doing. When you feel something so strongly, it's hard to stop yourself from doing it."

The girls tried to imagine letting their emotions and desires lead the way. Every part of their lives was influenced by some restriction, and trying to imagine this absence of rules was like trying to picture themselves as someone else.

"Come on," Batsheva said gently. "It's time to go to sleep. We'll talk more in the morning." She walked them to the door and kissed each of them on the cheek before sending them off to bed.

If they talked about anything else, Hadassah wouldn't say. She had already revealed more than enough to her mother, and though she was still angry at her friends, she was worried that she would get into trouble with them.

When she had said good night to Hadassah, Ruth called Becky Feldman. If anyone would understand how upset she was, Becky would. "Have you heard anything else about the trip?" Ruth asked, trying to keep her voice calm.

"Why? Did something happen? Is there something you're not telling me?" Becky asked. She began to imagine the worst—perhaps Batsheva had a male friend meet them in Gatlinburg; perhaps they had shared a room.

"I'm not sure. Hadassah told me about a conversation the girls had with Batsheva. We shouldn't jump to any conclusions but it doesn't sound good."

Ruth filled her in on what Hadassah had said, not leaving out any details, even though she had promised Hadassah she wouldn't say anything. She felt a twinge of guilt at breaking her word, but it was for Hadassah's own good. She still saw Hadassah as a little girl, and she hated the idea that Batsheva was treating her as an adult. That would come soon enough. She would do whatever she could to keep her daughter innocent for a little longer.

"You let one thing slip by and before you know it, everything comes undone," Becky said, furious at herself for letting Shira go on the trip with Batsheva as the chaperone. Shira didn't need anything pushing her over the edge; she was dangling close enough as it was. And from the way Ruth had described the events of the trip, it certainly sounded like Shira had once again been a ringleader. When Becky thought Shira had been improving, she had been less strict with her. But now Becky resolved to clamp down. She would tighten Shira's curfew, impose tougher rules about when she was allowed to use the telephone and watch television. She would do whatever she could to prevent any future rebellion.

Fuming with anger, Becky hung up with Ruth and called Tziporah Newburger. "You'll never believe what's been going on behind our backs."

"Let me guess," Tziporah said. "This has to do with Batsheva."

"Who else?" Ruth asked. "I heard that Batsheva has been teaching the girls about sex."

"What!" Tziporah exclaimed. While she was certainly no fan of Batsheva, she had a hard time believing that even Batsheva would be so irresponsible. More than anything, Tziporah believed in modesty, privacy, decorum. The idea of sex being discussed so casually went against every value she cared about. This was how Tziporah had been raised. When she got her period for the first time, her mother tapped her on the face to ward off the evil eye, gave her a box of sanitary napkins, and told her that the beauty of becoming a woman was that it happened in private. And only right before she got married had her mother sat her down and asked if she had any questions.

"It's the truth. I heard it straight from Ruth Berner, who heard it from Hadassah," Becky said.

After hanging up with Becky, Tziporah called Mrs. Levy, who had the experience and wisdom to know what to do.

"We need to talk," Tziporah said, and Mrs. Levy realized that this was no ordinary phone call. "I've been hearing some upsetting news and I was hoping you'd know what to do."

"Of course, dear. Go ahead." She settled into her overstuffed sofa, prepared to listen for as long as Tziporah needed.

Tziporah took a deep breath. "I heard that Batsheva told the girls all about sex. She described to them in great detail her past experiences, and, if you can believe this, she encouraged them to have sex before they were married. She said it would make them feel freer."

No, Mrs. Levy agreed, that certainly didn't sound like a good thing. But now it was out in the open: the problem of Batsheva teaching at the school, the inappropriateness of what had happened on the trip. Mrs. Levy assured Tziporah that something would be done, and she began the task of spreading the news.

AFTER the events of the trip, what happened a week later should hardly have been a surprise. Tziporah Newburger was at her allergist's office, right next door to McDonald's, and she was walking through the parking lot and happened to glance inside, curious to see what it looked like—she had never, in her whole life, been inside a McDonald's. The last thing she expected to see was Shira Feldman sitting by the window eating a cheeseburger.

Tziporah froze. She tried to convince herself that it was just someone who looked like Shira. And even if it was Shira, maybe she was just having a soda—still a sin, but not a major one. Tziporah took her glasses out of her purse and put them on for a second look. This time there was no denying that it was definitely Shira and it was definitely a cheeseburger. That it was McDonald's made it worse. Big Macs seemed more nonkosher than any other food, singled out by God as the one thing above all else that we were not supposed to eat.

Once Tziporah had gotten over her initial shock, she noticed that Shira wasn't alone: there was a young man across the table from her. She took a closer look at him. He was no one we knew. He was a few years older than Shira, and he had sandy blond hair and green eyes. Even Tziporah had to admit that he was good-looking, in a non-Jewish sort of way. But he was certainly not religious, probably not even Jewish. She had no idea who he could be.

Tziporah decided to bang on the window and wave so that Shira would know she had been caught. She imagined Shira stopping midbite, the onions, cheese, and special sauce (whatever that was) spilling onto the table. But as her hand was inches from the glass, Shira stared directly at her and gave a little wave. Tziporah drew back in horror at Shira's brazenness. Then Shira leaned closer to this boy, put her arm around him, and kissed him on the lips. This was too much. Tziporah had never seen such chutzpah in her whole life. She withdrew her hand and lowered her head as she passed by.

Safely home, Tziporah wasn't sure how to proceed. Doing nothing would condone Shira's behavior, and she was sure that, in the eyes of God, that would be as bad as eating the cheeseburger herself. She tried to imagine that it was her daughter who had crossed such a line, making a break with her people and her past. She would have to tell Becky; there was no way around it.

She called Becky and instead of gradually mentioning the reason for her call, Tziporah brought it up right away. "Hello, Becky? Are you sitting down?" Then she jumped right in with the bad news. "I thought you'd want to know that I happened to pass by McDonald's today and I saw Shira in there eating a cheeseburger."

On the other end of the phone, Becky was silent. Every day she thought that things had bottomed out, and every day she discovered that it could always get worse. It was as if her daughter was drowning and she was trying to hold on to her with her bare hands. But this was the final straw. She wrapped the phone cord around her fingers, tightening her grip on the receiver. Things were going to change, she vowed; this would be the last time she'd get a call letting her know about one of her daughter's infractions.

"Thank you for telling me," Becky said and was about to hang up the phone.

"Wait, there's one more thing. She was with someone, a boy, and I didn't know who he was. He was no one I've seen before, but they seemed very . . . close." Tziporah couldn't bring herself to say that she had seen Shira kiss that boy. She hoped Becky would be able to read between the lines and understand what had gone on.

Becky quickly thanked Tziporah and hung up. At first she considered waiting for her husband to come home so they could deal with this together. There might be strength in numbers. But she knew he would go easy on Shira. Even with something as big as this, he would take Shira's side. Becky would deal with it on her own and not even tell her husband. He was always at work and he had no right to come home late at night and act like he was still in charge.

Becky went upstairs to Shira's bedroom and walked in without knocking. Shira was lying on her bed, the radio turned up loud. Becky shut it off and Shira looked up.

"What do you want?" Shira asked.

Becky braced herself against the doorway. "I just got off the phone with Tziporah Newburger, who saw you enjoying lunch at McDonald's today," she said.

"So what?" Shira asked.

"So what?" Becky repeated.

"Yeah, so what if that spying busybody bitch says she saw me somewhere?"

Becky's face grew red. "Don't you ever talk that way to me again. I won't stand for it. Tell me right now who you were with. Tziporah said she saw you there with some boy."

"I don't have to tell you anything."

"Tell me who you were with or you're going to be sorry."

Shira didn't say a word. She just stared at her mother.

"You listen to me, young lady. As long as you are living in this house, you are going to follow our rules and be religious in the way we tell you to be."

Shira jumped up, her cheeks burning red, the same shade as her mother's. "Fine. If that's what you want. I'll pretend to be religious. I'll go along with it but you can't control what I think. I don't believe in any of it. I don't even believe in God."

"You're just saying that," Becky said. "You're doing this to hurt me."

"You can think whatever you want, but I see through everything here. It's all fake. It doesn't mean anything to any of you. All you and your friends care about is what people think."

What was Shira talking about? How dare her daughter speak to her like that. Before she could stop herself, Becky slapped her daughter across the face and ran from the room.

A few weeks later Hadassah Berner and Ilana Salzman were, believe it or not, caught smoking marijuana. It seemed impossible that this could be happening, and we would never have given it any credence had there not been an eyewitness.

"Seeing anyone was the last thing I expected," Yocheved Abraham reported. "It was cold outside and I was only there because I needed some fresh air. I smelled a strange burning, and I was worried that, God forbid, the school was on fire. I went in the direction of the smell and I saw Hadassah and Ilana. I ran over to them and asked them what was going on. They insisted that nothing was, but I wasn't going to be fooled so easily. They had their hands behind their backs and I ordered them to show me what they were holding. At first I thought it was cigarettes, which would have been bad enough. But then I saw that Ilana was hiding a small plastic bag full of something that looked like I don't know what."

Yocheved was stunned. When she was in the high school, this never would have happened. The most serious offense was an occasional missed class, usually when Loehmann's was having a sale. She and her friends heard about the problems at public schools, but they didn't know anyone there. In fact, Yocheved couldn't remember ever talking to a non-Jew the whole time she was in high school, except of course to salespeople and grocery checkers. How the girls had gotten their hands on marijuana was beyond her. Even if she had wanted to try drugs, she wouldn't have known where to find them.

Yocheved marched the two girls into the office, gripping their arms in case they tried to escape. She tried to think of an appropriate lecture but nothing came to mind. This wasn't a situation she was prepared for, and she hoped her silence would sufficiently convey the seriousness of their offense.

The office was in its usual hustle and bustle: sick children waiting for mothers to pick them up, teachers complaining about photocopying not completed in time for classes, two maintenance workers fixing the heat which broke every winter. Doreen Sheinberg, the school secretary, was at her desk presiding over the activity. Despite the presence of a principal and two assistant principals, everyone turned to Doreen to get things done. Last year, after a fight with Rabbi Fishman, the principal, she had quit and stayed away for a full month. No one knew where anything was, students roamed the halls, even the teachers came and went as they pleased. When the school was threatening to crumble under the weight of so much disorder, Rabbi Fishman had gone to her house and begged her to return. Doreen had never felt so needed, so important as that first day back. Finally, everyone in Memphis would know where the real power lay.

"I need to see Rabbi Fishman," Yocheved announced in a voice that towered above the other noise in the office, and everyone, even the maintenance workers, looked up.

"I'm sorry but he's booked for the next few hours," Doreen said. "He's with the Ladies Auxiliary executive committee right now, and after that he's supposed to handle a dispute between the two nursery school teachers." She scanned his calendar. "Can you come back tomorrow?"

"This is an emergency. If you don't tell him that I need to see him, I'm going to have to march in there myself."

Normally Doreen didn't tolerate *anyone* telling her what to do, particularly in that tone of voice, but she had a soft spot for Yocheved, not to mention the fact that she was distantly related to her, on both her father's and mother's side of the family.

"Sit down and I'll see what I can do," she said.

Hadassah and Ilana hadn't said a word and Doreen was starting to get the feeling that they were in big trouble. She stuck her head into the principal's office and mouthed that there seemed to be a problem. As soon as Yocheved told Rabbi Fishman what she witnessed, he had a fit. In between yelling at Ilana and Hadassah that they were a disgrace to the school and the community, he called their mothers and asked them to please come get their daughters.

"I assumed that Ilana was sick," Arlene Salzman said about her initial reaction. "Now that I think of it, I suppose it was unusual that Rabbi Fishman would call. But I couldn't think of any other reason. Ilana is a good girl."

Ruth Berner was home organizing the publicity for the school's Annual Goods and Services Auction, and when Rabbi Fishman called, she assumed there was a mistake. Maybe he was confusing Hadassah with Shira Feldman, who was always in trouble. She put down the flyer she was designing and headed over to the school to straighten things out.

Arlene and Ruth ran into each other on the way in, and at first they didn't make the connection that they were there for the same reason. The two of them went into the office and asked to see the principal.

"He's waiting for y'all. I had to cancel three of his meetings for this," Doreen said and gave them her most serious look, hoping to prepare them for the gravity of what lay ahead.

The principal suspended both girls for two days and gave them a warning: this kind of thing was never to happen again; what kind of message did this send if girls from our school were caught with marijuana? We were known in Jewish communities across the country for being special and we were proud of this, especially when we heard about yeshiva high schools in New York where the kids were so wild it was almost impossible, we were told, to tell the difference between them and public school kids.

In case that wasn't enough, the principal said that if there were any such problems again, he would call the police. Ruth and Arlene shuddered. The idea of their sweet girls involved in anything that would concern the police was shocking. Hadassah's and Ilana's futures could be ruined; who would marry girls with criminal records?

As Ruth Berner walked home with Hadassah, she couldn't believe this was happening. Hadassah looked so sweet and wholesome, hardly the kind of teenager to be involved with something as outrageous as drugs. Every night, she had tucked Hadassah into bed and asked her how her day was, what was on her mind, if things were okay at school. And she had always answered that things were fine, everything was fine.

Fed up with Hadassah trying to act like everything was normal, Ruth stopped suddenly. She turned to face her daughter and put her hands on her shoulders.

"Hadassah, what were you thinking?" she asked.

Hadassah started to cry. "I don't know. Ilana kept talking about how she wanted to try it and I was so sick of always being a goody-goody so I gave in."

Hadassah told her how the girls had been angry at her for telling her mother too many details about the trip. She had felt more left out than ever, and trying the marijuana had seemed like the only way to show that she could be as cool as the other girls. Hearing this, Ruth's anger mixed with guilt. She pulled Hadassah to her and hugged her.

Arlene Salzman didn't participate in the conversations swirling about. She didn't answer the phone, which was ringing off the hook. She called her husband to tell him what had happened and he came home from work early. They sat together on the living room couch and held each other. Everything they had assumed about their daughter was called into question. They could no longer read the paper with the same detached sympathy. Any article talking about the alarming rate of drug use, the overdoses, and anything-goes culture was now about Ilana. They had joined a larger segment of society that they had always considered themselves immune to, and its problems were now theirs.

In shul that Shabbos, it was all we could talk about. Nothing this outrageous had ever happened in our community, and it left us feeling like we didn't know ourselves anymore. We tried to treat Hadassah and Ilana the same as we always did. But our eyes rested on them for too long as we searched their faces for clues to explain what had possessed them. Hadassah returned our probing looks with a blank one. Ilana had a hardened expression on her face; when Mrs. Levy wished her a good Shabbos and tried to pat her arm, she cringed and pulled away.

"Did you see that?" Mrs. Levy said to those around her. "I've known Ilana her whole life and here you would think I was a perfect stranger."

Batsheva was the only one the girls were talking to. Mrs. Levy watched with exasperation as Shira, Ilana, Hadassah, and a few of the other girls gathered around Batsheva. Batsheva even had her arm on Shira's shoulder, something Shira never would have let us get away with.

"We were just seeing what it was like," Ilana said. "It's not such a big deal."

"I don't know about that," Batsheva said. "I think it's a pretty big deal. And I'd be willing to bet that you do too."

Ilana looked away and Hadassah blushed.

"Come on, Hadassah. You're not going to pretend like smoking marijuana is a run-of-the-mill activity for you," Batsheva said.

"No," Hadassah admitted.

"Trust me, you don't want to get involved with marijuana. But maybe it was good that you tried it, because it opens up a great opportunity to deal with this issue."

We had no idea what Batsheva hoped to accomplish by talking about the marijuana use so openly. If anything, the girls should talk to us, their parents and elders, about it, but if they wouldn't, there was no reason why Batsheva had to put herself at the center of it. They were still our daughters, no matter who Batsheva thought she was.

Not taking any chances, Doreen Sheinberg forbade Nechama from hanging out with Shira and Ilana and Hadassah. That way her daughter wouldn't be adversely affected. Inspired by this decision, Rachel Ann Berkowitz decided to impose a stricter curfew on Aviva. She had always assumed she could trust her daughter, but now she wasn't sure. No doubt influenced by Batsheva, Naomi Eisenberg went so far as to suggest having a drug counselor come speak to the girls. But that was just like Naomi: take a bad situation and make it worse by letting everyone know that a problem existed in our school. It was so much better, the rest of us knew, to keep the marijuana incident under wraps and salvage what we could of the school's reputation.

The one question that kept coming into our minds was why, what had caused this latest round of rebellion? Every time we turned around something else happened. The walls of our community had sprung a leak and we were frantically trying to plug the holes with our fingers. Who knows who thought it first, whose wondering to herself became a wondering out loud, a softly whispered rumor, a passing idea. But all we could think was that Batsheva had brought something new into our community and she was leading our children astray. These incidents added up, becoming a sharp reminder that Batsheva was, after all, not one of us. The seeds of suspicion which had been swirling through our minds took root, and we watched her with newly opened eyes.

13

ONCE WE STARTED LOOKING for additional reasons to be suspicious of Batsheva, we found them everywhere. It was as if she had pulled a curtain of invisibility over her transgressions, blinding us to what she was exposing our children to, and only now that we had pulled aside this veil could we see what was really going on.

We sorted through our memories. Helen Shayowitz recalled that at the Donor Luncheon a few weeks back, she had been sitting next to Batsheva, and everyone had been discussing the terrible story that had been in the news about sexual abuse at a daycare center downtown.

"We, thank the Good Lord, don't have to worry about such things, being religious and all," Helen had sighed with relief.

"I don't know about that," Batsheva had said. "When I lived in New York, I heard about a teacher in a yeshiva abusing his students. Everyone tried to pretend like it wasn't true, but in the end, he admitted it."

"No," Helen had said. "I can't believe that."

After that somber turn to the conversation, it had been difficult to enjoy the luncheon; not even Bessie Kimmel's pecan pie could lighten the mood. As irritated as Helen had been then by Batsheva's comment, she now looked at it with more suspicion.

"I think it was her way of telling us that she can do whatever she wants and there's nothing we can do about it," she explained.

What upset Mrs. Levy about Batsheva's comment was the sheer bluntness of it. Maybe they talked that way in the North, but not down here. We preferred a softer approach. Even if there were problems in our community, we understood the need to emphasize the positive.

Seeing how eager Mrs. Levy was to discuss Batsheva, Helen decided to reveal what she had overheard the week before when she was at the boys' high school. Helen had peeked in at the boys eating lunch, at their baggy pants, unruly hair, and unshaved faces. She would never get used to the fact that these were yeshiva boys; they certainly didn't look the part.

"I think Batsheva likes me," Avi Dresner was saying.

"Yeah right," the other boys laughed.

"Really. I saw her giving me the look the other day when I was walking by her classroom, like she was very happy to see me."

It made sense that the boys looked at Batsheva in this way—they were at that difficult age, and someone like Batsheva would no doubt pique their interest. She was pretty and she had made it perfectly clear that she had had quite a past. No wonder the boys had gotten ideas. Whether she had really given anyone a look or not, Batsheva was clearly a disruptive influence on the boys as well. Thank God we had had the foresight to have her only teach the girls. Who knows what we would be dealing with now had the boys been in contact with her every day.

As long as we were on the subject of Batsheva, Becky Feldman mentioned what she had overheard. She hadn't realized that her daughter, Shira, was on the phone with Ilana Salzman, and she happened to pick up the kitchen extension and heard them talking about the marijuana incident. Ilana was saying that she had taken Batsheva up on her offer to talk about the marijuana, and Batsheva had told her that she too had experimented with it when she was in high school and college. Becky wasn't surprised that Batsheva had been involved with drugs, but she couldn't believe she would tell the girls about it. How could we teach our girls one thing when Batsheva was an example of behaving in the opposite way?

The time had come, Becky decided, to find out all that she could about Batsheva's past. That was the only way to predict what the girls might try next. And she did, after all, have that friend from college,

Sarah Klein, who lived in the neighborhood of the Carlebach Shul in New York, where Batsheva had gone. Maybe she had known, or at least heard of, Batsheva. Feeling a little uncomfortable—she hadn't spoken to Sarah in years—she placed the call. Sarah was naturally surprised to hear from her, but Becky explained the purpose of her inquiry.

"I'm only asking because the girls are so taken with Batsheva. There have been some unusual things going on down here, and we just want to be sure that she is who she says she is."

"The name sounds familiar, but I'm not sure I can place her," Sarah said.

Jewish names always sounded familiar, as if we had, at one point or another, come across every other Jew in the world. We might not know someone ourselves, but we certainly knew someone who knew someone, never more than a degree or two of separation. Once Becky described Batsheva—her long blond hair, her unusual clothing, her spirited manner—her friend realized who she was.

"Maybe you heard something about her and a man," Becky prompted, to jog her memory.

"That's right, I do remember. Starting about a year after her husband died, there was some talk about her and someone from the shul. No one knew for sure what was going on between them, but they were always together, involved in these intense conversations. But we felt so terrible for her after the accident that no one wanted to make a big deal about it. After a few months, we stopped seeing them together and a little bit later, we stopped seeing Batsheva altogether."

"Really? What do you mean?" Becky asked.

"Batsheva stopped coming to shul and we were concerned about her. No one was sure if she was religious anymore. She stopped going to the rabbi's class, and once someone saw her in a nonkosher restaurant, but who really knows for sure if it was her. Maybe we should have expected this after all she had been through, but she had seemed so sincere in her conversion."

"She stopped being religious?" Becky asked incredulously.

"That was what we assumed, and then one day, we heard that she had moved away."

Becky had expected to hear confirmation of Batsheva's affair, to maybe hear that there had been another man or two in her life, but even in her most suspicious moments, she hadn't considered that Batsheva had stopped being religious. Becky thought of the people she knew who were no longer religious: her third cousin, an acquaintance from college, and of course Helen Shayowitz's brother David. She saw these people as cut off, no longer part of the world the rest of us belonged to.

When Becky relayed this news to the rest of us, everything came together. With the few things Batsheva had said about how hard it had been to stay religious after Benjamin died and of course what she had told Naomi about her affair, we were able to envision what her life had been like before she came to Memphis. Batsheva had converted, that much was true, but she had apparently left out a few important details of what happened later. She had an affair, she stopped being religious, she had exposed Ayala to God-knows-what else, and only now was she trying to be religious again. Batsheva had acted like being religious came so naturally after she wandered into shul one Friday night, but apparently, that wasn't the case. She too had her doubts, she wasn't perfect either. Even though she had come back to Judaism, her having left once created the possibility that she would do so again. There was an open door in front of her that could never be fully shut and that could beckon her out, on to new places and new lives.

It made us think—what did it mean that Batsheva seemed so sincere about being religious? If she had been minimally involved, if she had only been going through the motions, we would have understood that she had never really wanted to be Orthodox, her conversion a convenience for the sake of marriage. But we remembered how moved we felt as we watched Batsheva daven, how we really believed that her heart was in her words. We thought of her enthusiasm for building the sukkah and how excited she had been about her learning. We couldn't imagine that she had been faking it, but we also didn't think of religion as something you could move in or out of. People were supposed to be either religious or not; we had never before entertained the possibility of an in-between category, never considered any shades of gray.

Tziporah Newburger understood how dangerous this news about Batsheva's past was. Not that she knew from personal experience, but she imagined that after the first time, breaking God's word wasn't such a big deal. If the girls heard about this, they might realize how easy it was to stop being religious: a little here, a little there, and then you were no longer observant. Tziporah also knew that the only way to counter such transgressions was to instill a renewed commitment to keep the whole Torah. She needed to remind the community that it was full-fledged observance, not intention, that counted. Batsheva may have seemed sincere, she may have been spiritual and sung and danced, but if she was having affairs and frequenting nonkosher restaurants, she wasn't being an Orthodox Jew. Tziporah had tried to be a good example, but perhaps she needed to do something more active to hit home her point about the need to be scrupulous in every aspect of observance. Perhaps the recent problems with the girls were even God's way of telling us that we were too lax. By pointing this out, Tziporah could strengthen her own position of communal role model. She would be like a commander in God's army, offering sustenance and support to His weary troops.

With this image strong in her mind, Tziporah decided to convene a special class for the women. It wasn't the first time she had done this. From time to time, she organized classes on topics important to her—a refresher course in the laws of modesty, the laws of mikvah, even a two-part series on hair covering. But this class was different. Here, the very future of the community was on the line.

As she did before every class, she called Mimi to let her know what she had in mind. She liked the security of knowing that Mimi had given the class her stamp of approval. Usually Mimi praised her for her activism, for creating an opportunity for the other women to learn. Tziporah expected a similar reaction this time, maybe even a little extra praise for working so quickly to put a stop to an ever-growing problem. She told Mimi that she wanted to give a class that addressed the recent problems with the girls. She would explain the concept that everything happens for a reason, that there is no punishment without sin, and then she would encourage everyone to look for areas of observance where we were lax. If there were any women who had real reasons to repent, this class would offer them the proper motivation, sort of like a Weight Watchers meeting. And, Tziporah said, she hoped this renewed commitment would help us to combat the forces that were causing our girls to rebel.

Mimi was quiet when Tziporah finished. She offered none of the praises Tziporah had expected. When Mimi finally spoke, she made sure to emphasize the positive first; that was her way. "I'm glad you want to have a class. It's always a good idea to work on our own levels of observance." And preparing for what Tziporah wouldn't want to hear, Mimi lowered her voice and tried to tread as gently as possible. "But I'm concerned about the possibility of placing blame. It would be very harmful for our community if we started pointing fingers at each other."

"No one said anything about blame," Tziporah said. "But we don't have to sit by and let the girls get wilder. We need to try to understand why it's happening."

"Of course we need to try to understand what's going on with the girls. I'm also extremely concerned about them. But there's a difference between working on our own observance and working on other people's observance."

Tziporah tried to strike a compromise with Mimi: what if she had everyone focus only on individual observance and left out the planned discussion about general areas in which the community was weak? Mimi sighed and said that the important thing to remember was that the class should be a way for us to come together, not something that would tear us apart. Tziporah took this as a green light, and she began making her phone calls, asking us if we could meet that Wednesday night for an hour or so.

In an especially generous moment, Tziporah even invited Batsheva. There was no reason why Batsheva couldn't change her ways. Maybe it was too late to repair the damage she had done and that would remain a blemish on her permanent record, but Tziporah could prevent her from doing anything else. To her surprise, Batsheva said she would love to come, and Tziporah smiled with satisfaction.

On the night of the class, Tziporah's living room was crowded with folding chairs. Small plates of pastries and a pitcher of iced tea were laid out on the coffee table. But there were none of the usual pleasantries or gossip. We were there for a serious purpose and this feeling was palpable in our tight-lipped expressions and stiff postures. Waiting to begin—it was already ten past eight—Tziporah took stock of who had shown up. She was pleased by the turnout. Even women who didn't usually come to this sort of function were there: Anna Weinberg, who had taken her three children out of the Hebrew Academy last year and sent them to public school, was sitting next to Mrs. Ganz, who rarely left her house. Even Naomi Eisenberg, who usually offered flimsy excuses for not attending Tziporah's classes, was waiting for her to begin.

"I don't see Batsheva, do you?" Mrs. Levy whispered to Helen Shayowitz.

"No, and I've been watching the door," Helen said.

The idea that Batsheva wouldn't show up left us more on edge than ever. Her absence would cement in our minds the fact that she was up to something and that she didn't even have the decency to try to cover up her transgressions. For all we knew, maybe she was deciding once again that she didn't want to be religious.

"I guess we ought not be surprised," Mrs. Levy sighed. "It's definitely the direction that things have been heading in."

As usual, Helen had no choice but to agree. "I suppose so," she murmured.

We were growing impatient, feeling our seriousness of purpose wilt in the stuffiness of the crowded room, when Batsheva arrived. She knocked loudly on the front door, not knowing to go around to the side one, which was always left open on such occasions. Helen was the closest, so she ran to answer it.

"Hurry up, Batsheva. We're fixing to start," she cried out when she saw who was there, unable to mask her impatience.

When Batsheva walked in, we tried to smile as we usually did, to be polite no matter how upset we were, anything to avoid an out-and-out confrontation. Better to let her get the hint on her own, to realize through our cold eyes and tight smiles that we were displeased. Then it would be up to her to decide how she might make amends and stop the terrible trend of rebellion she had started. But Batsheva didn't seem to notice that anything was different. She smiled at us as she looked around the room for an empty seat. Mimi waved and motioned to Batsheva that there was a seat next to her. Batsheva went over to her and squeezed Mimi's hand affectionately as she sat down. Then she turned around to say hello to Helen Shayowitz and Mrs. Levy. Because there was no other choice, the two of them nodded politely. Jocelyn

Shanzer looked down and folded her hands in her lap. Leanna Zuckerman tried to wave, but with so many people around, she decided to greet Batsheva later, in private. Batsheva looked at her with curiosity, but she didn't say anything and the moment passed.

Tziporah stood before us. "I have arranged this class because we are losing our children. When there is so much trouble in one place, it's up to us to take a look at our lives and our community. God forbid that I would question the work of God's hand. But we are not helpless. God's commandments are His way of showing us the right way to live. If we better ourselves and strengthen our observance of the mitzvoth, then we'll be closer to God."

There was so much more Tziporah wanted to add: about the importance of rooting out bad influences, the need to look for sources of rebellion and remove them from our midst, the command to offer rebuke when in the presence of sin, that the prohibition against adultery was one of the Ten Commandments. But Mimi's presence prevented Tziporah from making any of these more direct allusions to Batsheva. Every time she thought about saying something, she imagined the disapproving look Mimi would give her and she restrained herself.

Instead, she told a story from the Talmud that her husband had looked up for her: Four hundred jugs of wine belonging to Rav Huna turned sour. The other rabbis came to visit and advised him to examine his behavior to understand why this was happening. Surprised, he asked if they suspected him of a sin. Not to point fingers, the rabbis said, but we have heard that you are occasionally a little stingy. Upon hearing this, Rav Huna resolved to mend his ways. After that, some reported that the vinegar became wine again. Others reported that the price of vinegar went up and sold for the same price as wine.

The story made sense to us. If Rav Huna's situation could be resolved, then why not ours? We too would mend our ways, so that whatever was sour in our community would become sweet again. We didn't have to be helpless; we could do something to stem the tide of rebellion and unrest.

Pleased with the murmurs of agreement she heard, Tziporah passed around sheets of paper and a box of sharpened yellow pencils.

"I want each of you to write down one mitzvah that you'll work on in the upcoming months," she said. "You don't have to show it to anyone. This is between you and God."

Tziporah decided to be brave and add a special message subtly intended for Batsheva. "Remember, there's no sin so great that you can't do teshuvah." What she didn't add was that waffling back and forth between being religious and not being religious would certainly require a great deal of repentance.

We examined our lives for the area most in need of improvement. We didn't want to pick a mitzvah that was too easy, one that would make us seem unwilling to push ourselves. But if we listed a mitzvah that was too major, if, for instance, we said we needed to be more strict with the laws of Shabbos, we worried it would imply we weren't already doing so.

"Help me," Helen whispered to Mrs. Levy. "I can't think of anything to write."

"Shush, Tziporah will hear you. Put down anything. It doesn't matter what," Mrs. Levy said.

We felt as if we were bargaining with God, offering our good deeds like collateral against our children's souls. We promised to be more careful in giving the required ten percent of our earnings to charity, we would learn more Torah, be more careful with keeping kosher. We would better honor our parents, pray with more feeling, feed the hungry, clothe the poor. And with these changes, we could save our children and our community.

There was no doubt in Jocelyn Shanzer's mind what she should write. Tupperware containers of shrimp salad danced in her head, and she wanted to cry for the hungry nights that would lie ahead. But the time had come. She could finish the last batch she had in the freezer, but that was it; she would make no more.

For Tziporah Newburger, the decision wasn't as clear-cut. She certainly didn't have to work on being more meticulous with Shabbos or kosher. In fact, as far as she knew, she might have mastered all 613 of God's commandments. As she felt pride spread through her body, she recoiled in self-disgust. Internal modesty probably counted nearly as much as external modesty. She would adopt a humbler attitude, she would be modest in her thoughts as well as in her dress, like Moshe Rabeinu, God's most devout yet unassuming servant.

"I'm putting down 'No gossip.' That's always a good one," Bessie Kimmel said.

"Me too," Doreen Sheinberg decided. "We'll have to be careful when we talk on the phone from now on."

We looked over our shoulders to catch a glimpse of what Batsheva was writing. But she was staring straight ahead, lost in her own thoughts. We wondered if she knew what we were feeling, if that was why she looked a little sad. We felt a pang of guilt, and we tried to push it away. Batsheva snapped out of whatever daze she was in and quickly wrote something on her paper. What it was, we couldn't tell, but we came up with many possibilities. Surely she could repent for her affair, for drifting away from religion. Or if she wanted a more up-to-date sin, she could consider the way she dressed or the way she was disrespectful to the rabbis at the school, joking around with them, calling them by their first names. And she could of course repent for the inappropriate things she had said to the girls.

"Keep these pieces of paper and look at them every night to remember the promise you made to yourself," Tziporah said.

There was a light feeling in the room as we folded over our sheets of paper and put them into purses and pockets. As if a vicious storm had passed, we breathed in a new optimism, and we left Tziporah's house feeling hopeful for the first time in weeks. But this is where, at least with regard to Batsheva, things took a turn for the worse. According to Helen Shayowitz, Batsheva folded up the slip of paper and placed it in her skirt pocket. Mrs. Levy swore that as Batsheva walked out of the house, deep in conversation with Mimi, she dropped the piece of paper onto the front porch (whether by accident or on purpose, no one, not even Mrs. Levy, knew). She happened to be a few paces behind Batsheva, and she stooped down, picked it up, uncrumpled it and smoothed it out against her thigh. With the porch light to guide her, she discovered that Batsheva had not written a single word on that paper.

Who knew what to make of it? Maybe Batsheva hadn't been able to think of anything. Maybe she was afraid to put a horrible sin in writing. Maybe she still thought she could pretend that her past had nothing to do with who she was now. Or maybe she didn't believe in repentance, maybe she was laughing at our attempts to better ourselves. No matter what the reason, Batsheva's omission left a sour taste in our mouths.

With this latest incident fresh in our minds, we began to discuss the best way to handle the situation. We discouraged our daughters from spending time with Batsheva. "Weren't you at her house yesterday afternoon? Don't you think you should be spending more time with friends your own age?" we asked when they told us that they were going to visit Batsheva. If they insisted on going, we set strict rules about when they needed to be home: before it got dark out, early enough to set the table for dinner, no more than an hour after they went over there.

We also began to think about the problem of our daughters being alone with Batsheva during art class. We realized that we had no idea what really went on: for all we knew, Batsheva could be having them do nude drawings. We imagined the conversations that went on, how free they probably felt to say whatever was on their minds, to make fun of school, religion, maybe even us. And what if she was giving them details of her time off, so to speak; what if she said that year was a much-needed vacation from so many rules and restrictions? What if she recommended that they do the same?

Thank God, though, for Yocheved Abraham. She had a free period when the girls were at art, and usually she sat alone in the teachers' lounge, drinking one cup of coffee after another, brooding over her sad, single state. Luckily, the lounge was right next door to the art room and the interior walls in the school were notoriously thin. When the problem was presented to Yocheved, she was eager to help out. There was no reason, she said, why she couldn't keep her ears open and try to overhear what Batsheva and the girls talked about. We were relieved. At least this way there would be some responsible presence keeping an eye on Batsheva until we could come up with a better, more permanent solution.

But however we were feeling toward Batsheva, we were determined not to let it affect the way we treated Ayala; the sins of the mother would not be visited on the daughter. She was still invited over to our houses to play with our children, we still gave her hugs at shul and offered her seats on our laps. Mrs. Levy made sure that the chocolate chip cookies she baked for Ayala every Friday afternoon were still delivered without fail. In the past when she had brought them over, she had gone inside and chatted with Batsheva, enjoying the chance to see Ayala open the tin and gobble down a cookie or two. Mrs. Levy was no longer comfortable with these visits, so instead, she left the cookies by the back door with a Good Shabbos note for Ayala inside.

Whether Batsheva noticed these changes, we couldn't say. She didn't confront us if she did. But she seemed a little sad; we could see that in the wistful look she gave as we passed by with perfunctory hellos. And she was keeping more to herself—there were no invitations to come sit out back with her and watch the sunset, she didn't ask us in to taste the new vegetarian dish she was experimenting with. She was being careful, as if she knew she had somewhere along the way stepped out of bounds, only she still wasn't sure where those lines had been drawn. But still, we recognized the look of gratitude in Batsheva's eyes when we did something nice for Ayala, and we imagined that this was her way of sending us a message, reminding us that no matter what happened between her and us, Ayala could still be part of our world.

FOR Leanna Zuckerman, the tension was unbearable. She was like a double agent in the midst of a spy game—not wanting everyone else to know that she sympathized with Batsheva and not wanting Batsheva to know what people were saying about her. But she was sick of the duplicity and she decided that she was going to publicly continue her friendship with Batsheva; for once in her life, she wasn't going to care what people said about her. She was unwilling to believe that Batsheva was the cause of the problems in the community and she hated seeing how alone Batsheva looked, her growing puzzlement as people gave her the cold shoulder.

Leanna asked Batsheva to have lunch with her, and Batsheva jumped at the invitation; she said she had been feeling down lately and maybe this would cheer her up. Batsheva didn't say more specifically what was bothering her, and Leanna wondered whether she had noticed the talk that was building up around her. As uncomfortable as the conversation might be, Leanna promised herself that if Batsheva asked her why people were looking at her with suspicion, she would be honest and tell her what was being said.

When Leanna and Batsheva got to the Posh Nosh, it was crowded. In the corner sat Alvin Shayowitz, Helen's husband. He had been sitting there for more than an hour, as he did on most weekdays, making us wonder if in fact he did have a job. Next to them was a seventieth birthday luncheon for Bessie Kimmel, her daughter and two daughters-in-law squeezed around the small table. In the other corner were three girls from the high school on an extended lunch break.

Even though Leanna hadn't planned to raise the subject of the community's feelings toward Batsheva unless she was asked, now that she was sitting across from her, she couldn't put it out of her mind. She had to know what Batsheva was thinking. Whether she knew or not what people were saying about her, surely she had an opinion about what was happening with the girls.

"So, what do you think about what's been going on?" Leanna asked.

"What do you mean?" Batsheva asked.

"You know, with the high school girls," Leanna said softly. "Everyone seems so upset and thinks we need to do something." She looked around. "Don't repeat this, but I don't think it's the biggest deal. The drugs are different, but everything else, I don't know. They're teenagers and they want to experiment. I definitely wanted to when I was their age."

But Leanna hadn't experimented with anything. She had been too concerned with what people would think. In college, she and her friends had been such good girls, no staying out late, never stepping foot into a bar, no wild parties. "I don't know," Leanna said. "Maybe it's just me, because I don't have kids in the high school."

"What the girls are doing is nothing compared to what most teenagers do," Batsheva said. "When I was in high school, among the people I knew, three girls got pregnant; one guy shot his father, who had been abusing him for years; two people were killed in a drunk driving accident; and another two died of drug overdoses."

"But those kind of things aren't supposed to happen here," Leanna said.

"Who says they aren't? I've learned that the same things happen everywhere, just in some places they're talked about and other places they're not."

"You really think those things happen in religious communities?"

"I'm just saying that we need to be proud of how good our kids are and not drive them crazy by forcing them to be something they're not.

That's certainly not going to make them be religious," Batsheva said. "I know it's not my place to say this, but sometimes I think the girls would turn out better if their parents eased up on the restrictions they place on them and let them figure things out on their own."

Leanna nodded in agreement. It was nice to hear such an open point of view. "I felt the same way when I was their age," Leanna confessed. "Sometimes I still do."

As they were talking, Mrs. Levy had walked into the restaurant. She overheard almost everything, and the anger that had been rising inside her reached a crescendo. It was time to take action. She wasn't going to be ugly, but there was a way to subtly and tactfully get her point across. If that didn't work, there would be time at a later date for a more forceful confrontation.

"Hello there, Leanna. Hello, Batsheva," Mrs. Levy said. "How nice to see the two of you. It's somewhat crowded here, which I suppose is a sign that business is good."

Leanna was about to agree that it did look unusually crowded, but Mrs. Levy held up her hand.

"It's important that we support our local institutions, don't you think? I was just this minute thinking what a nice community we have here. Most of us would do anything to keep things the way they are. We have certain things we expect from our children, and we would hate it if anyone was trying to change that."

With that, Mrs. Levy wished Batsheva and Leanna a good day, and she moved on, stopping at every table she passed to comment that the broccoli soufflé didn't look quite as fresh as usual, that Alvin Shayowitz had better get more sleep, he looked exhausted.

Leanna burned with anger at Mrs. Levy and everyone she spoke for. But Batsheva's expression was partly confused, partly amused. Maybe she thought it was just Mrs. Levy's way. If you hadn't lived here for a long time, it could be hard to decode what people said. When Leanna had first moved to Memphis, it had taken her a while to figure out that people were upset that she wasn't making the obligatory pre-Shabbos phone calls to all of Bruce's relatives. After several weeks of her mother-in-law mentioning their names loudly and giving Leanna a pointed look, she had caught on. But Batsheva was different; she wasn't from this world and didn't seem to comprehend its inner workings.

"Batsheva, I need to tell you something." Leanna looked down at the plaid pattern of her skirt, at her well-chewed nails and cuticles. "People have been talking, and they think that you're a bad influence on the girls," she said in a whisper.

"What!" Batsheva said.

"It's because you're different than everyone here. Your background, and the way you are," Leanna stammered.

Batsheva was stunned. She stared at Leanna, trying to make sense of this. "I don't understand," she finally said.

"I think people are assuming that the girls are feeling free to experiment like you did and that maybe you encouraged them."

Batsheva's face flushed. "That's ridiculous. I've helped the girls. They come to me with things they would never talk to their parents about."

"I think that's probably what everyone is worried about. Haven't you noticed that people have been acting a little strange?" Leanna asked.

"I guess people have been a little standoffish, but I figured it was some small thing that I did that I wasn't even aware of, and sooner or later, everyone would get over it. It never occurred to me that it had to do with the girls," Batsheva said. "How long has this been going on?"

"A month or two maybe. When things started getting out of control with the girls, no one knew what to do. And people started talking about how after Benjamin died you had that relationship and then you stopped going to shul and . . ." Leanna looked at Batsheva, hoping she would fill in what she didn't want to have to say.

"I can't believe people are talking about that. Those things have nothing to do with my relationship with the girls," Batsheva insisted. "It's true that after Benjamin died, I did drift away, but it wasn't like I made a thought-out decision that being Orthodox was no longer what I wanted. I just didn't have the strength to keep everything. All I thought about was getting through each day. In my heart I was always religious, but it was just a matter of regaining the commitment."

"I think people felt like you were intentionally hiding your past, like maybe you were pretending to be something you weren't," Leanna said.

"Not that anyone has a right to talk about my past, but I haven't kept any of it a secret. I just didn't go around publicizing certain parts of it because I thought it would be taken the wrong way and that everyone would assume I wasn't religious now."

That was exactly what had happened, Leanna knew. There had been little things all along the way that made people uneasy and then this cemented their suspicions, so that when the girls started acting up, Batsheva was the natural scapegoat.

"Maybe no one here would admit it, but everyone goes through stages of being more or less connected to religion. I'd like to see how people here would react if they were in the position I was in," Batsheva said.

"You're right," Leanna said. "It's easy to judge when you're not in the same situation. But no one is thinking about it like that."

"After Benjamin died, I thought about going back to the small town in Virginia where I had grown up. But I knew I would never fit in. Ayala and I would always stand out and be talked about," Batsheva said. "Maybe I was being naive, but I thought that in a community like this, where people are supposed to be thinking about how God wants us to treat each other, it would be possible to make a place for myself. I thought that people would be more accepting and understanding. But I guess I was wrong."

"Batsheva, some of us see it your way," Leanna said. "I know that you're doing a great job with the girls. And with other things too, you've made such a difference. It's like you've reinvigorated us. I think the only thing you can do is keep doing what you're doing and this will eventually blow over."

"Do you really think so?" Batsheva asked.

Leanna smiled at Batsheva. "I do. It might take a while, but things will work out. You'll see." Even if she wasn't sure this was true, she hoped it was. Seeing Batsheva reminded her that you could be Orthodox and still be different, that religion didn't have to be a mold turning out clones. But to really fit in, that was something else. As Leanna had discovered, sometimes you had to shave off any rough edges, rounding yourself into an easier size, a more manageable shape.

They finished eating, quickly and mostly in silence. Something inside Batsheva had changed, some of her enthusiasm deflated. She seemed struck by her realization that despite our rules and rituals, the way we treated one another wasn't necessarily better than anywhere else. And Leanna too had to wonder what this meant. Did she disagree with Batsheva? Should she be asserting that our community did stand on a higher moral ground? Or did Batsheva have a point? In the betrayal Batsheva was feeling, Leanna began to see that maybe we really were no better. Maybe we were like any small town, with small town ideas and small town fears.

14

EVEN THOUGH WE WERE upset about Batsheva's negative influence on the girls, we hadn't really believed that anything improper was going on between her and Yosef. Even if she had been willing, we never imagined that Yosef would be involved in anything inappropriate. They were still learning together, either in the morning or in the evening, depending on her teaching schedule, and we had assumed that that was all. But now, we no longer viewed anything with the same naiveté, and what we were first able to overlook as a case of overzealous friendliness stuck in our minds and worried us.

Yosef seemed different, even though it was hard to put our finger on exactly how. To some of us, he looked a little sick. He was no longer as friendly and open as he used to be. His eyes didn't burn as intently, his shoulders slumped when he walked, and his face looked pale, tired, like he was working hard to shield some terrible secret. But others of us thought his eyes blazed with some newfound passion. In fact, his whole body seemed looser, made of more supple bone, more flexible skin. That we could look at Yosef and see such different things was puzzling, as if we were looking at two separate people.

He had begun leaving his house late at night, after his parents fell asleep. Yosef got into their car, an old brown station wagon with wood paneling, and backed slowly down the driveway. He always turned right, around the corner to Batsheva's house, and paused for a few seconds. If her lights were on—usually they were, she rarely went to bed before midnight—he would stay longer, leaving the engine on and the headlights burning. Then he would drive down the street, pressing hard on the accelerator until he was out of sight. We didn't know where he went so late at night; even the traffic lights started blinking at ten-thirty. No stores were open, the park was deserted and dark, and we couldn't believe that he would go to a bar. Because we couldn't come up with any place for him to go, we imagined Yosef driving restlessly through the empty streets.

He brought this restlessness to everything he did. Even though he still learned with his father, he no longer seemed interested. When he read the Talmud out loud, his voice had a lackluster quality. Our husbands told us that at davening in the morning, he would stumble in late, barely able to keep his eyes open. He no longer volunteered to go grocery shopping with Mimi, and he stopped keeping her company on the other errands she ran as well.

At least Yosef was still visiting Edith Shapiro on Shabbos afternoon. Thank God he was; she didn't deal well with disappointment, and any time she felt let down, she withdrew further into her memories and declared that with her husband dead and her four sons living so far away, she had no reason to be alive. Edith was as bothered as the rest of us by Yosef's behavior, and one time when she had him in her living room, she resolved to get to the bottom of it.

She asked Yosef the same questions she did every week. To change this would have been too much; he had been visiting for years, and their routine had taken on the weight and permanence of Jewish law. But she paid closer attention to the answers he gave, hoping to detect some departure from the ordinary.

"How's your learning?" Edith asked once Yosef had settled comfortably into her sofa and was eating a piece of cake.

"It's okay," he said and in these two words, she detected a moment of hesitation, a flicker of uncertainty.

"And are you enjoying your time in Memphis?"

"Sure," he said.

Here she was absolutely sure that he hesitated, and from his two answers, she formed a hypothesis: Yosef was bored with Memphis. He had grown tired of this slow city where so little happened. He was weary of the same people who never had anything new to talk about. Edith sighed with sadness. Good things always came to an end. It won't be long, she thought, before he leaves us behind.

We watched him for signs that this theory was true. One day at the end of February, Batsheva was taking a walk and Yosef left his house and walked toward Batsheva's. They weren't supposed to be meeting at the shul until later that evening, so we had no idea what he was doing. Maybe he was dropping off a book for her, maybe Mimi had asked him to pick something up. But instead of knocking on her door and stating the reason for his presence, he stood on the edge of her unmowed lawn and kicked at her dry grass.

When Batsheva finished her walk and rounded the corner of her street, she saw Yosef in front of her house. She waved and Yosef flushed with embarrassment. Ever since Leanna Zuckerman told Batsheva what was being said about her, she had been withdrawn. She still talked to Leanna and to Naomi Eisenberg, confiding in them what a hard time she was having. Even though she was determined to do her own thing, she was always wondering what people were saying when she turned her back. She was quiet when we ran into her, no longer greeting us with a smile as she used to. And when she did speak to us, she was on her guard, carefully weighing each word that came out of her mouth.

But Batsheva was glad to see Yosef; she had told Leanna that he was one of the few people she could trust. "Hi," she said enthusiastically, as if he could offer her relief from the loneliness she must have been feeling. "It's nice to see you."

"I was passing by," he began saying. "I wasn't planning on staying but . . ."

"You don't need a reason to visit. I'm glad you stopped by," she said.

They walked up the driveway, and at the doorway Yosef stopped, knowing it was improper to enter the house. As far as we knew, they had never been alone together behind closed doors.

"I'll wait here," he said and sat down on the wooden porch swing.

"Suit yourself. I'll be back in a second," Batsheva said.

It was warm out, especially for late February, but this wasn't so unusual in a city where the weather varied widely from day to day. Yosef swung back and forth, enjoying the time outside. When Batsheva reappeared, she had taken off her shoes and socks and tied her hair away from her face. She handed Yosef a glass of iced tea and sat next to him on the swing. Yosef took a sip from his glass, and she watched him, shaking her glass so that the ice cubes tinkled against the sides. Batsheva stretched her legs out onto the wooden porch railing. We'd assumed that Yosef had a specific question to ask her, something that couldn't wait a few more hours. But he didn't say anything, and they seemed perfectly content to swing in silence.

"What's it like to be home for this long?" Batsheva asked finally.

"It's okay, I guess," he said.

Batsheva laughed. "That doesn't sound very enthusiastic."

"It's a little boring. I don't have any friends here. I like learning with my father and with you, but that's all I'm doing."

"Why did you decide to stay?" Batsheva asked.

He looked away. "I don't know."

"You're not the kind of person who does things without a good reason. I can tell, you think about everything before you make a decision," Batsheva said. "Do you want to talk about it? I'll bet you haven't told anyone what's really going on and I can see it eating away at you."

He looked around, expecting someone to pop up behind him, to be hiding behind the swing or in the bushes lining the driveway.

"I just didn't want to go back, that's all," Yosef said.

"Did you actually want to be in Memphis, or was it that you didn't want to be in yeshiva?" she asked.

"I don't know," Yosef said sharply.

"It's okay. You don't have to tell me if you don't want to," Batsheva said quietly and sighed.

He looked at her. She lacked her usual smile, and her voice didn't have the same lightness it normally did. "Are you okay?" he asked. "You seem pretty upset yourself."

Batsheva shook her head. "Nothing is working out like I thought it would. I guess you've heard that people are saying it's my fault the girls are rebelling."

"That's crazy." Yosef shook his head in amazement.

"I know," Batsheva said. "I'm trying not to let it bother me, but it's hard. I'm realizing that this isn't the place I thought it was."

"Are you sorry you moved here?" Yosef asked.

"I don't know. I still hope things will work out for me in Memphis. And Ayala loves it here. Maybe that's enough of a reason to be here. I thought that I could create this wonderful Jewish home and she could have all the things I didn't. I imagined we'd have so many friends, that it wouldn't matter that I don't have a single relative that I'm close to."

The two of them stared at the street spread out before them. While we looked at this view as a sort of paradise, we couldn't be sure what they saw. We hated the idea that anyone might be thinking something negative about our community, and we wanted to throw open our doors and call out to Yosef that he needed to get going, it was past time for him to learn with his father. Bessie Kimmel wanted to beg him to remember that he wasn't just anyone, he was our Yosef. Mrs. Levy had a clogged toilet and she wondered how inappropriate it would be to ask Yosef to take a look at it—anything to get him away from Batsheva.

As if he had heard our silent pleas, Yosef looked at his watch. "I have to go."

"Late for your father?" She smiled at him sadly.

"Yes," he said. "He's waiting for me."

"It's been so nice talking to you. I feel like I've known you for a long time. Maybe it's because you look like Benjamin. I'm sure you've been told that before."

"No," Yosef said.

"Your face is the same shape, you have the same smile, even the same build. Even Ayala noticed it."

He stood up. If he didn't leave then, it seemed like he would never be able to. He said good-bye and walked away, looking back a few times until he could no longer see her sitting on the swing, rocking back and forth.

AT the shul, the Rabbi had been checking his watch, glancing nervously over his shoulder, expecting Yosef to walk up behind him. His face showed a mix of worry and anger, alternating with each minute that ticked by. He couldn't come up with any reason to explain Yosef's lateness—he surely didn't imagine that he had been sitting and talking with Batsheva.

Arlene Salzman and Helen Shayowitz were picking up the last of the decorations from the Chanukah dinner; no one had bothered to collect them all these months, and they had been gathering dust in the back of the social hall. Finally, Arlene and Helen had decided to take care of the situation; they had, after all, been co-chairs of the event. They bumped into the Rabbi in the foyer where he was waiting for Yosef, their arms loaded with three-dimensional dreidels cut from Styrofoam, decorated with gold and silver glitter.

"Hi, Rabbi. How are you doing?" Arlene asked.

"Have you seen Yosef?" the Rabbi asked, not bothering with the usual pleasantries.

"Today?" Helen inquired, because as a matter of fact, she had seen Yosef the day before, sitting alone in the dark sanctuary. He had looked so sad, so deep in thought. But it was probably best not to mention that to the Rabbi; he looked concerned enough as it was.

"I thought maybe you saw him while I was in my office," the Rabbi said.

"I don't think I've seen him today at all," Helen said, struggling to keep her grip on the dreidels. Already her hands and dress were covered with glitter, and if she dropped a dreidel on her newest pair of shoes, she would never be able to clean them off.

"I haven't seen him either," Arlene said. She wished she had seen Yosef and could tell the Rabbi that he was on his way. After all she had been through with Ilana, she was more sensitive to anyone who was worried about a child. She knew that there was nothing worse.

"I'm sorry, let me help you with those," the Rabbi said.

"Don't you worry, Rabbi. We can make it out to the car just fine. You see to your son," Arlene said.

The Rabbi returned to his office to wait, and Tziporah Newburger called just then to ask a question. She was having her parents over for dinner and had been trying to cook early in the day. She had accidentally grabbed the wrong pan and ended up cooking mushrooms in her dairy frying pan. She had been planning to serve them with hamburgers, and she needed to know if she could still do that. As Tziporah was explaining that she had never been this careless before and she was ashamed of herself, Yosef knocked on the door.

"One minute, Tziporah," the Rabbi said, putting the receiver down on his desk. "Come in," he called, and Tziporah couldn't tell from the Rabbi's voice whether he knew it was Yosef or not.

Yosef opened the door gingerly, afraid of what might jump out at him. "Hi," he said softly.

"Where have you been?" the Rabbi asked.

"I was at home and lost track of time," Yosef said.

The Rabbi didn't think to cover the mouthpiece of the phone, and Tziporah could hear every word.

"I'm sorry," Yosef said. His voice was that of a small child begging forgiveness from an angry parent.

"Go review what we did yesterday," the Rabbi said, "and I'll be there in a few minutes."

The Rabbi finished with Tziporah. Because they had been cooked in a dairy pan, she couldn't use the mushrooms with the hamburgers. But since it was only the pan and not the ingredients that were dairy, she could eat the mushrooms immediately afterward; she didn't have to wait the usual six hours between meat and dairy. Tziporah hung up, trying to decide what to do with those mushrooms.

Yosef went into the bet midrash and waved to the old men as he sat at the last of the long tables, his regular spot.

"You're late, young man. Your father was worried about you," Mayer Green said. Mayer was always at the shul, and even though he didn't have an official job, he saw to the details that needed to be taken care of: changing lightbulbs, buying wine for kiddush, straightening out the rows of siddurs and chumashes before Shabbos.

"I was running errands for my mother," Yosef said.

Usually Yosef would make conversation with Mayer, but this time he averted his eyes and didn't say anything else. He opened his Talmud to a random page and pretended to be looking intently at it. But his eyes wandered and the troubled expression he had had on his face at Batsheva's house was still there. If anything, he looked more upset than ever. Batsheva hadn't said that much to him, but somehow just a small dose of her had been enought to rattle his concentration.

"Where did we leave off last time?" the Rabbi asked when he walked into the room.

Yosef quickly flipped pages back and forth, looking for the right place. He started reading and his tongue flew smoothly over the Aramaic. The words were close to Hebrew, but not close enough to make any sense to us. We didn't study Talmud; that was a world reserved for men. Our only knowledge of these sacred texts came from the snatches of conversations overheard from our fathers, husbands, brothers, and sons. But even so, it was our connection to the past. Sometimes, in this day and age, it was hard to believe that the Temple had once stood, that God had really revealed himself in our midst, that rabbinical courts had been the highest authority in the land. And that our most famous scholars had sat in yeshivas in Babylonia and debated the oral law that was passed on to them by the men of the Great Assembly who received it from the prophets who received it from the elders of Israel who received it from Yehoshua who received it from Moshe who received it from God at Sinai.

To hear Yosef read the Talmud, it was possible to think that there had never been any interruption in this transmission, that the events of history had never caused any confusion, any loss of tradition. He translated every word correctly, explained every opinion, every argument. His face relaxed and the disturbing events of the afternoon disappeared; he was, once again, the Yosef we had always known. The Rabbi's proud smile spread across his face, and it was in these moments that we saw his love for Yosef.

"Finish translating until the end of the page," the Rabbi said.

They learned like this for several hours, with no breaks, not a single interruption. They were swept into a dialogue with the generations of scholars before them, lost inside this ancient world that remained closed to us.

"Very good," his father said at six o'clock.

As Yosef and the Rabbi walked home, they discussed what they had been learning, their hands gesturing in time to their excited voices. It was starting to get dark, and as we set tables for dinner, chopped vegetables for salad and stirred boiling pots, we watched them pass across our front windows like two identical shadows.

15

SNOW WAS A RARE OCCURRENCE in Memphis. Years could go by without flurries. But this year, everything was happening in extremes. The summer had been hotter than any we could remember, and in autumn, the leaves had turned fiercer shades of red and yellow. When the snowflakes danced down around us in mid-March, filling the air with an unearthly whiteness, we were hardly surprised.

Yosef left the house a few hours before he was supposed to be at the shul to learn with his father. It had been snowing for hours, and to Yosef too, it must have looked like a different neighborhood. The houses, lawns, and streets were covered by a layer of snow not yet interrupted by footprints or tire tracks, leaving open fields of white as expansive as the blue of the sky. Yosef's feet were the first to make tracks, creating a lonely pattern from his house to Batsheva's.

He walked up her driveway and knocked on the door. Batsheva answered, wearing only a white T-shirt and sweatpants. She spoke to him in the doorway, the white snow accumulating in his dark hair. He brushed it off, creating a miniature blizzard as the snow landed at his feet. She laughed at the bewildered look on his face, and after a second, he shrugged his shoulders and laughed with her. She motioned for him to come in, and he hesitated. She waited, as if daring him to step inside. Even though he knew it was wrong, he looked both ways as if crossing the street, shrugged his shoulders, and went inside. Batsheva closed the door behind him and we felt as if we had been slapped.

With this latest development, all we could think was that Batsheva was seducing Yosef, that she had hooked him into some terrible, illicit affair. We tried to reassure ourselves that it was impossible. She was more than ten years older than him. And he was religious, even if we weren't so sure about her. But these assurances did little to soothe our worries, since we could come up with no other explanation for them to be spending so much time together. Maybe in another world, their behavior wouldn't have been cause for concern, but in our world, single young men didn't go around being friends with older, single women; it just wasn't done.

Batsheva and Yosef stayed inside for an hour and we could only imagine what was going on. Though we tried not to think about it, we had visions of the two of them entwined on her couch and in her bedroom, her flimsy T-shirt and his starched white button-down shirt in a pile on the floor. We wanted to march over there and pry Yosef loose, to place anonymous phone calls to the Rabbi and in disguised voices tell him to get over to Batsheva's house right away. But because there wasn't anything we could really do, we just watched her house in between attempts to busy ourselves with housework.

A little after noon, Batsheva received the same phone call as the rest of us: school was canceled. It only took a few flurries to shut down Memphis, and already there were a good two inches on the ground. The city only owned one snowplow, and though there was talk of buying more, it hardly seemed necessary since the last snow had been five years before. Even so, the school had a snow plan; when it came to our children we could never be too careful. Each class had two room mothers to help with driving on field trips, checking for head lice, ordering cupcakes for end-of-the-year parties, and, in the unlikely event of snow, making sure the kids got home safely.

The kindergarten room mothers were Leanna Zuckerman and Rena Reinhard, and as soon as they received the call that school was canceled, they pulled boots out of closets, buttoned up long wool coats, and made their way there. Despite the emergency plans we had in place, the school was chaotic, with all the room mothers trying to reach the other parents, and the teachers trying to keep track of which students had already gone home. Instead of having everyone venture out, Rena called to let us know that she would walk home the children who lived close by. Leanna would drive those who lived farther out—no point in the rest of us taking our chances on the slippery streets.

When Rena spoke to Batsheva, her voice didn't sound out of the ordinary, but then, it was so noisy in the front office, it was hard to hear anything. Rena gathered the children and walked them home, stopping to brush snow off the face of her daughter, to scold Moshe Newburger for throwing snowballs at the girls. When she got to each house, she stopped the group and waited until the child trudged across the snow, knocked on the front door, and was taken inside.

When she got to Batsheva's house, Rena walked across the lawn holding Ayala's hand, instead of letting her make her way through the snow alone. Ayala seemed so much smaller than the other kids and Rena didn't want her to fall. Even though she hadn't spoken to Batsheva in a while, she still felt an obligation to protect Ayala.

Rena rang the doorbell, and as she was waiting for Batsheva to answer, she grew uncomfortable at the prospect of an awkward conversation. She had been angry at Batsheva because of the affair, but Leanna Zuckerman had told her what Batsheva had said about how easy it was to judge without being in someone's shoes. This resonated with Rena; she certainly didn't want anyone judging her. But even so, she hadn't resumed her friendship with Batsheva. She felt too vulnerable to be associated with her. The possibility of getting divorced made her unable to risk giving anyone another reason to talk about her. But when Batsheva opened the door, Rena's resolve to protect herself lessened and she realized how much she missed their conversations.

"Who ever heard of such a thing, a blizzard in Memphis? But then you must be used to it, having lived up north," Rena said nervously.

"How are you doing, Rena? I've been thinking of you," Batsheva said.

"I don't know. I guess I'm okay. The same, at least," she said.

"I'm still here, you know, if you ever want to talk," Batsheva said and looked Rena straight in the eye, as if to let her know that she knew what was being said about her and that there was another side to the story.

When we asked Rena if she happened to see Yosef inside Batsheva's house, she insisted that she hadn't. As far as she could see (into the living room and part of the kitchen), no one was there. But we had been keeping a careful watch and knew that Yosef hadn't left. Whatever they were up to—and we were pretty sure we knew what that was—he was still there.

Forty-five minutes later, Yosef, Batsheva, and Ayala emerged from the house. Batsheva had changed into turquoise ski pants and a silver ski jacket that looked like it had been made of aluminum foil, the kind of heavy winter clothing that only northerners, or former northerners, own. By this time, our kids were also outside building snowmen and having snowball fights, their footprints dotting the once perfect white. After bundling our children up, making them put on a third pair of socks and add another long-sleeve shirt under a sweater, we put on pots of soup for dinner and prepared hot chocolate for when our children came home, frostbitten and exhausted.

Ayala didn't run off to join the other kids. Instead, she attached herself to Yosef, placing her hand in his and laughing.

"Watch me, Yosef," she said.

Ayala did a tumble in the snow, and Yosef clapped for her. He picked her up and brushed the snow out of her hair. Batsheva watched the two of them, and we imagined that she saw Yosef as a new father for Ayala. Batsheva went over to join them, and the three of them scooped up snow and pressed it into a ball. They rolled it on the ground and watched as it became bigger. They did this a second time, then a third, until they had a full-fledged snowman. Clearly Batsheva had some experience; our children, who had never seen this much snow in their lives, were still struggling to put together a single ball of snow.

"Our snowman still needs something," Yosef said. "Don't you think so, Ayala? Maybe a hat."

Ayala nodded excitedly, and when Batsheva wasn't looking, he snatched her purple ski hat and stuck it on top of the snowman.

"Perfect," he said.

"You don't think I'm going to let you get away with that, do you?" Batsheva asked. "Come here, Ayala." She bent down and whispered something into her ear. Ayala laughed and made a face at Yosef.

"You're in trouble now," Ayala told Yosef.

Batsheva and Ayala made snowballs, and threw them at Yosef. He was caught off-guard and soon was covered in white. He ran across the yard and they chased him. Ayala shrieked with excitement, and Batsheva too seemed to lose herself with abandon.

When Batsheva and Ayala were out of breath from so much running, they stopped and began laughing. Yosef grabbed a handful of snow and ran toward Batsheva. He was going to throw it at her, but when he neared her, he stopped. He stood in front of her and lightly sprinkled the handful of snow into her hair. She made no effort to move away, and the white of the snow mixed in with her blond hair. She shook her head, letting the flakes fall all around her. Batsheva and Yosef stood so close they were almost touching. The snow was coming down harder than ever and the wind blew stronger. But they were frozen in place; neither of them moved, and on their faces, we saw so much feeling, such intensity and confusion and desire.

When Ayala came up behind them, Batsheva pulled herself away. She reached for Ayala, and exhausted and wet, the three of them fell into a pile in the snow. They lay there, Ayala between Yosef and Batsheva. Ayala reached out her snow-caked red mittens to take hold of their hands. They moved their arms and legs back and forth, creating three snow angels on her lawn.

It was past time for Yosef to meet his father. As he stood up, Ayala hugged him, holding his legs so he couldn't leave. He hugged her back, looking over her at Batsheva. After a few seconds, Batsheva took hold of one of Ayala's hands that was planted behind Yosef's knee and he stepped free. He leaned down, kissed Ayala on top of her ski hat, and with what we thought was a deliberately casual wave to Batsheva, he started down the street.

EVER since Yosef had started spending so much time with Batsheva, we barely had a chance to talk to him. He left kiddush before we had a chance to wish him a good Shabbos. If he answered the phone when we called Mimi, his voice was curt. He never looked us in the eye if we happened to run into him. This thing between him and Batsheva was stealing him away, and we felt desperate to speak to him, to somehow knock some sense into him and return him to the person he had always been.

We looked for any opportunity. We stopped by the shul on the off chance that we might run into him. We planned out what we might say: that this kind of behavior was beneath him, that he should get married to an appropriate girl and forget about Batsheva. But all the times we hoped to run into him, he was either with Batsheva or with one of his parents, and we wouldn't dare say anything in front of them. We wanted to spare Mimi and the Rabbi; if we could hardly deal with what was happening, how would they be able to?

We soon realized, though, that we couldn't protect Mimi; she was too perceptive to miss these changes in her son. A few days after the snow had melted due to the unseasonably warm weather, Mimi was at the shul, organizing the food pantry. This was a project Mimi had started a few years before when she worried that we weren't involved enough in helping the larger city that we lived in. She had tried to get volunteers to help her that morning—she had called Mrs. Levy, Tziporah Newburger, and Becky Feldman—but everyone was busy with one thing or another and so she was doing it by herself.

Esther Abramowitz, the Rabbi's secretary, was taking a break from her duties, and she came across Mimi sitting alone in the back corner of the social hall, surrounded by cans of vegetables and fruit, boxes of instant mashed potatoes and rice. Figuring that the typing and mailings could wait a little longer, Esther sat with Mimi and helped sort the food. Right away she noticed that Mimi didn't seem like herself—instead of the positive attitude she usually exuded, she looked worried.

"Mimi, are you okay?" Esther asked.

"I am. I just have a lot on my mind."

"Do you want to talk about it?" Esther remembered their long talks over the years. Esther had confided how hard it was to be alone in a community where everyone else was married, how she had watched her friends get married, always assuming she would be next. But she never was, and as she grew older, she began watching her friends' children get married, and now she was watching their grandchildren get married. And Mimi had talked to her about the pain of so many miscarriages, four in a row before Yosef, how with each pregnancy she had held out the hope that this one would survive. Even though the pain of these losses was unbearable, she hadn't wanted to give up hope.

Mimi looked at Esther, remembering these same moments. "I'm worried about Yosef," she said.

Somehow Esther had known this was what Mimi would say. She couldn't imagine that Mimi hadn't noticed what we had this past month or two.

"He doesn't seem like himself," Mimi confided. "When Yosef came home for the summer, I didn't dream that anything was wrong. He was learning with his father and teaching Batsheva. It was working out beautifully. And when he decided to stay home, I was worried, but he was sure that this was best for him. But lately, he's been different. I don't know what it is, but he looks so sad, like he's wrestling with something and doesn't know what to do."

Esther wanted to add her own observations to what Mimi had said: that Yosef came late to learning, that his eyes wandered during davening, that he was spending too much time with Batsheva.

"What does the Rabbi think?" Esther asked. The Rabbi was supposed to know everything, and Esther hoped that maybe he would know what to do.

Mimi sighed. "He doesn't see it. I've tried to talk to him about it, but he only sees that they're learning so well together and that Yosef says everything is fine. I wish I could see it that way, but I know something is bothering him."

"Have you talked to Yosef about it?" Esther asked.

"Not in so many words. I've let him know that I'm here for him, that he can talk to me about anything. It used to be that if he had a problem, he would come to me. But now he looks away, and I don't want to push him."

Esther put her hand over Mimi's. "Yosef is a special boy," she said. "He'll come around."

Even though Mimi hadn't explicitly mentioned Batsheva, Esther had the feeling that Mimi was starting to worry about her relationship with Yosef. The old Yosef would never have spent so many hours with Batsheva, not caring what the community thought. She saw how this worry was tearing Mimi apart—Mimi was never suspicious of people, she always gave them the benefit of the doubt. But when it came to her own son, it wasn't so easy.

THIS conversation with Mimi made Esther even more determined to speak to Yosef. She looked for any opportunity. A few days later, she was in the empty sanctuary, dropping off the typed pages of the Rabbi's speech; even though he didn't read directly from them (after so many years, he knew his speeches by heart), he still liked to have the pages as a reference, just in case. She saw Yosef sitting by himself in the middle of the room and she jumped.

"Oh, my stars!" she cried out. "You nearly scared the living daylights out of me."

Yosef stood up quickly, looking as if he had been caught doing something he shouldn't. "I'm sorry," he said. "I was just sitting here, thinking."

Esther understood. She too loved these quiet moments alone in the sanctuary. All the lights were off, except for the ner tamid, the single light over the ark which was always burning, a symbol of God's constant presence. Standing among so many empty seats, she felt like she was in God's private home after the other guests were gone.

"I'll sit with you for a minute," she said. "I need to catch my breath after all this excitement."

Out of the corner of her eye, she stole glances at Yosef. He looked so sad she could barely stand it.

"I wasn't going to say anything," Esther said hesitantly, "but as long as we're here, I may as well. I don't want to intrude, you're a grown boy and your business is your business, but I'm only doing this because I care."

Yosef drew back. His eyes seemed to be begging her to let things be. She felt a rush of sympathy for him, but she knew she had to say something.

"I'm worried about you, Yosef. You don't seem like yourself," she said. "You're not at yeshiva like you should be. You seem like you don't know what to do with yourself."

"I wanted to learn with my father, that's all," Yosef said.

"Learning with your father is one thing. But maybe it isn't a good idea for you to be spending so much time with Batsheva. People might get the wrong idea."

Yosef looked down. "We're friends, that's all," he said.

"Friends," she repeated with a question in her eye.

Yosef blushed. "It's not like what people are thinking. She's not like that."

Hearing this, Esther realized that Yosef must not know anything about Batsheva's past. It made sense that she wouldn't have told Yosef such sordid details about her life. She obviously wanted to portray a certain image.

"Now Yosef, I know this may come as a shock to you, but Batsheva isn't who she seems to be. She may seem sincere now, but a few years ago she was involved in an improper relationship and it's even possible that she stopped being religious."

Esther was going to say more when Yosef cut her off. "I know all about that, and it's nobody's business."

"How do you know about it?" Esther asked, taken aback.

"We talk about things. We're friends. She's not pretending to be someone she's not. But she's here trying to start over and she deserves that chance," Yosef said.

Esther had never seen Yosef like this, his voice so desperate, his eyes hazy. He looked lovesick. It made her remember the time a man had looked at her like that. Years ago, Esther had gone on vacation alone to Miami Beach and had stayed at a kosher hotel. In the lobby she had met a nice widower, and they had had a lot to talk about. They walked on the boardwalk, ate their meals together, and when it was time for her to return home, he had asked her to stay. But she had said no; she was too afraid to give up her life in Memphis.

She wanted to advise Yosef to push aside his feelings for Batsheva and do what was right in the long run. She wanted to repeat to him all the things she had told herself: emotions were not to be trusted they were here one day and gone the next. What if she had stayed in Miami with that man and things hadn't worked out? What would have become of her? She knew that this entanglement with Batsheva could only end badly, and she wanted to urge Yosef to spare himself that pain.

"Yosef, remember that you're special. You have a wonderful future ahead of you." But as she spoke, she felt a terrible regret for the opportunity she had passed up in Miami, and a small part of her longed to tell Yosef to follow his heart, to take the kind of chance she had been afraid of.

THE next week, Mrs. Levy was at to the shul to begin preparations for the Memphis-in-May Kosher Barbecue Contest. The rest of Memphis had its contest the first weekend in May, and chefs came from all over the world to prepare hundreds of pigs for the roast. Mrs. Levy had spent years watching the city go all out for an event that, because we were kosher, we couldn't be part of, and she hated being left out of such a big to-do. Then one year, she realized that there was no reason why we couldn't have our own contest, complete with local celebrity judges, door prizes, and fancy booths designed by each team. The only difference was that instead of pork roast, our teams—the Alte-Cookers, the Memphis Mavens, and the Holy Smokers—would barbecue brisket.

With all the upsetting events going on in the community, it was hard to care about anything, even the barbecue contest. Mrs. Levy still couldn't get over the fact that Batsheva had talked to Yosef about such inappropriate topics as her affair; who knows what kinds of thoughts that must have stirred up in him? But she also knew that sometimes you had to force yourself to focus on the positive, or else the bad would eat away at you and you'd get nothing done. So even though the event was weeks away, she threw herself into her work, consoled by the fact that no matter what happened between Yosef and Batsheva, at least the barbecue contest would be in order.

As she marched into the shul, her heels clicking sharply against the floor, she was determined to put aside her worries and replace the disturbing images of Batsheva and Yosef with thoughts of special barbecue sauces and new grills. But on her way to the office, Mrs. Levy happened by the bet midrash, where she came across Batsheva and Yosef learning together. From her initial glance, Mrs. Levy noticed that Batsheva and Yosef were sitting too close together. From her vantage point, they couldn't have been any closer unless Batsheva was on his lap. The anger she had been trying so hard to suppress came back full force. It was bad enough that they were carrying on at Batsheva's house, but they didn't have to bring it into the shul as well; some places ought to be left sacred. She longed for an excuse to interrupt them. She imagined bursting in and grabbing Yosef by his collar, forcibly dragging him out of the shul, ordering Batsheva to stay away from him or else. As satisfying as that image was, she knew she couldn't give in to these fantasies. She was a lady after all.

Then, as luck would have it, she remembered that she had a bundt pan sitting in her car that she needed to return to Mimi. She ran out to get it, and when she came back, she hid behind the door, waiting for the right moment.

"Telling my father that I didn't want to go back to yeshiva was the hardest thing I've ever done," Yosef was saying. "I went to his office planning to say that I wasn't sure I wanted to go back at all. But when I looked at him, I couldn't do it. Instead, I told him that I wanted to stay home so I could learn with him. When I said it, it was like the words were coming out of someone else's mouth."

"So he doesn't know the real reason?" she asked.

"No," Yosef said and shook his head. "I couldn't bring myself to tell him."

"You really think he wouldn't understand if you explained everything to him? It seems like there has to be a way to make him see what you're feeling," Batsheva said.

"You don't know him the way I do. When I was a kid, I'd wake up early to go to shul with him. Before I went to sleep every night I would repeat over and over, 'I will wake up at six-thirty, I will wake up at six thirty.' I only overslept once. When I woke up that morning, he was in the kitchen eating breakfast. He wouldn't look me in the eyes. He said that apparently I was too tired for God today, and could I imagine what would happen if one day God decided he was too tired to take care of the world?"

"That's a heavy load for a kid," Batsheva said.

"I was this miracle child that wasn't supposed to be born, and my whole life I've tried to live up to their expectations."

Mrs. Levy couldn't bear to hear any more; she would scream if she didn't do something. She cleared her throat as she stepped out of her hiding place, and Yosef and Batsheva looked up.

"I'm sorry to interrupt y'all, but I wanted to give you this. It's your mother's," she said to Yosef and held up the bundt pan. Batsheva didn't look up to acknowledge her and Yosef only gave her a quick glance.

"How do you do, Batsheva?" Mrs. Levy asked through clenched teeth, to let her know that politeness was still required, no matter how ugly things had become.

"Fine," Batsheva said softly.

"Glad to hear it," Mrs. Levy said. She set the pan down on the table and left the room without another word. Before she was fully out of earshot, Batsheva and Yosef resumed their conversation.

"What about your mom?" Batsheva asked. "I feel like I can tell her anything. She's so tuned in to what people are feeling. You should talk to her. I'm sure she'd understand."

"She knows something is wrong. I can tell by the way she looks at me that she's waiting for me to confide in her. But I don't know if I can bring myself to say anything."

Hearing this, Mrs. Levy decided that if Batsheva was the least bit responsible, she would go straight to Mimi and the Rabbi and confess that she had seduced Yosef. It was the least she could do and maybe if she came clean, the Rabbi would be able to work something out. He could arrange for Batsheva to leave the city in a hush-hush manner, and we would be able to pretend that none of this had happened.

A few days later, when Mrs. Levy was at Kahn's buying groceries for Shabbos, she ran into Mimi. The two of them were the only ones there at the time, and this, Mrs. Levy believed, was no accident; nothing short of destiny had brought them together. She and Mimi had had their problems in the past, but it was time to put these differences aside. She marched over to Mimi, who didn't see her until she was nearly standing on top of her.

"How are you doing?" Mrs. Levy asked.

"Just fine," Mimi said. "How about you—is everyone well?"

"We're all, thank God, doing fine."

Mrs. Levy peered into Mimi's shopping cart: there were four challahs and two cakes and enough chicken to feed an army.

"I see you're having a lot of company this weekend," she remarked.

"No more than usual. We're having Batsheva and Ayala for dinner, and the Zuckermans are coming for lunch," Mimi said.

Mrs. Levy couldn't believe that Mimi was still having Batsheva over. You would think she wasn't interested in protecting her son.

"You know, Mimi," she began, "I've been thinking about Yosef. He doesn't look right to me."

Mimi looked down at her basket of food, feigning great interest in the cakes and raw chicken. "He needs his space right now," she said. "He'll be okay, though."

Needs his space, Mrs. Levy harumphed. She had never understood what that was supposed to mean. If anything, Yosef had been given too much space. That was how this whole situation with Batsheva had begun in the first place.

"Mimi, sometimes you can give kids too much space, and one day you realize that they're not turning out the way you intended." Mrs. Levy kept her voice gentle. She wasn't out to embarrass Yosef or Mimi; on the contrary, she hoped that she might spare them greater embarrassment in the future.

"Or sometimes you can smother them and they'll do anything to break away," Mimi said.

Mrs. Levy nearly dropped the jar of gefilte fish she was holding. This was too much. It almost sounded like Mimi was implying that her child-rearing techniques were less than perfect. It was time to take a more aggressive stance. Luckily, she had anticipated this possibility and she had her arguments ready and waiting.

"Listen, Mimi, I happen to know that Yosef is not at home to learn with his father. He didn't want to go back to yeshiva, and from the way it sounded, I'm not sure he's ever planning to," Mrs. Levy said, finishing with a flourish.

Mimi wasn't used to anyone speaking to her with such force, and she nearly recoiled in surprise. Mrs. Levy leaned closer to her, waiting for a response, and Mimi's fingers gripped the handle of her shopping cart. "Don't you think I know my own son?" Mimi said. "I'm not blind, I can see with my own eyes what's going on."

"No, obviously you don't know what's going on with him," Mrs. Levy said. "Because if you did, you certainly wouldn't be having Batsheva over for Shabbos. You would be doing whatever you could to keep her away from your son. Batsheva is the reason he doesn't want to go back to yeshiva. She's trying to lure him into her arms. She's going to take him away from us, and then what will you have to say?" All rules of behavior had been cast aside, and Mrs. Levy's voice had risen to its most dramatic level.

Mimi looked stunned. "No, that can't be. You don't know that."

"Yes, Mimi, I do. And it's time for you to face the truth about

Batsheva and Yosef before it's too late," Mrs. Levy said. Yosef may have been Mimi's son, but this community belonged to all of us. There was no way Mrs. Levy was going to sit back and let Batsheva destroy it. No, that wasn't the way it was going to be at all. Either Mimi would think over what Mrs. Levy had said and realize that she was right, or else this was war; it was plain and simple. There was nothing else to be said, and Mrs. Levy excused herself and stormed off.

Mimi stood in the middle of the store and let out a sigh. We had always believed that she saw everything that happened in the community, that she always knew the right thing to say or do. But she seemed as confused as any of us, maybe even more so. Our sense of security that she would always be guiding the way had vanished, and we were left on our own.

16

AS IF THINGS COULDN'T GET any worse, Batsheva invited the girls to her house for Purim seudah. The holiday of Purim celebrates the deliverance of Queen Esther, Mordechai, and the Jews in Persia from the wicked Haman. It is our day to let loose: we wear costumes, send shaloch manot baskets filled with food to friends, and have festive meals with singing, dancing, and drinking until we no longer know the difference between righteous Mordechai and evil Haman. But no matter how topsy-turvy a holiday it is, there was no way we were going to let our daughters go to Batsheva's house.

"Absolutely not," Arlene Salzman told Ilana. "Absolutely not."

"Please," Ilana begged. "I won't even stay long."

"I'm sorry, but this is what your father and I have decided," Arlene said.

"I don't understand," Ilana said. "What do you think is going to happen? It's a Purim seudah, for God's sake."

Growing exasperated—the conversation had been going back and forth for half an hour—Arlene asked why it was so important to her. If it was going to be like any other seudah, why was it crucial that she go?

"I'm sick of our Purim seudahs. They're always the same. We just sit around and eat and no one talks to each other."

Had they been too busy to take the time to make each holiday special? Arlene wondered. Had holiday meals become no different than any weeknight dinner? Now her daughter was grown up enough to see these flaws; she no longer assumed that the way her family did things was the only way.

Arlene kissed Ilana on the forehead. "Go to Batsheva's," she said, hoping her daughter would choose to remember the best times the family had had and not let the bad stain everything.

Once Arlene had given in, Ruth Berner decided to let Hadassah go as well. She had been grounded since the marijuana incident, and Ruth didn't want her to be left out. Doreen Sheinberg, Judy Sussberg, and Rachel Ann Berkowitz eventually agreed as well. They were tired of fighting with their daughters, tired of sulking and silence. They hoped that if they gave in on the seudah, they would have more leverage when it came to bigger issues down the road.

As the holiday approached, we tried not to let Batsheva spoil our fun. We helped our younger children plan their costumes. They had been King Achashverosh last year and Kermit the Frog, Queen Esther, and Snoopy in the years before. This year they wanted to be Spiderman, Wonder Woman, Darth Vader, Raggedy Ann. We cut crowns from posterboard and covered them with aluminum foil. We bought yards of fabric to sew superhero capes, white clown makeup, and red yarn for hair. We also busied ourselves with preparing our shaloch manot, making lists of whom we would send to, trying to remember everyone who had sent to us last year. The one thing we included in our shaloch manot every year were hamentashen, the triangular cookies reminiscent of the three-cornered hat the evil Haman wore. But no two recipes were the same. The trick was in the filling. We used prune and poppyseed, apricot jelly and chocolate chips. Rena Reinhard had even come up with a peanut butter and jelly recipe that our children loved.

We scoured through cookbooks trying to come up with new ideas for what else to include in our packages. Every year, our shaloch manot grew more elaborate, and we could only dream of what next year's would be like. The most exciting shaloch manot ever was the one Bessie Kimmel made a few years ago. In each box were two genuine New York bagels (FedExed to her by her daughter-in-law Devorah), a container of cream cheese, and individual packets of lox. Rivaling this was what Ruth Berner made last year. Purim had fallen on Friday, and she had sent everyone homemade challahs, small spinach noodle kugels, and carrot cake.

Besides the food, there was the packaging to consider; no one sent shaloch manot in plain brown bags anymore. We used colored cellophane, patterned paper plates, hand-decorated bags and wicker baskets. Mrs. Levy bought Easter baskets (removing, of course, any pictures of bunnies) and filled the bottoms with Easter grass, feeling lucky that these two holidays fell at similar times. Tziporah Newburger started saving the green plastic containers from cherry tomatoes months ahead of time. Rachel Ann Berkowitz filled glass jars with layers of different candies, creating a shaloch manot so beautiful that we felt bad eating it.

On the eve of Purim, we went to shul, trying to get ourselves into the proper mood. The day before the holiday was a fast day, commemorating the danger the Jews had been in in Persia, and we were struck by the sudden change of mood, from somber and repentant to wild and free. We tried to loosen up, to push our worries to the backs of our minds and breathe in the joyousness of this one day of the year when we were commanded to be free-spirited, when nothing is supposed to be as it usually is; just as Haman's decree against the Jews was reversed and he was hanged on the same gallows he prepared for Mordechai, we celebrate this day where everything is turned upside-down.

The shul had been decorated with this theme in mind. In the seats in the front of the room where the board members usually sat, someone had placed stuffed animals wearing cartoon character masks. And there were streamers hanging from the ner tamid, a red-and-white polka-dot tablecloth across the bima. Even the Rabbi was wearing a Hawaiian print shirt. Mrs. Levy wore a pair of rhinestone-studded sunglasses, and she had encouraged Helen Shayowitz to tie a yellow ribbon in her hair. Tziporah Newburger had brought along a floppy rainbow-colored hat to wear over her wig, if she worked up the nerve. Batsheva was the only adult who wore a full-fledged costume, and by now, this wasn't surprising. She was dressed as Queen Esther, the heroine of the Purim story. Her hair was elaborately braided underneath a construction-paper gold crown, and she wore a long purple dress covered with tiny beads and sequins. Around her neck she had tied a silver, sparkly piece of fabric, creating a dramatic flourish behind her when she walked.

We tried, though, not to think about Batsheva as we listened to the reading of the Scroll of Esther. Achashverosh, the King of Persia, held a feast in Shushan, his capital city, and ordered his wife, Vashti, to appear. She refused, and in his drunkenness, he had her killed. The next morning, he awoke, filled with sorrow at what he had done. His minister Haman advised him to assemble all the maidens in the land and select a new queen. In the end he chose Esther, who, unbeknownst to him, was a Jew. Later, when Mordechai, Esther's uncle, would not bow down to Haman, Haman was furious and conspired to kill all the Jews of Persia. Hearing of this decree, Esther went before the king, revealed that she was Jewish, and pleaded for her people. The king granted her request, hanged Haman, and appointed Mordechai as minister in his place. The Jews of Persia took revenge on their enemies and they were joyous and happy.

This year, though, the story was transformed, and we saw Memphis as a modern-day Shushan. A terrible decree had been sent forth against us, and only we had the power to turn it around. As much as Batsheva thought she would save our daughters, we knew that we were really the Esthers of our story, good and righteous and beautiful, trying to save the community we had worked so hard for. Each time Haman's name was read, the shul erupted in boos and hisses, the sounds of graggers twirling back and forth, feet stamping, even a trumpet blaring. These were our attempts to blot out Haman's memory, to show that we could overcome any enemy who rose up to destroy us, and this year we added a special hope that we could wipe out all the troubles that were befalling us.

The next morning, when Mrs. Levy dropped off her shaloch manot at Naomi Eisenberg's house, she asked her how she was handling the fact that her daughter was going to Batsheva's seudah later that day.

"I don't have any reason to mind," Naomi said. She had asked Batsheva if she realized that people were unhappy that their daughters were going to her seudah. Batsheva had shaken her head and said she couldn't do anything about that. The girls had complained for the past month how the rabbis had the boys over for Purim seudah and let them drink as much as they wanted, while the girls never had anywhere to go. Batsheva had promised that she would have them over, and she wasn't going to let them down. Even though she realized some people would be unhappy, she said she had to do what she thought was right. And she hoped that when everyone saw how much she was doing for the girls, they would come around.

Naomi told Mrs. Levy what Batsheva had said, and Mrs. Levy wasn't surprised. She had noticed the way Batsheva was trying to act like nothing had happened, as if she could carry on despite what we were thinking. It wouldn't be this way for long, Mrs. Levy resolved. Sooner or later, we would be able to put a stop to what Batsheva was doing. She handed Naomi the bag of goodies she had prepared and marched down the street.

Arlene Salzman had her shaloch manot in the back of her car, the yellow bags sliding off the seat each time she braked. Her son, David, was bringing them to each door, but she was driving him because there were too many to carry by hand. Becky Feldman was delivering hers by herself—Shira had laughed and rolled her eyes when Becky asked her to come along—and she pulled up next to Arlene's car.

"What are you doing for seudah?" Becky called out through her rolled-down window.

"Going to my parents," Arlene said. "But the kids won't be with us. David will be at the Fishmans' and Ilana is going to Batsheva's."

"Shira is going too," Becky said, "and I'm not happy about it. But she's been so upset recently and I was afraid that saying no would push her over the edge."

When we returned home from our deliveries, we found on each of our front steps a small package of food with just our daughters' names, not the whole family's as we were used to. When the girls opened the cards, there was no message, no Happy Purim. There was only a small B at the bottom of a white card, drawn so that it looked like a butterfly. The fact that we had been left out only added to the feeling that this day wasn't like all others. It was as if our daughters were the adults, with friends all their own, and we were the children, too young to be included.

As our Purim celebrations continued throughout the day, a carnival-like feeling descended over the community. Our usually orderly neighborhood seemed to be painted with wilder, almost garish colors, deeper shadows, thicker brush strokes. Littering our yards were candy wrappers, curls of ribbon that had been used to tie shaloch manot, pieces of hot pink and orange tissue paper. Our husbands came home from work early and began drinking with their friends, a Purim mitzvah that was always scrupulously observed. We could barely recognize our children: boys were dressed as girls, girls as boys. They wore multicolored wigs and grotesque masks. Clown makeup had become smudged, turning once neat faces into blurs of white and red and yellow and blue.

When it was time for the seudah, our girls were getting ready to go to Batsheva's house. Batsheva had somehow convinced them to dress up in costumes, even though most of them had abandoned this practice by the time they entered high school. On this day when they could do whatever they wanted, they transformed themselves into punks, their hair teased high above their forehead, spray-painted with glitter and temporary green dye. They wore leather jackets, neon dresses, multiple strands of silver necklaces. They clipped rows of earrings onto their ears. They became rock stars, caked eyeshadow onto their lids, and painted their lips bright red. And there was nothing we could say. There was no sense, at least for this one day, of how things ought to be.

Rachel Ann Berkowitz, whose daughter, Aviva, was dressed as a hippie, decided to walk her over to Batsheva's so she could see the girls' costumes. To get into the spirit of the day, she dressed up as well. She wore the cowboy hat her husband used to wear for fun, a long jean skirt, a denim blouse, and a red-and-white-checkered scarf.

Rachel Ann and Aviva knocked on Batsheva's door. Batsheva answered, wearing the same Queen Esther costume as the night before. She greeted Aviva with a hug, but when she saw Rachel Ann, she drew back almost shyly.

"Don't worry, I'm not planning on staying. I know you don't want any of us old folks around. I just wanted to see the girls in their costumes," Rachel Ann said.

They stepped inside and Rachel Ann took a look around. Batsheva had transformed the place. The dining room table was covered with a silver paper tablecloth, silver plates and silver plastic cutlery. She had sprinkled confetti on the table and draped curly ribbon over paper cups and plastic wine glasses. It was a table set for a feast, as elaborate as Achashverosh's party in Persia. But that was as much as Rachel Ann saw. Batsheva was perfectly friendly to her, but she got the sense that this was a party for the young. Even in her costume, she felt out of place. She kissed her daughter good-bye and went home to tend to last-minute preparations for her family's seudah.

When all the girls had arrived, Batsheva's house was full of activity. Shira Feldman was the only one not there; she hadn't been in school for the few days before and when her friends called, Becky had said that she was under the weather. But her absence was quickly forgotten. The girls knew what was going on between Batsheva and us—there was no keeping secrets from them—and being at Batsheva's was their personal victory, an assertion that they could do what they wanted. They felt like it was finally their turn—after years of hearing the boys talk about the wild times they had at their rabbis' seudahs, they were now having a seudah of their own.

The seudah started out almost as any of ours did—Batsheva had made an effort to cook a nice meal, and she looked so proud of herself as she served it. She had made carrot soup and potato kugel and vegetable pies. The only unusual dishes were the vodka tofu and the pasta salad dyed green with food coloring, which she presented to the girls with a laugh, trying to encourage them to get into the topsy-turvy spirit of the day.

After eating, Batsheva started singing Purim songs, and the girls joined in, so much excess energy running through them. Then Batsheva stood up to dance. She wrapped her cape over her arms, so that when she raised them over her head, the silvery fabric shimmered. She grabbed Ayala's hand and lifted her onto her shoulders. Our girls got up too, their feet stomping loudly and their voices rising in pitch. In the middle of this exuberance, someone turned on the radio to a rock station. They were no longer celebrating God's deliverance of the Jews. Instead, they were dancing to rock songs, celebrating God knows what. Shira arrived somewhere in the middle of the dancing, but she barely spoke to anyone, nor did she join the other girls as they danced, doing moves we didn't know they knew, hips shaking, bottoms wiggling. The girls danced until they could no longer see straight and everything was a fast, uneasy blur. They collapsed exhausted onto the couch and floor, catching their breaths, their heads still spinning.

The high school boys hadn't been invited to Batsheva's, or at least none of the girls would admit to telling them to stop by, but as the dancing stopped, they arrived. They gathered on Batsheva's front yard, and when the girls realized that they were there, they went out to join them. Soon the entire party had moved outdoors. Our children were milling around Batsheva's yard, sitting on the porch, a few bottles of beer that the boys had brought with them visible here and there. The girls were so happy to see the boys that Batsheva told them they could come inside and continue the party there; if they were going to be outside together, they may as well be inside, she had said with a nervous laugh. When they shuffled into her house, she seemed overwhelmed—her house was wall to wall with high school kids and they were rowdy and carrying on. But Batsheva seemed determined not to ruin the fun, and she tried to laugh along with them and look the other way as they sprawled out on her couch and floor.

There were so many versions of what happened next. The story we wish to believe came from the girls who were known to be the wildest, which did little to set our hearts at ease. It was also the hardest version to believe, with so many facts out of place, unsubstantiated, downright contradictory. They claimed that nothing had happened. Sure the boys came over, sure the boys had been drinking, sure it was late, but nothing earth-shattering took place. But the more reliable girls confessed that the boys pulled out more bottles of beer and passed them around. The girls swigged freely from them, growing tipsy. One of the boys, so drunk he couldn't tell the difference between night and day, started to dance to the music that was still blaring. One of the girls got up to join him, and soon a group of our boys and girls were dancing together in the middle of Batsheva's living room.

While such things were going on, we were home wondering where our children were. Our husbands, drunk from their own Purim celebrations, had conked out, and we were left to handle this situation on our own. We kept glancing out our windows. It looked like there were too many people over at Batsheva's house, certainly more than the eighteen high school girls who were supposed to be there. But we couldn't be sure and we kept waiting, hoping they would show up. Every time we heard a creak, we were sure it was our children, and every time we were disappointed. When midnight passed with still no sign of them, Arlene Salzman and Becky Feldman decided that it was time to go over to Batsheva's. By this time, the neighborhood had quieted down, but even so, Arlene and Becky felt afraid to be out so late at night. The porch lamps seemed to glow an eerie yellow, and they worried that someone in costume might jump out at them from behind a tree or a drunken figure might chase them around the block.

When Arlene and Becky arrived at Batsheva's house the party had quieted down. A few boys appeared to be sneaking out, but when Batsheva opened the door, looking tired, only the girls were there. They were lying across her couch, sitting on the floor, deep in conversation. The room looked like there had been a wild party going on. The coffee table had been pushed aside and the throw pillows were on the floor. The confetti that had been sprinkled on the tablecloth was now on the sofa and in the girls' hair. There were plates of food scattered around the room and enough empty cups for a crowd much larger than just the girls.

"What is going on here?" Becky exclaimed. "Do y'all have any idea what time it is?"

"I don't know who you young ladies think you are," Arlene said, "but this is not a free-for-all."

Becky and Arlene looked around. None of the girls offered the excuses they had expected to hear, that they had lost track of time, that they were about to leave, that they had just been gathering up their things to go home. There was just a horrible creeping silence. Then it hit Becky.

"Where's Shira?" she asked.

Becky's sharp, nervous question snapped the girls out of the dreamy haze they had been in, the craziness of the past day coming to an end. They blinked as if they had just woken up and looked around.

"She must have gone home," Batsheva said. "I haven't seen her for a while."

"No, I would have heard her come in. She must still be here," Becky insisted.

Under normal circumstances, Becky might not have been so worried. There had been other times when Shira wasn't where she said she would be. But their relationship had hit an all-time low these past two weeks. Even though Becky had forbidden Shira to apply to any college besides Stern, she had done so anyway. That week her first acceptance had come, from Brown (who had even heard of such a school? what kind of nice Jewish girl went there?), and Shira had been thrilled. But Becky had heard too many stories about religious kids who went to college and were forced to read the New Testament and secular philosophy. And then the gradual decline: they would start eating in the nonkosher dining hall, first just a salad, then pizza, and soon they would go to parties on Friday nights and football games on Shabbos afternoons and live in coed dorms with coed bathrooms. By the end of the semester, religion would be thrown to the wind. Becky would not have this happen to her daughter. She tore Shira's acceptance letter to shreds and made Shira write a letter saying she wouldn't be attending.

Since then, Shira hadn't spoken to her. She refused to go to school. She wouldn't help prepare shaloch manot and she hadn't gone to megillah reading. All she did was stay in bed and watch television. As angry as Shira had been in the past, Becky saw that this was different, and she didn't know if there would be any turning back.

"Please tell me where my daughter is," Becky said again, her voice pleading.

Batsheva looked at the girls, but they too seemed to have no idea where Shira was. Faced with this silence, Batsheva turned to Ilana. She and Shira were best friends, and if anyone would know where Shira was, Ilana would. With everyone looking at her so intently, Ilana burst into tears.

"I didn't know what to do. She had already made up her mind. There was nothing I could say to convince her to stay," she wailed.

"What are you talking about?" Becky demanded.

"Ilana, if you know something you're not telling us, you're going to be in big trouble," her mother threatened.

Her voice shaking, Ilana described what had happened. Shira had arrived late to the party and wasn't in costume like the other girls. All she wore was a silver mask in the shape of a star. She tried to act like she was into the party but Ilana could tell something was wrong. When Shira pulled up her mask, her eyes were red and swollen.

"Come outside," Shira whispered. "I need to talk to you.

Ilana followed her outside, worried about her. "Shira, what's going on?" she asked.

"I'm leaving," Shira had said. "Matt and I are getting out of here."

Matt was Shira's non-Jewish boyfriend, the one Tziporah had seen at McDonald's. They had met at the mall and had started going out secretly. Matt was twenty-one, and according to Shira, they were in love. She didn't know where they were going, only that they wanted to be together and this was the only way. Even though Ilana had known about Matt, she never thought Shira would do something like this. She and Shira had spent hours complaining about the school, about their parents, about the community, but Ilana still couldn't imagine running away from it. As constricted as she felt, it was the only life she knew.

"Are you sure you want to do this? Maybe you can try it here a little longer," Ilana begged Shira. She was suddenly terrified for her friend, and she wished there was some way to stop her from leaving.

"I can't stand it anymore. If I don't go now, I'll never have the chance to get out of here. Matt will be here any minute. My stuff is already in his car."

Ilana started to cry and when Matt pulled up, she hugged Shira good-bye. Shira's tough demeanor shook, and she too began to cry as she got into Matt's car. As he pulled out of the driveway, Shira turned back and waved to Ilana. Ilana stood there watching them go, until the car had turned the corner and was out of sight.

"I'm sorry," Ilana said to her mother and Becky and all the girls who were staring at her. Batsheva was as surprised as everyone else. Her face went white and her eyes looked as if they would spring from her face. "But I didn't know what to do. She said she had to get out of here."

"What do you mean?" Becky asked, her voice nearing the point of hysteria. "What do you mean she left? And you let her go? You stood here and let her go?" Ilana started to cry harder and Becky turned her fury on Batsheva. "How could you do this? What's wrong with you? Is this what you wanted to do to us?"

Batsheva didn't say anything—she was too stunned to speak—and this only angered Becky more. She put her hands on Batsheva's shoulders, wanting to shake her, as if this strange woman in front of her was a phantom that had snuck in during the night and stolen away her daughter. If she could shake her, shake her harder and harder she might reverse this terrible nightmare. But instead, Becky let go of Batsheva and sank into a pile on the floor.

THE next morning, we woke up and rubbed our eyes. We felt like we had been participants in some nightmare, and even upon waking from this strange slumber, it wasn't easy to sort out what was real and what wasn't. We kept expecting to hear that Shira had changed her mind and come home, that her leaving had been part of the craziness of the holiday, no more real than a passing shadow or figment of our imaginations.

But this didn't happen, and as Shira's running away became more real, we did what we always do in times of tragedy: we brought soups and casseroles over to the Feldmans'. We sat with Becky, taking in her red eyes and exhausted face and tried to think of something to say. Helen Shayowitz chattered on about how the weather was warming up, spring wouldn't be too far off now. Rena Reinhard tried to turn the conversation to the subject of Pesach, how much work there was to prepare for it. But each of these conversations was punctuated with gaping silences. For once in our lives, we were quiet. We couldn't think of a single thing to say.

The Feldmans called the police, but because Shira had turned eighteen and had left voluntarily, there was nothing they could do. Becky had taken to calling Ilana each night to see if Shira had called or written. But no one had heard from her; she had simply vanished. We thought of stories we had read about runaways, living on the streets in New York or Los Angeles, eating out of garbage cans, begging for money, doing things we couldn't bring ourselves to say. We had heard of such cases, but we never thought that that could be one of our own. We worried about our own children too. We felt as if they could slip away at any time; we were discovering that the safety net underneath us had holes in it large enough for them to fall through.

We tried to talk to our daughters. We sat at the edge of their beds and asked what was on their minds. We wanted them to pour out their hearts, to tell us that they were confused and needed our guidance and wisdom to help them through these rocky teenage years. We wanted to hold them in our laps and wrap our arms around them as we had done when they were little girls. But they said that they didn't feel like talking. We could see through their makeup and trendy clothes that they were anything but these savvy adults they were pretending to be. We kissed them on the tops of their heads and left their rooms, wishing there was some way to break through this façade.

In the grocery store that week, Helen Shayowitz couldn't stop fidgeting at the checkout counter. She scraped price tags off boxes of cereal, she peeled off the corners of labels. Shira's leaving had made her more nervous than ever. "Who would have thought this could happen?" she said and sighed.

Rachel Ann Berkowitz was behind her in line. "I dropped Aviva off at Batsheva's house, and I could tell right away that things didn't look right. Batsheva had gone to all this trouble, and she acted like she didn't want me to be there, like I was ruining the fun."

At the dry cleaners, Naomi Eisenberg ran into Ruth Berner, both of them dropping off their children's Purim costumes, stained with chocolate and poppyseed filling.

"Quite a Purim, wasn't it?" Ruth asked.

"I spoke to Batsheva this morning and she was beside herself," Naomi said.

"But Batsheva must have known Shira was up to something. She was so close to her," Ruth said.

"She swore to me that she had no idea. She said she was as surprised as any of us. In fact, I think she's taking it harder than anyone. She could barely move this morning, she's so sick over what happened."

"But even if she wasn't directly responsible, I'm sure she had some kind of influence on Shira. The girls are so crazy about her, they would jump off a roof if she told them to. And she stopped being religious for a while. So what's to prevent the girls from wanting to do the same?"

A few houses down, Rena Reinhard and Tziporah Newburger were having a similar conversation.

"I hate to be the one to say I told you so," Tziporah began.

"If you were so certain that something like this was going to happen, why didn't you do something?" Rena demanded.

"I tried, but no one would listen to me. Everyone thought I was being narrow-minded, but see, in the end I was right."

Even though Tziporah felt a tiny sense of gratification that she had seen such a disaster coming, she also felt guilty. She had been up all night worrying that she hadn't done enough, especially after she saw Shira in McDonald's. Maybe she should have marched in and insisted that Shira come home with her.

When Leanna Zuckerman heard that Shira had run off, the first thing that came to her mind was the conversation she had had with Batsheva at the Posh Nosh. Was this the price of freedom? she wondered. She looked down at her daughter, Deena, reading a book. She was such a good child, dutiful and sweet and studious. Maybe Batsheva had been right: the more restrictions you placed, the more the kids would rebel. Shira especially seemed to have so many rules and maybe that was why she'd run off. But if you let children do whatever they wanted, there was no way of knowing what would happen. Of course it was possible to strike a balance, but who knew where to find that perfect combination?

Mrs. Levy was home trying to busy herself with other tasks. She longed to lose herself in cooking, to allow the rhythmic beating of the electric mixer to soothe her. But everything seemed inconsequential. What good were homemade challahs and fresh apple cake if there were no children left? She was trying to save this community, but so far, nothing was working. Filled with the fear that maybe even she did not have what it took to fight this battle, she turned off the mixer, put down her spatula, sank into a chair, and prayed. She begged God to save this community that she had worked her whole life to build. With all that had happened, she could almost feel it sinking to the bottom of the Mississippi. This is how the Jews must have felt when the Holy Temple was destroyed. Like the martyrs who wept at the sight of their city in flames, Mrs. Levy realized that she would risk her life to preserve this Jerusalem of the South.

WHEN the girls went back to school after the holiday, everything was in disarray. They spent most of their time talking to each other by the lockers, saying over and over again how they couldn't believe Shira had actually left. None of the teachers knew what to do. The girls were so upset that no one had the heart to make them study math or chumash.

Realizing that this was her moment to shine, Yocheved Abraham decided to step in and exert some leadership. The girls had been furious at her ever since she turned Hadassah and Ilana in for smoking marijuana, but with Batsheva under such a veil of suspicion, she could redeem herself; she could become their new confidante, the new cool, young teacher. She spoke to the principal, and, baffled about how to handle the situation, he gave Yocheved permission to deal with the girls however she saw fit.

Yocheved's first act was to have the girls' class schedule rearranged so that they wouldn't have art for the next few weeks. The official reason given was that the girls were too busy for art, and it was partially true. They were supposed to be planning a hamburger and hot dog dinner for the night before Pesach, when our kitchens were already kosher for Pesach and no bread or non-Pesach food could be brought into our homes. Now they would have more time to plan the menu, shop for ingredients, and keep track of the reservations that were flowing in. But the real reason was that Batsheva could not be allowed to exert any more influence on them. Any progress Yocheved made would be counteracted by their contact with her.

Her next move was to come up with a way to get the girls to open up to her. She remembered a movie she had once seen about a teenager who committed suicide. At school the next day, the principal had called an assembly and had the students share their pain and confusion. Yocheved imagined getting the girls to open up. They would pour their hearts out, they would lament how they had gone off the proper path; undoubtedly there would be tears. Unable to control their grief, the girls would turn to her for advice. Yocheved would hug them, she would comfort them, she would help them subdue their evil inclinations which had lately been given such free reign.

Once this had happened, Yocheved could ask them for more information about Shira and that terrible boyfriend of hers. They would be so grateful to her that they would tell her whatever she wanted to know. And then Yocheved would be able to go back to the parents and tell them what she had learned. Not only would she be beloved by the girls, but she would be a hero among the women. And maybe then they would stop viewing her as poor Yocheved Abraham, the soon-to-be-old-maid. Maybe they would stop setting her up with whatever random man they could think of and concentrate on quality, not quantity.

With all the girls assembled in a classroom, the desks pushed into a circle, Yocheved waited for the sharing to begin. She had brought along a tape recorder and some soft Hebrew music to get them into the right mood. Yocheved had thought of bringing music because it seemed like the kind of thing Batsheva might have done, and she realized that she had to take what she could from her. But even with the music playing, no one volunteered to go first, and Yocheved realized that as the teacher and confidante-in-waiting, she would have to.

"What has happened to our community is devastating," Yocheved began dramatically. "What Shira has done affects each of us and we must grapple with what she has left behind in her wake. We must try to learn from this experience—we must finally realize the true dangers of exposing ourselves to outside influences. We must acknowledge that we can never trust ourselves when it comes to the evil inclination present in each of us," she said, trying to finish with a flourish.

The girls stared at her.

"Why do you care that Shira's gone? She wasn't your friend," Ilana said.

"We're the ones who miss her," Ariella Sussberg said.

They began talking about Shira, how they couldn't imagine school without her. They had grown so dependent on her sense of humor, her sarcastic take on everything. Ilana talked about how she and Shira would stay up late on the phone, trying to imagine what next year would be like when they were finally away from Memphis. Ariella said that she had known Shira would get into every college she had applied to—she was so smart, she could read something complicated and understand it right away. The girls talked as if Yocheved wasn't there. Not once did they turn to her for guidance or ask her how to mend their ways.

Trying to regain control, Yocheved turned the music louder and demanded that they tell her what they knew about Shira and that boy. But they would only tell her what they had already revealed to their mothers. They had known Shira was dating someone older and not Jewish. She met him six months ago, and he started calling her, hanging up whenever Becky answered the phone. Shira would pretend to be going out with the rest of the girls, and he would meet her at the bowling alley or the movie theater, and the two of them would leave from there. Sometimes Matt would hang around with them, and the girls talked about how Shira would come to life. Her usual glum mood would disappear, and she became animated and flirtatious. They remembered the time Shira said that she and Matt wanted to go away together, to just drive with no set plans, nowhere she had to be. The girls hadn't said anything because they didn't want to betray Shira. A few times, they thought of telling someone, maybe Batsheva, but they worried it would get back to Shira.

Yocheved stared at them. "Girls, if you know where Shira is, you are committing a grave sin by not telling me."

This argument did little to sway the girls. They insisted that they didn't know where Shira was. They said they hadn't believed Shira would really leave; they never thought she'd have the guts to go through with it. In the way they spoke about Shira, Yocheved detected a surprising tone. As worried about Shira as they were, they also sounded a little jealous. When the tape ran out and the girls still weren't saying anything helpful, Yocheved called the event to a close. The girls walked out of the room, as unhappy as ever.

EVEN though Batsheva wasn't teaching art to the high school girls, she was still busy with her elementary school classes. To our outrage, most of the girls still stopped by her room and talked to her. Only a few of them had been convinced of the need to stay away from her. Batsheva talked to Ilana most, the two of them sharing how worried they were, how they hoped Shira would figure things out and come back. Ilana said that Shira still hadn't called her, but she promised that as soon as she did, she would tell Batsheva.

Batsheva also called the Feldmans and tried to talk to Becky. But as soon as Becky heard who was on the other end of the phone, she slammed it down. Every time the phone rang, she prayed it was Shira, and when it wasn't, her heart sank in disappointment. If it wasn't Shira, that was bad enough, but the last person she wanted to speak to was Batsheva.

The next day, Batsheva walked over to the Feldmans' house and knocked on the front door. Becky opened the door a crack and peered out.

"Becky," Batsheva said, "I know this is a nightmare for you, but we need to talk."

Becky started to close the door. No matter what Batsheva had to say for herself, Becky knew that she was to blame. She had seen the way Shira admired Batsheva's free spirit, how she longed to reinvent herself as Batsheva had done. Even if Batsheva hadn't been so open with the girls and unlatched the door to a foreign world, her very presence in Memphis would have been enough.

Batsheva put her arm against the door. "I want you to know that I'm doing everything I can," she said. "I've been talking to Ilana and I'm hoping she'll open up more and tell me if she knows anything else. And I'm sure Shira will call her or me at some point."

Becky didn't want to hear about the efforts Batsheva was making to find Shira. "If it weren't for you, Shira would still be here in the first place," Becky said.

"I had no idea what Shira was planning. There were so many kids at the Purim party, and I was trying to keep track of who was where and who was doing what. I didn't expect the boys to show up, but the girls really wanted them to come in so I said it was okay. I didn't think it would be a big deal. Maybe I shouldn't have done that, but that has nothing to do with Shira leaving. During the party, I asked Shira how she was, but she didn't want to talk. She hung around with Ilana, and then she told me she was going home, that she had an early curfew. I know she's been upset, but she never even hinted that she was thinking about running off."

Becky turned scarlet. Anger rushed up in her throat. "But why do you think she decided to do this?"

"I don't know why," Batsheva said. "But I do know she felt so constrained here. I'm not saying that justifies what she did, but I've been worried about how unhappy she seemed. I feel terrible that I wasn't able to help her. I wish I could have done more."

"Help her? Done more?" Becky screamed. "I suppose you know better how to raise children? What, would you have her run wild like you did? You have no idea how hard it is. You don't care about being religious like we do. You act like you can come and go. This is how we've spent our entire lives, and we're not going to have someone teach our daughters that they can throw away everything we've worked so hard to give them."

Batsheva looked down at the ground and didn't say a word. She no longer knew what to say. Even though she thought she knew what was best for the girls, with Shira running off, she too had to question what she had thought was true.

Becky slammed the door and went back to bed, where she had spent the past week. It was still too early for her to feel the full extent of what had happened. Mostly she was numb. She played over and over in her mind the moment when she realized what had happened, the exact second that she understood that Shira had run away. She constructed scenarios in her mind that could have prevented this: if only she hadn't let Shira go to the party, if only Batsheva had never moved here, if only Batsheva had never converted in the first place.

All along, Becky had tried to stop something like this from happening. She had seen it coming; she had known to recognize the signs. She hadn't wanted to admit this to herself, but she had been so hard on Shira because she knew how alluring this kind of rebellion could be. As a teenager, Becky had been just like Shira. She had snuck out of the house on Friday nights and gone out with non-Jewish friends, she too had eaten nonkosher food. After high school, when she and everyone else assumed she wouldn't end up religious, her parents had sent her to seminary in New York, one last-ditch effort to reform her. And to everyone's surprise, it had worked. She began to find meaning in observance, she found that she wanted to keep kosher and Shabbos. After a year in seminary, no one would have guessed what she had been like as a teenager. With Shira, she had hoped to prevent her from making the same mistakes she had: why have her daughter go out so far only to return in a few years? But now Shira had taken it farther than Becky ever had, and there was no way of knowing if she would ever find her way back.

If this had happened in her parents' generation, they would have sat shiva and said kaddish, acting as if Shira had died. Becky had never understood before how parents could do this, but now she did. Sitting shiva gave a certain finality; it tried to impose closure on a grief which would never really subside. Becky wasn't going to sit shiva, but she could still show what a loss this was. Of all the rituals for death, the most powerful to her was the rending of one's garments over the heart to show the tear that was left there. That was what she would do, she decided. In her own private ritual, Becky tore the edge of her blouse, under the collar where no one could see.

BY Shabbos, we knew we had to take action. What was going on between Batsheva and Yosef was horrible enough, but with Shira running away, we saw that there would be no end to the havoc Batsheva would wreak. When our husbands had settled in for their afternoon naps and our children were involved in their games, we gathered at Mrs. Levy's house, the task of saving the community falling to us.

"There must be something we can do," Mrs. Levy said. She was certain that by banding together we could put a stop to all this rebellion.

"I don't know who Batsheva thinks she is," Tziporah Newburger said, "but when I saw Shira eating in McDonald's, I knew it was time for something drastic."

"Yosef is the one we should be worried about," Edith Shapiro said. "Shira's always been a problem, but Yosef is something special."

"Maybe Shira is coming back. And maybe Batsheva and Yosef are just friends," Helen Shayowitz said.

"Helen, you don't have the sense God gave a goose," Mrs. Levy said. "Anyone can see that a lot more is going on."

"I don't know," Helen said, "It seems so ugly."

"Sometimes life is ugly," Mrs. Levy said.

On the couch, Mrs. Ganz was talking to herself and to anyone else in the vicinity. "I don't understand," she said. "Can someone explain to me what in God's name y'all are talking about?"

"Shhh, dear," Jocelyn Shanzer said. "We're talking about why the girls are rebelling."

"Oh," Mrs. Ganz said. "Rebellion. That's bad."

"I'm sorry to say that I think Batsheva is going to have to move," Mrs. Levy announced. "It's not working out with her here. We need to come up with a way to let her know what we've decided."

If Batsheva moved, so would Ayala, and Mrs. Levy hated the idea of losing this child she had grown so close to. But that, she knew, was the risk she took when she became close to children and grandchildren not her own. Ultimately she had no say in their lives; Batsheva was responsible for Ayala, even if Mrs. Levy was the one who knew what was best for her. But she would accept this loss with grace. It would be her personal sacrifice for the sake of the community.

"We can't make Batsheva move," Helen exclaimed. "She wouldn't have to listen to us if she didn't want to."

"We're not going to force her. But there's a way to gently suggest something to someone so they realize what a good idea it is." Mrs. Levy was becoming frustrated with Helen. Until recently, Helen had always listened to whatever she said and she had grown used to this constant support. But now it appeared as if Helen was trying to break loose. She would have to see to this problem once the situation with Batsheva was resolved.

"We can't tell Yosef what to do, but there has to be a way that we can at least limit her contact with the girls," Jocelyn said. "That way we can contain the problem."

"I can tell Ilana what to do until I'm blue in the face and she still does whatever she wants," Arlene Salzman said.

"And Batsheva is teaching in the school, for God's sake. How can we get them to stay away from her if she's one of their teachers?" Norelle Becker asked.

"But if it's not up to the parents to decide who should teach in the school, then who is it up to?" Tziporah asked.

"Exactly," Mrs. Levy said. "Exactly right, Tziporah."

Mrs. Levy and Tziporah looked at each other: They were thinking the same thing. Firing Batsheva, effective immediately, would be the only way. There was only another month or two left to the school year and it wouldn't be hard to fill that one class period for such a short amount of time: the girls could have a double period of chumash or Jewish law, even a study period. And next year, they could have something more useful in its place. Mrs. Levy imagined the art room empty, boarded up. Whatever negative influence Batsheva had had would not be allowed to contaminate the rest of the school. Tziporah Newburger envisioned a wrecking crew coming in over the summer to demolish any trace of what had been. And then the room would be turned into a home economics classroom, with a brand-new gas oven and a built-in microwave, gleaming silverware, several state-of-the-art sewing machines, cookbooks and decorating magazines lining the shelves where paint and charcoal used to be.

Mrs. Levy and Tziporah turned to Rena Reinhard. She was the Ladies Auxiliary president, and at a time like this, it was up to her to exert her leadership; this was precisely what she had been elected for. If the Auxiliary didn't want to sponsor the art program anymore, then there would be no way Batsheva could teach in the school.

"Why are you looking at me?" Rena had barely been paying attention to the conversation. She was preoccupied with her own problems and she didn't have the energy to think about anyone else.

"Maybe the Auxiliary has other priorities besides art," Mrs. Levy said. "If you know what I mean."

"I don't know," Rena said. "I'm not sure I want to get involved." What she didn't say was that she liked Batsheva, even after all that had happened. She still hadn't fully resumed her friendship with Batsheva, but she did feel personally indebted to her for her support throughout this horrible year. And she had her doubts as to whether Batsheva really was responsible for the girls' rebellion. If she had learned anything from the situation with her husband, it was that the problems of the outside world—divorce, drugs, and the rest—didn't stay at bay because you were religious. Maybe religion was a buffer, but eventually these things found their way around it.

"No one is asking you to get personally involved, but the Ladies Auxiliary does belong to all of us," Mrs. Levy said. As a three-time past president, she knew for a fact that this was true.

"And we should at least have the chance to discuss it," Tziporah said.

With everyone staring at her, Rena didn't have the strength to disagree. "Okay, if y'all feel like we need to have a meeting, I suppose I can arrange it," she said, knowing full well that she was going to regret this.

It was settled: if we wanted to end Batsheva's influence on the girls, we would have to fire her. If she was no longer teaching, the girls would have no excuse to always be hanging out with her. Then it would only be a matter of time before Batsheva moved away from Memphis. She would pile her belongings into her car and drive away, following the same road out of town that she had taken in so many months ago. And our community would finally be able to go back to the way it had always been.

With that taken care of, we turned to other subjects. Pesach was approaching so rapidly, how would there ever be enough time to clean? We discussed whether there were any new Pesach recipes. We were sick of making the same potato kugels and sponge cakes. And Helen Shayowitz gave us the weekly wedding update: the big event was now fifty-three days away. The crisis of the week was that Tamara had somehow gotten it into her head that she wanted to wear white Keds for the dancing, instead of the beautiful lace-covered high-heeled pumps Helen had selected. Helen couldn't understand it: she would rather die than wear tennis shoes to her own wedding.

THAT evening, when three stars were visible, our husbands ended Shabbos with the havdallah, praising God who separates between holy and secular, between light and darkness, between the seventh day of rest and the six days of work. The braided candle shone before us, leading the way into this new week. We smelled the besamim, the cinnamon and cloves meant to console us as Shabbos was leaving, and we dipped the candle into the wine, watching the blue flames crackle and then go out. Now that Shabbos was over, there was work to be done. We flipped the lights on and picked up our phones.

Each of us had been assigned a different task, to call the principal, the head of the board, and the rest of the Ladies Auxiliary executive committee. At the last minute, it was hard to come up with a good time to have the meeting. Mondays were mah-jongg night, a tradition longer and more steadfast than the Ladies Auxiliary itself. Thursday nights were never good; we had too much to do with getting ready for Shabbos. Finally, after consulting numerous schedules and community-wide calendars, the meeting was set for a Tuesday night, two weeks away.

Until then, our world hung in the balance. Everything important to us had been placed on a thin wire suspended over nothing, and there we were waiting to see which way it would tip. The world was frozen for the few seconds before the sun fades, when it is neither day nor night. And in a way, there was a certain peacefulness to those moments, a resignation when there was nothing to do but wait.

17

THE LADIES AUXILIARY MEETING was scheduled for the week before Pesach, and we were running around cleaning our houses, planning menus, and inviting guests. There really was no time for meetings. But the issue simply could not wait. In every corner we cleaned, in every cabinet we scrubbed, we saw Batsheva, as if she had become the chametz we were commanded to seek out and remove from our possession.

There had been no keeping secret from Batsheva what was planned for this meeting. It was everywhere, on the tips of our tongues, flowing from our lips, in the air itself. She learned that we would be discussing whether to fire her from the looks the other teachers gave her, ones that mixed sympathy with relief that they were not the subject of such a meeting. And she gleaned her knowledge from the special memos sent home with our children, reminding all mothers once again of the time and date for the meeting. It was so central in our minds, so pervasive in what we talked about, that we half expected to pick up the *Memphis Commercial Appeal* and see an announcement of it in a banner headline across the front page.

As she had been doing for the past month, Batsheva took refuge in her friendship with Yosef. We would have expected her to be extra careful about everything she did, to avoid anything that would strengthen the appearance of wrongdoing. But apparently she didn't care, because we saw her taking a walk with Yosef one evening as the sun was setting. They were heading west towards Shelby Farms, the park two miles from our neighborhood, and all around them the sky was turning pink and purple. Batsheva's walk seemed angry; there was no free-flowing amble or arms swaying loosely by her side.

We had expected to see Batsheva talking to Mimi, for her to try to lobby Mimi to her side. But Mimi seemed to be avoiding her as well as us—never rudely, never obviously, but she had retreated into her own routine of home and shul. We all saw the worried look that had recently shown up on her face whenever Yosef went over to Batsheva's house. We noticed how she would wrap her arm protectively through Yosef's when Batsheva came up to the two of them at kiddush. She too no longer knew what to think.

All week before the meeting, Batsheva spent hours on the phone with Leanna Zuckerman and Naomi Eisenberg. Batsheva told them that she couldn't believe it had come to this. She had never, in her wildest dreams, thought something like this would happen. Naomi and Leanna tried to cheer her up—they promised to do everything they could to defend her. Batsheva would of course not be present at the meeting. What kind of meeting could we have if she was listening to every word? And it was customary (though rarely enforced) that the teachers not attend the Ladies Auxiliary meetings, in case there was a sensitive issue to be discussed.

We tried to imagine how we would feel if we were the subject of such an inquiry. How would we be able to face anyone? We imagined locking ourselves in our houses, hiding under our covers, our faces scorched with embarrassment. But Batsheva wasn't like that. When we saw her, she held her head high. She still taught with as much enthusiasm as ever, maybe even more than ever. She seemed determined not to cower or allow the upcoming meeting to dictate her behavior.

It was only in her eyes that we saw the pain this was causing her. Instead of looking away when we passed her, she would stare at us, her eyes probing for some explanation, demanding that we remember the good she had done here. She also tried to talk to a few of us. She told Rena Reinhard that she was being judged unfairly, and Rena had blushed with shame that she had allowed herself to be talked into calling the meeting. And Batsheva tried to convince Ruth Berner that she hadn't done anything to cause Shira's leaving, that on the contrary she had done her best to help her. But Ruth didn't want to hear it. She was too worried about Hadassah to care about anything else. Batsheva even tried to talk to Mrs. Levy. She went up to her after shul and said that she wanted to talk to her, that there were several things that needed to be said. But Mrs. Levy looked her squarely in the eye and said it was a little late for that.

ON the night of the meeting, we put aside our housework and left our husbands in charge of easy tasks that we thought they could handle: shaking out the bread crumbs from the toaster, lining the silverware drawers with shelving paper, checking the books for stray pieces of food that had wandered over from the kitchen. Now that we thought about it, there was no reason why the men shouldn't help get ready for Pesach; they too had been taken out of Egypt.

We untied our aprons and went outside for the first time in days. During our hibernation, the weather had started changing. Spring had arrived in Memphis in time for Pesach. Even at night, when we couldn't see the daffodils that were coming up in our flowerbeds or the pink and white buds appearing on trees and bushes, we felt it in the air. The nip that had been there all winter was gone. The sky wasn't as dark, and even the smell was different, as if a bottle of perfume had been dabbed in our yards.

The meeting was in the school library, and as we walked through the hallway, we couldn't help but notice the elementary school kids' paintings that Batsheva had hung. They, like everything these days, were about Pesach. Batsheva had asked them to imagine what kind of work they would have done had they been slaves in Egypt, and they had drawn with great creativity: They would be pyramid builders and snake charmers and water carriers and straw gatherers.

"Batsheva certainly knows how to get the kids going," Bessie Kimmel commented.

"That she does," Mrs. Levy answered, smoothing out the silk scarf she had tied around her neck for the occasion. In truth, she did think the paintings were kind of cute. But she couldn't be distracted from the issue at hand. Batsheva being good with the younger kids was not reason enough to keep her in the school.

Bessie had gotten a ride over with Mrs. Levy, who felt it was her obligation to ensure the highest possible turnout. But with this meeting, she didn't have to worry. No one would have dreamed of missing it.

The school library was the site of all official meetings, and even though the room was plastered with posters of cartoon characters encouraging the students to read, it took on a serious feel when the entire Ladies Auxiliary was gathered. The official meeting decorations were in place. The Ladies Auxiliary banner—in blue and white, the school colors, with a touch of pink, to show our influence—had been hung. The portraits of past Ladies Auxiliary presidents, which had a permanent home on the back wall of the library, had been dusted off, so that our predecessors stared back with a new shine. And the plaque presented to the Ladies Auxiliary by the Memphis City Council commemorating thirty years of dedicated service was proudly displayed on the librarian's desk.

While the library was usually large enough to accommodate our meetings, tonight it was filled to capacity. We sat in all corners of the room, crowded against bookshelves, squeezed into the small orange chairs used for story time. On this night, so many of us were present that there was no need to worry if we would reach a quorum, if we would have the proper ratio of executive members to general members, life members to new members.

The room was crowded and hot. We shifted in our seats, fanned ourselves with the agenda, and talked among ourselves, whispering excitedly as we anticipated what this night would hold. We felt a sense of history, the soul of every past Ladies Auxiliary member watching us and guiding us toward a wise decision. We wondered if this was the first time in history such an important meeting had been convened on such short notice, at such a busy time. Mrs. Levy, who had served as Ladies Auxiliary historian for the past thirty years, said she had looked into the official chronicles and discovered that indeed it was a first—there had never been a meeting this close to Pesach—and not since 1972, when the science teacher had been caught teaching an unauthorized sex education course, had there been a meeting to recommend that a teacher be fired in the middle of a school year.

At five minutes to seven, we could stand it no longer. It was time, past time really, to deal with this issue. But Rena Reinhard, PTA president, would not be rushed. She was taking a moment of privacy in a stall in the girls bathroom, trying to collect herself and prepare for the challenge of presiding over such a charged meeting.

Rena had thought long and hard over how to run this meeting. "The way I see it," she had said, "my job is to remain objective. I don't have to tell anyone how to vote. I just need to make sure all voices are heard."

"You'll be wonderful. I know you will," her mother had replied. (While no one ever, God forbid, doubted Rena's skills as president, her mother was certainly less than partial.) "What are you going to wear? Personally, I think you need to wear a suit, maybe your navy one."

She had taken her mother's advice, and as always, it was right on target. Rena was the portrait of presidentiality. There was no way to see that underneath this smooth veneer was so much unhappiness. When the library could hold no one else and the room threatened to burst from so much pent-up expectation, Rena made her grand entrance. She approached the podium, straightened her shoulders, smoothed her hair, and cleared her throat. Right away all the whispering and rustling of papers came to a stop. There was a perfect silence, unlike any ever heard during our meetings.

"We have many important things to discuss tonight and this is a busy time, so we'll get started," Rena said.

With that, the Ladies Auxiliary meeting was officially under way.

Making use of the business sense she had no doubt inherited from her father (the owner of a very successful paper-bag manufacturing company), Rena had placed the issue of Batsheva last on the agenda. First, the minutes from the previous meeting were read, the results of the newspaper recycling program announced. Then there was the candy sale to discuss, followed by the plans to purchase a new sign for the front of the school.

"I wish they'd get on with it already," Helen Shayowitz muttered.

"These items of business are as important as anything else," Mrs. Levy shot back. She too was eager to get to the subject of Batsheva, but this was one more opportunity to keep Helen in line.

"Oh, I know they are. I didn't mean it that way," Helen said, embarrassed at having been heard making a negative comment. Why did she always say the wrong things at the wrong moment?

"I don't know about the rest of you, but I have three cabinets and an entire pantry to clean tonight," Tziporah Newburger said and checked her watch.

"We are all familiar with the issues concerning the art program and the teacher of those classes." Rena paused, enjoying the spotlight fastened on her; it was the only time she felt like she had any power. "We would like to say, of course, that we appreciate the hard work Batsheva has put into the art program. We know how dedicated she has been and she has certainly done more than her fair share of work."

She paused again, giving us time to nod our heads and murmur in agreement. It was important to Rena that all teachers, no matter how successful they had been, receive some thanks at the end of each year. In fact, she was personally responsible for instituting Teacher Appreciation Day, complete with personalized mugs and a lovely luncheon for all.

"With that said, we'll move on to the question of whether Batsheva ought to continue teaching given some of the issues that have arisen."

Rena warned us that we would have to be polite, speak in turn, and extend the same courtesy to others that we expected for ourselves. She opened up the floor to discussion, and at first no one said a word. Then everyone's hands shot up. We were all eager to have our say, feeling that if only we could make everyone listen to us we could somehow make sense of the situation we were in.

Mrs. Levy was the first to speak; as a former Auxiliary president, she had seniority. "I have been involved in the school for many years, since before some of you were born," she began, "and when it comes to an issue like this, I feel I have a certain perspective." She cleared her throat and hoped this was coming out right. "I have nothing against Batsheva personally. But sometimes we want a certain thing for our children, while someone else might want something different. We're lucky to be part of a community that goes back many generations. And sometimes that means we have to fight to keep things the way they've always been. Batsheva has exposed our children to ideas and values that we do not believe in. And that can be confusing and dangerous and we need to put a stop to this before it's too late."

An onslaught of hands was waiting when she finished, but Rena called on Helen Shayowitz, her second cousin once removed; family is family, after all.

"Batsheva is a very nice person, but that's not what this is about. I don't know if I'm comfortable with how close she is with the girls. They're very impressionable, and maybe they should be spending more time with someone like Yocheved Abraham. I can't imagine anyone would have anything bad to say about her." Lately, Helen had been noticing that her relationship with Mrs. Levy was tenuous, and she hoped that by agreeing with Mrs. Levy, she would be able to remain in her good graces.

Roslyn Abraham, Yocheved's mother, nodded in approval. Finally someone had come up with a sensible idea. Her Yocheved was a lovely young woman and it was bad enough that she was unmarried; she didn't need to be overlooked by her own community as well.

"Maybe we can give Batsheva another chance," Jocelyn Shanzer said when she was finally called on. "I'm sure she didn't mean any harm. We could explain to her what we expect and she could tell the girls that she didn't mean any of the things she said about needing to explore what they think about religion. Then maybe they'll realize that they need to settle down. Everything will work out and we can pretend like none of this happened."

"What's done is done," Edith Shapiro said. "There's no way for her to take back what she's already said."

"Really we know nothing about Batsheva. She just turned up one day out of the blue," Rachel Ann Berkowitz realized.

"But we have some obligation toward her. She's a fellow Jew after all—nothing we can do about that," Norelle Becker said.

"She seems nice enough to me," Mrs. Ganz said to no one in particular.

Naomi Eisenberg, in the back of the room, stood up without waiting for Rena to recognize her. "The girls love Batsheva and I've never seen them happier." She looked at all the faces that had turned her way: did anyone agree with her? Probably not. No one ever did. But she was so angry, she didn't care. "My daughter, Kayla, says that Batsheva is the only teacher she can talk to. Usually she's ignored because she's so quiet; the rest of the teachers hardly notice she's there. But Batsheva took a special interest in her. She's been such a good influence on her—she got her to open up and feel more comfortable with herself."

"Her Purim seudah sounds like it was a good influence," Tziporah Newburger called out sarcastically. "Maybe that's what you want for your daughter, but it's certainly not what I want for mine." Tziporah didn't understand how some mothers could be so lackadaisical. This wasn't a question of whether you liked a particular teacher or not. Maybe people like Naomi Eisenberg would laugh, but she felt as if the well-being of her children rested on the outcome of this meeting.

Naomi stood back up, her anger years in the making. "I feel ashamed to be from Memphis right now. All this talk about how friendly we are as a community, what a special place this is—what does any of it mean if we treat someone who's a little different than us in such a close-minded way?"

These accusations were too much and Mrs. Levy jumped up. She had had enough of Naomi Eisenberg. She was always making trouble, always maligning the community. She thought back to the time Naomi had convinced that family not to move here by saying such terrible things about us. At the time, she had held her tongue, but she would do so no longer.

"Who do you think you are!" she exclaimed. "If you don't like it here, you are free to move. And in fact, I would suggest that you consider the idea very seriously. But I've lived here my entire life and I won't stand for you insulting our community. We have done too much good for you to go around saying such terrible things." Mrs. Levy was visibly shaken—she nearly lost her balance as she returned to her seat. For all she knew, she had almost fainted.

"But what has Batsheva done wrong?" Leanna Zuckerman said. "Everything is based on rumors and gossip. Can anyone name a single thing we know she's done wrong? Is there even one thing we know for a fact?"

"If you don't care if your daughter is religious, I don't have anything to say. But look at what happened to Shira Feldman. Do you want your daughter to end up like her?" Tziporah asked. She no longer felt the need to hold back: when something this important was at stake, she believed in fighting with every weapon she had.

Rena saw that the meeting was getting away from her. She held up her hands. "Ladies. Please. I am going to have to ask for complete silence if this meeting is to continue," she said in her most authoritative voice.

But it was too late. At the mention of Shira, the meeting had come undone. Jocelyn Shanzer was saying how awkward it was to have to say these things publicly, how out of character for us and the Auxiliary. And Arlene Salzman whispered to Ruth Berner that they were lucky it wasn't their daughters being mentioned, at least so far, but for all they knew, Ilana and Hadassah would be named next. Naomi Eisenberg was wondering out loud whether it was possible to cancel a Lifetime Ladies Auxiliary Membership and Leanna Zuckerman was practicing the breathing techniques she had learned to keep herself calm in stressful situations, and meanwhile Becky Feldman was scarlet. She felt like she was going to throw up right then and there. If she could have, she would have reached over and slapped Tziporah across the face.

And all at once, Rachel Ann Berkowitz was saying what a shame it was that Batsheva hadn't tried to stop Shira from running away, and Ethel Zuckerman was lamenting the negative influence Batsheva had had on her own daughter-in law, Leanna, and Tziporah Newburger was reminding anyone who would listen that Batsheva was *still* using the mikvah, despite the terrible inappropriateness of it, and Helen Shayowitz was trying to flatter Mrs. Levy by saying what a wonderful opening statement she had made, so articulate and forceful and ladylike all at the same time, and Norelle Becker was trying to figure out if we knew anyone else who had had an affair, and Edith Shapiro was sharing a memory of how darling Yosef had been as a little boy and how important it was to do whatever we could to save him, and . . .

"Quiet," Rena screamed. She banged the gavel, the first time in Ladies Auxiliary history that the small silver hammer needed to be used.

We stopped talking. We breathed slowly. We attempted to reign in the feelings that were coursing through us. We tried to remember that we were at a Ladies Auxiliary meeting. We tried to allow the hallowed history of this institution to return us to our well-behaved selves.

Taking advantage of this lull, Mrs. Levy stood back up. She saw how disorganized the meeting had become, and she realized that it was up to her to step in. Even though many years had passed since her reign as Auxiliary president, people still commented that no one had been able to run a meeting like Mrs. Levy. And that was why she had been elected to that unprecedented third term.

"May I?" she asked, turning to look at the rest of us.

We nodded; if there was ever a time for Mrs. Levy, this was it.

"Now Becky," she said. "I don't mean to make you uncomfortable, but the reason we're having this meeting is so we can prevent what happened to Shira from happening to the other girls. Maybe we can't bring your daughter back, but we have an obligation to protect the rest of our children."

Becky lowered her head. She still didn't want to look anyone in the eye, but Mrs. Levy had certainly put it more delicately than Tziporah Newburger had. She tried to think of it this way, Shira a sacrifice for the sake of the community, and only with her disappearance would the other children be saved. But it didn't make her feel any better; all she wanted was to have Shira home, safe and sound.

"I was all set to be Batsheva's friend," Arlene Salzman called out. "Right from the start I liked her. But my daughter is my first priority and if I don't protect her, then who will?"

"Even if Batsheva hasn't done anything wrong, it's confusing for the girls to have her as a teacher. She gives off the impression that you can do whatever you feel like and that you don't have to worry about communal norms," Rachel Ann Berkowitz said.

"I'm so worried about Hadassah, I can hardly sleep. It's like I don't know her anymore," Ruth Berner said.

"I feel the same way," Judy Sussberg said. "These are our children we're talking about. Ariella is my first priority and I'll do whatever I can to make sure she turns out okay."

We thought of our children and grandchildren. What was the point of thousands of years of Jewish history, just to end up with our girls running off with non-Jewish boys? That it could end with our children's generation made us feel as if we, on this night, at this meeting, were holding history in our hands.

And then we thought of Yosef. We remembered all the time he and Batsheva spent together. No matter how much we wanted to believe the best of him, we couldn't put aside these disconcerting feelings. We could only hope that removing her from the school would have some impact on him as well. We didn't mention Yosef outright—we wanted to avoid the ugliness of having to discuss him in front of Mimi. But even so, he was present in the creases of every word said here this night.

We turned around to look at Mimi. She was sitting in the back corner of the room. The hard work of the past few weeks had taken their toll, and she looked tired and worn-out. Usually, whenever something controversial was going on, we would all have our say, and then Mimi would quietly raise her hand to speak. She would look warmly at us and tell us what she thought and suddenly the issue would come into focus. All the arguing back and forth, the irritation we had felt toward each other, would fade in the shadow of her wisdom. We checked our watches. If we voted now, we would still have time to scrub one more cabinet. But Mimi hadn't yet said anything, and we couldn't leave until she had spoken.

As we waited for her to raise her hand, we tried to imagine what she would say. Mrs. Levy nodded her head in anticipation. Here it comes, she thought. Mimi's going to tell us that we have to get rid of Batsheva, for the sake of our children, including her own; somewhere along the way she had come to her senses. She wondered if her conversation with Mimi played a part in this, if her bluntness had managed to return Mimi to reality.

Leanna Zuckerman was definitely voting in favor of Batsheva, but she hoped that she wouldn't be the only one. She had seen the way Mimi had befriended Batsheva, not just like someone trying to be nice, but like someone who really cared. Mimi and Batsheva even had a similar sensitivity and perceptiveness; Leanna felt comfortable with them in the same way. Certainly Mimi was planning to say that Batsheva had been a positive influence on the girls.

Helen Shayowitz felt as if her body were being ripped into two. She had been planning to vote with Mrs. Levy against Batsheva. It hadn't occurred to her to do anything else. But what if Mimi defended Batsheva? For the first time in her life, she wouldn't be able to listen to both Mrs. Levy and Mimi.

We sat there, biting our fingernails, fidgeting in our seats, waiting for Mimi to stand up. But she bowed her head and looked at her lap. She wasn't going to say anything. She had been so close with Batsheva, she had befriended her, gotten her the job teaching at the school, she had defended her when our suspicion had grown. But now that her own son was involved, now that she too no longer knew what there was between him and Batsheva, her usual clarity was blurred and she didn't know what to say.

With Mimi offering only her silence, Tziporah Newburger made a motion to vote. The vote was by secret ballot; several women had phoned Rena ahead of time and requested it. In the name of fairness and privacy and democracy, Rena had agreed. We turned away from each other, trying to create a private space for ourselves so no one could see what we were writing, and on the small pieces of paper Rena had prepared, we cast our votes.

Rena gathered the pieces of paper and unfolded them. We waited anxiously and in silence as she tallied the votes. She counted them once and then twice. When she was finally satisfied, she looked out at us and announced that the vote had gone against Batsheva. No one was surprised by the outcome. But what was surprising was how close it was: nearly half for her and half against. We looked around the room, trying to figure out how everyone had voted. But no one was saying anything. We realized that we didn't know anymore what anyone felt. We were split, each part of us with a voice as strong as ours together had been. This realization made us see each other for the first time, and it was as shocking as looking at our faces in a mirror and seeing, suddenly, a stranger.

18

AFTER THAT, THE MEETING wrapped up quickly and, truth be told, a little awkwardly. We stood around in the hallway and thought about going over to Mimi, but we found that we didn't know what to say. Mimi avoided meeting our eyes as she walked through the hallway and out of the school building toward home. Before she went inside her house, she turned back to face the neighborhood. What did she see when she looked back, we wondered, still this same community that she was a part of, or something else, an unraveling group of people turned in against itself?

We had assumed that Mimi would be the one to break the news to Batsheva. She was closer to Batsheva than anyone, and coming from Mimi, the news that she had been fired would somehow sound softer, more bearable; if we had to hear bad news, we would want it to come from her. But Mimi went straight home, her confusion still evident on her face.

Naomi Eisenberg and Leanna Zuckerman looked at each other: the task of breaking the news to Batsheva had fallen to them. They didn't say anything to each other as they walked over to her house. There was no point rehashing what had happened or planning what to do next; there would be no nice way to tell Batsheva that she had been fired. They knocked softly on Batsheva's door and she opened it right away. She had on her white silk robe, and the way her sleeves hung loosely made her look like she was about to fly away. Before going inside, Leanna and Naomi hugged her, the light overhead shining on them so they seemed to be all that existed on the darkened street. By looking at their faces, Batsheva seemed to know, and when she invited them in, her voice cracked with sadness.

They sat down on the couch and Naomi took Batsheva's hand. "We wish we had better news," she said, "but people felt it would be better if you didn't teach the art classes anymore."

"I guess that's it," Batsheva said sadly.

"It was close. It really was," Leanna said. "A lot of people supported you, but some people kept insisting and . . ."

Batsheva shook her head. "Don't tell me. I don't want to know who said what about me."

Leanna hated seeing Batsheva so resigned, stripped of the desire to be part of the community. She thought back to Batsheva's first days here, and she could feel Batsheva remembering the same time, her first view of this well-ordered place, how in its closeness, it seemed like everyone could be taken in and cared for. She wished there was some way this could still happen; she hated the idea that Batsheva would leave Memphis, taking with her the energy and creativity she had introduced here.

"Batsheva, you've done some wonderful things here, more than most people could ever imagine doing," Leanna said. "You can't let this take away from what you've accomplished."

"You should know that you still have a lot of friends here. I know this doesn't change anything, but we're here for you," Naomi said. "And it will get better. I really believe that."

"I can't stop thinking that it didn't have to turn out this way," Batsheva said. "In the beginning, everything was going so well, and then later, I still held onto the idea that it would take time, but soon I would be part of this community."

"Do you know what you're going to do now?" Naomi asked, unable to imagine that Batsheva would want to stay here.

"I don't know yet," she said. "But despite what's happened, I feel like this is our home now, and it's not so easy to pick up and leave. I don't even know where I would go."

Neither Naomi nor Leanna knew what to say. Even though they had both spoken in support of Batsheva and had voted in her favor, they felt uncomfortable. It was as if they were still responsible for the decision that had been made; by belonging to this community for so long, they couldn't extricate themselves from any part of it.

When Naomi and Leanna stood up to go, Batsheva squeezed their hands and said good-bye, but she didn't get up to walk them out. She curled up on the couch and covered her face with her hands. Leanna and Naomi closed the door, leaving Batsheva alone with her sorrow, and they went home to their own.

WHILE Naomi and Leanna were talking to Batsheva, the rest of us also went home. We didn't feel any of the relief we had expected to feel now that the decision was made. Instead, we felt a gnawing sense that nothing was as simple or clear-cut as it had once been. When we arrived home, tired but hoping to do a little more cleaning before turning in for the night, our daughters were waiting.

"We couldn't let this go on any longer," Rachel Ann Berkowitz explained to Aviva. "It's nothing personal against Batsheva, but things were out of control."

"Wait until you have children. Then you'll understand why we did this," Ruth Berner said to Hadassah.

"You don't realize the danger of what was happening. You were too caught up in it," Arlene Salzman told Ilana.

"You don't get it," Ilana screamed. "Batsheva was helping Shira. She was the only person Shira could trust. She was the only one she really talked to."

"I realize that you like Batsheva, but sometimes parents need to do what's best for their children."

Ilana shook her head. "You think you know what's going on in the school, but we've hated it long before Batsheva came. Maybe you didn't want to see it, but that doesn't mean it wasn't there."

"Ilana," Arlene said, "you don't understand."

"No, Mom, you don't understand. What happened on the class trip and the marijuana and Shira leaving, none of it was Batsheva's fault. It's your and your friends' fault. Y'all think you know what's best, but why do you think Shira left? She couldn't stand it here anymore, everyone talking about her and telling her what to do. I just wish I went with her." Ilana broke into tears and ran to call her friends.

Alone in her house, her husband asleep and her daughter not speaking to her, Arlene glanced out her front window. Kitchen lights were on up and down the street, and she knew that similar conversations were being played out in each of these houses. Arlene tried to take comfort in the fact that she belonged to this community, that she had friends in all these houses, but it made no difference. She felt more alone than ever.

"I don't know what to do," Arlene said to Ruth Berner the next day, when she called to ask for her recipe for triple layer chocolate matza cake. "Ilana hasn't been out of her room all night. I knocked an hour ago and she yelled that I should go away."

"We did it for their own good," Ruth said. "They need to realize that."

"That's what I told Ilana. But she wouldn't listen to me." Arlene said. "I'm expecting a house full of company and I can't have Ilana refusing to leave her room."

"She'll come around. Hadassah tried the same thing, but I walked into her room and let her know that she was responsible for lining the pantry with contact paper. After a few minutes of arguing, she gave in, and now she seems fine."

"I hope that works because I don't know what else to do. The last thing I have time for is a temper tantrum," Arlene said and listed the other things she had to do—make two roasts, a turkey, a potato kugel, and, of course, the chocolate matza cake.

As we finished our cleaning, our daughters' words came back into our heads, making it hard to concentrate on our clean floors and countertops. We saw how they looked at us with scorn, how their anger burned against us. We wished we could say that it was only because of the Ladies Auxiliary meeting, but as we thought about it, we realized that these expressions had been on their faces for some time already. There was no pinpointing when we had first seen them, but by now they had become the norm, so much so that we almost hadn't noticed it.

What made us feel even worse was that Batsheva and Yosef seemed to be unaffected by the decision. Not that we expected the Ladies Auxiliary to have jurisdiction over them, but we assumed Batsheva would take it as a warning and stop spending so much time with him. And even if Batsheva ignored us, we hoped this would make Yosef return to his senses, that he would see, like we had, that Batsheva was a bad influence.

Late one night, Batsheva and Yosef were spotted by the Mississippi River. Norelle and Michael Becker were celebrating their sixteenth wedding anniversary and had gone to the Peabody Hotel for cocktails. They had a lovely evening. Of course they couldn't eat anything—it wasn't kosher—but they had a drink in the beautifully decorated lobby, right next to the fountain where the world-famous Peabody ducks swam. (They had even been on *The Tonight Show* a few years back, that's how famous these ducks were.) On their way home, the Beckers decided to drive by the river for a view of the bridge and the skyline of Memphis on one side and West Memphis, Arkansas, on the other. They drove down Riverside Drive, along Jefferson Davis Park, in front of the bridge that spanned the river in the shape of an M; even though it technically stood for Mississippi, we knew in our hearts that it was for Memphis.

From their car windows, they saw Yosef and Batsheva walking along the river. They both looked sad, their shoulders drooping, their pace slow. Yosef pointed to some far-off star and they looked up, as if they were both longing to be somewhere else. Then they stopped and sat on the grass a few feet from the water. Norelle and Michael watched Batsheva and Yosef for ten minutes, until they had to head home, afraid of being late for the baby-sitter.

The next day, Helen Shayowitz came across Yosef and Batsheva on the playground behind the school. They were sitting on the peeling wooden benches watching Ayala as she turned flips on the jungle gym.

"I feel like this has as much to do with our spending time together as it does with the girls," Yosef said.

"Who knows?" Batsheva said. "But I'm sure they would have found something else to be upset about even if we weren't friends. People need a way to make sense of Shira running away, and rather than taking a look at themselves, they're looking at me."

"I should have seen it coming. I've lived here my whole life and I know how things work." Yosef shook his head, full of anger at himself and the community.

"Don't let what happened affect the way you're feeling about being here. You're from here. This is your home. It's different for me. I can see it with more distance."

"But how can it not affect how I feel? I used to think that this was the best place to grow up. I couldn't imagine not living here. Everywhere I went, people would tell me that they had heard what a special place Memphis was, and I'd feel proud to be from here. But now I feel like I'm seeing what this community really is for the first time and I can't believe I never saw it before."

"Don't be so hard on yourself, Yosef. There are still a lot of good things about this community, and it's hard to question the things you're raised with."

"You did," he said.

"Well, look where that got me," Batsheva said and laughed. "It's okay. You're figuring things out for yourself, and Ayala and I are going to be okay too."

Batsheva looked up at her daughter. Ayala was balancing herself on top of the jungle gym, her body outlined against a blue sky that seemed flawless. In the past few months, Ayala had grown taller and her body no longer seemed as if a heavy gust of wind could blow her away.

"Look at her," Batsheva said. "I've never seen her this happy. She's like a different child since we've been here."

It was true. Even if Batsheva hadn't fit in here, Ayala had thrived. It was hard to imagine a place where she could have been happier. Helen walked home, the pieces of their conversation heavy on her mind. She had wanted to go over and explain to Batsheva and Yosef why we had done what we had. But as she tried to figure out how she would say it, she found that she didn't have the right words. She didn't know how to make it sound as clear and justified as it had in the past, and for the first time, she felt a strange stirring in her chest, almost like a cold, but deeper inside her body. When she got home, she took two aspirin and an antihistamine, but it didn't make a difference. All day, that unsettling feeling stayed inside her, an ache she couldn't name or describe.

We tried to block these incidents from our minds. We threw ourselves deeper into our Pesach preparations, scrubbed floors and cabinets harder, dusted with more force, mopped with more fervor. Our family members who lived out of town would be returning to Memphis for the holiday, and we tried to cheer ourselves with the prospect of having them home. We remembered Pesachs of the past, when all was happy and good, the biggest excitement over what we had bought new for Pesach, who would wear what on which day. In those days, we had looked forward to the holiday, excited to try out a new recipe, to make the matza balls and homemade gefilte fish, to polish the seder plate, turn the horseradish root into the bitter maror. But this year, we were so worn out that we felt like the slaves our ancestors had been before God took them out of Egypt.

We finally finished cleaning, certain not a drop of chametz was in our possession, not between the pages of any books, not in our children's toys, our coat pockets, between our couch pillows, behind our beds, in our cars, our mailboxes, our garages, our bathrooms. Now it was time for the cooking. We took out our Pesach dishes from the closets, attics, and cabinets where they had been stored since the year before. After we finished each recipe, there wasn't time to pause; we pulled out the ingredients for the next dish. We did what we could to get by without flour and other chametz; we made cakes with matza meal and potatoes in every possible form—fried, mashed, boiled, and stuffed. The more adventurous among us made Pesach bagels and rolls and donuts, although they all tasted somewhat the same, that familiar matzo flavor always detectable.

ON the evening of the first seder, when our families had gone off to shul, we breathed a sigh of relief. For Mrs. Levy, the Pesach seders were the most important part of being Jewish. If she added up the rituals she did every day, the Shabbos meals she prepared and classes she attended, they would not equal the importance of these two nights. It was the only time she had all her children and grandchildren together, and from her position at the head of the table, she loved to look out and see them all at once. She imagined that this was what God must have felt the night He took the Jews out of Egypt, looking down on this mass of people and seeing a nation to call His own.

Leanna Zuckerman wished she could share this enthusiasm. She used to look forward to the seders. But since she had gotten married, she had stopped enjoying them. Her father-in-law droned on as he read, only taking a breath when one of his sons had something to say. All these years, Leanna had barely participated in the seders. But next year, she resolved, she and Bruce would make their own seder. They would lead it together, and she would make sure everyone had a turn to speak. Maybe they could even do something creative, the kind of thing Batsheva would do.

Ever since her daughter had gotten engaged and scheduled her wedding only a few weeks after Pesach, Helen Shayowitz had known that this would be a holiday of taking short cuts. There was too much to do for the wedding to worry about anything else. Even as she tried to focus on the holiday preparations, the wedding was never far from her mind. The red wine she poured into the charoset made her remember to triple-check with the caterer that there would be white wine, not red, under the chupah to prevent a stain on the wedding gown. The brand-new white tablecloth that she spread over her seder table only reminded her of the white gloves the bridesmaids were refusing to wear, even though Helen had spoken to each of them personally and begged.

Bessie Kimmel considered this evening of the first seder her personal triumph. Everything was ready, and she took satisfaction in how beautifully she had prepared. The house was spotless, and her refrigerator was filled with enough food to feed her family for at least three Pesachs. The table had been set for the past two days: the place cards were laid out and the seder plate was ready. She hadn't cut corners, she hadn't resented the work she had to do, she hadn't complained to her husband and her friends. She had gone beyond the bare minimum; she had fulfilled God's commandments with love.

Tziporah Newburger didn't have the strength to think. She was just hoping to stay awake. At her house, seders ran longer than anyone else's. At shul there was always a competition as to whose had gone on the longest, the lateness of the hour testifying to the closest extended family, the most educated children, the best food and most enlightened conversation. Tziporah had the distinction of always winning this contest—last year they had finished at three in the morning. But she was too tired to enjoy it, and she found herself wishing that they had one of those speedy seders her husband made fun of. With four children under the age of seven, she decided that she was not making Pesach again. She would insist that they go away to Florida or New York or Aruba or San Juan, anyplace that had Kosher-for-Pesach Hotels. No house to clean, no food to prepare. Now that would be a real exodus into freedom and redemption.

For Becky Feldman, this was hardly a holiday. She wasn't having any company, except for her older daughter, Leah, who was at Stern College. As a teenager, Leah's behavior had been exemplary. Given Becky's own history, she had been shocked to have such an angelic daughter; she kept waiting for some genetic wildness to surface. But it hadn't until Shira. Becky looked at Leah, who was busy helping with the preparations, and she realized that she saw herself in Shira in a way that she didn't with Leah, and, for the first time, she felt a terrible guilt. Not only had she been unable to prevent her daughter from making the same mistakes she had, but maybe she had even driven her to them. Becky forced herself to prepare the seder plate. The house was taken over with the holiday, but Becky knew there would be no celebrating this year.

These musings were interrupted by the mad rush of husbands, children, and grandchildren home from shul, ready to begin. We filled wineglasses for the first of the four cups and opened our haggadahs. Once the seders began, there was no turning back: The washing of hands, the parsley dipped into saltwater to remind us of the tears our ancestors shed, the telling of how we were slaves in Egypt and with an outstretched arm God took us out. The ten plagues, the bitter maror and the charoset, the apples, nuts, and wine to remind us of the mortar we used to build bricks in Egypt.

Toward the end of our seders, we filled the cups of wine for Eliyahu the Prophet. According to tradition, he never died; he was swept up to heaven in a chariot, and from time to time he returns to make appearances on earth. In fact, some of us even suspected that we had come across him. Mrs. Levy loved to tell the story of the time she had let her son-in-law talk her into going on a canoe trip down the Spring River in Arkansas. She and her eleven-year-old grandson shared a canoe and had gotten separated from the rest of the group. After hours of paddling and no end in sight, Mrs. Levy was nearing ready to give up and die. Just then, a wrinkled old man with a long white beard came by in a motorboat and told her that they were almost there, the end was around the next turn. That bit of encouragement was enough to get her to paddle to shore. When she looked back, the man had disappeared. Only once she was safe and dry did she realize who this mystery man must have been.

But on the first night of Pesach, we knew where to find Eliyahu. He winds his way through every seder in the world, taking a sip of wine from his cup, a sign that he has indeed been there. Opening our doors to welcome Eliyahu into our homes, we looked out at the dark streets and all was still, except for a cool breeze that entered through our open doors. We moved closer together, trying to keep the warmth inside our homes.

Our seders ended as they did every year—half the family asleep at the table, the final songs sung by the few still awake. When we sang the last song, wishing for next year in Jerusalem, we cleared away the dishes and matza crumbs, leaving the wine-soaked tablecloths for later. That night we slept well, knowing we were more protected than any other night of the year. Just as God slew the Egyptian first-born sons on this night and passed over the Jewish houses, all subsequent generations of Jews are guarded on this night of watching.

EVER since the Ladies Auxiliary meeting, we had had little to do with Batsheva. Naomi had invited her for the first seder, but she had declined, saying she wanted to be alone while she thought things through. We tried to imagine a seder for two, no extended family squeezed around a long table, no place cards, no boisterous singing. We thought of Batsheva and Ayala singing the seder songs by themselves, their two voices alone against the background of all our voices singing together.

In shul on the first day of Pesach, we saw Batsheva. She and Ayala were there early, sitting in their spots in the front row. We tried to pretend that we didn't notice them, with all the out-of-town company filling in the usually empty seats. But Batsheva made no effort to pretend that she didn't see us. The sadness we had grown accustomed to now seemed different. She looked angry. She no longer probed our eyes for understanding. She had given up on this, and now when she saw us, her jaw hardened and she gave us a look that told us how betrayed she felt.

Even so, there was a feeling of festivity in the air. We had our new Pesach clothes on, and this was the first time we wore straw hats, such a nice change after a long winter of dark wool. Our daughters too were dressed in their new outfits, our younger ones wearing the white Easter bonnets with pink and baby blue ribbons that had come with their dresses. We didn't think there was anything wrong with that—we decided to think of them as Pesach bonnets instead.

At kiddush, as we were eating from the few plates of Kosher-for-Pesach cookies, we greeted each other's guests, welcoming everyone home to Memphis. Mrs. Levy was surrounded by her family, basking in the joy of having them home where they belonged. She had been so involved with them that she hadn't given any thought to Batsheva these past few days. She had wondered how Ayala was doing, but with all her own grandchildren here for the week, she didn't have much emotional space left.

Batsheva and Ayala were standing alone at the edge of the crowd. It was, in some ways, like their first Shabbos here before we had known them. But when Ayala saw Mrs. Levy, she ran over to her. Mrs. Levy was taken aback, but she hugged her, not wanting to hurt the poor child's feelings; there was no way Ayala could understand what was going on. All along, Batsheva had been gratified when Mrs. Levy had taken an interest in Ayala, but now her face tightened as she saw Mrs. Levy hugging her daughter. Mrs. Levy decided to ignore Batsheva and go on talking to Ayala.

"Are you having a nice Pesach, sweetie?" she asked.

"Yes," Ayala answered.

"You'll have to come over this week and try the macaroons I bought. It's been so long since you've come to visit me."

This was too much for Batsheva; she was being reminded that she would never be able to fit in the way Ayala could. Batsheva walked over to them. "Come Ayala, we should be going home," she said.

Mrs. Levy let go of Ayala and Ayala looked up at her mother, confused. Seeing Ayala like this, Mrs. Levy felt fury rise through her chest and settle right next to the heartburn she had been feeling all morning from so much matzo and grape juice the night before. Ayala could be like any of us here. She could grow up to be a nice Orthodox young lady, if only she was given the chance. Why should she have to spend her life as an outsider just because her mother was? She worried that Batsheva's anger would rub off on Ayala, that she would grow up thinking that there was no place for her here or in a community like this.

Knowing that she had the support of her family and friends, Mrs. Levy decided to say something.

"I know that a lot has happened, Batsheva, and I realize that you may not be happy about it. But as long as you're still here, there's no reason why Ayala can't be part of the community. It would be a real shame if you tried to prevent that," Mrs. Levy said.

Batsheva breathed in sharply; her face flushed with anger. "And what about me? I guess I'm supposed to pick up and leave now that I've been officially declared off-limits"

Her angry response shocked Mrs. Levy. She hadn't expected a confrontation, certainly not in public and certainly not on a holiday, in front of her entire family. But maybe Batsheva was right—it was time to have it out, in public or not, holiday or no holiday, family or no family. All these months, Mrs. Levy had been holding back, trying to be subtle and ladylike. She had suspected that the time would come when that would no longer be sufficient and here it was.

"If you must know, that is exactly what we want. We've had enough of all these problems. It was never like this before you came," Mrs. Levy said.

"I realize that you're unhappy with what's been going on in this community, but that doesn't mean it's because of me," Batsheva said.

"Well, we'll have to let God be the judge of that, won't we?" Mrs. Levy said.

Batsheva laughed. "That sounds like the best idea I've heard in a long time."

Mrs. Levy wasn't going to stand for Batsheva mocking her. "If it weren't for you, Batsheva, the high school girls would still be behaving properly, Shira would still be here, and Yosef wouldn't be gallivanting around the neighborhood with you when he's supposed to be learning with his father."

"Why? Because no one can be wrestling with their own questions and doubts? No one could possibly be unhappy in this community for their own reasons? If there's a problem, I must have planted the seed, right?" Batsheva was speaking loudly, almost shouting, and she angrily threw up her arms. She looked at all of us standing awkwardly by. We tried to continue on with what we were doing, but it was impossible to pretend that we weren't anxiously listening to every word. What Batsheva had to say was equally directed at us.

"How dare you?" Mrs. Levy said. "We are a very religious community. We were raised this way. It's our whole lives. All we wanted was to keep our children religious. Is that too much to ask? We weren't trying to hurt anyone, we didn't set out to be ugly. But we didn't work this hard our whole lives just to have you waltz in and destroy everything. We won't stand for it, Batsheva. We just won't stand for it." By now Mrs. Levy was yelling and her voice was shrill and shaky.

We stepped forward, forming a circle around the two of them. But no one made a move to stop them. We couldn't believe this was happening. It wasn't just the indecency of an open confrontation that stunned us. We were shocked by what Mrs. Levy was saying, even though many of us had made these same arguments ourselves. Hearing them played back to us made us want to recoil. Was this what we really believed? Was this how we too sounded?

"You can't force your children to stay here. You can't make them be religious. It doesn't work that way," Batsheva said.

For the first time, Mrs. Levy saw her own children watching her. She expected that they would feel proud of her, that they would admire the lengths to which she would go to save the community. But when she looked to them for support, she realized that they seemed horrified. Rebecca was glaring at her, Raphael was shaking his head back and forth in exasperation, and Anna Beth/Chana Bayla looked mortified, the same look Mrs. Levy had seen on her face so many times as a teenager. Even her grandchildren were staring open-mouthed at her. And Mrs. Levy finally understood: her children's practical reasons for living away were excuses. The truth was, they wanted no part of her, no part of Memphis. Her own children had taken a look around and not liked what they had seen. Mrs. Levy couldn't stand it; she just couldn't stand it.

"Yes it does work that way. It has to, or our whole lives have been wasted," Mrs. Levy shouted.

In desperation, she slammed her fist down on the table by her side, knocking against a plate of cookies. It fell to the floor and shattered, pieces of white china and crumbs landing at their feet. Ayala was still standing between Batsheva and Mrs. Levy, and she burst into tears.

They stopped shouting at each other, and Batsheva picked up Ayala and hugged her. Mrs. Levy stood there, staring at the mess at her feet. No one came over to her, not her son or her daughters, not her grandchildren, not even Irving or Helen Shayowitz or Bessie Kimmel or any of her nieces or nephews or cousins or lifelong friends. They let her stand there all alone.

WHILE Mrs. Levy was home recuperating from her fight with Batsheva, Helen Shayowitz ran into Batsheva at the park. Batsheva was with Ayala, and they were having a picnic with cream cheese and jelly sandwiches on matzo. Helen was with her sister and brother-in-law, her two sons and their wives and children. She still heard the words of Mrs. Levy's and Batsheva's fight replayed in her head as she watched Ayala sing a song that she had learned in school. Batsheva was clapping along with her, looking so proud of her daughter. Helen felt a terrible pang of regret for what had happened—it was hard for her to remember what exactly this woman had done that was so terrible in the first place. She knew that if she went over to them, Mrs. Levy would never forgive her; in times of trouble, she counted on Helen's support more than ever. But Helen wanted to cry seeing Batsheva and Ayala alone like that, and she decided to follow her own heart.

"Hey there, Batsheva. Hey, Ayala. I saw y'all over here singing, and I wanted to say hello and wish y'all a happy Passover."

Batsheva seemed surprised that Helen had come over, but if she was angry, she didn't show it. "I see you have your whole family here. That must be nice," Batsheva said.

Her voice was wistful, and it struck Helen that Batsheva would never have all the things she took for granted, that she would never have a big family of aunts and uncles and cousins that she could summon for every holiday and simcha. She felt sorry for her, and she understood why it had been so important to Batsheva to be friends with the girls.

"Why don't y'all come over and join us? We brought a whole lunch with us and Ayala can play with my grandchildren. That would be fun, don't you think?" Helen said.

Batsheva started to say that they were fine by themselves, but Helen wouldn't hear of it. "I even made Pesach bagels. I'll bet you've never tasted those before."

As she helped Batsheva and Ayala gather up their things, something became clear to Helen and she understood the aching feeling that had been nagging at her these past few weeks. For the first time, she saw herself from a distant perspective and hated what she saw: a woman who had followed the crowd, who hadn't stopped to think for herself. Her whole life, she had passed off other people's opinions as her own.

When she returned home, the phone was ringing. Helen picked it up and heard Mrs. Levy's voice on the other end, chattering on about God knows what, and she couldn't stand it. She hated having the same old conversation, talking about who had done what tiny new thing in the previous half hour. She made an excuse to get off the phone and longed for something bigger and more important to care about.

DESPITE these incidents, the holiday passed in a flurry of meals, sleep, and shul: for eight days, we did little else, and by the end, we were so stuffed full of food, matza, and wine we could barely walk. When Pesach was over, we put away our special dishes and tried to feel newly invigorated. The city was budding with pink-and-white magnolia trees, our front lawns sprouting azalea bushes. We lifted storm windows, we opened our screen doors, and we stepped onto our porches, hoping that our lives would now go back to normal.

These next seven weeks were a bridge that linked the holidays of Pesach and Shavuot. On Pesach we left Egypt, and on Shavuot we received the Torah at Mount Sinai. The time in between transformed a group of slaves into a nation about to meet its God. In the time of the temple, the omer offering was brought during these seven weeks. Later, the students of Rabbi Akiva began dying during this time, a plague let loose in their midst, punishing them for not treating each other with respect, for not loving their neighbors as they loved themselves.

All these years later, we still count each of the forty-nine days: Today is the first day of the omer, today is the second, the tenth. To remember the students of Rabbi Akiva, we refrain from live music, weddings, and haircuts, from any joy and happiness. On Lag Baomer, the thirty-third day of the counting, the students stopped dying and we too breathe a sigh of relief and celebrate this day, a respite from harm and punishment.

On Lag Baomer, Helen Shayowitz's daughter, Tamara, was getting married, and we all volunteered to help out. We would house the out-of-town company, make Shabbos meals, show the visitors around the city and prepare hospitality baskets filled with a schedule of events, home-baked goodies, and souvenirs of Memphis. The out-of-town company couldn't get over our efforts. What a wonderful community this was, so friendly and warm, such genuine southern hospitality.

The wedding was at the Peabody Hotel, with a special kosher caterer, and it was the fanciest affair we had ever attended. Helen had truly outdone herself. Instead of beginning with a simple cocktail party as we were used to, Helen had a full-fledged smorgasbord, like they did in New York. There were carving stations with beef and chicken and turkey, Chinese vegetables stir-fried on the spot, and seemingly endless platters of smoked salmon, chopped liver, and vegetable crudité. The flower arrangements were equally lavish: the chupah had a wrought-iron frame and flowers were wrapped around it, so many roses, tulips, and lilies that it was as lush as the Garden of Eden must have been. The dancing was so lively that our feet ached for days afterward. The band, seven pieces in all, was flown in from New York, and even they had never seen such dancing.

A week later, Bessie Kimmel's daughter, Adina, gave birth to a beautiful baby boy. It was her first grandchild, a much-heralded event. While no one could say for sure, most of us agreed that the baby looked just like Bessie. He had the same round face, full cheeks, and small forehead. The bris was in the Kimmel's backyard on a crisp spring day. After the circumcision, the party began. The baby blue helium balloons that rose from the center of the tables matched the napkins and tablecloths exactly. Hors d'oeuvres were passed around—potatoes in puff pastry and spinach knishes and fried vegetables and thinly sliced lox on miniature bagels with flavored cream cheese and fresh-fruit skewers. We ate, full from the knowledge that a son was born into our midst, the newest member of the House of Israel.

19

WE AWOKE ONE MORNING A few days later, our houses coming to life with their usual bustle. The Reinhards' lights went on first, then the Newburgers' and the Zuckermans'. Half an hour later, after Naomi Eisenberg had snoozed through every alarm in the house, her lights flickered on. And then right afterward, the sounds of water running, kettles whistling, children asking where their shoes were, their book bags.

Mimi's house was the only one that was still. The kitchen lights were on, but Mimi hadn't pulled open the blinds like she always did. The Rabbi didn't make his way toward the shul for morning davening. Nor did Yosef come flying out of the house, trying to catch up with his father. At the shul, our husbands stood around waiting to begin davening. No one could think of a time the Rabbi hadn't shown up. But as fifteen and then twenty minutes passed, they started to realize that the Rabbi and Yosef weren't coming, and reluctantly they began without them.

We went through our morning routines hoping and praying that nothing was wrong. Every time our phones rang, we jumped, waiting for bad news, maybe about Mimi's father in Birmingham or the Rabbi's older sister in New Orleans, who hadn't been well these last few years. We would have been concerned no matter what, but these days we were more nervous than usual; we were trying so hard to hold on to the idea that everything was finally back to normal, and we didn't want anything to jeopardize that.

The Rabbi appeared around noon. He walked slowly down the driveway, and as soon as he passed our houses, we knew something was wrong. He looked old; it was that simple. His salt-and-pepper hair now looked mostly gray and his cheeks sagged with worry. When he got to the shul, he went straight to his office and closed the door. He didn't stop to say hello to Esther Abramowitz, his secretary. He didn't leave letters for her to type or ask her to get one or another of us on the phone.

Something was wrong and we needed to know what it was. We called the house, hoping Mimi would answer and reassure us that the Rabbi had slept late, that she and Yosef were coming down with colds. But how nice of us to call, she would say; she could always count on us to look after one another. We would bring over chicken soup to heal their ailments and everything would be as it used to be. But no one answered the phone, which rang and rang in a house that we knew wasn't empty. Mrs. Levy knocked on Mimi's front door, but no one came to open it. Helen Shayowitz went over a few minutes later, and though she thought she saw someone move aside the curtain and peek out, no one answered for her either. The day dragged on; we counted the hours, we looked for any way to contain this growing anxiety. But nothing helped and all we could do was wait.

AS the sun was starting to set on this terrible day, Esther Abramowitz was beside herself. Something was amiss, she could feel it in her bones. Everyone else had assumed that after Pesach life had returned to normal, the strangeness of this past year finally over. But Esther hadn't been able to shake this worried feeling. The night before, she had woken up with a start and had the feeling that something was wrong with Yosef. It was all she could do to prevent herself from calling over there at four in the morning. But she couldn't make it through another night like that, especially now that she had reason to be concerned. Determined to find out what was going on, she went over to Mimi's house.

"Mimi, it's me, Esther," she called as she knocked on the door. "Can I come in? Please, I need to talk to you."

She tried the door, thinking that it would be unlocked, but it refused to budge. Esther wasn't going to leave until she spoke to Mimi. She was prepared to wait all night if she had to. "Please, Mimi, let me in," she called again.

After more knocking and pleading, Mimi came to the door. Her brown hair was uncovered; she hadn't had the strength to pull on a beret or a scarf. Mimi's eyes were streaked with red, with half-moons of purplish gray underneath. Esther reached for Mimi's hands. As she held them, she noticed for the first time how thin they were, childlike and delicate.

"Mimi, what in God's name is going on?" Esther asked.

Mimi stared out past Esther's shoulder, to the street behind her. "Yosef is gone," she said.

"Gone?" Esther shook her head. "No. He can't be."

"He is," Mimi said.

"When? Why?" she managed to stammer.

"He left Memphis this morning," Mimi said and shut the front door, leaving Esther standing there in tears, not knowing what to do.

HEARING that Yosef was gone was like hearing the news of a death. Some of us cried, some of us screamed, and some of us said nothing. We couldn't believe that we had lost Yosef as well. We tried to come up with possible scenarios. We wondered if maybe, just maybe, he had gone back to yeshiva. Though we would miss him, we would take comfort in the fact that this was the path he needed to follow and that in a few years, it would lead him back to us. We tried to cling to this hope, tried to convince ourselves that maybe this was one more sign that our community had returned to the way it had always been. But we realized that his having returned to yeshiva was unlikely. If that was where Yosef was, the Rabbi and Mimi wouldn't have been upset. And there were only another few weeks before the summer break; there would have been no reason for him to go back for so short a time. And surely we would have known about it in advance. We would have made him a going-away party, we would have showered him with farewell gifts.

With a sinking feeling in our hearts, we realized that Yosef and Batsheva must have run off together; there could be no other explanation. We imagined them driving away from Memphis with Ayala in the backseat, the luggage once again piled on top of her car. They would have left when it was dark, trying to sneak away unnoticed. Maybe they would get married, maybe they wouldn't, but either way, Yosef would be gone for good.

These past few weeks, we had stopped thinking about Batsheva with as much intensity as we previously had. We had hoped that if we pushed her from the forefront of our minds, she would eventually disappear and the safe, secure Memphis we had always known would return. But now, once again, we couldn't erase her from our thoughts. We looked at her house. The windows were closed, the curtains were drawn, there was no sign of anyone inside. The garage door was also down and we couldn't tell whether her car was there. None of us could remember seeing Batsheva or Ayala all day; there hadn't been any reason to look for them, but still, it was one more ominous sign.

Even though our kids had already come home from school, and our husbands were on the way home from work, we couldn't pull ourselves away from our windows, waiting for some confirmation that it was true, that Batsheva and Yosef had run off together. The more time passed without any sign of Batsheva, the more certain we were. Despite all we had done to prevent it, Batsheva had managed to steal Yosef away. The neighborhood was never as still, never as quiet as it was that evening. As it started getting dark and the street lamps flickered on, the shadows of trees and mailboxes looked sinister as they fell across our lawns, as if to laugh at us for being unable to save Yosef.

AS we were beginning to give up hope that something would happen, Mimi emerged from her house. We thought about rushing outside to besiege her with questions, to offer our own sadness and disbelief. But the look on her face told us that this wasn't welcome. Her usually open expression, her always-present smile, her kind brown eyes, were gone, and had been replaced by a face that looked empty and tight.

She walked by our houses, without glancing at our lit windows to see if we were there. We still clung to the hope that she would stop, that she had been on her way to tell us what was going on. But she passed each of our houses without slowing down, and as she neared Batsheva's house, we assumed that was where she was going. Maybe she had to see for herself that Batsheva was gone as well, maybe that was the only way she could accept what had happened. At Batsheva's driveway, she paused and looked at the house, but she kept walking.

She didn't stop until she reached the shul. Even though it was late, the back door to the shul was open for the men who would be davening maariv in the bet midrash. Esther Abramowitz was there too, in her office. After leaving Mimi's, she couldn't bear going home to her empty house. Her job at the shul was all she had, and she had decided to catch up on her work. Mimi went inside and walked straight to the sanctuary. She opened the double doors; it was dark, only a few squares of light coming in from the skylight above the ark, projecting shadows across the purple carpet and silver walls. This was where Yosef had spent so much time these past few months, thinking and brooding, and maybe she wished she could find some physical remnant of what he had been feeling, some stray thought swept under a chair.

As Mimi stood in the doorway, so many memories of so many years flooded her: when she stood in shul pregnant with Yosef, praying that this would be the baby that would make it; Yosef as a little boy on her lap as the Rabbi made his speech. And later, Yosef's bar mitzvah, how he stood up in front of the whole shul and in a loud, perfectly clear voice, chanted the Torah portion; and when he came home from yeshiva, how he met her eyes and smiled from across the mechitza.

Mimi's eyes adjusted to the dark, and she looked around and realized she wasn't the only one there. In the far corner of the room, seated in one of the chairs, was the outline of someone. Mimi started walking down the stairs, holding on to the unlikely hope that it was Yosef. But she drew closer and she saw that it wasn't Yosef at all. Instead, there was the long blond hair, the familiar tilt of the head, the long flowy scarf trailing down her back.

Batsheva heard her footsteps and jumped up. The two women stood there and looked at each other.

"Mimi, I'm so sorry," Batsheva finally said.

Her face, like Mimi's was tear-stained. She tried to give Mimi a hug, but Mimi pulled away.

"You know Yosef is gone," Mimi said, in a half-statement, half-question.

"Yes," Batsheva said.

Mimi had been holding so much in, and now face-to-face with Batsheva, her reserve withered. With her voice breaking, Mimi described how last night, when she and the Rabbi were about to go to sleep, Yosef came to them and said how confused he was. He said he didn't know if he wanted to go back to yeshiva, if he wanted to be a rabbi. He said he wasn't sure if he wanted to be religious. He had been questioning what he had always assumed he wanted; he worried he had never thought things through on his own, never arrived at his own conclusions about what he wanted and who he was. And the only way for him to do this would be to leave Memphis. He said he couldn't think clearly here, he felt so much pressure and expectation.

He had made plans to stay with friends in New York until he could figure out what to do next; maybe he would go to college, maybe he would get a job, maybe he would travel, he just didn't know. The Rabbi had been shocked—he hadn't realized that anything was wrong. But Mimi had known, and now she understood the restlessness and sadness she had seen on Yosef's face these past few months. The Rabbi had tried to convince him to stay, he couldn't believe that his son would not become the rabbi here, that he would maybe not even end up religious. But Mimi had known that as much as they wanted to hold onto him, they needed to let him go.

Batsheva nodded as Mimi spoke; she had known all along that this was what Yosef was feeling. "It's true, Mimi. He knew he had to go away," she said.

"But I need to know why," Mimi said.

"He said he had been thinking about this for a long time, and that it got worse this year. When we first started learning together, he thought that everything made perfect sense to him. But after a while, he said his answers didn't feel satisfying."

"But why didn't he confide in me?" Mimi asked.

"He wanted to, but he was afraid. He tried to tell his father, when he said he didn't want to go back to yeshiva for the year, but he couldn't bear to disappoint the two of you. At the end of last year, he was so tired and he assumed that he just needed the summer off from yeshiva. But after a few months away, he still didn't want to go back. He needed time to figure out what he wanted. And then when people started talking about him, he couldn't stand it," Batsheva said and shook her head.

"Mimi, I wish that he hadn't left. Believe me, I do. But we both know that this is what's best for him."

Mimi heard the pain in Batsheva's voice, how much she too would miss Yosef. She thought of the long talks Batsheva and Yosef had had on her front porch, how Yosef had looked so tired, so heartsick. As much as she hadn't wanted to think it was possible, everyone else had seemed so sure that the two of them were involved in an inappropriate relationship. "Please, I need to know what there was between the two of you," she said.

Batsheva looked at Mimi, surprised that she would give any credence to what had been said about her. "Mimi, no. It wasn't like that between us."

"Then what was it?" Mimi asked.

"I'm not saying I never thought about it. I did, I felt close to Yosef. Besides you, he was the only one here who understood me. And I was the only one he could talk to, and that made us have a special friendship. But we didn't act on it. I came here to start over. I knew I couldn't get involved with him. I would never do that to you, or to him, or to myself either," Batsheva said. "Mimi, please believe me. I don't care what anyone else thinks about me anymore, but you have to trust me. I would have told you if I could, but I promised him I wouldn't say anything, that it would be up to him to decide what to do, when he was ready."

Mimi looked at Batsheva. She remembered how close they had been all these months, how she had chosen not to listen to the talk that had circulated about Batsheva. This same trust and understanding came flooding back to Mimi and she burst into tears.

"I was so worried about Yosef that I didn't know what to think," Mimi said. "I was so worried that maybe everyone was right, that you and Yosef were involved and that was why he looked so confused and didn't want to go back to yeshiva." Mimi looked pleadingly at Batsheva. "I'm so sorry," she said.

Batsheva took hold of Mimi in a hug, and they stayed there like that in front of the ark, rocking each other back and forth.

WHEN we heard what had happened between Mimi and Batsheva, part of us still wanted to blame Yosef's leaving on Batsheva, to hold on to the idea that they had had an affair and that was the cause of all our troubles. But we found that it was getting hard to believe our own version of events. Maybe Batsheva's presence had played some role in his decision and maybe it hadn't, but either way, we realized that so much more had been going on. We thought about Yosef, how sad he had seemed, how he had avoided us whenever we tried to talk to him, and we understood that it was true. He had left because he no longer knew what he wanted, because he didn't know who he was.

In some ways, we found ourselves wishing that Batsheva and Yosef *had* had an affair. That would make everything easier to explain. We could reassure ourselves that these things could be prevented if we tightened the barrier between the sexes even more. It would be an isolated incident, something that might never happen again if only we were careful. But now, everything could be called into question. It wasn't his leaving as much as it was his rejection of our community and what we believed in. In leaving like this, Yosef was saying that he wanted no part of us.

All we could think about was Yosef. We still expected to see him, to be looking out the window as he walked past, to be getting our newspapers as he was getting his. Or to come across him at the shul, at the school, or the grocery store, as if nothing had changed. When we didn't see him, our eyes played tricks on us: any dark-haired young man we saw, anyone in dark pants and a white shirt, was Yosef.

We tried to imagine feeling what Yosef felt, seeing himself as a stranger in this city that embraced him. We tried to imagine taking a look at the community we had loved so dearly and seeing only the smallness of this world, the lack of any broader view to the outside. Instead of viewing the roots we had set down here as nourishing and supporting, we tried to imagine seeing them as twisting round and round each other in overly close, strangling connections.

And we tried to imagine calling into question the assumptions and beliefs that had shaped our lives. We reminded ourselves that somewhere along the way, we too had had a choice about whether we wanted to be religious, that we still had a choice, even if we didn't usually think about it like that. All the moments of doubt that we had had over the years came together now, and we thought about how hard it sometimes was to be religious, how elusive this God of ours could be, how lonely it was to always be different. We conjured up images of Yosef sleeping late without davening, getting dressed without his yarmulke. We imagined him breaking Shabbos and eating whatever he wanted. But this person we were seeing was no longer Yosef. Separated from our world, it was as if he had ceased to exist. Even though we never believed that Shira Feldman would take it as far as she had, she had always been rebellious. But Yosef was our best and our brightest. Not only was he supposed to return to Memphis, he was supposed to become our leader. If he could leave Memphis and all that we believed in behind, then any of our children could.

"Maybe he's coming back," Helen Shayowitz said in desperation. If only she had woken up earlier, maybe she could have been a positive force in the community; maybe she could have helped it to be as special and as warm as we had always thought it was. She remembered a story she had once heard: a woman had gossiped about her neighbors and later regretted what she said. She went to the rabbi and asked how she might take back her words. He instructed her to take a feather pillow to the top of the highest hill and tear it open, letting the feathers fly every which way. Then, the rabbi said, she should return to him and he would tell her what to do. She did as he said and when she returned, he told her to go outside and gather the feathers. But that's impossible, she cried. They're already scattered all over the village. He looked at her and smiled. The same is true of your words, he said. Helen imagined herself as this woman, trying in vain to chase down every feather that had flown from her mouth.

"Give it up, Helen," Mrs. Levy said, her eyes cold, her voice colder. "Even you can't possibly believe that. It's time for you to open your eyes and see what's really going on. Remember, I'm the one who knew from the start that things weren't going to turn out well."

It hadn't turned out well at all. It was worse than even Mrs. Levy had suspected. As far as she was concerned, this wasn't the same Memphis, Tennessee. Before this year, Mrs. Levy had assumed that the community would carry on as it always had. This was the point of tradition, that each generation was connected by bonds so strong that it was possible to build something lasting for children, grandchildren, and every generation forevermore. That everything could be lost made her feel smaller and less important.

"You're always saying that things aren't going to turn out well," Helen exploded in anger, no longer willing to accept what Mrs. Levy said as if it were the word of God. After so many years of doing so, her resentment spilled over; it was time to voice her own opinions. "Did you ever stop to think that maybe you're one of the people who caused that to happen?"

Mrs. Levy drew in her breath. Helen had no idea what she was talking about; she never had and never would. If it weren't for Mrs. Levy, Helen would still be a nobody. "At least I take an active role in this community and try to do things to help. Which is more than I can say for you," she said, putting an official end to this thirty-nine-year-old friendship.

"No one believed me," Tziporah Newburger was saying to herself and to anyone who would listen. "All along I knew we shouldn't trust Batsheva." Even if nothing improper was going on between Batsheva and Yosef, the very fact of their friendship proved that there were certain lines not to cross. Tziporah had always known that it was dangerous to be too open; once the mind was exposed to foreign ideas, who knows where it would wander. Maybe now everyone would realize that once you start down the slippery slope, there was no escaping its icy descent. But she would no longer bear the responsibility of trying to get everyone to see this. The only answer was to pull inside as tightly as possible, to build an ark around her family which would protect them from the flood of hard times that lay ahead.

Leanna Zuckerman was glad that Yosef had left and she wasn't afraid to say so. She felt sorry for what we had lost, but not sorry for him. She hoped that one day Yosef would find his way back, that he would sort things out and preserve what was meaningful to him. But for the time being, all she wished was that he find his own happiness, that he go in peace and return in peace, wherever it was he eventually landed.

For Becky Feldman, Yosef's leaving had been pushed into the background. Shira had finally called that morning. Becky had cried as soon as she heard Shira's voice on the other end of the phone and she begged her to come home, no punishment meted out, no questions asked. Shira too had started to cry as she told her mother that she and Matt were in California, that they had been driving around for the past few weeks, trying to think of their time away as a vacation from real life. Shira hadn't agreed to come home, at least not yet, but she said she would call again in a few days, and for the first time, Becky felt a sense of hope.

Instead of joining in any of these conversations, Rena Reinhard was home. She had finally come to a decision. That evening, she had gone to her husband's study, knocked on the door, and told him she wanted a divorce. He had been shocked—he never thought she would have the courage to do this. When Rena had imagined this moment in the past, she envisioned herself unable to stop crying. But, to her surprise, she was dry-eyed; she was calm and still. She wasn't worried what the community would say, she no longer cared if she was the subject of everyone's conversations. She was only interested in seeking out a new life for herself.

Naomi Eisenberg was thinking about how she had seen Yosef and Batsheva together the night before he left. Naomi and her husband had decided to take a walk. It was past eleven, and Batsheva and Yosef were standing under a street lamp, its light catching them in its glow. They were talking and both of them looked sad; they must have been saying good-bye. Yosef had jumped when he saw the Eisenbergs coming, and he stepped back from Batsheva. As they passed, Naomi felt a kinship with Batsheva and now Yosef. They formed a silent community of outcasts that lived outside the walls of the established one. As she and her husband continued their walk, Naomi looked around the neighborhood, turned to her husband and told him to go ahead and accept the job he had been offered in Atlanta. Knowing that she would finally be leaving washed away a glare from her eyes and she saw that she had never belonged in Memphis. This had never been a real home to her, even if she had spent her whole life here.

In our minds we imagined the scene of Yosef leaving, over and over again, like a movie projected on a giant screen set up on our lawns. For months he had been thinking about this. The more he and Batsheva learned together, the more he heard the hollowness in his voice as he answered her questions, the more he realized he didn't feel the conviction he was professing to have. And when he learned with his father, he no longer felt as connected to this line of tradition as he once had.

He would hope that each twinge of doubt would go away, would be nothing to worry about. But they only got worse, and this wondering if he really believed in the life he lived ate away at him, giving him the troubled, preoccupied look we had come to know so well.

Even so, he wasn't sure he would be able to break away; it takes a lot to question your entire life and even more to do something about it. When he started making plans, calling friends in New York to see if he could stay with them for a while, making a plane reservation, he still wasn't sure he would go through with it. But he would think of all that had happened and he would long to go somewhere he could be on his own, where he didn't feel the breath of so many people looking over his shoulder.

We added on to what Naomi Eisenberg had seen of Batsheva and Yosef saying good-bye under the street lamp, until we could almost hear them talk about what there had been between them. How they had had feelings for each other, but they had held back. And how Yosef had to go off and discover what he really wanted. Batsheva hated to see him leave, she would tell him that it was hard to imagine being in Memphis without him. But even so, she would stay here; it wouldn't be as she had imagined, seamlessly being part of the community, but it could be enough, at least for now. And who knows, she would have said with a smile, maybe their paths would cross again, there was no way to know what the future held. Yosef would long to hug her good-bye and, before he turned to leave, he would put his arms around her and bury his head in her long hair.

And we saw Yosef returning to his house, wiping away the tears from his good-bye to Batsheva. We imagined how he must have forced himself to finally tell his parents what he was feeling; after months of hiding it, the time had come to say that he had stayed home because he was no longer happy at yeshiva, that instead of having a short break from that world, he now wondered if he ever wanted to go back. One question had led him to another, like pulling a thread on a sweater until the whole thing eventually comes unraveled. His father would react as Yosef had known he would. He would be shocked, he wouldn't have seen it coming. This would make it worse, that his father had known so little of him, that he had been so successful at hiding himself. Yosef would feel torn in two, having to choose between his loyalty to his father and his loyalty to himself. But his mother, she understood, she would let him go. She would kiss him on the forehead and say that if this was what he needed to do, they would have to accept it. But he should remember that they loved him, they would be here for him when he wanted them.

The next morning, when it was time to leave, he would sling his bag over his shoulder and walk out the door. As he started to close it behind him, when it was still open a crack, he could see a narrow line of his mother's kitchen. He paused and tried to gather every detail into his head, wishing he could pack his memories the way he had his clothing. He pulled the door shut and stepped outside into the early morning light, the time of day when anything feels possible.

We didn't envision him ever arriving anywhere. The road before him always grew longer, any fixed point of land ahead a mirage, so that he was always moving further away from us. But even if we could imagine exactly how he left, even if we could fill in every blank space in between the last time we saw him and when we discovered he was gone, we couldn't fill in all that had taken place inside his head over this year. We had thought we could see inside him, and now we understood that we hadn't seen anything; all we saw in the brown of his eyes was what we had wanted to be there.

Yosef's absence created a hollowness in the middle of our neighborhood, as if during the night, a line of bulldozers dug a pit that stared back at us. With each day that passed, that hole grew larger, expanding against the bedrock of our foundation, until our houses circled dangerously close to its edges. For the next few days, no one had the strength to speak, let alone think about the holiday of Shavuot that was fast approaching. Everything reminded us of Yosef. Our own children too, we couldn't look at them without seeing his features ghosted over their faces.

20

SHAVUOT MARKS THE GIVING of the Torah on Mount Sinai—the central event in our history—but the holiday always receives short shrift. There are no Sukkahs to build, no houses to clean, no Menorahs to light. There are just blintzes and cheesecake, and those are only customs.

We plowed ahead with preparations for the holiday. Everything was a chore; we could hardly bring ourselves to do the bare minimum and instead of feeling like we were all in it together, we felt alone. We saw less of each other. The walls of our houses had become thicker, more solid and impermeable, so that we were divided inside private domains of immediate family and individual lives.

On the first night of the holiday there is a custom of staying up all night to learn Torah, to re-accept God's word on the anniversary of our receiving it. We had never done this though. It was for the men; someone had to be awake to serve lunch the next day. But this year, Mimi had announced that she would be giving a class for the women. We had barely spoken to her since Yosef left. Mrs. Levy had seen Mimi walking with Batsheva, the two of them almost the same height and with the same slender builds, so that from the back they looked like sisters. But Mimi had had little to do with any of us. She was never rude, she would still say hello when we saw her, but she had distanced herself.

Without Mimi, we were confused, a mass of people with no leader and no direction, like the Jews in the desert, aimlessly wandering in search of some elusive place. We were excited to hear that Mimi would be giving a class, hoping that this was a sign she would be returning to our midst. We wished that we could restore things to the way they used to be. But as much as we wanted this, we knew it was too late. So much had happened in this past year, and there was no pretending that the community could go back to the way it had been.

When we got to the shul, the bet midrash was crowded with our husbands and sons. They were learning in pairs, only breaking to grab a cup of coffee and a few cookies from the refreshment table the sisterhood had set up to keep everyone going late into the night. Mimi's class was in a small room off to the side, and we took our seats and waited for her to begin.

Batsheva was there too, sitting in the front row. We had seen her around, but none of us had yet spoken to her; who knew where to begin or what to say? Ayala was curled up on her lap, asleep. Leanna Zuckerman and Naomi Eisenberg were on either side of her and a few of the high school girls, Ilana and Hadassah and Nechama, were sitting close by too. Batsheva scanned the room, not angry or uncomfortable. Instead, she was looking beyond us. With Leanna and Naomi and the girls, she had created her own version of a community, smaller, but all her own.

Mimi stood before us. Her face was glowing with purpose; she no longer looked delicate and vulnerable. She had prepared a class on the Book of Ruth, which would be read in shul on the second day of the holiday. Though we knew the story, we rarely thought about it; it didn't command the same attention as the Five Books of Moses.

Mimi began re-telling the story: In the days of the judges, there was a famine in the land of Israel, and Elimelech and Naomi left for the land of Moav, where their two sons married Moabite women, Ruth and Orpah. They lived happily until Elimelech and then his sons died suddenly. With their husbands gone, the women had nothing left, and they set out to return to Israel. As they traveled, Naomi urged her daughters-in-law to return to their land, their people. Orpah kissed Naomi good-bye and set off toward home. But Ruth clung to her mother-in-law. "Where you go I will go," she said. "Your people are my people." When they reached Israel, the town was abuzz: is this Naomi the rich woman who returns to us empty-handed? And who is this Moabite woman she brings with her? Naomi cried out that she had returned with nothing, that she was bitter and used up.

Ruth went out each morning to glean in the fields of the rich. One day, Boaz, a landowner, noticed her and sent her home with a basket of food. When Naomi saw this, she was relieved because Boaz was a distant relative and maybe he would fulfill his religious obligation and marry Ruth. When night fell, Naomi told Ruth to go to Boaz and she did as Naomi said. She lay at Boaz's feet and he woke with a start. "It is Ruth," she said, "searching for my redeemer." Boaz and Ruth were married and they had a son, and in the eyes of the people, this was good. This son was Oved who bore Jesse who bore David, the king of Israel.

Mimi reminded us that the kingship of Israel was passed down through Ruth. Even though she had initially been regarded with suspicion because she was a descendant of Moav, God saw fit to reward her for her righteousness by having the future kings of Israel descend from her; it was her personal qualities, not her past, that mattered. As we listened to Mimi and saw how she looked at us, the events of the past year became part of this text. We saw ourselves as characters we didn't want to be and we wished we could change what we had said and done. We avoided meeting each other's eyes. Everything that had once seemed so clear had lost its sharpness; a lens had been turned in the wrong direction and everything in front of us and behind was fuzzy.

WHEN Mimi's class was over, we said goodnight to our husbands and sons and started walking home. It was ages since we had been out this late. We were surprised at how cool the air was, sharp and piercing, without the humidity which was already beginning to fill the days, another summer come round.

We looked at our watches. It was a few minutes before midnight. We remembered something we hadn't thought about since we were children. At midnight, every year, on this night, the sky was supposed to open and reveal a flash of heavens. In that one quick moment, the scene of the giving of the Torah was replayed, allowing all Jews of every generation to witness the covenant between God and His people.

We were all there: Mrs. Levy, Helen Shayowitz, Leanna Zuckerman and Rena Reinhard, Naomi Eisenberg, Tziporah Newburger, Jocelyn Shanzer and Becky Feldman, Arlene Salzman, Bessie Kimmel, Edith Shapiro, Esther Abramowitz, Yocheved Abraham, Norelle Davidson, and Rachel Ann Berkowitz, all of us waiting for the sky to open, for God and his Heavens to be revealed in our midst.

Our daughters were walking behind us, talking and laughing, their voices loud and untired; they were used to being up this late. We could hear snippets of their conversation, about summer plans and the excitement of next year when they would finally be far from here. Batsheva had made her way outside as well, and she and Mimi were walking behind us. Batsheva was carrying Ayala fast asleep against her shoulder. When we stopped walking, they did too and they looked at us, wondering what we were waiting for.

We craned our necks and looked at the sky, hoping we might see something. We longed to cry out to God and beg him to renew us as in days of old, when the city was fresh, full of so much possibility. But we saw nothing up there. Even though we hadn't really expected to, we were disappointed. Maybe it was only a legend, something to keep the children awake.

Just as we had given up and were about to turn away, there was a flash like lightning opening the sky. We looked up, expecting to see Mount Sinai in the midst of the desert, the soul of every Jew standing at the foot of the mountain, waiting as one nation, with one heart for God to descend. We expected pillars of fire and smoke, the trumpets sounding, and then a still silence as the Ten Commandments echoed through the air. But instead of this vision, all we saw was ourselves.

There was Memphis high on this bluff and the Mississippi River winding its way around us. Our houses were lined up in neat rows, their lights on as if we were inside going about our lives. Our shul was there and our school, and the restaurant and the kosher grocery store and the shops we frequented. Everything looked exactly as we saw it everyday, only against the backdrop of so many stars, it seemed smaller and less important.

In the sky above these places was a chain of hands, our ancestors on one side, holding on to each other, our grandmothers and great-grandmothers, stretching back to Sarah, Rivka, Rochel, and Leah. We were part of this line of women, connected to them by the daily routines of our lives, the Shabboses we had prepared, the holidays we had celebrated, the homes we had made. Even Batsheva was there, holding on to Mimi's hand. But when we looked at who was on the other side of our long line, our daughters were off somewhere in the distance, some closer and some farther away, and only if we stretched out our arms as far as they would go could we maybe begin to reach them.

Before we had time to think or look at each other, the vision was gone. We studied the sky for more, hoping it would reveal some answer, some way to turn. But the heavens were still, and all we saw was the mistiness of hazy nighttime clouds and the silvery white of the moon above and the blackness of a sky that extended forever. We looked down and went on home. It was late and we were tired. We could no longer be sure what we were seeing.

Acknowledgments

There are many people who have provided me with help and guidance in writing this novel.

I want to thank my teachers at the Columbia School of the Arts, particularly Rebecca Goldstein, Mary Gordon, and Binnie Kirshenbaum for their wisdom and encouragement.

I am very grateful to my editor, Jill Bialosky, who has been wonderfully supportive and has offered me invaluable editorial advice. Nicole Aragi has been a blessing of an agent. First as her intern, and now as her client, I have seen the wonders she has done.

I want to thank David Wolf for reading numerous drafts and offering a critique that was always unflinchingly honest and insightful.

My parents, Lynnie and David Mirvis, encouraged me at every step of the way. I am grateful to my father for offering me his intelligent advice and for teaching me how to press on, and to my mother for giving me a love of stories and for sharing hers with me. I also want to thank Shoni Mirvis, my sister, for her perceptiveness, her insight into theme, and for being there for me always; my brother, Simmy Mirvis, and my sister-in-law, Elisheva Kagan, for their encouragement and helpful advice; and my grandmother, Dotty Katz, for being my southern-language consultant.

I am especially indebted to my husband, Allan Galper, for his constant support and love, for his eagle eye as a line editor, and for his suggestions that opened up new ideas. I will always be grateful to him for allowing the ladies of the "we" to live with us for three years.